STRANGE BEASTS

"A whip-smart, lusciously atmospheric adventure through the dazzling theatres and chilling catacombs of turn of the century Paris."
—Frances White, *Sunday Times* bestselling author of *Voyage of the Damned*

"A propulsive collision of historical fiction and fantasy, all tied together with an opulent gothic bow. A terrifying delight."
—Signe Pike, author of The Lost Queen series

"Engaging and delightful, *Strange Beasts* draws the reader into a gothic setting that seems all too real. I was at once intrigued and a little spooked by all the familiar names, especially when I began to realize just how effectively Susan J. Morris has used our own nightmarish archetypes to trap us in her tale."
—Troy Denning, *New York Times* bestselling author of more than forty science fiction and fantasy novels

"Morris cleverly weaves together historical, literary, and mythological threads to create the endlessly rich world for her supernatural sleuths in this gripping mystery. With gorgeous prose and an unforgettable pair of heroines, *Strange Beasts* romps through the opulence and intrigue of turn-of-the-century Paris, offering an exploration of femininity, power, and the nature of monsters—as well as a thrilling adventure full of wit and heart. I can't wait for the sequel."
—Kate Alice Marshall, *USA Today* bestselling author of *What Lies in the Woods* and *Rules for Vanishing*

"In *Strange Beasts*, Susan J. Morris gives readers a subtle alchemy of beauty, poetry, suspense, and horror, nestled perfectly in Paris during the belle epoque . . . Hel and Sam are a stunning pair, fighting monsters in the darkest catacombs, while at the same time fighting against a world that would make monsters of them. A delightfully wicked read."

—Jaleigh Johnson, *New York Times* bestselling author of *The Mark of the Dragonfly*

"A magnificent book . . . of gas lamps and murders, of Paris, of secrets and love, and of finding yourself and trust. I treasure this tale. I hope it's the first of many, and until those many start appearing, I'll reread this one. Often."

—Ed Greenwood, creator of the Forgotten Realms

STRANGE BEASTS

A Novel

SUSAN J. MORRIS

Published by Inky Phoenix Press, an imprint of
Bindery Books, Inc., San Francisco
www.binderybooks.com

Acquired by Kathryn Budig

Edited and designed by Girl Friday Productions
www.girlfridayproductions.com

Cover design: Charlotte Strick
Image credits: Zach Meyer

ISBN (paperback): 978-1-959411-64-2
ISBN (hardcover): 978-1-959411-91-8
ISBN (ebook): 978-1-959411-65-9

Library of Congress Cataloguing-in-Publication data has been applied for.

First edition

This is a work of fiction. Names, characters, places, and incidents are
either the product of the author's imagination or are used fictitiously and
not to be construed as real. Any resemblance to actual persons, living
or dead, organizations, events, or locales is entirely coincidental.

Printed in China

To Mom, for reading to me when I was a child,
and then reading my writing in turn.

And to Dad, for showing me that science is the closest
thing to magic, and encouraging my love of monsters.

CHAPTER ONE

The Royal Society for the Study of Abnormal Phenomena, London Field Office
September 1903

Samantha Harker's heels rang on the fine marble floors as she hurried past plaster reliefs of scenes torn from myth. Gas lights illuminated the carvings, and in their shifting shadows, the Gorgons and Furies and men fighting the Minotaur in his maze seemed to almost *move*.

Despite the fact that she saw the reliefs every day, Sam couldn't deny the thrill that shivered through her at the sight of them. In a world filled with mysteries and monsters, Sam was a hunter.

Or rather, the field agents of the Royal Society for the Study of Abnormal Phenomena were hunters. Sam was more of an Ariadne herself, spending her days surrounded by books, uncovering the secrets of the Labyrinth, and giving her assigned field agents the threads by which they'd find their way to their monsters and then safely home.

Usually, anyway. That thrill shivered through her again, only this time, with an undercurrent of fear.

Sam patted her curls, which had come undone despite the best intentions of her pins. Her borrowed shoes pinched—her mother's feet being far daintier than her own—and her sodden skirts clung to her legs on account of London being London and so rather wet. But her attire would do. It would have to. Touching the St. Brigid medal at her throat for luck, she called out.

"Mr. Wright!"

An older gentleman looked back at her from across the marble foyer, his foot on the stairs that swept up to the Society's private offices. Mr. Wright always looked as if he expected to dispatch a ghoul in the morning and treat with ministers in the afternoon, with a neatly trimmed salt-and-pepper beard and flared moustache to match King Edward VII's own. In his diorite hand—gone to stone courtesy of a misadventure with a cockatrice—he'd wedged a crumpet heavy with marmalade of that bitter British variety that Sam's American tastes just couldn't get used to.

His right hand, as of yet unpetrified, held a briefcase—a dark, heavy thing that looked as if it could withstand an explosion. Which, given that he was the director of the Royal Society for the Study of Abnormal Phenomena, might not be far from the mark.

"Ah, the Harkers' girl. Samantha." A fond smile cracked his face, although he barely knew her beyond the occasional research request. She, however, knew him.

When she was eight, he'd visited her family in Chicago. Crouched in the dumbwaiter, where the walls were thinnest, Sam had eavesdropped on Mr. Wright imploring her father, Jonathan Harker, to join the Society. Or, at the very least, for Sam's mother, Mina, to allow the Society to study her. Mina was one of the few people who'd fallen under a monster's sway and come out the other side, entirely herself save for the angry red scar on her forehead, where the Host had burned her when she was under Dracula's influence.

Jonathan and Mina Harker had refused of course. They had Sam and her brother to think of, after all, and the Society was no environment in which to raise a child. But Sam had become obsessed.

"Research department, second level, isn't it?" Mr. Wright said as she crossed over to him. "You're the very spit and image of your mother."

Sam blushed prettily for him, as she was sure he'd intended. Mr. Wright had adored Sam's mother—still did, even if his fixation on the monsters that had touched her life had warped that affection. He'd been at university with Sam's father, and before the Harkers had moved to America to have Sam, he'd been a frequent dinner guest.

Really, Sam didn't see any great similarity. Oh, she supposed she could pick out her mother's rabbit-brown eyes and her father's slightly crooked lips. But any resemblance was certainly heightened on account of her donning her mother's old tartan skirt and white shirtwaist—as *she'd* intended. She'd even fixed her blonde curls with one of her mother's precious tortoiseshell combs, entrusted to Sam when she left for London, to complete the effect.

Sam needed all the leverage she could get.

Mr. Wright took a bite of his crumpet as he gestured for Sam to fall in beside him. "What can I do for you, Miss Harker? I'm afraid I don't have long—there's apparently a *glaistig* sleeping under my desk, getting wet goat everywhere—but I'm yours until we get there."

"I'd like to put in for the Paris case," Sam said at once, not even bothering to ask why he might have a half woman, half goat in his office. "As a field agent."

Mr. Wright choked on his crumpet. "The Beast attacks?"

Sam could sympathize: the Paris case wasn't exactly breakfast fare.

Four brutal murders in less than two weeks, all in different locations: an art gallery's washrooms and a private dining salon, a moving carriage and a box at the ballet. Every day, the papers reported finding new pieces of the victims—a finger here, a liver there. Though, strangely, they'd never found their hearts. Sam was of the opinion the killer was eating them.

"That's a bloody business, and no place for a woman."

"The victims are all men," Sam said, sparing him an education in just how bloody a woman's business could get. "All Parisian, and of considerable means. The killer has a type, and I'm not it. I'll be as safe in Paris as I am on the streets of London."

Mr. Wright acknowledged the point with a *humph*. "Still, you're a researcher, and a promising one at that. Why on earth should you want to abandon that for the field?"

If she were honest, Sam *didn't*. She loved the library. It had more the feeling of a temple than any earthly office. Fanciful scenes from myth leapt across the vaulted ceilings, heavy bookcases lined the walls, and disturbing oil paintings of queens bathing in blood and gods devouring men hung between them in gilt frames.

Sam could spend reverent hours in the stacks, combing the archives for obscure references by the flickering light of gas lamps, surrounded by that comforting old-book smell and the memories of lazy summer afternoons spent hidden among the towering shelves.

But the library didn't hold the answers she needed—she'd had two years to be sure of that.

"Do you know what it's like in the research department, Mr. Wright?" Sam said, by way of answer. "It's like trying to unravel a mystery with a wineglass, absent the wine, the person who drank it, and the company in which they did so. The field team sends us clues, but the best clues simply can't be bagged. They must be seen, heard, *smelled*. I can help you solve this case, but not from here."

Like all the best lies, it was partly true. Half of solving a mystery was knowing where to look. And that meant learning to listen, and not just to what people said out loud. You had to learn the secret language of glances and quirking lips and the whole library of gleams that could be found in a man's eyes. You had to listen like your life depended on it, because it just might.

The field agents were good at killing things, Sam would give them that, but good listeners they were not.

That was not, however, why Sam needed Mr. Wright to assign her to the Paris case.

"Smelled?" Mr. Wright burst out laughing. "Miss Harker, your passion is to be commended, and I know from your reports that you have a fine set of senses, but you're no Baker Street detective. You couldn't possibly learn anything from the way someone *smells*—"

Sam smiled.

"I can smell you have a mistress," she pointed out, and Mr. Wright shut his mouth. "You wear a wedding ring, but your suit smells, quite strongly I might add, of jasmine, gardenia, and wild roses—scents that represent romantic trysts, secret love, and pain mixed with pleasure."

Sam was cheating, of course. Some of this she'd noticed,

but the wild roses bit? Not even a bloodhound could distinguish that much. The particulars of the lady's perfume were something she'd gathered from the whisper network of women who did the dull work of the Society—cleaning, sorting, archiving, delivering coffee—all without ever being noticed, as if they were some tame variety of ghost.

Sam was a researcher after all; she'd done her research.

"The fashion for respectable women," Sam continued, "is fragrance of a single note, and never on their person, only on their artifacts, meaning the traces that transfer to others are faint. Certainly your wife is a lady, meaning this perfume originates from someone else. The triple-odor extract implies that someone is a younger woman, which the choice of notes supports. In addition, the sheer suffusion of the scent on your person implies she was quite *penetrated* with it—"

"That's enough," Mr. Wright said, his face flushed. "I suppose I asked for that."

Sam inclined her head. "You may count on my discretion."

Mr. Wright turned to face her fully for the first time, his dark eyes piercing right through her. He was an entirely different beast when he was engaged, as if he'd been sleepwalking before, and had only now awoken.

Sam forced herself to stare back at him, for all it unsettled her.

"Very well, Harker," Mr. Wright said at last. A rush went through her at the lack of honorific: *she'd passed.* "But I'm afraid I haven't been entirely open with you—the Paris case has already been assigned."

"What?" Sam said, startled. "To whom?"

"Miss Helena Moriarty."

"Lady M?" Sam's heart sank. The only person more famous

than Mr. Van Helsing in the London field office was the notorious Lady M, or, more properly, Dr. Helena Moriarty. She had a reputation for being brilliant and more than a little terrifying, and she never took partners anymore—not that they would have her.

The only daughter of the infamous Professor Moriarty, the man Scotland Yard had nicknamed the Napoleon of Crime, the man whispered to be behind half the criminal activity in the West, from the theft of priceless French oil paintings to the selling of Egyptian mummies on the underworld's shadow market. The man who had snuffed out London's brightest light, Sherlock Holmes.

The criminal mastermind had nearly buried Dr. Watson along with Holmes, but the stalwart doctor had survived to tell of Professor Moriarty's crime, driving the man from his post at the university into hiding. Rumor had it, Professor Moriarty persisted in running his shadow empire, but no one could prove it. In fact, no one could find proof of the man's continued existence at all.

"What do you know of her?" Mr. Wright asked.

"She's a field agent and an Oxford-educated chemist, specializing in supercritical fluids, though she recently published a paper on liquid chromatography. I, ah"—Sam chose her next words carefully—"I hear she's very clever."

What she'd actually heard was that Dr. Helena Moriarty, when faced with a man who wouldn't stop harassing her, had taken up beekeeping, distilled the queen bee's scent, and slipped it into the offending man's shaving cream. After that, bees had swarmed him—impossibly finding him no matter where he went, wriggling and squirming through cracks and keyholes, air vents, and chimneys. It was enough to drive a man mad.

They just want to be friends, Dr. Moriarty was said to have echoed back at him. For indeed, he was only stung two or three times.

Needless to say, he left her alone after that.

"Right. Well, that makes this simple," Mr. Wright said briskly. He handed her the stern-looking briefcase he'd been carrying. It was even heavier than she'd expected, but she managed to keep from lurching with its weight. "Take this down to Miss Moriarty. If you can convince her to partner with you for this case, I'll speak to Mrs. Martin about covering for your responsibilities in the research department. But if she won't have you, you're to return to your work directly, without complaint."

"Of course." Sam's stomach fluttered with nerves and excitement. A not insignificant part of her had assumed she wouldn't succeed. "Thank you, Mr. Wright."

"Happy to have been of service. Do send my regards to your mother," Mr. Wright said, his hand closing on his office door. "Heavens, I can smell the goat from here."

There was no doubt in Sam's mind that Mr. Wright expected Sam to give up upon the revelation of her intended partner, for Dr. Moriarty had not always worked alone. Three times she'd taken a partner. And each and every time they had come to a mysterious end en route to the case site. Granted, gruesome and mysterious ends were hardly uncommon in this line of work, and Dr. Moriarty had been thoroughly investigated and absolved of all guilt. But three in a row, and with a father like that . . .

People had begun to say she was cursed. That even saying her last name was enough to invoke misfortune, as if she were a character in a Shakespearean play.

Curse or no, Sam wasn't about to give up now.

She found Dr. Moriarty in the firing range—a slender figure in a black suit and a long tan coat, a slash of crimson at her neck.

Gun smoke hung in the air and six bullet holes were clustered in the painted heart of her monstrous target. Sam was impressed: the last time she had tried shooting, she'd nearly taken out a light fixture. Dr. Moriarty paused to reload her revolver.

"I don't know where he is," Dr. Moriarty called without looking up. "But if you find him, do me a favor and punch him in the mouth, will you?"

"Where who is?" Sam said.

Dr. Moriarty looked up. She had a slightly crooked nose and shockingly short ginger curls that escaped her black trilby hat in a cloud. Her eyes were sharp as splinters, and focused entirely on Sam.

"My father, of course," Dr. Moriarty said. Holstering her revolver, Dr. Moriarty strolled over to Sam, peering at her, curious. Sam caught a hint of rosin under the stench of gunpowder, leading her to wonder if Dr. Moriarty played the violin, or if Sam was thinking too much of the romanticized detective stories she'd indulged in as a girl. "But you're not here about him, are you?"

"I'm Samantha Harker, research department, second level. I'm here about the Paris case," Sam said, gathering herself and holding the briefcase out. Dr. Moriarty took it, and Sam couldn't help but notice that it didn't look as if she'd found the briefcase heavy at all. "I want on."

"Ah, so you're the one they sent to spy on me. A researcher this time, and a woman—he's getting better, I'll give him that." Dr. Moriarty leaned back as if everything made sense now. "Of course, he won't have told you yet. He must have been worried I'd read it in your face. He'll tell you after—watch for it."

"I very much doubt it," Sam said. "I expect Mr. Wright thought I'd give up at the prospect of working with you."

"And why haven't you?" Dr. Moriarty inquired, her lilting

accent unmistakably Irish. "Surely you've heard the rumors about the curse of Lady M. I could repeat a few, if you're interested, though I fear I haven't heard the most colorful. The one about the bees perhaps?"

"Is it true?" Sam asked curiously.

Dr. Moriarty shrugged. "Does it matter?"

"Not insofar as my interest in this case."

"Hmm. And what *is* your interest in this case?"

Seventy-four. Ten. One hundred three. Twenty-eight, eight, twenty-seven. Forty-four, one, fifty-six . . .

"Solving it," Sam answered, tucking the numbers back inside her head. Dr. Moriarty didn't need to know about the personal reason for her interest. As far as Sam knew, it was just a ghost of a suspicion haunting the bones of a half-forgotten trauma.

Dr. Moriarty laughed. "Touché. Well then. Let's see what you make of this." She settled the briefcase on the firing range wall and clicked it open. There was a puff of escaping gases and the scent of rotting meat.

Sam recoiled. Inside was a severed human arm, lying there like a piece of butcher's meat wrapped in the sleeve of a suit jacket, the diamond cuff link smeared with blood.

"Oh. That's"—*dreadful, terrible, horrific*—"a lot, isn't it?" Sam said, covering her nose with her sleeve.

"There's a world of blood and pain and death outside your books, Miss Harker," Dr. Moriarty said. "If you can't deal with this, then you certainly can't deal with the Paris case."

"I can feel things and still deal with them," Sam said, a shiver working through her just imagining the power it would have taken to rip an arm clean off at the shoulder. There was probably a book in the library in which she could look that up. "What kind of a person would I be, if this didn't horrify me?"

"What kind of person indeed." Dr. Moriarty's smile pulled crooked, and the rumors of Lady M whispered in the twists of Sam's mind. "Then tell me, what does this piece of evidence reveal about the attacker? Other than that the crime they committed was horrific."

Reluctantly, Sam abandoned her examination of Dr. Moriarty and peered closer at the bloodied arm.

"The attacker is strong—unusually so," she murmured, and Dr. Moriarty snorted. That much was obvious. She turned the briefcase slowly. There were small divots on the humerus, as if the attacker had gnawed on it, the marrow sucked clean from the end of the bone, and she felt a quiet satisfaction at being right, even as her stomach turned over. "The attacker likely ingested part of its victim. There are calluses here, on the finger, from what I assume would be a wedding ring, but given the dismembering of the corpse and his continued possession of a diamond cuff link, I doubt theft was the primary motivation."

"Is that all?" Dr. Moriarty crossed her arms.

It couldn't be all. If Sam couldn't bring more to the investigation, there was no incentive for the doctor to accept her onto the case. She had to find something else, something even the incisive Dr. Moriarty had missed.

There was . . . one other thing Sam might try. She risked a glance at Dr. Moriarty, who was staring at Sam as if she were a puzzle in want of solving. If Sam were caught—

Fear tightened around her neck. She couldn't get caught. Couldn't let Dr. Moriarty know who she was. *What* she was. But she couldn't leave her analysis there, either.

Before she could think better of it, Sam reached out to turn the man's arm over, hoping Dr. Moriarty might mistake the tremble in her hand for mere horror. The moment her fingertips brushed his jacket, a chill went through her. Suddenly she could *feel* her fingernails ripping on the floorboards, could feel teeth tearing into the softness of her belly. And behind it, the sound of someone weeping.

And then the sensations were gone, as if they had never been. Sam found herself clutching the dead man's hand—its nails splintered and torn—and hurriedly let go. Dr. Moriarty stared at her in frank fascination. Sam flushed with fear and embarrassment at once.

"A vivid imagination," her mother had lied when Sam was a child, holding her tight and stroking her hair. "They're just dreams that strayed from the night. Ignore them. Trust in logic. Trust in the rules. They will keep you safe."

"She's a *channel*," her doctors had said when boarding school had failed to set her right and her father had demanded answers.

"It means that you're susceptible to the influence of evil," Jakob Van Helsing had whispered poisonously to Sam when they were still just teenagers lurking in the library at a Society party with their parents. And this, she was to learn, was what most people thought about channels. "You'll get visions from monsters, like your mother did. They'll lead you astray and everyone you care for will suffer for it."

Which was to say, if she wasn't careful and someone caught her channeling a vision, she might be committed to an asylum. She couldn't precisely fault them. The visions came from monsters—as had been well documented in the wake of the Transylvanian affair. If she let the wrong one in, it might corrupt her; it had happened when her mother had channeled visions from Dracula. Worse, it might turn her monstrous herself, like the Harkers' late friend Lucy—transforming her into the very thing she'd sworn to fight.

Still, Sam needed to present Dr. Moriarty with something, or she would leave Sam behind, and then Sam would never solve the mystery of those numbers. With a twist of guilt, she lowered her face to the jacket sleeve, and sniffed.

There—beneath the putrid smell of meat rot and the sharp, coniferous scent of the dead man's cologne was the faintest whisper of salt. It was unsettling, like catching the scent of the ocean in the dark heart of the forest. It did not *belong.*

She felt a prickle on the back of her neck: her vision had been *right.*

"The attacker wept over his victim," Sam said slowly, unable to shake the sense that this was important, even if she didn't yet know how.

"Ah, yes. Harker . . . As in Mina and Jonathan Harker." Dr. Moriarty was watching her intently.

"The fabric on the back of his arm is stiffer than it should be," Sam went on. "But not on account of blood. It smells faintly of salt, and unless the victim was uncommonly flexible, his murderer was the one doing the crying."

Dr. Moriarty leaned in and took a sniff. Her eyes widened. "You're *right.*"

"But what sort of a person cries after committing such a vicious murder?"

"A very good question," Dr. Moriarty said, snapping the briefcase closed. "All right, Miss Harker. You have my attention."

"Please, call me Sam," Sam said on impulse.

"Then you must call me Hel."

"Like *A Midsummer Night's Dream*," Sam said at once, and a smile curled Hel's lips.

"I'm sure we'll be fast friends," Hel said. "Now you'd best pack your bags. We leave for Paris in the morning."

That, Sam thought, was too easy. Lady M never took partners. What had changed?

Sam had channeled, that's what had changed, she thought nervously.

Sam left the gun range only to find Mr. Wright waiting for her in the hall, smelling strongly of barnyard. He motioned her over, with a curtness that had not been there before.

"Miss Harker."

Sam's churning thoughts evaporated with the sudden awareness that her clever plan from that morning might have come across as rather threatening and that he could be sore about it.

She glanced through a window into the gun range at Hel, but Hel had resumed her practice, the gunfire more than sufficient to ensure a private conversation.

"If this is about what I said before—" Sam began.

"No, no, nothing like that," Mr. Wright said. Sam felt a welling of relief. "I take it Miss Moriarty has accepted you onto the case?"

"Yes," Sam said. "We leave for Paris in the morning."

"Excellent, excellent," Mr. Wright said. He was repeating himself more than usual. "I'll speak to Mrs. Martin, as promised. And in return . . . the Society would appreciate it if you'd keep an eye on Miss Moriarty for the duration of this expedition."

"You mean for me to spy on her?" Sam blurted. So this was why he'd let Sam on the case. Hel had been right. She glanced over Mr. Wright's shoulder at Hel again, who winked at Sam, though she couldn't possibly have heard. *Told you so.*

"Nothing so crass as that," Mr. Wright said. Reluctantly, Sam focused on him, her mind burning with questions. "But Miss Moriarty has had three partners on three separate cases, not one of which has returned. And here you are, not even a field agent.

So I am merely . . . suggesting you keep an eye out, for your own safety."

"It's a dangerous business, hunting monsters," Sam said, not quite sure how to feel, but certain she felt ill used. "I'm sure Dr. Moriarty and I will both need to keep an eye out for safety on this trip."

"Of course," Mr. Wright said smoothly, a twinkle in his eye. He pressed a folder into her hands. A bad taste bloomed in her mouth. This wasn't a personnel file—it was the case reports on the deaths of Hel's prior partners.

Of course. How much of this was because of what Hel had done, and how much was because of her father? From everything Sam had read, Hel was an exemplary field agent—solving more cases in six months than most agents did in a year.

But then, her partners *had* died.

"This file will explain everything," Mr. Wright said. "Now, I'm setting you up in a hotel that has installed telephones in every room. I'm told it's very modern, the height of luxury. I have eyes amongst the staff, but of course, they can't be everywhere all at once, so should you happen to see—or smell—anything that isn't precisely as it should be, no matter how insignificant it might seem, you feel free to let me know."

"Thank you," Sam said, mostly because he expected it.

"Don't thank me, I'm putting you in all kinds of harm's way with this." Mr. Wright clapped her on the shoulder. "Good luck, Miss Harker."

As complicated as things were getting, Sam was beginning to think she'd need it.

CHAPTER TWO

The Royal Society for the Study of Abnormal Phenomena, London Field Office

If the Society's library was like a temple, its war room was something else entirely. Sam had only ventured inside once before, when she'd located a rare tablet on trolls, which Mr. Wright had requested for an expedition he was leading into a remote forest in Norway, and she hadn't been allowed to linger. Even on the very morning she left for Paris, Sam felt like an imposter, as if the room itself might smell the books on her and refuse her passage.

The heavy iron door was inscribed with apotropaic symbols from the world over, the doorknob silver and embedded with a relic of a long-forgotten saint. Sam pushed it open.

Ghostly predawn light fell from a glass dome onto a bed of wild roses, garlic, wolfsbane, and sage. Behind the floral display, there was a heavy table of scarred mahogany, covered in maps and diagrams, scrolls and calendars, both esoteric and mundane.

A veritable armory covered the burgundy-and-gold walls: stakes hewn from mountain ash and ornate holy crosses, bolts of blackthorn dipped in all manner of poisons, knives edged with silver, and great iron chains. Apothecary cabinets crowded the room beneath them, their hundred tiny drawers brimming with exorcism salt, skeleton keys, silver bullets, and anything else a field agent might require.

This was where every hunter in the Society prepared for whatever may come. Now it was her turn.

She could scarcely believe it.

When Sam first told her mother she wanted to join the Society—albeit to research rather than hunt monsters—she'd expected her mother to be proud. Instead, her mother had been horrified.

"Why would you think I would be happy for my daughter to risk her life?" Mina said, looking so stricken Sam had the impulse to take it all back.

"But *you* hunted monsters," Sam protested.

"Oh darling," Mina said, taking Sam's hands in hers. "I did what I had to. The alternative was to become a monster—I had to fight for my soul. What mother wants that for her daughter?"

Sam's cheeks burned at the memory. Oh, what had she been thinking, channeling in front of the best field agent in the Society! Honestly, Sam was fortunate she hadn't proved her way into an asylum while she was at it.

Still, a small voice whispered, *it worked.*

Pulling out a drawer in the cabinet, Sam ran her fingers along the collection of oddments, picking up a dagger. The label claimed it had been forged with one of the claws of the Nemean Lion, which were said to cut through anything. Unlikely, Sam thought. It was far too long to be the claw of any lion Sam had seen, more like a tooth, and such an artifact would surely be kept in the vaults, and not where any hunter might—

The door opened. "Miss Harker?"

Sam fumbled the dagger. It fell point first and stuck in the marble floor next to her foot, like the legendary sword in the stone. Sam paled—*genuine after all, then*—and turned, coming face to face with Jakob Van Helsing.

The only son of the esteemed Professor Van Helsing, Jakob was tall and broad shouldered, with neatly trimmed brown hair and the straight nose of a Greek statue. His eyes lived in a state of perpetual crinkle, like a gunslinger ready for a shoot-out, though Sam knew he was quite thoroughly Dutch.

He was still wearing those ridiculous American-style cowboy boots he'd picked up on that giant flying lizard case in the Arizona territory, made of the sun-kissed bronze scales of the beast he'd slain. They jingled with his every step, like a bell on a cat.

"Mr. Van Helsing," Sam said, swishing her skirt over the hilt of the knife.

Van Helsing eyed Sam. "What are you doing here?"

"Same thing you are, I expect," Sam said evenly. She had a right to be there, she reminded herself, no matter how Van Helsing tried to unnerve her.

Van Helsing snorted. "That, I doubt."

To think Sam had once looked forward to seeing him again.

Van Helsing—*Jakob*—hadn't always been that way. All hunter and no heart. Sam remembered autumn evenings spent exploring the woods outside her home, when Jakob and his father had come visiting from the Netherlands, watching the wills-o'-the-wisp dancing between the dark trunks of the trees like blue candle flames. Jakob, still recovering from a near-fatal bout of scarlet fever, had liked to sketch the ghostly lights while Sam told him their stories. Until, that is, his father had caught them.

"Are you looking to die?" Professor Van Helsing had said, his eyes bright with fury. "To light a lantern of your own?"

"I think they're pretty," Jakob had said defiantly, stepping in front of Sam.

"You *think*." Professor Van Helsing snorted. "They're monsters. Spirits rejected by Heaven and Hell who wander the earth, tempting the unwary off the virtuous path. You know Samantha's vulnerable to their influence. It's your responsibility to keep her safe."

"Like you did Lucy?" Jakob said. It had been the wrong thing to say. His father had gone very still, and then there was a *slap*, and Jakob's cheek was red, his great blue eyes welling with tears.

Sam's mother had, in her own way, been worse, for all she hadn't so much as raised her voice. "Did you forget it was wills-o'-the-wisp that led your father to Dracula's castle? You, who have so much more reason to be careful?" It was a song she'd heard before. Even before her parents realized Sam was a channel, everyone who knew the circumstances of her birth had seemed certain something must be wrong with her, the girl conceived when her mother was under Dracula's influence. "You are never to follow them again. Do you hear me?"

"But I—"

"Swear it."

That had been the end of Sam and Jakob's evenings in the forest. She'd seen him on a handful of occasions after that, but it had never been the same.

By the time she'd crossed paths with him at that Society dinner, when they were teenagers, it was as if his father had scraped out everything of the boy she'd known, and poured himself into its place. A Van Helsing, through and through.

Van Helsing picked up the field agent assignment list off the scarred table, his eyebrows rising. "You've been assigned the Beast murders?"

"Jakob," Sam chided. "If I didn't know better, I'd think you worried about me."

"Don't call me that. We're not children anymore." *That* much was obvious. The Jakob she'd known would have been happy for her, or perhaps wanted to come along. Van Helsing scowled. "There is something else going on here, and you know it."

"Do I?" Sam said lightly.

The look Van Helsing gave her could have withered an orchard. "You really think they'd just give you the Beast murders? You, a girl, who has never been out in the field, and who screams when she sees a rat? You don't have the stomach for it. *Duendes*. They have me doing duendes. I should be on the Beast murders."

"The Beast doesn't murder women," Sam said, resisting the urge to clarify that his case dealt with *trasgu*—mischievous goblin-like creatures, which were in fact a subspecies of duende. "Besides, it's not like I'll be alone. I'll be with Dr. Moriarty."

"He put you with Lady M?" Van Helsing's eyes tightened. "That's even worse. Do you know who she is? What she's done?"

"I know she's solved more cases than you."

"Her partners end up dead," Van Helsing said flatly.

"It's a dangerous job," Sam persisted. "And she was cleared of all wrongdoing."

"That just means she hasn't been caught." Van Helsing shook his head, as if she were very slow. And perhaps she was. She couldn't seem to figure out what his aim was. First he seemed suspicious, then jealous, and now concerned. She wondered if even he knew what he truly wanted. "Go back to your library, Miss Harker. I'll clear this up with Mr. Wright. I don't know what could have possessed him to—"

"Don't," Sam said softly. Van Helsing paused, eyes narrowed. "We're not children anymore."

"Do you really think you can hide what you are from her?" Van Helsing drew nearer, so close the hot leather scent of him washed over her. "That she won't find out? What exactly do you think will happen, when the monsters are more than ink on old paper? When you are stuck on some enigma, and can't resist the pull of their voices? The secrets they promise?"

Sam cursed their spotted history—how well he read her fears on her face even now. Van Helsing was one of the few people who knew of her . . . *condition*. That Sam was a channel. She should have expected him to use it against her.

"You sound like my mother." Sam was unable to keep bitterness from edging in.

"Mina's a good woman. You should listen to her."

"Being good didn't save her." The mark on her forehead was proof enough of that.

"If you think I will hesitate . . ." To put her down, he meant. To end Sam the way their parents had Lucy.

She remembered the elder Van Helsing lecturing young Jakob that Sam was his responsibility. That if she died, or worse, became a broken channel, it would be his fault. Jakob might have cared what happened to Sam—they'd been friends, once. But the Van Helsing that stood before her cared only for his reputation. She would do well to remember that.

"Thank you, Mr. Van Helsing," Sam said coldly. The first rays of the sun glittered on the glass in the dome above. The carriage would be pulling up outside any moment, and it was past time she was on her way. "But I can take care of myself. Now, if you'll excuse me, I have a job to do."

And she swept out of the room, heels ringing despite the tremble in her limbs, leaving Van Helsing staring at the dagger piercing the marble floor behind her.

— —

The first thing Sam learned about Hel was that she didn't do small talk.

"How did you know?" Hel asked, leaning in so her voice would carry over the creaking of the carriage and the clopping of the horses' hooves. Just like that, without any nouns or anything.

Sam, offended on behalf of the English language, could only manage, "Sorry?"

Sam was snug in a white wool-and-velvet traveling dress with matching gloves she'd received from her mother, blonde hair piled up under a broad-brimmed white hat that was the first thing she'd bought for herself when she arrived in London. All of which, Sam was certain, were already suffused with that particular traveler's perfume of road dust, freshly oiled leather, and warm horse. They'd been traveling for eight hours and she was on her sixth newspaper puzzle of the morning—studiously ignoring the siren call of the file Mr. Wright had handed her on Hel, her past partners, and the chances Sam was going to be murdered.

Hel, by contrast, looked precisely as she had the last time Sam had seen her, in a black suit, long tan coat, and crimson necktie, her ginger curls electric in the falling light. It led Sam to wonder if Hel had gone home at all the night prior, or if, perhaps, she was nocturnal, like the monsters they hunted. It gave Sam something of the feeling of being an unnaturalist, scouting out the habits and habitations of monsters.

"How did you know that the killer had wept over the man's arm?" Hel clarified.

Oh. *That.* She'd been rather hoping Hel hadn't noticed.

She should have known better. Sam had known what she was risking going into the field with Lady M—and it wasn't just her skin.

"Just a feeling, really."

"A *feeling*?" Hel prompted.

"Don't tell me you don't have them," Sam said tartly.

Hel laughed. "All right, I won't."

From what Sam had read, preparing to leave London had once been tantamount to preparing for war. There had been a troll under every bridge, phantoms on every old battlefield, and highwaymen—most of them remnants of battlefields themselves—crying for you to stand and deliver at every bottleneck out of the city, which all sounded exciting and terrifying at once.

Now the primary danger would be Hel. Whatever people thought of Hel, she was, by all accounts, brilliant. What's more, Hel seemed intent on keeping that brilliance focused squarely on Sam, and in their small carriage, their knees almost touching, there was nowhere to hide.

It would take the rest of the day to make it to Dover, where they'd catch the ferry across the English Channel to Calais, and then they'd spend almost a full day on the train to Paris. As far as Sam could tell, there was nothing but heather and potholes and the occasional churring of a nightjar for miles. And the chances Hel would uncover that Sam wasn't just uncannily perceptive, but a *channel*, grew with every passing hour.

"Anyway, we don't even know for certain the tears are from the killer," Sam said, easing the conversation away from things that could get her committed. "As far as we know, the victim shed the tears himself, after his arm was torn off."

"Unlikely." Hel snorted. "The dead don't cry."

"Unless he wasn't dead yet," Sam said.

Hel waved a hand dismissively. "Oh, he was dead all right. There's no swelling, just a splash of blood in the suit fabric, and bruising on the skin where blood pooled. All of which strongly implies a postmortem amputation."

"It seems like you have it all figured out." Sam was beginning to feel quite unnecessary.

"On the contrary, I missed the tears," Hel said. "Was it something about holding his hand? Do you need to touch things to get these *feelings* of yours?"

Sam tamped down on a flutter of apprehension. Hel was just teasing, she told herself. That was something normal people did—unlike, say, holding hands with a severed arm, lacing fingers like lovers do.

"I could smell the salt," Sam said. Life, she'd found, was easier when you could slip inside the stories others told themselves about you—when you didn't challenge them or their views about the world. "I have a very good nose. Ask Mr. Wright about it sometime."

Hel's gaze flickered over Sam's face. "Am I making you nervous?"

"No," Sam said at once. But as she curled her fingers into her palms, her fingernails felt as if they might splinter. "Yes. Please. Let's just talk about something else?"

"All right then," Hel said, tucking whatever questions she had left under her tongue. Sam was absurdly grateful. "Tell me, what do you know of the Beast of Gévaudan?"

Sam perked up. She'd read quite a lot on the subject. "The Beast of Gévaudan reportedly ravaged the French countryside a century ago. It killed over a hundred people, until it was finally put down by a local hunter with a silver bullet." Sam hesitated, then added, "The origins of the Beast are still unknown. While the silver bullet implies a werewolf, it remains unclear as to whether it was in fact a pack of wolves, a monstrous beast, or a werewolf."

"Not that it stopped us from exterminating them," Hel said.

Fear of the lunar lycanthropes had caught on like wildfire across the continent, and then the world—hunters trading in their deer-hunting rifles for shotguns, melting down coins for slugs, stalking werewolves by the light of the full moon.

"So," Sam said, "are you saying you think there's a link to the Paris case?"

"The papers seem to think so," Hel said, showing Sam the headline of the morning edition of *Le Petit Parisien*: "Le retour de la Bête du Gévaudan." The Beast of Gévaudan Returns.

"But the victims are entirely different," Sam objected. "The Beast focused on women and children and lone travelers, always outside the town's limits. The killer in this case is focusing exclusively on adult men."

"And wealthy ones at that," Hel said dryly. "A most discerning palate for ravening wolves."

A werewolf could be discerning, Sam thought. Moreover, they could operate a *door*. But the last known werewolf had been killed, stuffed, and put on display at the then brand-new Museum of Natural History in New York City thirty years ago, ten years before Sam had even been born.

Unless, of course, they'd missed one. Sam glanced sharply at Hel, who was watching her with a crooked smile.

"A living werewolf . . . ," Sam breathed.

It was no certainty, but just the possibility of getting to study a living werewolf—even if that werewolf was a bit murderous—sent a frisson of excitement through her. For a moment, she forgot to be wary of Hel at all.

"Do you think—"

The carriage wrenched to a stop, pitching Sam and Hel forward just as the window burst right where Sam's head had been moments before. Sam shook her hair out of her face, glass tinkling down around her, to see a sinewy arm with mottled green skin pulling back through the broken window, her beloved London hat crushed in its gnarled grip.

Sam screamed as a bloodshot yellow eye took the place of the arm, roving the inside of the carriage and settling on Sam. She scrambled back as far as she could in the suddenly claustrophobic confines of the carriage—a *grindylow*. Except it couldn't be. Grindylows were amphibious ambush predators, denizens of lakes and rivers and fens. It could never survive the dusty southern heath. Not without help. But who—

Hel drew her revolver. Sam's eyes hooked on the gleaming barrel.

Oh, *Hel*.

CHAPTER THREE

The Road to Dover, England

As Sam stared down the barrel of Hel's revolver, she realized two things:

One, bullets didn't work on grindylows.

Two, which meant that gun was for Sam.

Oh, Sam had been a fool.

"Hold still." Hel cocked her revolver. Sam's heart winged into her throat.

Three partners had died before Sam. Each of them under mysterious circumstances, each of them on the way to their case—exactly as Sam was now. Had Sam thought she was special? That she and Hel had a rapport? Mr. Wright had tried to warn her.

Before Hel could shoot Sam, the driver's whip cracked. The horses screamed; the driver swore. The carriage didn't move; the monster did. Hel's and the grindylow's attention snapped to the front of the carriage, and with a green, sawtooth grin, the grindylow passed out of sight.

Sam didn't have time to think. She threw herself at Hel while she was distracted, wrapping her arms tight around her.

The revolver clattered to the bottom of the carriage and went off, punching a hole to the dusty ground.

"Get off me!" Hel tried to push Sam off, but she clung tight, refusing to lie down and die.

"And make it easy on you?" Her whole body shivered as one of the horse's screams cut off abruptly in a wet ripping sound. She had to get out of there.

"What are you—it's not me trying to kill you, all right?" Hel said. "If I'd wanted you dead, you would be."

Sam looked up, searched Hel's eyes for a moment. She believed her, heaven help her, but she believed her. Only, that meant Hel didn't know everything—a thought that was as reassuring as it was unsettling.

"It's a grindylow," Sam said quickly, releasing Hel, who recovered her revolver. "A water hag. A bullet won't work."

Hel looked at Sam sharply. "Impossible. They never venture this far from their lakes and rivers in the north, and its skin is dry as bone. It's some variety of ogre, surely."

Another of the horses' screams cut off. They were running out of horses.

Thinking fast, Sam pulled out the satchel of rock salt she'd tucked in her skirts in case of ghosts.

Like frogs, grindylows breathed through their skin when they were in the water, and their mouths when on land. But that adaptability came with a price. Salt burned grindylows' skin in small doses and it lethally dehydrated them in greater—like frogs left out in the sun, gone all leathery and stiff.

Ordinarily, the small satchel of salt Sam had pulled out would only antagonize the grindylow. But it was already parched—*dry as bone*—and the blood it was using to slake its thirst was in itself salty, the murderous equivalent of drinking seawater when you were too desperate to remember why it was a terrible idea.

It should only take a little to push it over the edge, provided they could get the salt to stick and not just fall off. Which, admittedly, Sam hadn't figured out yet.

She thrust the bag of salt out to Hel as another horse screamed and went silent, her hands shaking. "Trust me."

One of Hel's eyebrows rose as if to say, *Really?*

Sam's cheeks heated, acutely aware she was asking the woman she'd just accused of attempted murder to trust her. But whatever words Hel had for Sam, her response was interrupted by the *squelch-thunk* of the driver's head hitting the carriage window—his salt-and-pepper hair matted with blood, his thick eyebrows raised in disbelief—before sliding down the window and out of sight.

Outside, the grindylow was holding the driver's headless body above its mouth like an orange and *squeezing*. Its throat worked vigorously as blood poured out of the man in quantities seemingly bent on reminding you that humans were 60 percent water. Sam tore her eyes away, her gorge rising. They were out of time.

"Right." Hel snatched the salt out of Sam's hand and opened the door of the carriage. "Distract it."

"Wait, what are you going to do?" Sam cried. But Hel was already gone.

Even crouched, the grindylow was as tall as the carriage, its body roped with muscle. It tossed the driver's headless body aside like an empty bottle, its toad-like skin glistening with the blood that hadn't made it down its throat. Sam jerked back inside the carriage and out of sight. Then the grindylow lifted its nose to the air and started a strange, wheezy trilling. *Uh-ehe-ehe-ehe-ehe-ehe. Uh-ehe-ehe-ehe-ehe-ehe.*

At first, it sounded far away, like the churring of the nightjars in the heath. Then, as if it were right outside. She could hear its nose working, scenting Hel out. Sam had to do something before it did—distract it, pull its attention back to her. If she didn't, Hel's plan would fail, and they'd both be done for.

Sam's legs went limp as shucked stockings. She'd read about this phenomenon—how the body tried to help when it decided you were going to die. *Shhh, don't struggle. It will all be over soon. You won't feel a thing.* She'd found it reassuring at the time.

She did not find it reassuring now. How had Sam ever thought she could survive the field? She was a researcher for goodness' sake. Her biceps were entirely theoretical, her greatest adversary the occasional paper cut. Neither of which prepared her to fight *monsters.* Even her *body* thought she was going to die. And Hel had taken her salt. Sam squeezed her eyes shut, tears leaking between her lashes.

It's not enough, she thought. I'm *not enough.* What kind of diversion could Sam even accomplish, putting aside for a moment the fleeting diversion of her death—

Except wait, no, don't put it aside—that was it, wasn't it? *That* was the distraction.

Like a killdeer leading a snake from her nest, Sam's potential death would capture the grindylow's attention far better than anything else she might devise.

The hard part was going to be keeping it *potential.*

Sam stole a glance outside, her eyes lighting on the kerosene lantern, her mind catching with the reports she'd filed on Emma Livry and Mary Wilde—women who Sam was certain hadn't spontaneously combusted no matter what defenses Charles Dickens mounted for the phenomenon in excuse for his books.

Far more likely the young women's high-fashion, highly

flammable dresses had proved the architects of their demise. And a plan came together in the back of her mind.

It was just in time. No sooner had she opened the carriage door than the grindylow's arm came groping through the window, fingers scrabbling after her with thick, yellowed claws. Thinking quickly, Sam scooped up shards of glass from the broken window and threw them at the grindylow's eyes.

It only bought her a moment, but a moment was all Sam needed. The grindylow recoiled and Sam scrambled out the other side of the carriage, tearing the petticoat off her mother's dress as she ran, ripping pieces with her teeth and hands and then the little knife she'd somehow forgotten she had. She grabbed the carriage's kerosene lantern as she raced past, her feet crunching on glass.

The grindylow's bloodshot eyes were fixed on her as it loped around the far side of the carriage, making that horrible sound. *Uh-ehe-ehe-ehe-ehe-ehe.* It took every tendon of strength she could muster not to answer the urging of her heart and *run* as she frantically spread the shreds of her petticoat in a nest around her.

The grindylow's jaw gaped—so close, Sam could smell the coppery rot of its breath—and it lashed out with a hand big enough to squash her head like an egg. Sam held her ground and smashed the kerosene lantern down.

The effects were immediate. Glass shattered and fire burst up around her, flaring in the prepared circle of her petticoat. Sweat slicked her brow and dried in an instant. The grindylow shrieked, cradling its withering hand as the ring of flames danced around Sam.

It was uncomfortably like being burned at the stake—a destiny that might have been Sam's had she been born a hundred years earlier. Still, Sam sobbed in relief, her tears evaporating off her cheek. For a blessed moment, she was *safe*.

Hel, whatever you're going to do, do it now, Sam thought, not letting herself imagine what might happen to her if the other woman had already done it—abandoning Sam to be just another mysterious death on her list, probably filed under spontaneous combustion.

The grindylow paced the fire, a sack of skin on its neck pulsating with that horrible sound. *Uh-ehe-ehe-ehe-ehe-ehe.*

Then, almost thoughtfully, the grindylow plucked up half a horse, like a daisy from a garden. It squeezed it, absently, though it had been long since drained dry.

"What are you doing? No, put that down. Stop—look at me!" Sam shouted, waving her arms to distract it. But there was nothing she could do, trapped in her ring of fire, except watch as it tossed the horse's haunches onto the burning petticoat.

Deprived of oxygen, the fire beneath the half horse sputtered and went out. The grindylow's sawtooth smile spread. Sam turned to run, but the fire still raged behind her, and her dress was highly flammable. She thought of Emma Livry again—she'd died before she could be doused. Sam would die caught by her own cleverness.

Why hadn't she trapped the grindylow? Or just set it on fire, for that matter?

Mr. Wright had been right: she was no field agent.

The grindylow reached for her. Sam screamed, shielding her face with her arms.

Thump!

Sam cracked open her eyes, her vision hazy with smoke. The grindylow's claws had just missed her. As she watched, its leg crumpled beneath it, a crater on the back of its knee spilling duckweed.

Hel cocked the driver's coach gun as she walked fearlessly toward the monster, lining up another shot.

Bullets don't work! Sam tried to shout. Given sufficient hydration levels, the duckweed flesh of the grindylow could pull itself back together again and again. But all that came out was a wheeze, the flames wicking away even the air from her lungs. If she didn't get out of there soon, Sam knew, she'd have simply exchanged one death for another.

Howling with rage, the grindylow made a grab for Hel, but she deftly stepped past and, while it was off balance, shot it in the back of the other knee. *Thump!* It fell to its knees, hard, keening, as if in prayer.

At last, Sam saw the brilliance of what Hel had done.

Hel hadn't fired shot—she'd fired *salt.*

The grindylow was unable to heal its wounds. The duckweed shriveled around the salt, spilling to the ground like so much rice. And between the salt, the fire, and the blood, the already dangerously dehydrated grindylow swayed on its knees once, and then passed out. Hel tossed the coach gun aside.

"You came back." Sam stumbled out of the ring of fire over the charring remnants of the horse. "I half thought you'd run off on me—"

Hel turned to her and smiled crookedly. "There you are." She drew her revolver and fired.

Sam flinched as the bullet popped past her ear. Turning slowly, Sam saw a man rolling in the heath, clutching his calf and screaming as his brethren—six more men, bristling with armaments—scattered in all directions.

Hel holstered her revolver, striding over to the man collapsed in the heather.

"You bitch!" the man sputtered.

"Fetch our medical supplies, will you, Sam?" Hel said, not taking her eyes off him. "This man's been shot."

"Y-yes, of course." It wasn't until Sam had plucked the small black bag of first aid from the carriage and was heading back that she noticed something she hadn't before: gouges on the grindylow's back. Marks around its neck and ankles, as if from a spiked collar and manacles. Burnt flesh on its back: a brand of ownership in the shape of a barghest, a monstrous black dog.

Fury snapped through Sam as the pieces clicked.

The grindylow, so far from the lakes and rivers in the north—it must have been bought off the shadow market by the highwaymen responsible for that brand. They seemed too afraid of the woman who'd slain it to have caught the grindylow themselves.

Now that she thought about it, she seemed to recall hearing something about Professor Moriarty selling monsters to the highest bidder.

The highwaymen must have kept the grindylow chained and collared, beat it when it misbehaved, and kept it so desperately dehydrated that when they let it out of its cage, all they had to do was point it in the right direction, and it would attack, killing horses and humans alike, risking the salt of its victims' blood to quench its parched skin and leaving the highwaymen to collect the treasure left behind.

The cruelty of humans was far worse than that of literal monsters. At least the grindylow had a reason for acting the way it did. Like crocodiles pulling the weakest wildebeest into the river, they needed flesh to survive. Humans were their natural prey. The humans who had done this to the grindylow—buying it on the shadow market, dragging it from its home, torturing it, forcing it to murder passersby just to slake its terrible thirst—they had no reason at all but *evil*.

By the time Sam handed Hel the medical bag, she was glaring at the man so fiercely he actually flinched.

"Why did you attack us?" Sam demanded as Hel cut the trousers away from the bullet wound. Sam handed her tweezers.

"You all right in the head?" the man said. "That was a grindylow that attacked you, not—*argh!*"

Hel stabbed the tweezers into the sea of his flesh, fishing for the bullet. "I'd answer her question if I were you," Hel advised when he stopped screaming.

"All right, all right!" he panted, his shirt damp with sweat. "Word was there were a couple of wealthy, um . . . ladies coming this way. Large travel trunks, no men. It was an easy job, of course we took it."

"Was it?" Sam said acidly, and Hel gave her an amused glance. The bullet tinkled as it hit the pan.

"No!" the man said miserably, and then screamed as Hel poured iodine over the wound.

"Right, well, do your fellows a favor," Hel said as she expertly packed and bound the wound, "and let them know never to trust whoever told you about this job again. Are we clear?"

"Yes, ma'am," he managed.

"Good. Now get."

Sam scowled after him as he staggered after his "friends," but to her surprise, he didn't try anything.

"So, you have some bite after all," Hel said. "I was beginning to think you were applying for sainthood."

"Those men tortured and enslaved that poor grindylow and tried to murder us with it!" Sam exclaimed. "I should think the use of teeth well deserved."

"No doubt most men feel differently." Hel laughed.

"Is this like what happened to the others?" Sam blurted. "Your partners, I mean. Before me."

Is someone trying to kill me?

"It's probably wisest to assume so," Hel said. "But why are you asking me? Mr. Wright gave you my file—don't tell me he didn't, he always does. All your 'answers' should be there."

"I didn't read it," Sam said, and for the first time since Sam had met her, Hel looked surprised. Honestly, Sam was a little offended. "We're supposed to be *partners*, Hel. Reading that file would be like saying I thought you were guilty. And that's a terrible place to begin a partnership."

"Says the woman who tackled me in the carriage, accusing me of trying to murder her," Hel said dryly.

"How was I to know the legendary Lady M couldn't identify a common grindylow?" Sam retorted. "I thought that gun was for me." Her cheeks were burning again with the sharpness of her tongue, but Hel just laughed.

"When you put it that way, it sounds downright logical," Hel said. "You don't believe him then? Mr. Wright?"

"I intend to make my own decisions about such things," Sam said firmly. And then, after a moment's hesitation, she asked quietly, "Do you think those were your father's men?"

If it wasn't Hel killing her partners, perhaps they were simply casualties in the twisted war Hel's father waged against her.

Hel was silent for long enough that Sam was sure she wasn't going to answer. That she was just going to stop talking, and they'd make their way to Paris like that, and somehow solve the case by way of hand gestures and significant looks. Then Hel sighed.

"The thing you have to understand," Hel said quietly, as if the shadows might overhear, "is that someone like my father doesn't have 'men.' He's a whisper of information, a nudge on someone's baser instincts, a finger on a domino whose effects spiral out in unseen designs. He doesn't order attacks—he manipulates the circumstances so that the attacks happen without ever having to dirty his hands."

"So . . . those men," Sam said slowly. "If they were working for your father, they wouldn't even know it?"

"Of course not. Otherwise, he'd have to pay them," Hel said. "Worse, they could be traced back to him."

"But then, if he's not paying them, how could he be sure they wouldn't kill you?"

"He couldn't," Hel said. "Like I keep telling everyone, we're not close."

"But you're his daughter!" Sam burst out. "Even if you're at odds . . . surely he doesn't want you dead."

"A daughter who can't survive a half-dead grindylow is no daughter of his," Hel said. "My father places a great value on usefulness. I should be grateful to have so many opportunities to prove it."

Sam was stunned. "Hel . . . I'm sorry."

"Don't be. As I said—we're not close," Hel said lightly. But she looked away, and Sam saw her smile slip for a second, before she pulled it into place again. Sam's heart squeezed. Oh, she knew what that was like.

"The more relevant question," Hel said, "is how we're going to manage to make it to Dover in time for the ferry. We seem to be fresh out of horses. And coachmen."

"That poor man," Sam said, mortified that she'd forgotten all about him. She hoped his death had been quick, for it couldn't have been painless. "If not for us, he'd still be alive."

"If not for those men," Hel corrected. "You didn't do this. They did." Sam was about to protest—their carriage never would have been attacked if not for Sam and Hel—but something about the set of the woman's jaw gave her pause. How many times had Hel's father murdered those around her? How many times had she been forced to tell herself this story, just to survive it?

Sam imagined the corpses piled at Hel's feet, bodies enough to bury her.

Hel sighed. "We had better get walking."

"I might have a better idea," Sam said, making for her travel trunk and pulling out the case with her precious wireless telegraph. There was a receiver in Dover, if she remembered correctly.

"You have a wireless telegraph?" Hel leaned in for a closer look. "Not even Mr. Wright has one of those."

"My grandfather had an obsession with radiotelegraphy," Sam said, stroking the smooth grain of the wood. Wills-o'-the-wisp eased out of twilight heath to alight on the machine, floating above it as if on invisible currents, as they always did when radio waves were involved. Radio waves, she'd learned later, were the true reason there'd always been wills-o'-the-wisp behind her house. "I suppose I caught it from him."

Hel gave her a measuring look. "You are far more interesting than I gave you credit for, Samantha Harker."

You have no idea, Sam thought.

The memory of her grandfather's hands warmed her own as she carefully unpacked and set the wireless telegraph up, remembering the quiet way he'd talked, the way his big, calloused hands had managed to move so delicately. Remembering the way he'd never precisely contradicted Sam's mother, but offered Sam acceptance and the saint medal from around his own neck for protection.

Remembering the day she'd gone into her grandfather's attic to find him gone, the falling light of day catching on the dust in the air, and those numbers *tap-tap-tapping* over the radiotelegraph.

Seventy-four. Ten. One hundred three. Twenty-eight, eight, twenty-seven. Forty-four, one, fifty-six . . .

For Sam's mother, who had grown up thinking herself an orphan, it had been the second time he'd disappeared from her life. After the death of her grandmother, her grandfather had apparently been unable to cope and had left Sam's mother on the doorstep of a church. It was awful to think of—and difficult to align the protective, loving grandfather she'd known with one who would abandon his only child—but it gave Sam hope that perhaps her grandfather might not be dead, but had only disappeared a second time.

Though if he had, she wasn't sure how she was going to forgive him.

It was *ten years* before Sam saw those numbers again, in a newspaper photograph of the graffiti at the first of the Beast murders: a wolf under a five-pointed star, standing on a broken crown, over the words *Car la solde du péché, c'est la mort.* For the wages of sin is death.

And, extending from the star in rays that looked innocuous unless you knew what you were looking for: the dashes and dots of Morse code, spelling out her grandfather's numbers.

Sam didn't know the connection. She didn't even know if there was one. But she knew she needed to find out.

She should tell Hel, Sam thought, about her grandfather's

numbers, and her interest in the Paris case. Hel had confessed something personal—Sam ought to return the favor. That was how partnerships went.

But when Sam opened her mouth to talk about it, something in her resisted. She'd give herself a little while longer to get to know Hel, just to be sure she could trust her.

CHAPTER FOUR

Lapérouse, Paris

If Paris was the boudoir of Europe, then Lapérouse was everything that had given it that salacious reputation.

One of the finest dining establishments in all of France, it was said the literati of the Romantic era had written their magnum opuses in its candlelit corners. That jewels flashed in the shadows as the mistresses of the rich and powerful tested their diamonds on the Venetian mirrors, leaving behind scratches like the ones they left down their lovers' backs. That in Lapérouse, politics mixed with poetry and became pillow talk on velvet love seats the color of spilt wine.

It was also where they'd found the latest body.

A boy in a red uniform had chased them down the steam-wreathed train platform in Paris to deliver the telegram, and though it was late and Sam and Hel had been exhausted from the trip, the news had electrified them to new action: *Edouard Barrere slain at Lapérouse.*

It was a wretched thing to feel excitement at a man's murder, Sam thought, even if it was at least half nerve-eating fear. But it was as inescapable as the feeling that she was rushing up to a cliff. Everything was about to change in ways she could scarcely imagine. The hunt for the Beast, for her grandfather's numbers, for whatever connection ran between them—it all began *here*.

There was no turning back now, if there ever was.

Sam tilted her head back, the wind pulling through the curls that had escaped her hat. The moon was fat and golden in the night sky. A werewolf's moon, if ever there was one. And she found herself wondering if right then, a surviving werewolf might be looking up at that same golden moon.

Lapérouse was a jewel box of a building that gazed over the River Seine. It looked precisely as Sam had pictured it: the gilded cobalt-blue façade, the lanterns swaying on iron tendrils, and that infamous thorny *L* gleaming on the corner.

Sam's cheeks heated as she allowed her gaze to linger on its painted panels, each featuring a different fashionable young lady, trying not to imagine what her mother might say.

Louise, a young woman Sam had known who'd once worked in Paris, had told her about Lapérouse in a voice that was barely above a whisper, confiding in Sam about the buttons on the inside of the *petit salons*—the small, private dining rooms where senators met their mistresses. About how if you didn't push that button, no one would open the door, no matter what sounds might come from within.

"This is a waste of time," Hel murmured as they showed their credentials to the police—*gardiens de la paix publique*—guarding the door to Lapérouse.

Hel looked the same as always, in her crimson necktie and black suit, for which she apparently had some special dispensation, as women in Paris were forbidden to wear slacks.

"How is talking to the police after a murder a waste of time?" Sam, by contrast, had worn her Parisian best for the occasion—her blonde hair piled up under a white hat, her waist cinched with a pink velvet ribbon over a pale green dress. "It's standard practice."

"They obviously don't know what's going on, or they would have solved it already," Hel said. "They'll only infect us with their bad ideas."

They pushed open the door, and chaos greeted them. The scent of alcohol bloomed in the air, glass crunching under the officers' boots. Coats were abandoned on red velvet settees like the shed skins of snakes, and armless Grecian statues twisted amidst abandoned tables and toppled chairs.

And looming on the wall behind the bar, sketched in wild strokes of glistering black, a hollow-eyed black wolf under a five-pointed star, its legs dripping down onto a broken crown, over now-familiar words: *Car la solde du péché, c'est la mort.*

It was just like the one photographed in the newspaper article about the first murder, the one that had brought Sam here.

Except . . . not *just* like. Sam's brow knit as she searched the graffiti. Missing were the dashes and dots of Morse code in the rays of the star like the one in the newspaper. In fact, the star didn't have any rays at all.

No numbers.

"Romans 6:23," Hel murmured, frowning at the words. "For the wages of sin is death."

"How do you—" Sam broke off, then started again. "Do you just know that?"

Hel shrugged. "I go to Mass," she said, as if that explained anything.

Sam frowned. She went to Mass too, though admittedly with less frequency than her mother might like, and it had taken Sam an embarrassingly long time to track down the source of the verse. She certainly didn't have it memorized.

But before Sam could pry further, the lead officer came over, taking off his cap and wiping the sweat from his brow. He had a wiry build and warm-brown skin. Like the others, he wore a navy double-breasted suit with red piping. Unlike the others, he had striking eyes, so dark they were almost black, and cauliflower ears that stuck out beneath his tightly coiled hair.

"You must be what England has sent us," the officer said, looking them over like he'd send them right back.

"And *you* must be a detective—"

"*Hel,*" Sam chastised. She turned her best smile on the officer. "We received a telegram at the station. There's been another murder?"

"You're Irish," the officer said to Hel, and it was like lifting a needle off a record and setting it in a different groove. Right— the English and the French had a history. "And you're American. My apologies, mademoiselles, I am being rude. I am Officer Berchard. Welcome to the City of Lights—though, I am afraid it is not so very light at the moment."

Hel smiled crookedly. "That's why we're here. Dr. Helena Moriarty." Hel shook the officer's hand once, in the French fashion, then gestured at the disarray around them. "And this is Samantha Harker, my partner. Who's the artist?"

"They call themselves the Loups de Dieu," Officer Berchard said. "The Wolves of God."

"Are they a religious organization, then?" Sam asked.

Officer Berchard shook his head. "They'd like you to think so. But I know these men. A year ago, they were nothing more than common thieves working out of Montmartre. They like to work in packs—one to sneak up behind a man and wrap a cord around his neck, holding him fast while two more steal everything but his shadow." He flashed papers to the officers guarding the hall, then hesitated. "Are you certain you wish to see the body? It's not the sort of thing I would wish on my sister. And we have detailed sketches that might better suit—"

"The body," Sam and Hel said simultaneously, and they exchanged a glance.

"Right then." Officer Berchard cleared his throat and straightened his cuffs. "Follow me."

The floorboards creaked as Sam and Hel trailed after the officer.

The halls of Lapérouse were a gilded ribbon red. The effect was somehow carnal—as if they were walking through arteries and veins and not hallways at all. Every so often, they passed through a lingering trail of perfume. *Orange blossom, jasmine and neroli, and vetiver.*

"Do you think the Wolves of God are responsible?" Sam asked, feeling a bit dizzy. All her life, she'd been taught to blend in. The women of Lapérouse, by contrast, seemed intent on suffusing the air with the memory of their skin, taking up space long after they'd left, in a way that was almost scandalous. "For the murders, I mean."

"If the Wolves of God didn't do it, they're certainly bent on taking credit for it," Officer Berchard said.

"The wolf and the crown," Sam murmured.

"Exactement," Officer Berchard said.

Hel frowned. "That graffiti—it's at every murder?"

"Well, no," Officer Berchard admitted. It wasn't at the murder with the carriage, Sam remembered. Or at least, no one had seen it there. "But most."

"And you said the Wolves of God were thieves, not murderers," Hel pressed.

"Criminals escalate," Officer Berchard said. "We see it all the time."

"Do you know how long it takes to dismember a corpse, Officer?" Hel asked.

"Can't say that I do," Officer Berchard answered.

"It's an *uncomfortably* long time," Hel said, with unnerving certainty. "And it draws a lot of unwanted attention from people like yourself. There are a multitude of easier ways to steal a purse before you get to dismemberment and cannibalism. Something must have changed for them to escalate like that."

"What if the Wolves of God managed to get hold of a monster? Something like the Beast of Gévaudan?" Sam offered, thinking of the highwaymen they'd encountered and their captive grindylow. Historically, highwaymen called for you to *stand and deliver*, and should you do so, spared your life. The grindylow had changed all that—turned thieves into murderers. "Perhaps that's why the Wolves of God have changed their behavior."

"Is that why the English sent you?" Officer Berchard scoffed. "Of course the newspapers say the Beast has returned. It sells more papers, doesn't it?"

"You don't believe them?" Sam asked.

"The reporters, they don't walk the streets like we do. They don't see what we see," Officer Berchard said. "There has not been a single shred of evidence for any sort of Beast. How would they even get it in here, without someone noticing? Meanwhile, the Wolves of God are crawling over the crime scenes—"

"And yet, you catch the Wolves," Hel said, "and the rich and powerful keep turning up dead."

"Because there are thirty thousand of them against only

eight thousand of us!" Officer Berchard was getting heated. "Of course there are more murders. Catch one of the Wolves of God, and there's always another. If the French Senate weren't cowards . . ." At the last moment, Officer Berchard seemed to realize who he was talking to and his cauliflower ears reddened.

Another piece of the puzzle slotted into place.

Instead of empowering the police, the Senate had appealed to the Society—revealing France's weakness to their longtime rivals, the English. Even if the Society was their best chance at ridding Paris of a monster, it was a bitter pill to swallow.

Sam shot a sidelong look at Hel, but Hel was frowning at the carpet. No—at the dark stain spreading from beneath the door they'd stopped at. Sam's heart stuttered.

"This is it," Officer Berchard said. He dug a key out of his pocket and hesitated once more. "Are you—"

"We didn't brave the English Channel to look at drawings," Hel assured him.

Officer Berchard shook his head and opened the door.

A new scent spilled out to lap against the ribbon-red walls. Not the upsetting musk of animal rot that had bloomed from the arm in the briefcase, but earthen sweet and humid—as if all the moisture that had been contained within the man hung in the air, pressing against Sam's skin like a ghost.

Hel picked her way carefully inside, and Sam moved to follow, taking in the room in small little gulps. The dining table was upended, the white china like bits of bone in the blackening pool. There was a Venetian mirror covered in a tangle of graffiti-like scratches, a red velvet settee, and a fresco of lilies and monkeys splattered with blood.

And then there was the body.

"What do we know about him?" Hel asked.

"M. Barrere is the third son of minor nobility," Officer Berchard said from the hall. "He's a shareholder in the Company of the Upper Ubangi Sultanates, involved primarily in rubber production, and is well connected with the French Senate. Married, no children. He was shown to the petit salon he'd reserved at 9:00 p.m. By 10:00, blood was discovered in the hall by a server."

M. Barrere lay splayed on the floor in what must once have been a very expensive suit—belt undone, wedding band missing, eyes clawed out, ribs cracked open, lungs pulled out like strange fruit.

A wet cavity where his heart should have been—rough and uneven, as if it had been *chewed* out of him.

Acid washed the back of her throat. When her mother, Mina, was Sam's age, she'd come upon Mrs. Westenra savaged by a wolf under Dracula's power. It had been a gruesome encounter, the details of which Sam's father had edited for public sensibilities—papering over the worst of the violence and removing Mina from the scene entirely.

Sam wondered if this was how her mother had felt, staring at what the wolf had left of her best friend's mother. Except, of course, that would have been so much worse. Mrs. Westenra was someone Mina had loved. This was a stranger.

Come on, keep it together, Sam. You faced down a grindylow with nothing but a torn petticoat and a lantern. You can do *this.*

"Who was M. Barrere dining with?" Hel asked.

"M. Barrere's reservation was for one," Officer Berchard said.

Hel raised an eyebrow. "For *one*?"

"That's what the reservation was for," Officer Berchard maintained.

"His wife?" Hel pressed.

"In Provence, visiting her sister," Officer Berchard said. "We've sent a telegram."

Sam tried to keep her attention on the conversation, but her gaze kept slipping to the corpse on the floor. To his outstretched arm, still reaching toward a bloody handprint that trailed down the wall. To the fingernail, caught in the gilded moulding, just out of reach of that infamous button.

Sam pressed the back of her hand to her mouth, trying desperately not to be sick. Had Sam once found that button erotic? It was horrific.

"Is the mademoiselle all right?" Officer Berchard said.

"She's fine," Hel said, without looking.

Sam smiled weakly at Officer Berchard. "I just—I need a moment." She sat down on the settee, keeping her eyes fixed on the candle-smoke stains on the ceiling.

This was what she had asked for, Sam reminded herself. She'd been *so sure* if only she could be at the murder scenes in person, she would see something the field agents wouldn't. But now that she was here, it was all she could do not to be sick on the poor victim, who had, doubtless, already suffered enough.

Sam squeezed her eyes shut, tears of frustration leaking between her lashes, and sank her fingers into the cushions. A small, hard knot pressed against her palm, and the air left her lungs in a *whoosh*, leaving Sam gasping as sensations that were not hers crashed over her.

"Mademoiselle?" Officer Berchard exclaimed.

It isn't real, Sam told herself as she struggled to draw breath against a sudden crushing weight on her ribs. *None of this is real.* It was just a vision. Just emotional noise from the monsters in the vicinity.

But now the vision was crunching down on her windpipe

and raking the softness of her eyes. It was salt on her lips and teeth sinking into her heart, it was her entire body convulsing—

Sam was vaguely aware of shouts as she retched, of leaning on someone as they half carried her from the room, her fist clenched tight on whatever had triggered her vision.

"Mademoiselle." Officer Berchard knelt before her, looking well alarmed now. Hel was still in the room, sticking a hat pin into the man's wounds. Sam was back in the hall, sitting on a plush velvet chair that she was pretty sure hadn't been there before. She uncurled her hand to see a garnet bead. "Are you with me?"

Sam quickly closed her fingers. "Yes, I'm sorry, I'm fine. Thank you."

Officer Berchard's face went through a succession of emotions before landing on chivalry. "I will fetch you a brandy. Stay here."

Sam uncurled her fingers, revealing the garnet bead again. It was small—of the size and shape typically strung on necklaces with diamond centerpieces. It might have been lost between those cushions for ages, of no more relevance to the crime than the couch itself. Except the garnet bead still carried fragrance. Gardenia, jasmine, tuberose, and lily. And given the strength of that fragrance, it couldn't have been there long, an hour at most.

Hesitant, Sam turned and scratched the garnet bead on the mirror behind her, the stories of mistresses testing their jewels on the Venetian mirrors ghosting through her mind like a memory. To Sam's surprise, it didn't leave a mark.

The garnet bead is fake.

Sam didn't know what was more startling, the thought that M. Barrere, rich as he was, might have given his mistress fake garnets, or that the floor wasn't covered in them. Unlike fine jewelry, in which the necklace was knotted between each stone, a cheap necklace was strung with the stones one after the other. If snapped it would spray the floor with the glittering red gems, which any thief would know weren't worth the risk of collecting.

"There may be something to your captive-Beast theory after all," Hel said. Sam startled. Hel was leaning on the doorframe, peeling off her gloves. "I found a partial paw print in the blood, canid or felid, which means it's not a spirit, and the bite marks are from a large canine's incisors. Potentially lupine, only a wolf would have eaten the lungs on the way to the heart, not pulled them out of the—wait, what's wrong?"

"I—" Sam started, but found she couldn't finish.

Ignore them, her mother had said, fear eating her voice until all that was left was a whisper. *Trust in logic. Trust in the rules. They will keep you safe.*

You'll get visions from monsters, Jakob Van Helsing had said, *like your mother did. They'll lead you astray.*

But even if the source was monstrous, the vision about the tears had proved accurate—and lives were at stake. If her vision had even a chance of being true . . .

Van Helsing had been right: she couldn't resist. And she couldn't hide what she was. Not from Hel.

"You have to promise me," Sam said, startling them both by taking hold of Hel's hands. "Promise me you won't tell anyone what I'm about to tell you." If anyone back at the Society found out she was listening to the monsters, if they decided she was compromised . . .

"Of course." Hel searched Sam's eyes, as if she could pull the truth from them. Sam looked away lest she find it before Sam did herself.

"You were right. In the carriage," Sam said, haltingly at

first. "I'm a—" She couldn't bring herself to say it, she'd spent so many years hiding it. "Sometimes when I touch something, I get glimpses of the past. Images and sensations that aren't mine. I know I shouldn't trust them, that everyone says they're monstrous, dangerous to me and others, but—"

Hel leaned in. "You saw something just now, didn't you?"

"Before I smelled the tears on the severed arm, I had a vision, and it came—" Sam broke off as what Hel said registered. "Wait, you *believe* me."

Hel shrugged. "You were right about the tears."

"Yes, but . . ." This was not the way Sam had expected this to go. "You realize these visions come from monsters, right? That a vampire used my mother's visions to manipulate her?"

Hel snorted. "Van Helsing say that?"

"He said she very nearly became a monster herself," she said, swallowing the words he'd said about Sam. He was cruelty in cowboy boots, that one. "That she was a prayer from getting everyone killed!"

"So was Van Helsing's father," Hel said dryly. "I read the report. He never could have taken down that vampire without your mother's visions. Men like him are entirely too quick to call a woman mad or monstrous just because she can do something they can't. Don't do it for them."

"And if they're right?" Sam said quietly, unable to wipe away the echo of her mother's fear—the garlic flowers in the windows, the nights Sam would wake up to her mother watching her from the doorway, as if afraid she'd be drawn out in the night . . . the holy cross burned into her mother's forehead.

"I watched you fight the grindylow," Hel said with that crooked little smile. "If you turn into a monster, I'm pretty sure

I can take you. Now, are you going to tell me what you saw, or should I start guessing?"

Sam ended up telling her about both visions—slowly at first, in measured language that kept slipping as she remembered the feeling of teeth tearing at the softness of her belly, the ghost of pain shivering over her nerves.

"Lupine, certainly," Hel mused. "But captive Beast or trained wolf?"

"Or werewolf," Sam added.

Hel shook her head. "The moon is right for werewolves tonight, but that only means the moon was wrong the night of the first attack. Unless there's some new variety of lycanthrope."

Historically, werewolves only transformed when a full moon's light suffused the sky—three days on average. But what if werewolves had changed, *evolved* to escape mass extinction? Stranger things had happened.

Though perhaps she only wanted that to be true.

"There's one more thing." Sam held up the garnet bead. "I found this between the cushions." And she told Hel about necklaces, fine and fake, and what it meant.

"A mistress," Hel muttered. "Well, of course. No one comes to Lapérouse to dine alone."

"She might have seen something," Sam said.

"She might have killed him," Hel said. "We need to find her. If you're right, and there is some new variety of werewolf in play, she is the most obvious suspect."

"But Officer Berchard—"

"Might be in on it," Hel said.

Sam started to object, only to realize with a sinking feeling that Hel might be right. *Someone* had cleaned up the rest of the garnet beads. There was motive, too: Officer Berchard was un-happy with the Senate for calling in the English instead of em-powering the police.

Except her thoughts kept catching on Officer Berchard's kindness. He'd noticed she wasn't well, carried her outside when her legs wouldn't, brought her a chair when there wasn't one, and gone to get her a brandy to steady her nerves. . . .

He was taking an awful long time pouring it.

"He didn't seem especially religious," Sam protested weakly. Whereas the killer, whoever he might be, absolutely was. One didn't leave a Bible verse at every crime scene, judging the vic-tims for their sins, unless one wished to give at least the appear-ance of piety.

"It's France. Everyone's religious. The country is 98 percent Catholic," Hel said flatly. "Besides, he lied to us, and not to cover for Barrere. The man's dead. And even if he weren't, men like that, their mistresses are open secrets, signs of their virility. The mistress is the key to all this—we need to find her. Figure out how she slipped away without anyone noticing."

"Oh," Sam breathed, remembering another of Louise's whis-pered stories. "I might know. There are tales—rumors, really—of a secret door to an underground passage that goes all the way from Lapérouse to the French Senate, so that the senators can visit their mistresses without appearing to leave the building." The senators couldn't be expected to keep their indiscretions outside working hours. That was for paupers. But they couldn't let said paupers see them at it, either.

"Of course there is," Hel groaned. "Do those rumors happen to say where?"

The rumors didn't—but it couldn't be far. There were officers posted at the stairs, and the hall was a dead end. It had to be here.

They hurried down the passage, but behind every door was just another petit salon, and in one case, a cloakroom. Hel made impatient noises and had them checking the seams in the walls, the solidity of the floorboards.

Meanwhile, the mistress's trail was going cold. And Officer Berchard still hadn't come back.

The mistress could have killed Officer Berchard, Sam's mind whispered as she ran her fingers over the walls. He could have been returning, brandy in hand, and caught a glimpse of something he shouldn't. That would make him late.

Officer Berchard could be the Beast, killing M. Barrere and then the mistress—having realized, upon seeing the garnet beads, that there was a witness to his crime.

Officer Berchard could be in on it with the mistress.

They both could have been killed by the Beast.

They both could be innocent—Officer Berchard might have been called away by something more important than fetching a fainting woman brandy; the mistress might have fled the Beast.

Sam's head ached, possibilities spilling out at the seams. Unraveling a mystery ought to be easier with more information—but it wasn't. It was as if instead of solving one jigsaw, someone had mixed together the contents of three or four. It was up to her to pick out the right pieces, and then, somehow, put them together again, without ever knowing what the picture was about.

Sam had to focus. She didn't need to know any of that yet. All she had to do was find the secret door.

Sam glanced back at M. Barrere—at his hand, just visible from where she stood. If she touched it, would it tell her the path he'd taken to Lapérouse? Or would it only tell her how much less a person he'd become, how much more *meat*?

Haltingly, she walked closer, stretching out her hand toward his, willing herself to find out, when a scent hooked her.

Sam startled. "Do you smell that?"

Hel tipped her nose up and sniffed. "Flowers?"

"Perfume," Sam said. *Gardenia, jasmine, tuberose, and lily.* Four notes. Most exceptional—even Mr. Wright's mistress had only dared three. Breathing it in, a strange feeling fluttered in her chest, like a bird trying to escape the cage of her ribs. It felt dangerous and wild. "It's the same scent as on the garnet bead."

"Well done," Hel said. "Can you track it?"

That was the question. The halls were heady with a dozen perfumes, ebbing and flowing like ocean currents, mixing with one another in the drafts by the doors. But after a few false starts, Sam picked out the thread of the mistress's perfume and followed it past door after door, petit salon after petit salon, until finally it stopped.

Hel opened the door on a room full of coats.

Sam's heart sank. "The cloakroom. Oh, I should have known. It must just be from her coat. I'm sorry, I—"

But Hel wasn't listening—she'd grabbed a gas lamp from a nearby table and was shoving her way into the forest of coats. Sam hesitated only a moment before following, shushing past furs that closed in Hel's wake, to the very back of the closet, where the lamp's flickering light shone on a plain wooden door— entirely unassuming, save for a smear of blood beside the handle.

Hel flicked a finger into the blood. She held it up to Sam, red and glistening.

A thrill hollowed Sam's bones. She'd been right.

Even the spiders held their breath as Hel nosed open the hidden door in the cloakroom of Lapérouse, her hand on her revolver. For a moment, Sam could have sworn she saw skulls leering out from the walls like ghosts, begging, admonishing, praying—but no sooner had she gasped than they were gone. There was nothing there but a wooden staircase that disappeared into a claustrophobic tunnel carved from pale yellow stone.

"Shall we?" Hel said, and she offered Sam the light.

Sam led the way, holding the lantern against the dark, Hel covering her from behind with her revolver. She needn't have bothered. There were no turns, no obstacles—nothing to interrupt their passage. At one point, they came across a smear of what might have been blood on the wall, but it was dry and could just as easily have been a discoloration in the stone.

After what must have been half a mile, it let out in another closet that opened into the most ornate room Sam had ever seen. Sculptures stretched out of the pale stone between gilt and paintings that covered the ceiling and walls. Palais du Luxembourg—the Senate building. Or a back room of it, anyway. And one of the windows was gaping open like a scream, looking out onto the gardens beyond.

Sam and Hel dashed over, but the darkness swallowed the gardens and everything in it. Everything but a slip of scarlet silk caught in the wood, which smelled of gardenia, tuberose, jasmine, and lilies.

CHAPTER FIVE

The Streets of Paris

Cold-curled leaves tumbled down the cobblestone streets in the slant morning light. Sam wore a dress in a devastating ultramarine that shifted to peach with a clever bit of layering. Hel was in her customary suit and red tie, her long tan coat snapping behind her. They were returning from searching the Senate grounds a second time, having found no further trace of M. Barrere's mysterious mistress, other than the garnet and the perfumed slip of silk.

"Well, that's just a security hazard," Hel complained of the secret tunnel. "There weren't even any guards."

"It's not very *secret* if you post guards," Sam pointed out.

Unsurprisingly, what guards had been on-site the night before hadn't seen anything, and were remarkably unalarmed about the potential invasion of rogue mistresses. In fact, they seemed to find the whole affair rather amusing. As if a mistress couldn't also prove a murderer—or whisper word to one. She would hardly be the first spy to sharpen an assassin's aim.

"It's foolishness," Hel grumbled. "If security by obscurity doesn't work for vampires, it's certainly not going to work for the Senate, whose members are severely lacking in the Suggestion and Hypnosis departments."

"Unless, of course, some of them are vampires," Sam said. Though that was unlikely. The world had gotten much better at detecting vampires in the aftermath of her parents' Transylvanian affair.

"They could at least invest in a *lock*."

It was a strange thing, to hear the notorious Lady M grumbling. Not because she couldn't be irritable—Sam got the impression she very rarely wasn't—but because it meant she was here, with Sam, in the moment. Up until then, she'd always seemed a step ahead, daring Sam to keep up.

Hel, Sam decided with a private smile, had *feelings* about competence or the lack thereof.

And after she'd gone to such lengths to pretend she didn't have feelings at all.

"How are we going to find M. Barrere's mistress now?" Sam asked, rolling the garnet bead between her fingers.

"We don't," Hel said. "We follow other leads—the Wolves of God. Officer Berchard. The Freemasons."

"Freemasons? What do they have to do with anything?"

Hel shrugged. "You'd be surprised." Then she paused. "Where would a well-heeled man buy a suit in Paris?"

"Lars Larsen," Sam answered automatically. "He's Danish, actually, but M. Larsen has been featured on the cover of several prominent Parisian magazines just this year, and—"

Hel grimaced, shaking her head. "No, not that one. Something more traditional. More *Parisian*."

"House of Worth, perhaps?" Sam's brow furrowed. "Why? Do you think the *suit* he was wearing has something to do with M. Barrere's death?" Something similar had happened before—a dress suffused with nicotine had killed a woman. Sam's brother—who was as obsessed with medicine as she was with monsters—had talked of nothing else for weeks. But then, why had the body been mauled? It didn't make sense.

"Maybe," Hel said.

Sam frowned. If she didn't know better, she'd have said that was the first time the thought had occurred to Hel. Which couldn't possibly be the case. Why else ask about the suit?

"Le Temps, madame?" a paperboy asked Hel. She waved him away.

"I was thinking," Sam said, changing tack. "That perfume—it was unique, in all likelihood custom made. If we could find the perfumer who concocted it, we might be able to get the name of the mistress."

"That," Hel said, "is not something I ever would have thought of."

"Et pour vous, madame? Le Temps?" the paperboy persisted, trotting to keep pace.

Sam turned absently. *"Non—"* She inhaled sharply.

The boy's hands were covered in blood. Not the bright red of fresh blood, but dark and gloppy. It saturated the newspaper he was hawking, dripping onto the cobblestones with a familiar *tap-tap-tapping.*

Hel looked at her, then at the boy. The crowds parted around them, sweeping past in a murmur constant as the ocean waves. It wasn't real. It was just another vision. But how—?

Hel peeled Sam's fingers open and plucked out the garnet.

All at once, the blood was gone, and Sam was staring at the front page of the latest issue of *Le Temps*: a black-and-white photograph of the graffiti in Lapérouse from last night. That wolf under a star, its legs dripping over a broken crown, under the headline "Les Loups de Dieu ou la Bête du Diable?" Wolves of God or Beast of the Devil?

Except it wasn't the same graffiti. Not exactly.

"*Comme vous voulez.*" The boy was edging away from her, like a horse gone skittish at the scent of death on the wind.

Sam was scaring him. She couldn't help it. She was scaring herself.

Hel bought the newspaper. The boy fled. Sam wrapped her arms around herself.

"Another one of your feelings?" Sam startled to find Hel looking at her steadily.

The garnet rested in the palm of Hel's hand—an offering. Sam closed Hel's fingers around it, then drew in a shuddering breath. The world started to move again.

"I think so," Sam managed. It was easier with the garnet out of sight. Something about it pulled the air from her lungs, made the world seem to breathe around her. . . . She shook her head to clear it. "It's different. Before, it's always been things I'm fairly certain happened in the past. I've always imagined it to be emotions leaking out from spirits, caught in the amber of their memories. Nothing *intentional*. This, it was almost as if . . . as if it were trying to catch my attention."

As if it wanted to *tell her something*. But that was terrifying, and despite Hel's assurances, she still couldn't make herself confess something that seemed so likely to get her committed. One didn't listen to monsters who wanted to tell you something. It simply wasn't done.

"Fascinating," Hel murmured, staring at her as if she were a rare insect.

Color rose in Sam's cheeks. "I did learn something, though," she said, pulling the remnants of her professionality around her. She pointed at the photograph in the newspaper, at the dashes and dots radiating out from the star. "See these notations?"

Hel broke her gaze to frown down at the newspaper. "Yes, I—wait, is that Morse code?"

"Yes, it's a series of numbers," Sam explained. "They were also in a photograph I saw back in London of the graffiti at the first murder. The numbers here are different than the numbers at that murder, but it's the same pattern. And they weren't there last night. Someone added them to the graffiti after we left the crime scene."

"It's a cipher," Hel said. "Used to communicate with someone outside of Paris."

"Why outside?" Sam said. "The graffiti is in Paris."

"On an *interior wall*," Hel said. "Where it will doubtless be painted over. But you can get a newspaper anywhere. Have you translated them, these numbers?"

Sam hesitated, then reached into a pocket she'd sewn into the ribbing of her bodice and pulled out a well-worn notebook, still warm with the heat of her body. Hel stood behind her, leaning over her shoulder.

The pages fluttered in the wind. She smoothed the papers, parting them to the first page, where she'd written her grandfather's numbers—the same as she'd done in every iteration of this notebook since she was ten years old.

Seventy-four. Ten. One hundred three. Twenty-eight, eight, twenty-seven. Forty-four, one, fifty-six . . .

She'd researched them in every library she visited, every archive she had access to, but she hadn't seen that exact sequence of numbers again until she caught sight of that photograph in the newspaper, back in London.

Sam had to know what it meant.

Retrieving her pen from her bag, Sam carefully copied the new set of numbers beneath it.

"It's in sets of three numbers, just like the first sequence," Sam explained as she translated. "None of them larger than two hundred—though with only two sequences of twenty-odd numbers, any patterns we discover might prove nothing more than chance."

It was Hel's turn to hesitate. Almost at once, Sam realized her mistake. The paper of the notebook was fragile as autumn leaves, the ink of her grandfather's numbers faded next to the still-wet ink beneath it.

The numbers were older than this case.

But if Hel noticed, she didn't say anything, just frowned at the numbers like she was remembering a bad dream. Sam began to feel uneasy.

"I've done some research," Sam continued, not mentioning exactly how long she'd been doing said research. "They're not dates or coordinates or simple substitution formulas. Given the structure, I think it's—"

"A book cipher," Hel finished for her.

Sam looked at her sharply. "How did you know?"

"I don't," Hel said. "And you don't either. Not until it's been cracked. But it's the most common cipher that uses sets of three numbers—page, paragraph, word—and it's nearly impossible to break unless you know the title being used as a key."

"We should send it back to the Society," Sam said. "Now that we have multiple examples of the code, the researchers may be able to make something of it."

"No," Hel said at once.

"What?" Sam blinked. "Whyever not?"

"It's a waste of resources," Hel said, but Sam knew Hel well enough by now to read the lines of tension in her shoulders. "They'll never crack it, not without the key."

Hel hadn't wanted to ask the police what they'd found out either.

"Trying is exactly what the research department is here for," Sam said. She would have worn sodden skirts for a week to get a chance at a puzzle like that. "You don't have to do everything yourself. You can trust them."

Hel snorted. "Of course I can. Which is why you have to hide your gifts to win your way onto a case."

That was unfair.

It was also true. The Society would never have put her on this case if they knew the extent of her visions. And even so, Mr. Wright hadn't wanted to let her on. Not until she'd as good as threatened him. But was he wrong?

What Hel did took real strength. Logic. Calm under pressure. The ability to fire a revolver without taking out the furnishings, to stand down a grindylow and fill it full of salt, instead of trapping herself and nearly setting herself on fire.

Sam didn't have that sort of strength, as circumstances frequently took pains to remind her—most exquisitely when she was sixteen. She'd been in London with her father, who was there on business. She'd spent the summer lost in the Society's stacks, and had at the end of it decided to ask Mr. Wright if she might join. Jakob Van Helsing, who, as far as Sam could tell, lived in the Society, had come up behind her while she was gathering her courage. He was always suspicious of her in those days.

"You, join the Society?" Jakob crossed his arms. "The work is far too strenuous for a woman. Being a field agent takes real strength. And you—"

"Have feminine strength," Sam said, lifting her chin.

"*Feminine strength?*" Jakob scoffed. "Now there's an oxymoron if I've ever heard one. Besides, that would be like a fox joining the hunt. You might get away with it in the beginning, but we all know how it ends."

It had felt almost like talking with Jakob's father.

Sam hadn't asked Mr. Wright that day. Nor the next. It had been a full two years before she'd gathered the courage again.

Mr. Wright was taking a chance on her. If the Society found out she'd been listening to monsters, well, Sam doubted she'd be welcome at all—on the hunting side of the equation, in any event. Van Helsing had made it clear he'd be all too happy to set her on the other end of it.

"Can I borrow that?" Hel nodded her chin toward Sam's notebook. Flipping to the end, Hel copied down the numbers and ripped the page out.

"You follow up on the perfume," Hel said, folding the paper and returning the notebook. "I'm going back to Lapérouse."

"Wait, alone?" Sam said. The numbers were the connection to her grandfather. If they were to separate, Sam wanted to be the one who followed up on them. Not that she could tell Hel that. "Why? Shouldn't we go together?"

"We haven't the time," Hel said. "And you're the one with the nose for perfume. I'll meet you at the hotel."

Hel left Sam on the banks of the River Seine, the muddy scent of the water leaving the taste of silt on her tongue.

Hel wasn't telling Sam everything—that much was certain. This was *exactly* the sort of thing Mr. Wright had asked her to look out for. But whatever Hel was hiding, Sam got the distinct impression it wasn't malicious. She could easily have let the grindylow kill her, or even let her suffocate in the circle of her own petticoat, if she'd wanted her dead—another accident for the books. It was as if Hel thought that keeping Sam in the dark might somehow keep her safe. That she had to do this alone.

But ignorance, as far as Sam could tell, had never kept anyone safe. And Sam was already a part of this—had been since long before Hel had told Sam to pack her bags. If Hel wanted to keep Sam away from whatever she suspected was going on with those numbers, it was too late.

Still, there was nothing for it. Sam didn't fool herself into thinking she could track down Hel if Hel didn't want to be found.

Besides, absent the book that was the key to her grandfather's cipher, the numbers meant nothing. Solving this case, finding out who was writing the numbers on the wall, *that* was Sam's best chance of unpicking the riddle of her grandfather's disappearance.

Sam was just going to have to trust Hel, and do her part to the best of her ability. Which, Hel was right about one thing: Sam had a very good nose.

There were over two hundred perfumeries in Paris. But respectable women, such as Mr. Wright's wife, only wore scents of a single note—typically lavender, which was terribly unimaginative, but which also meant that most perfumeries wouldn't bother with custom scents.

Sam's French, despite the best efforts of her mother, left a lot to be desired. Fortunately, it proved sufficient. By the fifth woman Sam scented out, she was getting better at asking them what she needed to know. By the eleventh, a pattern was developing: *Arsène Courbet.*

Arsène Courbet created custom perfumes for all the brightest luminaries in the performing arts—including Évangéline St. Laurent, star soprano of the Paris Opera and unofficial queen of Tout-Paris, and all the socialites who followed in her footsteps. It was something of a scandal amidst proper ladies, appearing in newspapers as far away as America.

Arsène Courbet had a gift for combining recognizable scents into transformative experiences, taking you from Paris to Scotland's misty moors, so real you could feel the wind rasp your cheek.

He was an olfactory *artist*. Something Sam, to this point, had not known might exist.

He was also very selective.

"He won't see you," the last woman had said in heavily accented English. She was undoubtedly the most fashionable woman Sam had ever met. She wore lilac silk that set off her warm-brown skin perfectly, and her perfume was thick and green, as if Sam stood in a tropical garden and not the Gare Saint-Lazare with the sound and the fury of the trains leaving the station, the nebulous clouds of their steam caught beneath a cage of iron and glass.

"Whyever shouldn't he?" Sam said.

"He's *Arsène Courbet*," the woman had said, as if it were obvious. "He only works on canvases that will be displayed in the right places. Even if you could afford him."

Sam was a little offended. "And how do you know I'm not such a canvas?"

The woman had just shrugged. "I haven't heard of you, for one thing. Your dress is démodé—too structured, you can't see the natural body—you're wearing a Catholic saint medal, which is probably why, and you're definitely not French. By which I mean stop trying to speak the language, it's embarrassing, I'm embarrassed for you."

Sam had felt quite undressed. At the same time, each detail was a drop of color on the broad sketch of the mystery mistress. She was French (of course), not overly Catholic or at least not conservatively dressed, and a part of so-called Tout-Paris—a writer or artist or socialite—one whose passions became trends, whose opinions became the sentiments of all Paris.

Of which Sam was decidedly not. Fortunately, Sam wasn't going to see Arsène Courbet with the intent of being a canvas— which, what an awful phrase, it put her in mind of a serial killer, skinning women like rabbits, stretching their skin for paint. English wasn't the admittedly fashionable woman's first language, Sam thought generously. It was embarrassing, Sam was embarrassed for her. Still, the encounter encouraged Sam to be forthright about her purpose.

La Parfumerie du papillon was located near the Jardin des Tuileries. The young women who worked the luxury fashion houses of Paris sat on the park benches, laughing and chatting and eating their packed lunches. They looked exquisitely stylish in their shawl-collar blouses and dark skirts pleated tight around their hips, which they each made their own by way of bright scarfs, clever hand-ornamented hats, and daring glimpses of heels and stockings.

Nearby were all manner of expensive restaurants filled with the sorts of men who might prove the next victim, their eyes dark with avarice.

Reaching for the door of La Parfumerie du papillon, Sam heard a familiar footfall and jingle behind her. Like a bell on a cat. *Van Helsing*, still in those ridiculous boots of his. And here Sam had thought she'd finally escaped the man.

Sam turned on her heel, intent on asking Van Helsing what precisely he thought he was doing—skulking about in the shadows, spying on young women, more like a murderer than a Society agent—but when she did, no one was there.

Doubt crept cold fingers up her spine. She *had* heard it,

hadn't she? The jingle of his cowboy boots was perhaps the most distinctive thing about him—impossible to mistake for anything else, and as uncommon in Europe as peanut butter. But as Sam carefully catalogued the young women at their lunches, the men watching them, and the fashionable passersby, the man still refused to materialize.

The excitement from the prior evening must have gotten to her. Van Helsing was in Spain, Sam knew it to be true, had handed him the research on his next assignment herself—a duende infestation, as she recalled. What reason could Van Helsing possibly have for abandoning his assignment to follow *her*?

But Sam knew the answer to that. And suddenly, she was very aware of just how often she'd made use of her visions on this case, of what Van Helsing, who seemed determined to believe she would fall under the influence of evil, would do if he saw her inviting the monsters in. . . .

Uneasily, Sam turned back to the perfumery.

La Parfumerie du papillon had a small storefront, with an industrial-looking glass-and-steel butterfly worked into the window of the door. It had taken her a moment to find it, tucked away between fashion houses as it was. But though it appeared small on the outside, it stretched on narrowly inside.

Winnowing the store further were glass-caged tables, displaying a chic array of perfume bottles, punctuated by mortars and pestles filled with drops of ambergris and myrrh, like the blood of strange gods. Vast teak cabinets lined the walls with countless tiny drawers, each with their own equally tiny label. At the far end of the store waited a desk with two chairs—one for the chosen canvas, and one for the man sitting on the other side.

"Arsène Courbet?" Sam asked as the door shut, the bell

tinkling behind her. Crossing over to him, she drew out the slip of scarlet silk they'd found caught in the window, the memory of the perfume curling around her fingers.

The man looked up. His eyes met hers—dark as tourmaline. The perfume bottle in his hands beating like a living heart, the awful wet pulse of it drumming in her ears, blood pouring down his hands to splatter on the fine hardwood floors, filling the air with the scent of death.

It was all too much. Sam swooned for the second time in as many days, the silk slipping from her fingers.

Arsène Courbet dropped the perfume he'd been holding. It shattered on the floor, and he caught her in his arms.

"Mademoiselle!" The scent of sunflowers bloomed around her, earthy and resinous, as if she'd somehow lost her way and stumbled into a summer day. Fingers brushed the saint medal at her neck, so gently it might have been a breeze. Then strong arms wrapped around her, and she was being carried.

Another vision, Sam thought blearily, the world still dizzying around her as she was set down in a chair. Like the newspaper, it couldn't be literal. It was telling her something. Sam wasn't going to think about how nervous that made her—how much she doubted whoever or whatever was sending her these messages, or what their purpose was in doing so, because it meant she was right: the mistress had *been here*. Sam was sure of it.

"*Vous allez bien, mademoiselle?*"

"I'm sorry, I'm—"

The world resolved. The man kneeling before her had down-turned eyes that conspired with dark brows to give him a soulful look, and something discontent about the set of his mouth that put Sam in mind of Jane Austen's Mr. Darcy. He wore a slim silver waistcoat under a black suit jacket. His fingertips were cool as they tipped up her chin, and he checked her eyes for what she supposed must be signs of concussion.

Sam blushed. She was going to have to stop having visions in front of strange men. It was getting out of hand. "Just a little faint. I don't know what came over me."

"So many scents at once, they overpower the senses if you're not used to it," Arsène Courbet said. "What brings you here? You do not look like my clients, if you'll pardon me saying so."

Sam was uncommonly flustered—she'd known she wasn't one of his canvases, so why did it bother her? And this, it wasn't how she'd intended on beginning things. So very personal, when she'd been trying her hardest to be professional. "No, actually, I'm looking for someone."

He settled back on his heels. "And you think I might be able to find them?"

"She wore a particular perfume. One I've been led to believe might be something of your make." Sam closed her eyes, just for a moment, so she could concentrate without him staring into her soul. "It had notes of gardenia, jasmine, tuberose, and lily."

He raised an eyebrow. "You have an exceptional nose, if you can extract all that, mademoiselle—"

"Harker," Sam said. "Samantha Harker. I work for the Royal Society for the Study of Abnormal Phenomena. We've been asked to help with the murders."

M. Courbet frowned. "They sent a young lady, to hunt a Beast?"

"A Beast that doesn't murder women."

"And you think *she* is this Beast?"

"No, I don't," Sam admitted. "But I suspect she saw something. She was there the night M. Barrere died, and I imagine she's very scared. Will you help me?"

"The perfume—it is not one of mine, but I will try," he said gravely. He riffled through his drawers, flipping through cards of handwritten notes, his long fingers gliding over them like a spider over its webs. As he searched, he spoke. "Perfume is like the riddle of the sphinx: she has a dawning, a noontide, and a twilight. You think you know her, but after five to fifteen minutes, she changes, the top notes fading, and the heart emerging. The heart, you think, is the true perfume, but twenty minutes to an hour later, she changes again, the heart fading and exposing the base, which lingers for hours or even days."

Sam cocked her head. "But how can elements emerge that weren't there to begin with? Shouldn't they have been detectable from the start?"

He smiled, pleased with her insight. "That's the secret: they *are*, only we miss the signs because they're hidden beneath the notes that come before." He pulled a card from the stack and scanned it briefly, before tapping it neatly back in place.

"I'm afraid I cannot offer you the name of its maker," M. Courbet said. "Only who wears it. This is the perfume of the midinettes—that is, the women who work in the fashion houses and eat their lunches in the gardens. They are always young, always working class, and yet they are swimming in luxuries they cannot afford—falling into temptation and love and impossible ambitions of marrying above their social class. They are admired, yes, for their style, their savoir faire, but they are ephemeral. They often catch the eye of the businessmen who dine nearby, and sometimes, if they shine particularly bright, the eye of politicians."

"Like M. Barrere," Sam said. You weren't supposed to speak ill of the dead, but Sam could already tell she wouldn't have liked

M. Barrere—or, probably, most of the men the Beast was killing. Still, that didn't mean they deserved to die.

"Exactly so," M. Courbet said.

Sam furrowed her brow. "You don't sound as if you approve."

M. Courbet sighed. "I have known since I was a boy the effect that sort of woman has on a family." Sam got the impression this was more than a little personal for him. "Not to say it's entirely their fault. The midinettes—they are subject to temptations no woman should face. And these men, they have everything, including a wife and family. But the midinettes are determined to win them anyway. And so they spend their wages on cosmetics and perfume, to steal the hearts of men."

"Is perfume really that powerful?" Sam found herself asking. "Can it affect your emotions like that? Make you fall in love?"

M. Courbet stilled a moment, and then chuckled softly. "The midinettes' perfume? *Non*, I do not think so. But scent is a powerful thing, Mlle Harker. It transports us. Smell sun-warmed sand, sweat, and the sea, and you're at the beach, the surf rushing between your toes. Smell your grandmother's powdery perfume and see her smile again. Who is to say a scent cannot make you fall in love?"

Sam was skeptical. She had a feeling being extraordinarily attractive had something to do with it. At the same time, he was looking at her with those Darcy-dark eyes, the scent of sunflowers and lazy summers slipping around her like the first notes of a delicious daydream, and suddenly, it wasn't so far off a thought.

"Allow me to demonstrate," M. Courbet said, unfolding from behind his desk. "You are a stranger here, in Paris, I think. What place makes you feel most at home?"

"The library," Sam answered. And all at once, she missed it with her whole heart.

"The library," M. Courbet said, like a magician about to perform a trick. He was amongst the small drawers in his cabinet, his clever hands skimming the surface, drawing out vials labeled in his tight handwriting, putting back the ones that didn't meet whatever bar he had set.

At last, the perfumer set three vials on the desk. He selected a perfume bottle, no larger than the smallest of his fingers—made of dark green glass and covered in silver filigree. A small amount of liquid darkened the glass already.

With expert precision, M. Courbet pipetted extracts from the vials he'd selected. "Musk for that dusty scent all libraries have, with a hint of almonds and flowers," he murmured. "And oiled wood, for the bookshelves, warm with gaslight."

The perfumer held the vial to his nose a couple of times, adjusting the amounts of each extract, until at last his face shifted into satisfaction. Without speaking, he held it out to Sam.

Not knowing quite what to expect, and certain this was unprofessional, Sam took the bottle of perfume and, at his urging, breathed it in.

All at once, the library stretched out around her, as if it had been there all along, hidden in the folds of the world, so real she could almost run her fingers over the spines of her books. Embarrassingly, tears sprang to her eyes. Oh, how she *missed* the library—missed being good at something, at knowing what she was doing. It was almost enough to send her home.

"Thank you for your assistance," Sam said abruptly, pushing herself out of her chair. She should be able to track the mistress down from here. There was no reason to linger. Sam held out the perfume bottle with the secret library inside to M. Courbet. "You have been most helpful."

"Keep it." M. Courbet closed her fingers around it. "I made it for you."

"I couldn't possibly!" She knew how expensive his perfumes were—how *exclusive*.

M. Courbet shrugged. "I can hardly give it to someone else."

Her cheeks burned. Oh, what would Hel say if she saw her now? She was here to solve a murder, not flirt!

"Thank you," Sam managed, and she made for the door before she could get herself into any more trouble. He was entirely too distracting. She had a job to do.

Still, it had been pleasant to think about something that wasn't death or conspiracy for a moment, brief as it had been. A taste of the life she might have lived if her grandfather hadn't disappeared and left behind those numbers. If she hadn't had to coerce her way onto this case. If she hadn't been born . . . different, and if different didn't mean seeing ghosts in secret passageways and blood all over the morning news.

Sam was very good at playing normal. But that didn't mean she knew what it was like.

Sometimes she wished she did. That the biggest problems she faced were predatory men and not monsters. Then again, Sam could simply shoot the monsters. Or rather, Hel could, and Sam could shout encouragement. It was generally frowned upon to do the same with men.

"Of course," Arsène Courbet said gravely, his voice making her *feel things* she was determined to leave out of her report to Hel. "I am pleased to have been of service."

CHAPTER SIX

The Grand Hotel Terminus, Paris

The sun was slung low in the sky by the time Sam returned to the hotel. It was grander than Sam remembered—Sam and Hel must have horrified the staff, stumbling in exhausted and filthy the night before. Twin lion statues flanked the entrance to a gilded salon with fluted iron columns and grand electric chandeliers to chase away the night.

Their rooms were every bit as fine, boasting two electric lamps, a dusty bottle of Cabernet Franc in their chamber's vestibule, and a private telephone—a luxury at a time when most hotels didn't even have one. The only thing missing was Hel. Sam let out a disappointed huff and sat down on the bed. After a moment, she poured herself a glass of wine.

The midinettes outside the perfumery had known whom Sam meant at once when she'd asked after M. Barrere's mistress: Clotilde Auclair, one of the midinettes at Paquin. Of course, when Sam went to the manager of the Paquin store, he had denied any knowledge of Mlle Auclair or her whereabouts. But the midinettes had been only too happy to assist.

Mlle Auclair had been due to work that morning but had never shown up, one of the midinettes explained while several of the young women ran a distraction so that another of their number might steal into the manager's files. It wasn't like Mlle Auclair to miss a shift. She'd never even been late. The midinettes knew how easily they were replaced. They were worried.

The midinette who'd hunted within the manager's files returned triumphant, and the others pressed close, shielding the young woman from view as she slipped the address from her stockings, distracting onlookers with their laughter.

Sam was impressed: far from the easily tempted girls of the perfumer's fable, the midinettes were clever and fearless young women, their teamwork flawless and unspoken.

"She's one of us," the spokeswoman for their group said simply when Sam said as much, and the others nodded. "And no one else cares when we go missing. Bring her back safe for us, and we'll be even."

Sam understood the grim look in her eyes, filled with the knowledge that when women like them went missing, they rarely came home. The weight of their expectations settled over her.

Sam hoped fiercely that she might live up to them. That Mlle Auclair wasn't dead and wasn't a murderer. That those young women's faith in them both might be rewarded.

Speaking of faith—where *was* Hel?

Sam took a sip of her wine, dry as tea with notes of bramble and clove. She could only conclude that the Morse code hadn't been on the wall at Lapérouse. It must have been added to the photograph itself, rather than the graffiti. Which meant whoever had left those numbers was sloppy. Hel was probably tracing them.

Sam should be glad. It meant they were that much closer to stopping the murders and uncovering whether there was any connection between this case and her grandfather's disappearance.

And Sam *was* glad, mostly. Only, Sam had rather hoped they'd do this part together. Sam was a researcher for heaven's sake, she could do more than drink wine and speculate. She could *help*.

But Hel seemed intent on keeping Sam in the dark. Honestly, the way she'd reacted when Sam had suggested they send the cipher to the Society to see if they could crack it, it was a wonder Hel had let Sam on at all.

Almost as if it had heard her, the telephone started to ring. Sam snatched it off the hook.

"Hel? I think I've found something—"

There was the crackle of distance over the line. "Miss Harker, I'm happy to hear you made it to Paris intact. I take it Miss Moriarty isn't with you?"

"Mr. Wright!" Sam said, pulling her professionalism on like a coat. Of course it was Mr. Wright—with what telephone would Hel call her? Sam blamed the wine. "My apologies, I thought—I mean to say, Dr. Moriarty went out. I'm not sure where."

"Good, good," Mr. Wright said. He was repeating himself again. He was nervous. "It seems I was right to send you. You've made it farther than most, already. How was your trip?"

"We ran into some trouble on the way. Highwaymen with a captive grindylow. Apparently, someone told them we were coming." Even if whoever had sent them had left out a few pertinent details that might have made the highwaymen think twice. Still, Sam supposed, it was better they'd attacked Sam and Hel than anyone else. They—or rather Hel—knew how to deal with highwaymen. Others might not have been so fortunate. "They ruined our carriage and killed the coachman and horses. They would have killed me, too, if it weren't for Hel."

"Excellent, excellent," Mr. Wright repeated. There was the creak of his chair as he leaned back. Sam frowned. "Miss

Moriarty seems to have taken a shine to you. This is good news. But do not think for a moment this means you are safe—it may be a play to earn your trust."

"Don't you want to hear more about the highwaymen?" Sam pressed. "They're from Northern England, I think. They used a barghest as a symbol—"

"Not our department," Mr. Wright said. "Have you read the file yet?"

Sam knew what she was supposed to say next—it was there in the space between Mr. Wright's words. *Yes,* she was supposed to say, and if she couldn't say that, then *Not yet.* But something stopped it on her tongue.

"I'm sorry, bandits forcing grindylows into service isn't our department?"

"The way I hear it, the grindylow's dead," Mr. Wright said. But she hadn't mentioned the grindylow's death. "And you should read the report."

Sam frowned. "I prefer to work without biases, sir."

"You're a researcher, Miss Harker," Mr. Wright said. "If any-one can research a subject and keep an unfettered mind, it should be you. And I won't have you going in unarmed when I have the ability to ensure the contrary. Now, is there anything else of a questionable nature? Anything at all?"

Sam's conversations with Hel nipped at the edges of her mind—the things Hel had confided in her about her father, things Sam had guessed. The way she'd left Sam behind.

"No," Sam said shortly.

"Keep in mind, she may be attempting to conceal it from you."

Sam was beginning to get irritated. "Aside from apparently owning only one suit, being entirely incapable of small talk, and possessing a distressing aversion to nouns, I have seen nothing that warrants a report nor further questioning."

Mr. Wright cleared his throat. "Miss Harker, everything I'm doing is for your protection. People tend to die around Miss Moriarty. Your parents would never forgive me if the same were to happen to you."

"If anything, *Dr.* Moriarty has been overcautious in trying to keep me out of harm's way," Sam said. "With all due respect, I should think you're focusing on the wrong Moriarty. Sir."

The line was static for a moment.

"You're getting awfully close to this, Miss Harker," Mr. Wright said, his voice cold with warning, and Sam knew at once she'd made a mistake. Oh, what had she been thinking, defending Hel like that? It was Hel, throwing her off. She'd gotten used to saying every little thing that came to mind, instead of searching for the right words.

It had not gone unnoticed.

"In your opinion," Mr. Wright said, "are you able to continue to work 'without biases,' or do we need to reassign you?"

"I'm fine," Sam said, her face hot. "Apologies, I must be exhausted from the trip."

"Of course," Mr. Wright said, his voice warm again, as if all he'd needed was Sam back in her place. "Now, if there's anything else?"

Sam hesitated, remembering the sound of jingling footsteps outside the perfumery. "Do you happen to know if Mr. Van Helsing is in Paris?" she asked carefully.

"Van Helsing?" Sam swore she could feel his frown through the line. "You know he's not. He's been assigned a case in Spain. Why?"

"It's nothing," Sam said, that same uneasy feeling creeping

over her, as if she were, even then, being watched. Her eyes swept over the room's furnishings. She'd read of a man with a hotel filled with one-way mirrors, so that he might spy on its guests.

But there were no mirrors on these walls. No one was watching her. Sam was working herself up over nothing.

"Very well," Mr. Wright said. "Read the files, Miss Harker."

"Yes, sir," Sam made herself say, because she knew it wouldn't be over until she did. And she hung up before that could be anything less than the end.

Sam felt, uncharacteristically, like breaking something. But this was a very nice hotel, and if she broke something, Mr. Wright would have to pay for it, and then he'd *know*. And so tears came out instead. She wiped them away angrily before Hel could come in and wonder what was wrong with her and decide she had to leave Sam out of yet more things.

Sam tilted her head back toward the ceiling, as if that would help keep the tears from spilling, when she caught sight of something *off*—a faint watery reflection of light, delicate as spiderwebs, playing over the crown moulding. For a moment she just watched it, entranced. Then she crawled across the bed, poking her head over the edge to see light reflecting off the base of the lamp.

Dropping to the floor, Sam pressed her cheek to the cool hardwood. In the dark, narrow space under her bed was an eerie blue flame, dancing around the well-loved case in which she kept her radiotelegraph. Sam caught her breath—it looked simply *magical*. Like something she might have dreamed of as a child. But this was no dream.

A *will-o'-the-wisp*.

The best-known tale regarding their origins, the one Sam's mother told her when she was a child, was about a man named

Jack who tricked the Gentleman in Black three times. He had led such a ruinous life that neither Hell nor Heaven would take him, leaving his unclaimed soul with nothing but an ember with which to light his way. They said his lost soul traveled the endless twilight still, leading other travelers astray, as he tried to find somewhere that would take him.

Sam wondered sometimes if that was what drew wisps to radio signals: that connection, that signal that led them from the rock and dirt of Earth up into the starry heavens. Looking for a place to call home.

Then it hit Sam, as she watched the blue flame dance through the floor and away, leaving the room somehow so much darker in its wake: wisps were drawn to *radio signals.*

Sam pulled out the case, opened it, and placed her hand on the radiotelegraph. It was still warm.

A shiver went through her. Someone had used her radiotelegraph. More precisely, someone had broken into her room, set up her radiotelegraph, used it, and put it back exactly the way they'd found it, hoping Sam wouldn't notice.

Van Helsing, Sam thought immediately, forgetting for a moment in her fear that not only was he in Spain, he probably wouldn't have the slightest idea how to operate a radiotelegraph.

But then, the only other person who might have done it . . .

Her eyes fell on the file Mr. Wright had given her, the case reports on the deaths of Hel's prior partners. *If I'd wanted you dead, you would be,* Hel had said, and Sam believed her. She'd saved Sam's life.

But Hel had shut Sam out, nearly as thoroughly as she had the Society. She'd refused to send the cipher to the research department, when that was what they were for. She'd left Sam behind and used Sam's radiotelegraph to contact someone, when

Hel was Sam's partner. And then there was that line of questioning, about where a well-heeled man would buy a suit in Paris, which, as far as Sam could tell, had nothing whatsoever to do with the case.

All of which left Sam holding one question: What was Hel *really* up to?

A knock interrupted her thoughts. Sam frowned, opening the door to see one of the hotel's uniformed attendants, a thin-boned man with nervous, fluttering hands. His suit had once been nice, but was quite worn, as if it had been washed and carefully pressed many times.

"I'm sorry to interrupt you, mademoiselle," he said. "It is just, there has been another murder, and the police are certain you would like to know."

"Already?" Sam blurted. They'd barely started on the last one! But, she supposed, murderers didn't wait for you to be ready.

"Did the police happen to say where?" Sam asked, throwing on her white traveling coat. It was just a body, she told herself. Not a murderer. Just research, with a bit more . . . physical intensity than usual.

Sam thought about what had happened last time it was "just a body," and felt ill.

Oh, where was Hel when she needed her?

"Le Meurice," the attendant said. "In a hotel room."

Sam recognized the name at once. It was a hotel that looked out over the Jardin des Tuileries, with a reputation for lavish entertainment and clients who breathed rarified air. It was also perhaps the only hotel in Paris more expensive than the Grand Hotel Terminus.

There went Sam's captive-Beast theory. Lapérouse might have secret doors by which one could sneak a Beast into one of the petit salons, but from what Sam had heard, Le Meurice had none. Whoever had done this had come in walking like a man.

Sam thanked the attendant and wrote out a short note for Hel explaining where she'd gone, on the odd chance the habit might rub off on her.

Night had fallen by the time Sam hurried down the hotel steps and past the stone lions to the promenade, the light reduced to puddles under the electric streetlamps. The wind rose, reddening her cheeks and tugging her scarf behind her.

No sooner had Sam caught sight of the dark shapes of the shrubberies that marked the edge of the Jardin des Tuileries than she heard the sound again—those jingling footfalls.

Sam stopped beneath a streetlamp. Out in the dark, the footsteps stopped with her. Her pulse picked up, the sense of being hunted, of being *prey*, lacing her veins like poison. And suddenly, *not* knowing—wondering if she was hearing things, if she was losing herself to the influence of evil the way everyone always said she would—was so much worse than whatever might be hiding in the dark.

Sam took the corner as fast as she dared, then stepped out of the light and behind a bronze statue of a Grecian nymph caught forever in the act of putting up her hair. The bronze was still warm with the heat of day, and the soft, scratchy branches of a topiary caught at her dress.

Trying to still her breath, Sam counted her heartbeats until she began to suspect she'd been mistaken, when all at once, there he was—striding into the streetlight, like Wyatt Earp.

Sam stepped out from behind the nymph.

"Mr. Van Helsing," Sam said, her voice sharp, and Van Helsing tensed, the fabric of his jacket pulling tight across his shoulders. "Did you get lost on your way to Spain?"

"I finished the job in Spain," Van Helsing said, turning smoothly to face her. "Duendes. Hardly worth the effort."

A lie, it had to be. There hadn't been enough time to travel to Spain, and then to Paris, let alone dispatch the duendes. But why would he risk his place at the Society just to follow her? It wasn't for her sake; that much was certain.

"Is the Society not expecting you to return?" Sam said. "Surely you've not run through all the world's monsters quite yet."

"No, not yet," Van Helsing agreed, closing the distance between them, as if she were a shying horse. She half expected him to offer her a carrot—though she knew it would only be so he could fit her with a bridle and bit. The days when she'd trust him to do her a kindness were long over. "There's at least one in Paris. I should think you'd be grateful. It's late, and the streets are dangerous at night. No proper woman should be about unescorted."

"Escorted?" Sam had to struggle not to laugh. "Is that what you call skulking in the shadows?"

He raised an eyebrow. "Would you have permitted me accompany you?"

Before Sam could formulate a response, he stepped close—so close she could smell the dusty leather and sweat of him. Instinctively, she tried to step backward, only to be stopped by the bronze bulk of the nymph.

"You will slip up," Van Helsing said, his voice low. Her eyes fell to his boots. They were spattered with old blood. Here, in the dark, with him stalking her like a beast, it felt like a threat. "You will channel, like Lucy before you—you won't be able to help yourself, it's what you *are*. Your visions will lead you astray. And when they do, I will be here to stop you, like my father before me."

And then Sam would be fortunate if all she earned was a place in an asylum.

Sam forced herself to meet his gaze.

"Mr. Wright has entrusted Dr. Moriarty and me with this case," Sam said as evenly as she could, knowing any sign of weakness would be seen as an admission of guilt. "Until he assigns you to it, I expect you to enjoy your holiday, Mr. Van Helsing, and leave the hunting to us."

Without waiting for his response, Sam fled. She heard his curse behind her as he moved to follow. But Sam had escaped the light, hurrying as fast as she dared in the pitch black toward Le Meurice, keeping to the shadows like a creature of the night. Until finally she stopped and did not hear the sound of jingling footsteps behind her. "At last," she breathed.

Sam had glanced at the nearest street sign to orient herself, when a feeling broke over her like a fever. She looked around, only to find that nothing moved—passersby like figures on a music box, their scarfs frozen behind them; moths caught in their adulations of the light. It was as if the world held its breath, until her gaze fell upon a will-o'-the-wisp, winding into the dark like a lost star, before flickering and snuffing out.

Sam drew in a ragged breath, the cold air rough in her throat, and the world breathed with her, passersby and scarfs and moths all moving as they were meant to.

A vision. A will-o'-the-wisp's light could not be blown out like a candle.

Sam should ignore it, especially with Van Helsing out there somewhere, watching her, waiting for her to make a mistake. That's what you did with visions and wills-o'-the-wisp both: you ignored them. They were harmless, so long as you didn't follow them into the dark.

But her visions had been right so far. And Sam was already in the dark.

When she reached the spot where the will-o'-the-wisp had fallen, Sam knelt, touching the lingering sparks. That strange blue-green light smeared, illuminating her fingerprints for a moment before fading. She looked around.

It had led her to the mouth of a narrow alley, cobblestones buckling where they met the building. The streetlight was unlit above her, and it took a moment for her eyes to adjust.

"What did you want me to see?" Sam murmured as she stared into the dark.

Then, at last, something resolved. Deep in the alley, behind stacks of wooden crates, stood two shadowed figures, heads bent close.

Sam went still. She could think of a few reasons one might meet with another in a dark alley in the middle of the night, and they were none of them good. Then, one of the figures shifted, and the full moon's light poured upon her face.

Sam's breath caught in her throat. *Hel.*

She no longer had a choice: she *had* to find out what Hel was up to.

Please don't let Mr. Wright be right about you, Sam thought as she eased deeper into the alley, slipping into the hollow of a doorway. Hel had returned to her conversation with the shadowy figure. But they spoke in a hush, and try as she might, Sam couldn't make out what they were saying. The wooden crates, if Sam could just slip around to the other side—

A shadow separated itself from the wall, and a heavy hand fell on her shoulder. *Van Helsing.*

And Sam had been channeling.

Sam whirled, her heart a hummingbird's wings, and knocked the hand from her shoulder.

"Rien de tout cela ne vous regarde." Behind her stood a man in an exquisitely cut black suit, with a golden brocade waistcoat and a collection of rings on his fingers that would do a pirate proud. He had an almost delicate build, brooding eyes and a sharp jaw, and that astringent scent about him Sam associated with men who shaved. Witch hazel, Sam thought. He didn't look like a thief or murderer. He looked wealthy, and almost . . . bored.

Relief flooded her. Not Van Helsing, after all. Sam was going to have to be more careful.

"I'm sorry, I—"

Sam met the man's eyes, and the world fell away, and though she knew it was impossible, she could have sworn his dark eyes were hollow, that the darkness within was *moving*—thousands of tiny black legs crawling over one another inside his skull, as if he weren't a man at all, but a colony of spiders wearing a man's skin like a suit.

Sam's hands flew to her mouth, afraid even to scream, when the vision melted away.

"I—I'll just be on my way," Sam said, fear making her voice faint.

He was looking at her now, though, no longer bored. He grabbed her arm, searching her face. "You are a *channel*."

"I'm afraid you're mistaken," Sam said, trying to pull her arm free, but his hand only tightened. She considered screaming, but would summoning Hel bring help or harm? "I'm only looking for my friend."

"I saw the way you looked at me just now—you were

channeling something." There was a lean and hungry look in his eyes. "What did it show you?"

"Nothing," Sam said, knowing that she couldn't tell him about the spiders—no one wanted to hear that they were full of spiders. "Please, I didn't see anything."

The man's face darkened. "You channels never appreciate the gifts you were given. You do not know what I would do to be like you, to hear them like you." Still holding her with one hand, he drew a golden knife. Sam tried to wrench away again, but he held her fast. "Do not worry, I will be quick. Just a vial of your blood. That's all I need. You'll barely miss it."

This time, Sam did scream, and it startled him enough that she was able to twist out of his grasp, throwing her hands up in defense. But that only meant the knife went deeper, cutting a searing line across her palm. She fell to the cobblestones, but he seized her wrist, pulled out a glass vial, and—

The retort of a revolver split the night, and the vial burst in his hand.

The strange man and Sam looked back at the crates, only to see Hel, far closer than she had been, striding toward them, a reckless light in her eyes. She gestured with her revolver.

"Let her go." Sam didn't think she'd ever heard Hel so furious.

"My apologies." He raised his hands in surrender. "I did not know she was one of yours."

Hel pulled him away from Sam by the collar and knelt by Sam's side.

"Are you all right?" Hel murmured, looking over Sam's wound, her fingers gentle.

"Yes, I'm fine," Sam said automatically, trying to smooth her skirts with trembling hands, only to hiss at the sting of the cut, the blood smearing and ruining another of her fine dresses. "What are you doing here? You said you were going to Lapérouse to check on the graffiti hours ago. Not to an alley to consort with, with—" Men whose heads were filled with *spiders*.

She still couldn't say that.

Hel cursed when she saw Sam's hand. "You shouldn't have followed me," Hel said, pulling off her crimson tie and wrapping it around Sam's hand tightly, to stanch the bleeding.

Hel stood as the second figure from the alley approached. It was a woman—Sam didn't know why that surprised her—the sort who looked as if she might be more at home astride a horse, with a crop in her hand. She wore a high-necked blue riding habit and smelled strongly of hay and dust, which did nothing to dissuade Sam's impressions.

The woman didn't wear nearly so many rings as the man, but they shared one in common. It had a peculiar design—a golden triangle under a ruby-inlaid cross.

"Is the channel all right?" The woman's words were said perfunctorily, as if Sam were a prized possession and not a person.

All softness fled Hel. She stood, putting herself between Sam and the strangers. "Miss Harker is under my protection. She is not to be touched by you or any of your order. Do you understand?"

"Of course, Dr. Moriarty," the other woman said, inclining her head, her hands still clasped before her. "It was just a misunderstanding—M. Voland is new; he does not yet know our ways. We do not take what is not offered. We have more than enough with which to barter. It will not happen again."

M. Voland, however, didn't look ashamed. He just watched Sam with hooded eyes. The kind of man who, once denied something, only wanted it more. It put a black churning feeling in

Sam's gut, and left her so focused on determining whether or not they were being followed that they nearly reached the train station before Sam realized they were going the wrong direction.

"The hospital is the other way," Sam protested. She looked down at her ruined dress—the second in three days. Her mother was going to be in a state about it. Her parents were hardly pleased that Sam had joined the Society, but had grudgingly allowed Sam to tap her trust fund for fashionable attire—as an *investment*, they'd said.

Sam didn't want to imagine what her mother would say if she learned Sam was ruining her fashionable dresses in the field instead of finding love between the stacks of the library in London.

"We're not going to the hospital," Hel said. "We're going to the hotel."

Sam stopped in her tracks. "We absolutely are not." Hel and her infuriating need to do everything herself. "I need a doctor. My hand needs stitches."

Hel shook her head. "I can do better than they can."

"Can you? Because I am under the assumption that your doctorate is in chemistry," Sam said.

"I need you to trust me on this one, Sam," Hel said.

"I want to." Frustration bled through into her voice. "But you have to give me something."

"Not here," Hel said, and she kept walking.

Oh, Sam's curiosity was going to be the death of her. She made a frustrated sound in her throat and followed.

Once inside their hotel room, Hel led Sam over to the chair by the fireplace. Then she pulled a tin from inside her coat pocket.

"Mint tea," Hel explained at Sam's look. "It calms the stomach."

"My stomach is fine," Sam said, a little snippily, but that was the pain talking. "It's my hand that needs assistance."

Hel favored her with a flat look. "Trust me."

It took Hel a minute to heat up the water, which she did by placing a silver carafe over the fire, as if they were camping. Sam winced at the sight of the black creeping up the silver.

Still, she was glad Hel hadn't left her alone to fetch hot water from the kitchen. Sam accepted the tea with her good hand, the steam washing over her, and drank. The mint was crisp as frost-curled leaves, taking the edge off the cold and nausea both. This, at least, was an advantage to not being in a hospital. She closed her eyes, savoring the taste and listening to Hel root around in her bags.

When she opened them again, Hel had carefully laid out a needle and thread, wound dressing, and iodine on a silver platter Sam was fairly certain was meant for breakfast. At the last, Hel pulled out a small clay vessel sealed with a cork and wax.

Kneeling in front of Sam, Hel held out her hands, palms up. Reluctantly, Sam put her wounded hand in Hel's.

Hel unwrapped the tie from Sam's wound, her fingers cold but gentle. It was still bleeding, but then, hand wounds were notoriously leaky. She remembered her father slicing his thumb open while gutting a fish. It hadn't stopped bleeding until the next day.

"Why did you follow me?" Hel asked as she washed away the blood.

"I didn't." Iodine hit the wound, and Sam hissed, her toes curling into the carpet. A wave of nausea swept through her.

"Tea," Hel instructed, and Sam took a steadying sip before continuing.

"There was another murder," Sam said. "I was making my

way there when I—when I *saw* you. Hel, who were those people? They had a symbol on their rings. A golden triangle under a red cross."

"Members of the Golden Dawn." Hel put down the iodine and carefully threaded the needle. "They have means of obtaining information outside the usual sources."

Sam had heard of it—a secret occult organization whose members hailed from the upper echelons of society. They operated in the shadows and practiced the forbidden arts of alchemy, ritual magic, and prognostication. Most of all, they endeavored to connect with supernatural beings, which was to say, with *monsters.*

Small wonder M. Voland had wanted Sam's blood. The Golden Dawn wanted what she had—except without the inconvenient part about inevitably ending up in an asylum if she didn't stop.

Which Sam would, if only the monsters would stop being *right.*

"I was hoping they could divine the key," Hel said. It took Sam a moment to realize Hel meant the book that would crack the cipher. "They couldn't."

"*They're* the ones who you choose to trust?" Sam exclaimed. "Not me, not the Society?"

Hel snorted. "Who says I trust them? They're useful."

"They could be behind the Beast!"

"Them?" Hel scoffed. "They're not powerful enough to perform transfigurations. Besides, they're the ones who tipped me off to certain . . . irregularities in this case."

Sam shook her head wordlessly. She was beginning to suspect that for all of Hel's brilliance, she couldn't comprehend how to be partners with someone. Which—how could she? It wasn't like she'd had much time to practice. "Why didn't you tell me?"

"Because I didn't want you to get hurt," Hel said. "Now hold still."

Sam squeezed her eyes shut as Hel started stitching her together, needle working in and out of her skin deftly. Sam had never really thought of how a dress might feel when it was being made, and she wished now she had never been given reason. She was, however, suddenly immensely grateful for the tea.

It occurred to Sam then that this tea was something Hel needed often enough that she kept it on her person at all times. Sam studied Hel through the steam, bent over Sam's hand with a look of intense concentration, wondering what had driven her to seek it out.

"Hel," Sam said, when she could breathe again, "if we're going to be partners, we have to start trusting each other."

"I won't let anything happen to you again." Hel cracked the wax seal on the clay vessel and popped the cork. The scent of amaranth filled the room, blended with something sharper that made her a little lightheaded. It was yellow, thick as custard, and stung like nettles as Hel applied it to Sam's wound.

"That's not the same thing!"

"I know," Hel said.

Sam was about to respond, when something odd happened. The angry wound on her palm began to change—the ragged flesh on either side extending small threads, purling and knitting, as if her flesh were a torn sweater, mending itself. Until at last, all that was left was a pale, silver scar. Hel snipped the stitches and pulled them free, then ran her thumb across the new line on Sam's palm. A shiver breathed down Sam's spine.

"Alchemy," Sam whispered.

Arcane chemistry that used the flesh and blood of monsters to fantastic effect—and risked the corruption of those who employed it. The cautionary tales Sam had read in the Society's library talked of kings and Holy Roman Emperors who had fallen under its sway and come to violent ends. King Henry IV of France had been stabbed by a monk, as if the monarch had become a monster himself. All of which was to say alchemy remained highly illegal.

Hel knew Sam had been sent to spy on her. She had to have known the consequences if Sam told Mr. Wright about Hel's use of alchemy. At the very least, Hel would be thrown out of the Society. Most likely she'd be thrown in prison. And yet, when Sam was injured, Hel had used the alchemical unguent on Sam instead of taking her to the hospital.

It was, Sam understood, an apology.

Hel gave a half shrug. "Your tendons were damaged. You never would have recovered full use of your hand—and what you did recover would have taken at least a month." As if it were only practical. "Come on, let's go."

"Where are we going?" Sam said, standing slowly.

"I was under the impression we had a murder to solve," Hel said.

"Tonight?" Sam exclaimed. Hel was already threading a new crimson tie around her neck, loose as a delinquent schoolboy's—utterly unrepentant about changing the subject.

"Unless you wanted to sneak out after me again?" Hel suggested. Sam's cheeks burned, for all she wasn't the one at fault here, and Hel laughed. "Come on, the body is growing cold."

Hel was still hiding things from her—Sam could feel it.

Things that might be just as dangerous as the Golden Dawn. And her thoughts drifted to the file Mr. Wright had given her, to the secrets it contained.

No, Sam thought, flexing her hand. Not yet. Hel was trying, had trusted Sam with her use of alchemy. She had to give her a chance.

"All right," Sam said. "Let's go."

CHAPTER SEVEN

The Morgue of Paris

The body of the latest murder victim, it turned out, was not only cold but half-frozen by the time Sam and Hel found their way to it. But this, at least, was not the fault of the Beast.

Sam and Hel had arrived at Le Meurice too late the night prior: the crime scene had been closed at the behest of the hotel, the murder victim moved to the Morgue of Paris, and the morgue did not open until daybreak, not even for Hel.

So it was that they found themselves in the throngs waiting outside the morgue in the cold light of dawn for a glimpse of the latest victim of the Beast.

It was a brutal building, composed from large blocks of a stone like yellowing teeth, squatting at the edge of the River Seine. Three unornamented archways formed the entry, a door behind each, reminiscent of a museum if you sucked all the life out of it.

Rumor had it, the morgue had been built on the banks of the Seine in order to ease the transfer of the river's unknown dead, where they were exhibited for identification purposes. Which didn't, of course, explain why the victims of the Beast were on display.

When Hel and Sam had first arrived, there'd been only an old man with a dog-eared paperback and a pair of factory workers playing chess in grease-stained coveralls. Now it seemed all of Paris was outside the morgue—men in morning dress reading the papers, elderly women gossiping in clusters, and street hawkers selling oranges to children dressed for school—all jostling for position outside the rope that barred them from the entrance.

"We could be done with this already," Hel grumbled.

"We're *not* breaking into the morgue," Sam whispered back, so as not to draw the attention of the crowd. Not when Van Helsing might be watching them, for all she knew the argument wouldn't move Hel.

Sam had told Hel about her encounter with the man the night prior, and Hel had been remarkably unbothered. "Then we won't get caught" was all she'd said. As if it were that easy.

"It's a crime," Sam said instead, "and would compromise the case against the murderer."

Hel snorted. "You know as well as I do this isn't going to end in court."

Sam had been trying not to think about that. It wasn't that Sam didn't know what the Society's agents did in the field—she knew that perfectly well, being the one to file their reports. But it was quite another thing to have to do it oneself.

And if the Beast turned out to be a *living werewolf* . . .

Every schoolchild knew that lycanthropes had all been hunted to extinction. But now, with the possibility that one had survived, it was like a little bit of magic had been breathed back into the world, for all she knew that, werewolf or not, the Beast was a murderer.

And Hel was Paris's best shot at stopping it.

They both were, she corrected herself. They were partners.

And at that word, she forced herself to draw in a deep breath and push aside her suspicions. Whatever secrets Hel was keeping from Sam, she was certain it wasn't murder. And they needed to work together if they were going to stop the Beast.

"Come on," Hel said, shouldering her way through the crowd. Sam hurried to follow as Hel stepped over the rope barrier, amidst a scattering of dirty looks. "Let's see if we can't get in early."

Hel raised her fist to knock, then lifted her nose, taking an experimental sniff. She turned to Sam. "What is that smell?"

Sam lifted her chin. "It's my perfume."

"That's a perfume?" Hel said. "You smell like old books."

"The perfumer I told you about made it for me," Sam said, fidgeting with her cuffs.

Sam had Hel's full attention. "Did he now?"

This time, Sam couldn't keep the heat from flooding her face. "Are you going to knock, or should I?" she snapped, fighting the urge to cover her traitorous cheeks.

Chuckling, Hel knocked on the leftmost door to the morgue. It was at least twice as tall as she was and crafted from suitably somber wood. A single gas lamp was lit overhead. The knock resounded hollowly, followed by a burst of irritated French on the other side.

"M. Rossignol? Hello?" Hel called.

"The doors open at 6:30 a.m.," came a man's muffled voice, in English this time. "Not 6:15, not 6:25. 6:30. Knocking won't make the sun rise faster."

"Dr. Moriarty and Miss Harker," Hel said, "here to see the victims of the Beast."

"So is everybody else."

Sam and Hel exchanged a look. "With the Society," Hel added.

At last, there was the *clunk* of a key turning in the lock, and then the heavy wooden door cracked open. A man Sam assumed to be M. Rossignol peered back at them. He had leathery skin and a hellfire preacher's piercing gaze under wild, bushy eyebrows threaded with grey.

"Officer Berchard said you might be coming," M. Rossignol said, and he creaked the door wide enough for Sam and Hel to slip through. The folks in the crowd craned their necks, trying to get a look, but the man shut the door tight behind them, locking it. "I wasn't sure I believed him."

"Does he lie often?" Sam ventured.

"No," M. Rossignol said. "It just seemed too unbelievable. A couple of Englishwomen come all the way across the Channel to look at French corpses? It sounds like the start of a bad novel."

"American and Irish, actually," Sam put in, remembering the change it had worked on Officer Berchard.

He raised his shaggy brows. "Oh, well then, why didn't you say so? That's completely different, isn't it? Everyone knows how much American and Irish women love corpses."

Hel raised an eyebrow right back at him. "There are a number of women waiting outside to see these corpses."

"Of course," M. Rossignol said, waving for them to follow him deeper into the morgue. "But they are French. These are their dead."

The inside of the morgue was an expansive space with curtained window displays like you might find in a department store, and a clear circuit visitors could walk from the entrance on the left to the exit on the right. Behind the glass were large slabs of marble, tilted toward the windows, upon which were a variety of dead bodies.

Sam averted her gaze, torn between embarrassment and

nausea. They were all of them naked, their clothing hanging above them, as if set out on the line to dry. It was a ridiculous thing to get worked up over—some of them were missing heads, it seemed unlikely that they would care about their modesty. But Sam couldn't help it. She couldn't believe her brother went to places like this on purpose.

Though, she supposed, now so did Sam.

"I was under the impression only unidentified victims were displayed here," Sam said to distract herself as they walked past waterlogged corpses pulled from the River Seine, their features bloated and stretched like melting wax. "Why are the Beast's victims here?"

M. Rossignol shrugged. "The police have a theory. They think the murderer will come to see his work."

"Do they?" Sam said faintly as she thought about the people waiting outside. The factory workers and children and the old women gossiping.

What were the signs of a werewolf again? There were few enough signs of lycanthropy in human form. Eyebrows that met in the middle—but one could always pluck unwanted hairs. A hunger for raw meat—but it wasn't like they couldn't eat other things. A weakness to wolfsbane, but of course, everyone was weak to wolfsbane. It was, after all, a poison.

The only things that couldn't be disguised, so far as Sam could remember, were the speed of their healing, their weakness to silver, and the reflectiveness of their eyes when they were about to transform, which was terribly short warning.

All of which was to say it could be anyone.

M. Rossignol halted before the last window.

"All the victims of the Beast are in this display," M. Rossignol said, unlocking the door to one of the exhibitions with a jingle of keys. "I do not know what you think you will find that we have not, but you are welcome to it. Just so as you know, you have ten minutes before you'll have company. I have to let the crowds in at dawn."

Hel frowned. "Where are the rest?" The Beast had murdered six men, not three.

"We cannot keep the bodies long," M. Rossignol called over his shoulder, already on his way back to the door. "They begin to rot. Good luck, agents. I hope you find what you're looking for."

Behind the glass, the room had the damp iron smell of a butcher's shop with hanks of meat hanging on hooks. It was cold—the floor frosted, her breath clouding the air. Try as she might, Sam couldn't bring herself to look at the bodies—not right away—so she looked at their nameplates first.

M. Barrere, the victim from Lapérouse, was on the middle slab. To his left, the victim from the murder at the ballet, M. Toussaint. And to his right, the victim from the murder at Le Meurice the night prior, M. Gauthier.

Sam forced her gaze up to the men who bore those names. It was easier, somehow, in the cold sterility of the morgue, than it had been in Lapérouse. Sam could almost imagine them Anatomical Adams—meticulously sculpted wax models for surgeons to practice on. But of course, they'd never made Anatomical Adams, had they? Only Anatomical Venuses— women with painted lips and falls of golden hair, split open from pearls to pelvis. And these were no wax models.

Limbs were in various states of detachment. Bones sprouted out of forearms and thighs—a sight so irregular, Sam's mind kept skipping like a record at the sight. M. Gauthier was missing his right hand and a couple of the fingers from his left, and M.

Toussaint was missing all of his left arm, which, Sam assumed, had ended up in that briefcase.

But the core violence was uncannily similar: throat crushed, eyes clawed out, ribs cracked, lungs pulled out, a cavity where their hearts should be.

Werewolves ate hearts, Sam's thoughts whispered as she struggled not to be sick.

Hel reached over with tweezers and pulled a thick strand of fur from the cavity in M. Gauthier's chest. The hair was nearly the length of Hel's hand, too long and thick for a dog's. "Well, someone certainly wants us to think it's a werewolf."

"You don't think it is?" Sam said.

Hel didn't look up from where she was examining M. Gauthier's wounds. "The whole world knows werewolves were eradicated. If one had escaped, why would they want to challenge that?"

"What if you were going to die anyway?" Sam said. "Might you not risk it then, to get revenge on those who had slaughtered the rest of your kind?"

"You might," Hel allowed. "It's a good thought. We should search out whether there's any connection."

The men's suits were all of fine but not identical make, and there was nothing about them to invite concern, apart from the rips and blood and viscera. Sam searched the pockets, but they were all of them empty, except for one, which only had a crumpled-up note inside, so saturated with blood the ink had spread over the paper like a fungal bloom.

If there was anything useful to be learned there, it was beyond Sam's abilities.

Sam was just about to abandon the clothes when her gaze

snagged. There, on M. Toussaint's collar, just below where his ear would have been, there was the barest smudge of red.

It wasn't blood. Blood a day and a half old would be brown. In fact, Sam was nearly certain it was crimson lipstick.

Her fingers worked down his suit, intent now. On the breast of his jacket, she found a series of strange splatter marks in a soft, shimmery grey, like a moth's wing. *Eyeshadow.* She examined M. Barrere next and found a hint of that same crimson lipstick on his waistcoat, that same iridescence in the weft of his lapel. Then, M. Gauthier, who smelled faintly of pine, but otherwise had nothing of note.

"It wasn't just M. Barrere," Sam said. "M. Toussaint is also missing his wedding ring and has smears of cosmetics on his suit. Wives don't wear cosmetics. Not in shades that announce themselves. That's the realm of actresses and mistresses." As were private salons at Lapérouse and back rooms at the ballet.

"What about M. Gauthier?" Hel pressed.

Sam chewed her lip. "I don't know, he doesn't fit. His suit's clean, and he's still wearing his wedding ring."

Sam's thoughts flicked back to the wall at Lapérouse, to the message the Wolves of God had left there: *Car la solde du péché, c'est la mort.*

For the wages of sin is death.

If these men were being killed for their sins, then it seemed it wasn't just for the sin of lust. But then, there were plenty of sins to which powerful men like M. Gauthier might fall prey.

Hel looked over Sam's shoulder at the fabric. "Show me."

"Here—" Sam reached out toward M. Toussaint's jacket, toward the smear of eyeshadow. But no sooner had her fingers brushed the iridescence than the breath left her lungs in a punch, and suddenly, Sam could *feel* as teeth closed on her throat, as cartilage crunched, as she tried but could not scream. Distantly, she could hear sobbing as her head lolled, her finger dipping into the ragged mess of her chest and then falling to the floor, tracing something, tracing *words*.

"Sam—Sam!"

Sam gasped, sitting up. When had she fallen? Hel knelt on the floor beside her, her hands on her shoulders, her eyes locked on Sam's. Sam lay next to the body, her legs in exactly the same position, her fingers dragging through the frost on the floor—

Sam gave a little cry, pulling her fingers close to her chest and cradling them.

Hel looked past her, at the words Sam had roughed in the ice.

Je sens le sapin.

"He drew words in his own blood," Sam croaked, her fingers curling toward her palms. Her throat felt as if it had been scraped raw, her face wet. She'd been screaming. "He drew words on the floor as he lay dying, hoping someone would see them."

But no one had. Of that much, Sam was sure. Words written in blood would have made the case file, if not the paper. Which meant someone had destroyed them.

Hel frowned. "What does—"

Before she could finish, the display door slammed open. "What in the Lord's name!" M. Rossignol cried, his weathered face a mask of horror. It was only then that Sam realized they were being watched.

Children with their sticky fingers pressed against the windows or held up on the shoulders of parents craning their own necks above the crowd. Laborers in their stained uniforms, the elderly and the young, the fashionable and the frumpy, all pointing and staring at Sam. And there in the middle of it all was Évangéline St. Laurent—the shining star of the Parisian opera and unofficial queen of Tout-Paris. She looked exactly as she did in the papers, save her sultry brown eyes were wide with horror and fascination, her lips just parted, painted burgundy to match her dress.

Which meant, of course, that the sharply dressed gentleman on whose arm she hung was none other than M. Poulin, one of the most influential men in Parisian politics—and Évangéline's fiancé.

Ten minutes, M. Rossignol had said, and then he'd have to let the crowds in.

"How long have they been watching?" Sam whispered, horrified. Had Évangéline heard them discussing M. Barrere's and M. Toussaint's mistresses? Had she seen Sam touch the man and fall, dragging her fingers through the frost like a woman possessed? If she had, it would only be a matter of time before all Tout-Paris knew.

M. Rossignol stormed into the display and yanked the curtains over the window, before rounding on them. "You need to leave," he said as the crowd began to pound on the curtained glass and people began to shout.

"I'm sorry," Sam started. "I only—"

"Now."

"We were just finished," Hel said, as if screaming were a completely normal and essential part of any investigation. And, hooking Sam's arm, Hel pulled her from the morgue, through the throngs of people craning for a look at Sam's face.

They didn't know what they'd seen, Sam told herself. They didn't know she was a channel, only that she'd put on a bit of a display. A hysterical woman, unable to take the sight of blood.

But Van Helsing would. If word reached him about what she'd done, there was no way he'd mistake it for anything other than what it was, for he'd seen her channel before. Exactly once, to be precise.

Sam had been all of eleven, exploring the woods behind her house—Jakob swinging a stick at the underbrush like a sword, pretending he was Achilles; Sam debating whether or not to tell him Achilles had used a spear—when she spotted a feather. But the instant her fingers had brushed its vivid blue, she'd gasped, suddenly able to *feel* needlelike teeth in her neck, her arms stretching as she fell, bending like broken wings in the underbrush.

When her vision had finished with her, there had been a look on Jakob's face she'd never seen before or since. *Fear.*

"S-stay away from me," he'd said, backing away, eyes wide, as if she might take his neck between her teeth. And then, before she could so much as say his name, he'd turned and run.

Of course, Van Helsing no longer ran from monsters. Oh, she was such a fool.

"Now do you think we should have broken in?" Hel asked as they made their way back.

"No!" Sam said, then buried her face in her hands. "Maybe. Yes. But it would have been just as bad if we'd gotten caught. You heard him—they think the culprit will come to see his work. They'd have thought we did it."

"I don't think so," Hel said. "Their theory rests on the culprit wanting to see the world's *reaction* to his crimes, not the crimes themselves, with which one assumes he is acquainted."

Once they'd arrived back at the hotel, Sam pulled out her French book of phrases, hoping that at least their efforts should have given them something to work with. At first, she was stumped. *Sapin* was fir trees, and *sens* was from *sentir*, which was to sense. Until at last, Sam realized what she was missing.

"It's an idiom," Sam said as Hel passed her a mug of mint tea. Sam sipped from it gratefully. She hadn't realized how cold the dead had left her, and the warmth seemed to seep down into her very bones, even as the mint settled her stomach. "It's the equivalent of the English expression 'To have one foot in the grave.'"

"He spent his heart's blood to tell us he was going to die?" Hel said skeptically. "I should think that self-evident."

"Maybe he was a poet?" Sam offered. But she didn't believe that either. A poet would have come up with something more original.

It was a dead end, at least for now. Fortunately, Sam and Hel had other avenues of investigation.

"What did you learn of the graffiti?" Sam asked.

"The Morse code was added by someone else," Hel said. "The wolf was drawn in a heavy, frenzied hand by one of the Wolves of God taken into custody before our arrival. The lines of Morse code were thinner, more precise, and accomplished after our departure."

Which meant that someone had slipped into the scene of the crime late that night to contribute their own artistry without the police noticing.

"Officer Berchard," Sam said. No one would have noticed a fellow officer examining the graffiti, and he'd already covered for the mistress.

"My thoughts exactly," Hel said. The morning paper had held more graffiti, this time from Le Meurice. Sam had copied the lines of Morse code into her notebook. The pattern fit the rest, but she could ascertain nothing more from it. The one connection to her grandfather—and she couldn't seem to grasp it.

Solve the case, solve the numbers, Sam reminded herself. Sometimes the only way to achieve your goal was to come at it sideways, so it wouldn't see you coming. Her grandfather had taught her that, when she was younger and they were on a quest to catch moths. Crouched down in the long grasses at night, he'd shown her how if she moved too fast, the moth would feel her coming through the currents of the air and slip through her fingers. He'd also told her not to hold them too tightly—gently would do.

"What about you?" Hel asked. "Did you scent out our mistress?"

Sam forced the complicated mess of her feelings aside. "Of course."

"Her name is Clotilde Auclair." Sam handed Hel the slip of paper the midinette had given her. "She's a midinette with Paquin—or rather, she was. No one has seen her since the day before yesterday. She lives with her parents on the northern outskirts of Paris."

"That address," Hel said. "It's in Montmartre."

Montmartre—she'd heard that before. That was where Officer Berchard had claimed the Wolves of God were from. "You don't think she's one of the Wolves of God, do you?"

Hel grabbed her hat. "I think it's time we found out."

CHAPTER EIGHT

Montmartre, Paris

The Paris Metro cut under the skin of the city, rumbling the catacombs far below. It didn't extend all the way to Montmartre. The butte was riddled with old mining tunnels, rendering the ground notoriously unstable. Rumor had it the Basilica of Sacré-Coeur had required a foundation that ran nearly forty-four yards under the ground, just so it wouldn't fall into the depths of the earth. Which, Sam reflected, would be a bad look for a church.

And the tunnels weren't the only source of instability in Montmartre. It was also where the Wolves of God made their home—and it was whispered that Tout-Paris's fear of the Wolves of God was the real reason the Metro didn't extend to Montmartre. Not that it seemed to stop the Wolves from leaving.

But every carriage Sam and Hel hailed at the station refused to take them the rest of the way to Montmartre, until there was only one left.

"We'd like to secure passage to Montmartre," Hel said, impatience leaking into her tone.

The driver glanced at them briefly and set his jaw. "No."

Sam blinked. "I'm sorry?"

"No, I won't take you to Montmartre," he said. "It's not safe. Not for you."

Sam felt a chill. Her father's stories of Transylvania always began with how the locals had been terrified, how they'd warned him it wasn't safe. How he wished he'd listened. But that wasn't what was happening here—this driver didn't appear afraid.

Hel raised an eyebrow. "You don't even know who we are."

"It doesn't matter." The driver waved a hand. "You're outsiders. *Tourists.* Turn around and go home. Montmartre isn't like the rest of Paris. There is nothing for you there."

Hel opened her mouth, a look on her face that said she was about to be anything but subtle.

"Oh, but there is," Sam blurted, hooking Hel's arm before she could speak. "We're going to visit a friend. She missed work, and we're all so worried about her. Her name is Clotilde Auclair. If you won't take us, at least tell us if she's all right."

It was slight, but something shifted in the driver's face. "You're midinettes?" It explained their fine clothes, if not their terrible French.

"You know her?" Sam let hope brighten her face. "She was going to see . . . she had a caller. And we never heard back. We're worried he did something."

"*So* worried," Hel said unconvincingly. The driver frowned. She was losing him.

"We brought her wages," Sam said quickly, pulling the driver's attention back. "In case she's—in case she's in a *way* and can't come back." Sam bit her lip, as if worried she'd said too much, watching through her lashes as caution and concern warred on the driver's face.

It was a calculated risk. But Sam had a suspicion he wasn't

just turning them down to protect them, but to protect his town in the event something happened to Sam and Hel—for something like that would bring the police down on Montmartre in bloody force. Which meant this was a good man. A man who cared about his town deeply enough to lose a fare from women who would doubtless overpay.

What's more, the driver knew Mlle Auclair; knew what she did, the risks associated with it. And even if he had no concern for Mlle Auclair, downtown Paris wages went a long way in Montmartre. Mlle Auclair lived with her family—they likely couldn't afford to lose that money.

"All right," he said at last, a gruffness finding its way into his voice. "Get in."

"You're terrible at that," Sam whispered to Hel once they were safely ensconced inside, the jingle of the harness and the clopping of hooves covering their conversation.

Hel raised an eyebrow. "At *lying*, you mean? I should think you'd approve."

"At pretending to be someone you're not," Sam said indignantly. "And it has its uses." Not everyone had the luxury of being who they were all the time—not if they didn't want the asylum to claim them.

Still, Sam thought, watching Hel sidelong, she had to admit it was reassuring. Whatever Hel's game was, she was fully herself—even if only because she didn't know how to be anyone else.

A half hour of fatherly advice later, Sam and Hel stepped out onto the dirt streets of Montmartre, the driver clucking, his carriage trundling away.

The driver was right: Montmartre looked a far cry from the rest of Paris. It was practically provincial—or at least it would have been, if the dilapidated cottages hadn't been packed quite so close together. A few chickens pecked in the wide dirt roads, chased by laughing children in shapeless clothes.

Mlle Auclair's home was up a dirt footpath carved into the side of the butte. It was in better shape than most of the cottages in the area, boasting a picket fence and a small herb garden with an apple tree. Crows sat in the tree's twisted branches like an omen.

Sam looked over her shoulder. No one was paying them any mind, but she couldn't shake the feeling that they were being watched.

"So that's where the gifts from M. Barrere went," Hel murmured as they walked up to the house. The fence was the color of fresh honey, not greyed with age; there was a still-shiny patch on the sheet metal roof.

"How responsible." Sam began to feel uneasy, unable to fit the pieces of Mlle Auclair together with either the perfumer's description of a young woman seduced by a lifestyle she couldn't afford or the revolutionary assassin of the Wolves of God.

Hel looked at her sidelong. "Who says Wolves can't be responsible?"

"Well, Officer Berchard for one," Sam said.

"Of course he'd say that." Hel snorted. "Look around you, Sam. You've seen how *Tout-Paris* lives. This is what it's like for everyone else."

Sam shook her head. "Yes, but Officer Berchard said they're criminals—thieves and murderers—"

"You're a *researcher*, Sam," Hel said, the second time Sam had been accused of such. Sam rather thought those who weren't researchers should stop getting ideas about what should constitute those who were. "Tell me, when is the last time *asking nicely* resulted in real change? And since when have the police by any name called it anything other than criminal? Theft and murder."

"You sound almost as if you agree with the Wolves of God," Sam accused.

"I think they have reason to be unhappy," Hel said pointedly. "And that given your reaction to that poor grindylow, you might agree with me."

Not knowing what to say to that, Sam knocked on the Auclairs' door. She checked over her shoulder, the sensation of being watched crawling over her again. But no one was there.

No one answered the door either. Frowning, Sam peered in the dirty windows. The falling light caught on the dust in the air, the distortions in the glass stretching shadows into monsters before resolving into a lived-in sitting room. Nothing moved.

"We're too late," Sam said. First Lapérouse, then the Senate, now here, at Mlle Auclair's home. Every time they caught the corner of a clue, a way to track down the missing mistress, it slipped through their fingers. "Someone must have warned her."

"You may be right," Hel said, staring intently at the garden. More specifically, at a hollow in the apple tree, where a crow had just alighted. It rooted inside the darkness for a moment, then flew off, something clutched in its long black beak.

A few seconds later, a second crow appeared and the ritual repeated itself.

"There's something in that hollow," Sam said. "Isn't there?"

Hel hopped the fence, crossing the garden to the apple tree. Crows flapped out of its crown of branches, cawing and circling above. Sam hurried after—"Wait!"—catching up to Hel just as she plunged her hands into the hollow, withdrawing what for all intents and purposes appeared to be a braided loaf of golden-brown bread.

"Is that . . . brioche?" Sam frowned.

Hel ripped the bread in half.

"What are you doing?" Sam exclaimed.

"There might be a message inside it," Hel said, peering at each half, and then tearing them in half again. The crows circling above cried out their appreciation, swooping and diving. "Something to tell whoever she's working with where she went. It's what I'd do."

"You'd leave out *bread*?"

"*Lass es in Ruhe!*" came a gravelly voice in German. Sam whirled to see an older gentleman walking stiffly across the dirt road, shooing the chickens out of his path with his cane. He was the kind of slender that happens to a man who was once strong, his bones almost too big for his skin, his eyes pale as moonlight on the water.

"There you are," Hel said. Sam wondered for a moment if Hel knew the old man, until she saw the edge in her smile. "I was wondering when you were going to come out."

"Was he—" Sam began.

"Spying on us?" Hel finished for her. "Yes. Or rather, on whoever came hunting Clotilde. Where is she?"

"I don't know," the old man said, switching to English. "Do you always destroy other people's property?"

"It's *bread*," Hel said. "It's made to be broken. And I think you know where she is."

"It doesn't belong to you, or the man you work for," the old man said stubbornly. "And neither does *she*."

The man you work for . . . The German *knew* something about Clotilde, about whatever it was she'd gotten herself caught up in.

"Remind me," Hel drawled. "Who is it we work for again?"

Sam noticed flecks of flour on his clothes, the old scars on his forearms in the place ovens always seem to burn bakers.

"The bread isn't Clotilde's, is it?" Sam said. "It's yours."

The man's jaw tightened, but then he squinted at the ghost of the moon in the midday sky, and something changed in his expression. He looked almost . . . frightened.

"Keep the bread if you want. Miserable tourists," the man said, starting back toward his cottage door, taking his secrets with him. "But a word of warning: the sun sets early in autumn, and the wolves come out at night. I wouldn't get caught in the dark if I were you."

"Wait just a moment—" Hel shoved the bread at Sam, stalking after the old man.

Sam's fingers closed reflexively on the bread, and a *feeling* brushed along her nerves like a bow across the strings of a violin. Sam gasped, the welcoming warmth of kitchen ovens and baking bread sweeping through her like a breeze through an open window. Suddenly she could *feel* the dough under her hands, the sunlight pouring in the window strong enough to cast out any shadows.

"Hel, I don't think this bread has a message in it," Sam managed, the bread's magic leaving her feeling overwarm. It was a ward. She knew it like she knew her own name, even if she couldn't explain why. "I think he's trying to *protect* the Auclairs from the Beast."

Which, given that Clotilde might very well be the Beast, was ironic, to say the least.

"With . . . bread?" Hel demanded incredulously.

But the old man scowled, crossing the distance to rap Sam on the head with his cane.

"Ow!"

Hel's revolver was in her hand in a second. "Try that again."

"Foolish girl! None of that, not out here," the old man said sharply, ignoring Hel entirely. "In front of my good Catholic neighbors. And for a moment I thought you might be smart."

Sam and Hel stared after the old man stomping back toward his cottage. He paused on the threshold, not bothering to look back. "Well? Are you just going to stand there, or are you going to come inside?"

— —

The old man, who introduced himself as Moritz Knie, led them past the entry into a kitchen dominated by a formidable black iron oven, the heat off it reducing the sweat on Sam's skin to salt. A rough, hand-carved crucifix adorned a sizeable hood, and a cheerful kitchen towel embroidered with birds hung off the painted wooden fingers of a half-skeletal, half-fleshed man attached to the wall.

It was like stepping into the past. Sam shuddered, reminded of the fleeting vision she'd had of skulls in the secret passage between Lapérouse and the French Senate. Sam half expected to channel something equally macabre in the old man's home, the way she seemed to every time there was a clue to be had—blood oozing out of the oven perhaps, or finger bones in the bread—but there was nothing beyond the rough-hewn reminders that some-day she, too, would die.

"Here," Herr Knie said, setting a lump of dough on the flour-dusted table. There was, Sam thought, something powerfully reassuring about that heavy wooden table. He gestured for Sam to sit. "Knead this."

"We didn't come here to make bread," Sam said, anxious to get what they came for and get out.

"You want an explanation, yes? Then do as I ask," he said.

Sam cast a sidelong look at Hel, who nodded minutely. She began to work the dough. Satisfied, he turned to Hel. "You were nearly right outside—you just had the wrong verb form. This bread is not meant to be broken, it's meant to break."

"Break *what*?" Sam asked.

"If you're going to talk, talk to the bread!" Herr Knie rebuked, before proceeding to answer Hel, as if she'd been the one to ask: "Whatever is calling the wolves, of course, don't you know anything?"

"Best assume we do not," Hel said for the both of them.

Herr Knie nodded to himself. "That would explain why you were destroying my wards. I thought you might be with *them*. Well. I will explain it to you. Listen carefully: behind the fragile skin of our world is another."

"We *know*," Hel said. "We're with the Royal Society for the Study of Abnormal—"

"Hush," Herr Knie chided. "Everyone *knows* it, though they call it by different names. If they're lucky, they will only ever contact it through brokers—the priests and the midwives and the shepherds—who entreat that other world by way of ointments and rituals, wine . . . and bread."

"Shepherds," Hel said skeptically. "The people who herd sheep."

"Most know how to heal a sick sheep or cow," Herr Knie pointed out. "Some know how to keep away storms. And a rare few, the *Wolfssegners*, we ward people's flocks from disease and accidents, monsters and wolves."

Hel glanced at Sam—*Have you heard of this?*

Sam shook her head. While the Society claimed to be the repository of all things unnatural, it was becoming clear how very much the Society didn't know . . . or wasn't telling them.

"Say I believe you," Hel said. "What's a German Wolfssegner doing *here*?" On the outskirts of Paris, in a run-down town—as far from pastoral as it was from Tout-Paris.

Herr Knie shrugged. "The Church doesn't like competition. They accuse us of witchcraft, for all we are in the pews every Sunday and call upon the same saints they do! Of course my good Catholic neighbors believed them, for fear their souls would prove forfeit otherwise. And they say Wolfssegners are the ones doing the coercing! Well—they can pray to the Church to save their cows from now on, see how far *that* gets them."

"They threw you out," Hel said dryly.

"They threw me out!" the Wolfssegner confirmed. "And now I risk being thrown out again, if I don't bake enough bread to ward all Montmartre. But I won't let the wolves claim my new home—or my good Catholic neighbors, whatever they think of my methods."

The way he talked . . . Sam would have thought him mad or a charlatan. It didn't escape her that most people would probably think the same of Sam, should she be honest about the things she saw.

Yet the fact remained: there had been no Beast attacks in Montmartre. It could be chance, of course, but Sam had felt the power in that bread for herself.

Besides, it would hardly be the first time she'd heard of such a warding. Her mother still warded the windows with garlic flowers.

"Give me that." Herr Knie grabbed the dough Sam had been kneading and, with quick, sure motions, divided it into eight pieces and slid them into the oven.

"Who's behind it then?" Sam asked, brushing the flour off her hands. "Who is calling the wolves?"

"Why would I know anything about that?" the Wolfssegner said.

Sam resisted the urge to shake the old man. "You said you thought we were with 'them.'"

"Well, it just stands to figure," Herr Knie said, as if it were obvious. "Wolves don't like the city. So something must be calling them."

Oh—*oh*.

Mlle Auclair had met with M. Barrere in the petit salon at Lapérouse the night he was murdered. And it might be happenstance—she might be injured, or lying low from the investigation with the Wolves of God—but a Wolfssegner had warded her house against wolves, and Mlle Auclair *hadn't come home*.

"Would your wards work against werewolves?" Sam asked.

Herr Knie snorted. "'Course wards work against the weres, or they wouldn't be very good wards, would they? Only when they're in wolf form, mind."

Which meant that on the off chance Mlle Auclair *was* a surviving werewolf—she hadn't started the night as a wolf.

But could she have ended the night as one?

"You said something is calling them," Hel repeated. "You mean a Wolfssegner."

"Well, that's one possibility," he admitted.

"Could *you* call the wolves?"

"Are you accusing me?" the Wolfssegner shot back.

Hel crossed her arms. "I'm asking you a question. That you can't tell the difference says more about you than me."

Moritz Knie knew more than he was letting on—Sam was nearly certain of it. The theory he'd offered them was obviously incorrect. There was no way wolves, even magically summoned wolves, could break into petit salons and ballets on their lonesome, lacking thumbs and all, especially without being seen.

But he'd put his dough where his mouth was—baking enough bread to cover all Montmartre in antiwolf wards.

Sam was missing something—she could feel it itching at the back of her brain. But even as she opened her mouth to interrogate him further, her gaze snagged. There, hidden beneath a catastrophe of books, was the ragged edge of a broadside.

It was probably nothing. An advertisement he didn't like, or liked too well, ripped off the wall. But something about it drew her in as surely as radio signals did wills-o'-the-wisp.

Surreptitiously, Sam checked over her shoulder to see Herr Knie still engaged in heated dialogue with Hel about what, exactly, the Wolfssegner could do with wolves.

"You didn't see any bread at the murder scenes, did you?"

"You're the one who said it didn't have to be bread."

Sam edged the broadside out from under the disorderly pile of books. The moment she pulled it free, a wolf's face stretched the broadside like a burial cloth, as if it were trying to escape, snapping and twisting—

Sam swallowed a little gasp, the scent of burnt toast lingering in her nose as the broadside slipped from her fingers. She felt a flutter of nerves—the wolf's eyes had looked . . . human.

Whatever the broadside was, it had excited her visions. She flicked her gaze over at Hel and the Wolfssegner, but neither seemed to have noticed.

Gingerly, Sam picked it up again and examined it. It was strange, as broadsides went. It didn't have a lot of text. In fact, it only had a single line, printed in bold, black lettering:

Omnes angeli, boni et mali, ex virtute naturali habent potestatem transmutandi corpora nostra.

Sam frowned. She didn't know a lot of Latin, but she knew enough to know the words for *transformation* and *body*, *good* and *evil*. She turned the broadside over. On the back, covering the whole page, was an ink drawing of a hollow-eyed black wolf under a five-pointed star, its legs dripping down onto a broken crown, and the now-familiar words: *Car la solde du péché, c'est la mort.*

The Wolves of God.

Herr Knie clapped his hands and Sam startled, nearly dropping the broadside again, but managed to tuck it in her skirts.

"Now, let's see what we have here," Herr Knie said, his argument with Hel apparently over. Opening the oven, he took out the rolls Sam had kneaded earlier. The smell of fresh-baked bread filled the room, their golden-brown crusts crackling.

The Wolfssegner took a bite and chewed.

"Well, you're not a Wolfssegner, that much is certain," he said, staring at Sam, his eyes narrowed in thought.

"I never said I was," Sam said, making sure the broadside was well and fully hidden. "Wait—was that what this was about? The business with the kneading? Is this an augury?"

"Strange. Not a cunning woman either, nor a midwife. A channel, except, there's something else there. Or some*one*." The Wolfssegner continued to chew, his expression slowly changing, until he was staring at Sam with an intensity that reminded her uncomfortably of a wolf, until he shook his head. "Powerful magic, whatever it is."

"I don't know what you mean," Sam said, crossing her arms.

"You *know* what I mean," the Wolfssegner said.

The visions that seemed as if they were trying to catch Sam's attention—that seemed as if they wanted to *tell her something*. Had she caught a monster's attention, like her mother? Despair rippled through her. How would she even know? Even now, she could be under a monster's influence, doing its bidding.

The visions had all come true, Sam told herself. And besides, Hel would know—she wouldn't let Sam be possessed by a monster.

Hel, who believed in Sam's visions rather than feared them.

Hel, who had claimed the late Professor Van Helsing would never have defeated Dracula without Mina Harker's visions.

Hel, whom Sam had stumbled across in that dark alley, bargaining with a secret society that dealt in forbidden magic and attacked Sam for the power in her blood, all to get an edge on their case. And a horrible thought wormed into her brain: If Sam was more useful when she was possessed, would Hel even fight it?

"You sensed my wards—knew them for what they were," the Wolfssegner said. "You can do more, I think. Pretending you can't doesn't make it so. Tell me, can you sense other things as well? Magic perhaps, or people's thoughts, or glimpses of the future—"

"You don't have to answer him," Hel said.

"If not to me, then at least admit it to yourself," the Wolfssegner said. "The more you stack against the door you've locked against whatever is inside you, the more it will burn you out from the inside, until all that's left is that *door*, and then it will define you. Trust me, I have been down this road before. You do not want what's at the end of it."

"All right, that's enough." Hel's voice was a whipcrack. "Herr Knie, where is Clotilde Auclair?"

The Wolfssegner shrugged. "How should I know?" Sam could hear Hel's teeth grinding. "Though, come to think of it, that cousin of hers was sniffing around late the night before."

"What. Cousin."

"What's his name . . . ?" the Wolfssegner grumbled, scratching his beard. "He's one of those jumped-up gardiens de la paix publique. Tightly coiled black hair. Ears blown out. Eyes black as ink—"

"Officer Berchard," Sam said, and Hel swore.

Of course it was. Between the missing garnets, the late addition to the graffiti, his paltry attempt to lie about M. Barrere's mistress, and now this, it was beginning to look like he might be in league with the mistress after all.

"Yes, that's him," the Wolfssegner said, giving her a strange look. He reached for a second roll. Hel got their first—scooping it up along with the rest of Sam's rolls.

"We're done here," Hel said, somehow managing to look dangerous with her arms full of bread. "Thank you for your . . . whatever this was. Come on, Sam."

The moment they were outside, Sam broke. "Why did you do that?"

"He was stalling," Hel said, throwing the rolls to the crows. "You saw that Wolves of God broadside in his room."

Sam hadn't realized Hel had spotted it—the woman didn't miss a thing.

"The mistress got away once already," Hel said. "He was about to ensure she got away again."

"But he knew something about what's happening to me," Sam said, and she thought of that awful vision in the morgue. The way she'd ended up on the floor, without ever knowing how she'd gotten there, in the same position as the dead man, her hand tracing words of its own volition. "About whatever's wrong with me."

"There's nothing wrong with you, Sam," Hel said sharply. "And you don't need old men to tell you who or what you are. You decide that. No one else."

"Except you, is that right?" Sam said. Hel froze, her eyes

narrowing for a second in a way Sam recognized as Hel identifying a miscalculation. Well, Sam thought fiercely, let her recalculate. Yet beneath her anger, a part of her could not deny how strongly she wished for Hel to promise Sam that she would never use her, that of course Sam was more important than the case. That they were partners.

But even if Hel did, would Sam believe it? Trust wasn't something you decided—it was something that simply was, or wasn't.

"Well, come on then." Sam turned away from the house and started down the road. "Let's see what Officer Berchard has to say for himself."

CHAPTER NINE

The Préfecture de Police de Paris

The Préfecture de Police de Paris presided over an island in the middle of the River Seine—a neo-Florentine citadel, built out of the warm cream-grey stone mined in the tunnels that became the catacombs far beneath their feet.

No sooner had Sam and Hel crossed the bridge to the prefecture than they spotted Officer Berchard on the street in a short-sleeved button-down, and with him, a brown-skinned woman in a man's coat, her dark brown hair come undone. The wind gusted, and Sam caught a glimpse of torn scarlet silk.

"It's her," Sam said excitedly. *Clotilde Auclair.*

As if she'd heard Sam, the mistress turned, and Officer Berchard cursed, wrapping his arms protectively around her shoulders. Sam gasped. Blood ran down the mistress's face—not from a wound or dripping from her teeth, but from her *eyes*, as if she were crying. With a chill, Sam remembered the tears that had soaked that arm in the briefcase.

Then, all at once, the blood was gone, as if it had never been.

"Officer Berchard," Hel said, raising her voice. "I believe you owe us an explanation."

"Mademoiselles. It's good to see you well." Officer Berchard shifted like a boxer. "Clotilde, if you don't mind—"

"I'm afraid Barrere's *mistress* and the sole witness to his murder won't be going anywhere," Hel said sharply, and the woman stiffened. "Unless, of course, you'd like me to inform your colleagues, and do this by the books?"

Officer Berchard darted a look behind him. "Not here! For pity's sake," he hissed. "Come with me."

He ushered them into an alley, and then to the wooden door of an outbuilding. There, Officer Berchard pulled out bent metal picks while Mlle Auclair let out a small unhappy cry and turned her back to him, covering for him with the breadth of her skirts. It was so much like the midinettes, like partners in crime, that Sam felt an ache in her chest.

She stole a glance at Hel, only to find Hel staring back at her, her expression unreadable.

The lock clicked and their gazes broke. Berchard ushered all of them into the outbuilding. Rakes and gardening shears and thick leather gloves hung on the walls, illuminated by the bars of light that filtered through the narrow window. It smelled strongly of fertilizer and shorn grass.

Berchard put his broad back against the door—Sam curled her nails into her palms as it sank in just how bad an idea this was, letting themselves get locked in a small, out-of-the-way room with the two most likely suspects for a series of grisly murders. Two suspects to whom they'd just revealed their suspicions. She imagined what it would feel like to get those gardening shears— crusted in rust and dirt and who knew what else—through her throat and shuddered.

But Officer Berchard just sagged against the door, as if it were all that was holding him up.

"Explain," Hel demanded.

"I will," Berchard said, dredging his head up. "I swear it. So long as you leave my cousin out of this."

Hel raised an eyebrow. "It's hard to leave her out of it when she's the prime witness."

"You have no proof of that," he growled. But Sam held up the slip of scarlet silk.

Clotilde flinched. Berchard cursed, snatching for the silk—but Hel was suddenly between them, staring him down with eyes like knives.

"Give it to me," he demanded, his voice rising. Clotilde put her hand on his arm, the coat falling open, revealing the scarlet silk dress. The fabric was torn—not just at the hem, but at the shoulders and back—and stiff with blood. Her skin beneath was entirely unblemished, not a single cut or bruise to be seen.

It wasn't necessarily what it looked like. Sam's own hand had been healed at a speed normally reserved for supernatural creatures. But that didn't stop the hairs on the nape of her neck from rising.

Sam looked over to see Clotilde looking back at her. Her eyes had dark circles under them, which at first Sam had attributed to a lack of sleep, but which she came to believe were actually the remnants of a blue-grey eyeshadow, as few people were fortunate enough to have *iridescent* bags under their eyes. Likewise, her lips looked fresh-bitten, but upon further inspection, it was only the remnants of a devastating shade of crimson lipstick.

The same shade Sam had found on the suits of M. Barrere and M. Toussaint at the morgue.

"Listen," Berchard said evenly, "if people find out she was at Lapérouse, alone with M. Barrere, without a chaperone—if there's even the suggestion of it . . . We grew up together. She's a good Catholic girl. She wouldn't do this, I swear it. Have pity and let the girl go. I'll tell you everything you need to know."

Every word that fell from Berchard's lips was a puzzle piece, and the more that spilled, the easier Sam found it to fit them together.

They'd gotten it wrong—at least part of it. Officer Berchard's motivation wasn't getting away with murder. Or at least, not entirely. It was protecting his cousin. That was why he'd misled them about who M. Barrere had dined with. That was why he'd cleaned up the garnets. And that was why he'd left Sam wanting that brandy—to go to his cousin, to help her, while his comrades in arms thought he was helping Hel and Sam, and they thought he was fetching a drink.

Unless, of course, he was just telling them what he thought would sway them. But in that case, he'd underestimated Hel.

Hel crossed her arms. "A good Catholic girl who is a married man's mistress?"

"It pays better than selling dresses," Clotilde said, speaking for the first time. Sam was surprised at the sharp surety in her voice. But of course, she shouldn't have been. How many people thought Sam a delicate butterfly? Mr. Wright certainly had.

"Even butterflies drink blood, given the chance," Sam murmured.

Officer Berchard and Clotilde turned to stare at Sam.

"What? Butterflies? What are you talking about?" Officer Berchard said, and Sam bit her lip, realizing what she'd said—or rather, all the bits she'd left out. Normal, she'd forgotten to be normal.

Hel rolled her eyes, as if it were obvious. "Your cousin's the butterfly, *Detective*. And it means appearances can be deceiving."

Clotilde flushed. "That doesn't mean I'm a murderer, *or* a werewolf."

"What," Berchard exclaimed, but Clotilde ignored him.

"That *is* what you're thinking, isn't it?" Clotilde nodded her chin at Hel. "That's why you have that silver in your hand?"

Sam whirled to see Hel toying with a double-bladed knife, one blade silver, the other iron, the grip between carved with sigils that warped the air around them.

That wasn't from the Society's armaments, Sam realized. Those sigils—she'd never seen their like, not in the war room, and not in books. And yet, something about them itched at the back of her brain, like a half-forgotten dream.

She wondered if Hel had gotten the knife from the Golden Dawn, the way she had the alchemical healing unguent, or from one of her other contacts. Whatever it was, Sam had no doubt it was highly illegal.

"Clotilde, let me handle this." Berchard's voice cracked. He tried to push Clotilde behind him. But Clotilde wouldn't move.

"I'm not embarrassed of what I did."

"You should be," Berchard snapped, and Clotilde's eyes flashed. He appealed to Sam and Hel. "This could ruin her life."

"She could ruin yours if she's a werewolf," Hel said. "It's a simple test."

"Werewolves went extinct thirty years ago," Berchard said, but he sounded desperate, as if he thought his cousin might actually fail. "Which you should know—you are supposed to be the experts. What would the Senate think, if they heard you were wasting time chasing ghosts instead of helping us stop the thing that's murdering them one by one?"

"It never has to be public," Sam said quietly to Clotilde. "We don't have to tell the police. But if you're not the murderer . . . we need to know everything you saw, so we can catch them before they kill again."

"She wasn't even near the other crime scenes!" Berchard said. "On my honor—"

"Your *honor* has already lied once," Hel said grimly.

"She can answer for *herself*," Sam told both of them, at the same time as Clotilde said, "Lucien, stop."

And Clotilde turned to Sam. "I'll do it."

You would have thought she'd slapped Berchard. "What? No—"

"It's my decision," Clotilde said, not taking her eyes off Sam, and she shrugged off her coat. Sam caught her breath. She could see why M. Barrere had been drawn to her. Even in that darkened, dirty shed, with her dress all bloodied and ragged, she was a nymph in scarlet silk.

Up close, Sam could see where the dress had been expertly tailored, the chest taken in, the hips let out, tucked in around her frame. The stitches were small, but handmade, in a cheaper thread than the rest of the garment. This, too, was the skill of the midinettes. To take what they had and make it the envy of Tout-Paris.

Clotilde held out a skinny arm. Sam almost missed the woman's trembling, before the midinette's fingers curled into her palm. "Test me."

Even Berchard held his breath as Hel lowered the silver blade flat first to the back of Clotilde's hand. Nothing happened—no smoke, no burning, no hiss of pain. None of the signs that would have betrayed a surviving werewolf.

"Well, now that that's settled—" Berchard began.

Hel flipped the knife and Clotilde's hand, lightly slicing the meat of her thumb with the iron blade. Clotilde swallowed a little cry, gripping her hand. Berchard shouldered Hel into the shelves, clay pots clattering to the ground in a cloud of dust. But Sam and Hel's eyes were glued to the cut on Clotilde's hand, to the blood welling. To the wound not healing.

She isn't a werewolf.

Sam was uncertain as to whether she was relieved or disappointed. Clotilde let out a shuddering breath, as if even she hadn't been sure.

"Satisfied?" Officer Berchard said, shielding Clotilde with his body. Sam tamped down on a thread of annoyance—Clotilde was far more capable than he gave her credit for.

"Rarely," Hel said dryly. "But she's not a werewolf, if that's what you're asking." Hel retracted the knife's iron and silver blades, tucking it back into its sheath on her ribs, where it disappeared under her black jacket.

"Why don't you tell us what happened that night?" Sam asked Clotilde gently.

"I—I don't remember much." Clotilde wrapped her arms around herself. "Outside of the blood and—and the pain. And the sound Edouard, M. Barrere, I mean, made when his throat was crushed."

"That's all right," Sam said soothingly. "Anything you can remember, no matter how strange or seemingly insignificant. Start at the beginning. You were going to meet M. Barrere at Lapérouse."

"Yes," Clotilde said. "Edouard's wife, Mme Barrere, was in Provence. When I arrived at Lapérouse, Edouard was already drunk—he'd made some sort of deal that afternoon and was celebrating. He gave me a gift." Her hands drifted to her bare neck.

"Garnets," Sam said, eliding the fact that they were fake. But if Clotilde knew, she gave no sign.

Clotilde nodded. "Anyway, we, um, began to do what we'd come there to do, and then . . . there was this sound. This . . . I'm sorry, I can't do this"—she covered her face with her hands—"I can't remember. Don't *want* to remember."

Hel and Berchard looked away, uncomfortable.

Trauma, it could do strange things to the mind. A thing that was too dangerous, too painful to remember, the mind might take and lock away. It might even feel as if it were gone, your waking mind going months without thinking of it—but it would still be there. And it would poison you, twisting you in ways you wouldn't even notice were wrong, because your unconscious mind remembered, even if you had forgotten. It had done so to Sam's father, upon his return from Dracula's castle, giving him fits of brain fever, until he'd faced the monster at its heart.

"You don't have to if you don't want to." Sam reached out and held Clotilde's hands. "But if you want to try, I'm right here."

Clotilde took a deep breath and closed her eyes. "There was a . . . a searing pain."

"From where?" Sam asked. "Did you see what hit you?"

Clotilde shook her head, her brow furrowing. "I didn't see anything. Just—it felt as if a fishhook had been driven up into my brain. And this terrible rotting ache branched all the way through me. It *hurt*. I thought I was dying."

Berchard made a strangled noise in his throat, his hands clenching.

"Then, all at once, it *cracked*." Clotilde licked her lips. "I could taste blood in my throat. I was screaming. I'm not a fighter, not like my brothers. But I fought until the darkness took me. The next thing I knew, Lucien—Officer Berchard—had found me, and Edouard was dead."

Clotilde opened eyes red with tears. She was leaving something out, Sam was sure of it. But what?

"Why didn't it kill you?" Sam asked.

Clotilde brushed at her eyes angrily with the back of her hands. "Don't you think I've been asking myself the same thing ever since I woke up? I was helpless. There was nothing I could have done. It's like it *wanted* me to get caught, like it wanted me to take the blame."

That might explain why Clotilde's dress had been ripped, while she had been left unharmed, Sam thought. The killer was telling a story.

"Berchard showed you the secret passage to the Senate," Hel said; it wasn't a question.

"Yes," Clotilde said. And she looked at Officer Berchard. "If you had been caught—"

"We're family," he said roughly.

"Was there anything else?" Sam pressed. "A sound before the attack? Or an odd light?"

"No, I—" Clotilde caught herself and frowned. "I suppose there was something. There was this awful smell, right before the attack. I remember thinking the kitchen must have made some terrible mistake with our dinner, that we'd have to send it back, but . . ."

Sam felt a frisson of anticipation. "Awful how?"

"A rancid, burning, sulfurous smell." Clotilde shook her head, her jaw clenching at the memory. "I could have sworn it came from Edouard, but that's impossible. I remember thinking how nice he smelled earlier in the evening—like evergreens.

"I didn't really have a chance to find out more," Clotilde said, and Sam believed her. She shrugged helplessly. "It was over so fast."

"Are we done?" Officer Berchard said.

Sam shook her head. "There's one more thing."

"Oh, for pity's sake," Berchard burst out. "She's given you everything she knows!"

"This question's not for her—it's for you." Sam pulled out the newspaper article from the day before and held it out to him—the hollow-eyed wolf under a star, its legs dripping down onto a broken crown, and the words: *Car la solde du péché, c'est la mort.* "Does this picture mean anything to you?"

Berchard frowned. "Is this a test? It's the graffiti on the wall at Lapérouse. It looks exactly like the photograph."

"Not *exactly*," Sam said, searching his face for a reaction. But if he knew what she meant, he was hiding it well.

"The lines around that star," Sam said, tracing the rays. "They're Morse code. What's more, they weren't there when we arrived. We think someone's using them to communicate with whoever's behind the murders."

"Which means," Hel put in, "that *someone* involved with the murders put them there after we arrived, and before the photograph was taken. While Lapérouse was still in lockdown."

Berchard cursed. "So that's what she was doing. I should have known."

"She?" Hel raised an eyebrow. "You mean to say it wasn't you?"

Berchard had the decency to flush, his cauliflower ears going bright red. "It wasn't me. The other night, when I opened the door of the kitchen to fetch Mlle Harker that brandy, I saw one of the Wolves of God halfway out a window."

"Another one!" Sam exclaimed. "Not the one you had in custody?"

Berchard nodded tightly. "It's why I never came back. I shouted for my officers, and we chased her through half the city and down into the underground Metro station, before she slipped through a hole in the wall and disappeared like a rat. You can ask any of the other officers who were there that night. They'll confirm my story."

"You didn't tell me that!" Clotilde said.

Berchard looked away. "You know I don't talk about my work."

"How can you be sure she was one of the Wolves of God?" Sam asked.

"She had that wolf pelt on, like they all do," Berchard said. But his gaze flicked away. Sam frowned. "Besides, no one else is fool enough to go down there."

"And you?" Hel demanded of Berchard. "Were you fool enough?"

"Of course not," Berchard said. Sam and Hel exchanged a look. His eyebrows pinched. "You're not from here, so you don't know: it is not just the catacombs that lie beneath our City of Lights, those pretty corridors of bone you can visit to remind yourself death is near. The catacombs were built in the old mining tunnels, and the mines go on for kilometers—a maze of narrow, collapsing corridors, pitch dark, and old bones. You could travel for days and never see the light of the sun.

"So no, we did not follow her to the Empire of the Dead," Berchard said. "We sealed it up, like we do every entrance we find. But there are more—there are always more."

"Where exactly?" Hel asked.

"If I knew, I would have sealed them already," Officer

Berchard said, a note of steel in his voice. "Trust me, I know these people—"

Suddenly Sam understood. The disdain and familiarity with which Berchard talked about the Wolves of God. The way he'd picked that lock, and the unhappiness that had rippled through Clotilde when he'd done so. The way she'd automatically covered for him regardless, without a second thought, as if she'd done so countless times before.

"You *knew* them," Sam said. Officer Berchard flinched, Clotilde lifted her chin, and Sam knew she was right. "You were Wolves of God, once. Both of you."

"That was a long time ago," Officer Berchard said. "We were kids."

"They were our friends," Clotilde said, with the feel of an old argument.

"But we got out," Berchard said firmly, as if Clotilde hadn't spoken. "Clotilde has a proper job now—we both do. Nothing is worth risking that."

"I think it's time we had a talk with the Wolves of God," Hel said. Sam agreed. Whether or not they were responsible, they knew something. "Supposing we are fool enough to go down into the mines, could you lead us to them, preferably without letting on as to who exactly we are?"

Berchard scowled. "Weren't you listening?"

Clotilde bit her lip. "I could lead you."

Berchard whirled on her. "You said you weren't in contact with them anymore! You promised—"

"I promised no such thing," she said. "But I'm not . . . in-volved. One of the other midinettes is seeing Claude, and they're having a party tonight, in the catacombs. I can get her to tell me where you might find someone who won't think twice about inviting a couple of young women to the show. I trust you can take it from there?"

Hel nodded. "Thank you."

"No. It's too risky," Berchard said. "Clotilde, these people will be gone in a few days—but you and I, we have to stay. If the Wolves of God find out we're involved, we'll be pulled back in again, one way or another. This isn't what you want."

"This isn't what *you* want," Clotilde said. "You were the one who wanted us to leave the Wolves of God, to stop talking to the only friends we'd had our whole lives, friends who were there for us when we were sick, or when we needed to hide from the police, or needed a shoulder to cry on. You were the one who wanted us to get jobs serving Tout-Paris—as if they'll ever let us be a part of them."

"But—"

"I want to keep this *quiet*, Lucien," Clotilde said. "I would have thought you would too."

"All right," Berchard said heavily. He couldn't have looked more wounded if she'd carved her words into his flesh. Sam had the feeling he was seeing his cousin as she truly was for possibly the first time. But instead of rejecting her, instead of trying to force her back in the box he'd made for her, he accepted her, even as he disagreed with her. "If it's what you want."

It is, Sam thought, her chest aching.

"Thank you," Clotilde said.

Berchard let them out of the garden room, hooking Hel by the elbow as they passed. "Not a whisper of what she told you. Or I swear to you, what happened to M. Barrere will look a kindness after I'm through with you."

Hel barked a laugh. "I'd like to see you try."

"Of course we won't tell," Sam assured him, with a glare at

Hel. The man was just trying to hold on to the last shreds of his dignity. They could afford him that. And she nodded to Officer Berchard. "We gave our word."

Clotilde looked haunted but steady, pulling Officer Berchard's coat tighter around herself in the driving wind. "I will get a message to you with a location before sundown. Be ready."

CHAPTER TEN

The Streets of Paris

It was raining when Sam returned from her trip to the bakery. Sam hurried, head down under her umbrella, trying to drown out the sound of it with her footsteps on the cobblestones.

Sam never could listen to the rain. Somehow her grandfather's numbers always found her in the drops' *tap-tap-tapping*, and all at once, Sam would be ten years old and in that attic again, utterly alone save for the numbers tapping over the radiotelegraph.

Seventy-four. Ten. One hundred three. Twenty-eight, eight, twenty-seven. Forty-four, one, fifty-six . . .

I will find you, Grandfather, Sam promised, as she always did.

Sam found Hel standing on the edge of the Île de la Cité, in the rain, without an umbrella or anything. She was staring moodily across the River Seine, her red curls plastered to her neck. Across the river, umbrellas bobbed along streets glowing with reflected light—the citizens of Paris going about their day, entirely unconcerned about the monster picking them off one by one.

Tucking herself in close to Hel, Sam lifted her umbrella to cover them both, before handing over half a baguette spread with a generous portion of Chaource cheese. Sam took a bite of her own; the crust was still crackling, the cheese salty and buttery, and for a moment, Sam forgot about the rain, thinking of nothing but how fantastic they tasted together. Though the depths of her appreciation might have had something to do with the fact that she hadn't eaten since breakfast.

Sam looked over her shoulder to see Officer Berchard ushering Clotilde from the prefecture, across the Pont Saint-Michel, still arguing from the looks of it. Sam shook her head.

"Can you believe him?" Sam said.

Hel looked over her shoulder, then back at Sam, tearing off a crumb and throwing it to a disgruntled duck. "Who, Officer Berchard?"

"The way he kept answering for Clotilde," Sam said. "And not telling her what he knew about the murders, when she was the mistress of a man fit to whet the Beast's appetite. She's his cousin, and a woman grown, providing for her family, and he didn't trust her."

"He was only trying to protect her," Hel said.

"For all the good it did," Sam said. "She got hurt anyway and couldn't see it coming because he hadn't told her about it."

Hel gave her a shrewd look. "Are we talking about them, or us?"

Sam felt the heat rise in her cheeks, but she held Hel's gaze, in challenge and invitation. "Why do you need to know where a well-heeled man buys his suits?"

"Why is the first set of numbers in your notebook older than this case?" Hel countered.

But Sam didn't back down this time, not with her grandfather's numbers whispering to her in the rain. She was done with secrets. They needed to trust each other if they were going to solve this case. And given the whole business with Van Helsing . . . Sam needed an ally, now more than ever.

"Because they were playing over the radiotelegraph the night my grandfather disappeared," Sam said. "They're the only hope I have of finding out what happened to him. It's why I'm not in the library right now. It's why I'm on this case. Those numbers—I'd resigned myself to never seeing them again, to never seeing *him* again, until I saw that newspaper. That graffiti. That murder."

A complicated emotion passed over Hel's face, as if she hadn't really expected Sam to meet her demands and wasn't sure what came next. "I didn't know."

"Of course you didn't," Sam said, but the ache in her chest from holding in the knowledge of her grandfather's disappearance had eased slightly with the telling. "I didn't tell you. So tell me now: Why did you need to know about Parisian suits? You showed next to no interest in the victims' suits in the morgue, so it's not about how they were murdered, and you don't wear men's suits, so it's not on account of your wardrobe."

Hel grimaced. "I can't. It's not safe."

"No one was ever safer for being kept in the dark!" Sam argued. "The darkness doesn't mean the monsters are gone—it only means you can't see them coming."

"If you knew, in this case, you'd make an exception."

"Easily enough said, when you won't tell me," Sam said tartly.

"Would you rather I lie?" Hel asked.

"Of course not—"

"Yours isn't the only life at stake!" Hel burst out.

Sam let out a frustrated huff, but she was so surprised by Hel's show of emotion that she let it go. It was probably another disreputable entity, like the Golden Dawn. Except Hel wasn't scared of the Golden Dawn. Whatever she'd done, whoever she'd done it with, she was scared of them.

"All right," she said at last, letting Hel have her secrets.

The disgruntled duck quacked. Hel tore off another crumb and tossed it. A crumb from a baguette that Hel hadn't touched, except to tear off pieces to throw to the birds. Sam couldn't remember the last time she'd seen her eat.

"Is something . . . wrong?" Sam asked hesitantly.

"Who says anything's wrong?"

"You haven't eaten a bite," Sam said. "Since yesterday."

Hel grimaced, flicking her gaze down at the baguette in her hand. She took a bite, looking approximately as happy about it as the duck. "It's just a feeling."

"A feeling!" Sam said lightly. "And here I thought you didn't get them."

"We're missing something important," Hel said. "Let's head back to the hotel. I want to look at those numbers again."

"No need, I have the numbers with me." Sam slipped her notebook out of a pocket in her skirt. "Actually, while we're here, we should see if the prefecture has photographs from the other murder scenes, see if there are any additional numbers."

"Good idea. You do that," Hel said distractedly. "I'll meet you back at the hotel."

Before Sam could stop her, she was striding off toward the bridge across the Seine, her long tan coat whipping behind her.

Sam's fingers curled into her palms.

I won't let anything happen to you again, Hel had said. And Sam could see why she thought she was protecting Sam. After all, look at what had happened the last time Sam met Hel's less reputable associates. But that had only happened because she hadn't told Sam where she was going.

Yes, Sam would have argued against it strenuously, but stumbling into it was so much worse.

Sam shivered, recalling the lean and hungry look in M. Voland's eyes, as if he saw her more as a resource than a person. It was worse, somehow, than how Van Helsing looked at her.

Sam wanted to chase Hel down, except she was, down to her bones, a researcher, and if there was any hope of breaking the code, they needed the rest of those numbers.

Sighing, Sam climbed the steps to the prefecture.

The prefecture looked more like a grand salon than what Sam associated with American police. A mirror took up almost the entire wall, she saw as she walked in, her heels clicking on the diamond-patterned salmon-and-cream floor. The doors were the same ecru color as the walls, with intricate moulding above them.

A young officer whose brilliant smile reached his eyes greeted her almost as soon as she entered. A plaque on the desk named him Officer Phan. "Bonjour." His accent was thoroughly Parisian, but he looked as if he might have Vietnamese heritage.

"Bonjour," Sam said with a smile to match, pulling out the credentials Mr. Wright had given her. "I'm with the Royal Society for the Study of Abnormal Phenomena. We've been working with Officer Berchard on the investigation into the Beast murders."

"Ah yes, the American and the Irishwoman who hunt monsters!" Officer Phan said, leaning forward. "Is it true you have a dragon in Maryland, one that sucks the blood out of children and livestock? I heard it can be warded off with a seven-pointed star. . . ."

"The snallygaster?" Sam said, grateful for the summer nights she'd spent with Jakob, listening to her grandfather spinning stories of North American monsters, then screaming at every sound until dawn. Her brother had thought it ridiculous, but then he'd done much the same with a book of infectious diseases, and all by himself. "Its name comes from the German for *fast ghost*, so it's unclear as to whether it's actually a dragon or a ghost. But yes?"

"That's the one!" Officer Phan slapped the desk. "Thank you, I was arguing with a friend over whether there were any dragons left in the world—or whether there ever were any to begin with, if you can imagine that!—and I'd forgotten its name. What was it again?"

"Snallygaster," Sam said.

"Snallygaster," he said, and he repeated it a few times. "If anyone asks you, it's a dragon, all right? None of this ghost business."

Sam laughed, charmed despite herself. "Of course."

Officer Phan beamed. "I knew I could count on you! But you didn't come to talk about snallygasters, did you? How may I be of assistance?"

"I was hoping to look at the files you have on the prior murders," Sam said. "Just to see if there's anything we missed."

"Of course. Right this way, please." He waved for her to follow him through reception to their offices in back. The floor turned from inlaid marble to herringbone wood. The simple wooden desks were mostly empty, but a few uniformed officers bent over their tasks. Filing cabinets lined the back wall.

"I'm afraid I can't let you take them with you," Officer Phan apologized. "But you can look through them as long as you'd like here."

"That is more than adequate," she assured him. Then, hesitantly, she asked, "How familiar are you with immigrants to the area?"

"That depends," Officer Phan said. He slowed his picking through the files in the cabinet. "Which arrondissement?"

"Montmartre."

"Ah, let me guess," he said. "You are referring to Moritz Knie, the Wolfssegner."

"How did you know?" Sam asked, impressed despite herself.

Officer Phan chuckled. "We are all well familiar with that one. Is he giving you trouble?"

"No, not at all!" Sam said, though that wasn't quite true, was it? The hollows of her mind still echoed with the things he'd said about her, about her visions. "He said he thought the wolves were being summoned. Have you seen anything like that at the crime scenes? Loaves of bread or anything that might hold a spell?"

"Did he tell you he was kicked out of Germany?"

"Yes, on suspicion of witchcraft," she said.

Officer Phan laughed. "Is that what he told you? He was kicked out on suspicion of attacking the flocks of his neighbors— the better to sell his services."

"He was summoning wolves to attack his neighbors?" Sam exclaimed. "And you let him into France?"

"*Non*, they claimed the Wolfssegner himself was attacking the livestock," he said. "Transforming into a wolf."

"They claimed he was a *werewolf*?" Sam said.

"He really had them going, didn't he?" Officer Phan laughed again. "But that's the beauty of bread as a medium, isn't it? The evidence of the spell is eaten by birds before it can be found out. Needless to say, we tested him—just to be safe—and he's as human as you or me. So we let him know that anyone's cattle or sheep go missing in Montmartre, for any reason, and we kick him out of France, too. And fewer animals have gone missing in Montmartre than anywhere else in Paris since."

So that was why the Wolfssegner was so intent on protecting

Montmartre—not out of selfless care for his neighbors, but for fear that he'd be kicked out of France.

"Here." Officer Phan handed her a thick manila file. It smelled so like the library that Sam was struck with homesickness. "This is everything we have on the Beast murders."

"Thank you," Sam said. "I won't need them long."

Officer Phan led her to an empty desk, and then disappeared back to the salon. A few of the other officers looked up at her briefly but otherwise left her to her own devices. Gingerly, Sam opened the file, spreading out handwritten reports and photographs over the wooden desk.

The photographs showed no sign of the Wolfssegner or his bread. Officer Berchard apparently hadn't even been at the first two crime scenes—having been assigned to the investigation of the Couronnes Disaster—and Clotilde Auclair wasn't listed at any of the crime scenes, not even the one for which Sam knew she'd been present. Of course, Clotilde could have escaped, the way she had Lapérouse, but Sam didn't think so.

It left an ill taste in her mouth, which only worsened as she read more about M. Barrere and the other victims. About the tunnels they'd made for the trains in Paris, too small for the trains in the rest of France, to keep those less fortunate than they from sullying their city. About Tout-Paris's expansion into Montmartre—forcing out the people who had scrabbled together a rural life to make it *civilized*. About the wives they promised to honor unto death only to betray them with mistresses they used and discarded as fast as the fashions they sold.

And she remembered what Hel had said about the Wolves of God—about how the working-class people of France had reason to be unhappy, about how she'd thought Sam might agree, if she considered it.

Sam's heart squeezed. It had been so easy to tell monster from human back in her library.

It didn't matter, anyway. The Society's jurisdiction didn't cover monstrous men—only monsters. And whether or not M. Barrere had been monstrous, the one who murdered him was most definitely a monster. You don't chew someone's heart out of their chest and get to be anything less.

Sam was able to determine a few things about the victims.

Firstly, they hadn't been involved in the eradication of werewolves, so that was the end of the vengeful, evolving lycanthrope theory. Which, Sam had to admit, probably ought to have been put to bed already.

Secondly, none of the victims were religious in any capacity. France might be 98 percent Catholic, but parliament, it turned out, was that remaining 2 percent, which did explain their recent push for the separation of church and state.

And finally, each of the victims was deeply involved in the effort to crack down on the shadow market, particularly the parts of it that trafficked in magic and monsters. This largely meant increasing the police presence in the poorer arrondissements like Montmartre, as well as raising the cost of living there, forcing the residents out of their homes. Just last week a shipment of sixteen casks of alchemical concoctions had been seized at the docks in Calais and emptied into the sea, along with a captive kelpie, far from the freshwater lochs from which it came. The kelpie had died an agonizing death—desiccated, not unlike the poor grindylow—in under ten minutes. Nearly a dozen men had been arrested in the incident.

All of which meant there wasn't just one possible motive for the murders—there were several, and suspects to go along with them. The working class, who had reason to be unhappy. The faithful 98 percent, forced out by a faithless parliament. And the shadow market, whose wares were being dumped into the sea.

Sam flipped away from the page detailing the victims, looking for anyone who had been at all of the crime scenes, anyone who might have been behind the graffiti, but the names didn't line up. If it was an officer or a witness, they'd covered their tracks well.

Reluctantly, Sam pushed the notes aside and pulled out the photographs. She was in luck—someone had thought to photograph the graffiti at the crime scenes. Sam studied the lines of the hollow-eyed wolf, that broken crown, and the star above. The words scrawled beneath them: *Car la solde du péché, c'est la mort.* They were all the same, and yet, each one looked different. The first, almost mournful, the lines of the wolf sweeping and variable like a calligrapher's brush. The second, murderous, with jagged, thick lines. The third, lost, with slender, hair-thin lines that overlapped each other.

Different hands, every one. Which agreed with the recorded arrests of a Wolf of God at each crime scene, for defacing property.

But the numbers . . . the Morse code around the star swelled under Sam's magnifying glass. The lines were thin, precise, with a wobble near the end of each stroke—exactly the same on each photograph.

Which meant not only was the Morse code added on later, but that whoever was doing so had never been caught. And Sam remembered the woman in a wolf's fur that Officer Berchard had chased to the mines.

To the Wolves of God.

Carefully, Sam transcribed the numbers into her notebook.

— —

Hel was gone when Sam returned to their hotel room, the reflections of wills-o'-the-wisp dancing across the ceiling. She pulled out the radiotelegraph and found it still warm to the touch.

Someone had used her radiotelegraph again—and recently.

"For heaven's sake, Hel," Sam said. She was probably going to meet more shadow market, secret society strangers, any of whom could absolutely be the Beast, in a dark alley somewhere, without telling anyone where she was going.

Why did Hel trust them, and not *Sam*?

Sam was her partner. Sam should be by her side. Instead, Sam was lying to Mr. Wright, covering for Hel, without knowing what she was really up to.

She closed the radiotelegraph's case and pushed it back under the bed—and her eyes hooked on Hel's case file, just visible poking out of the top of her bag.

Sam fished the file out, then hesitated a moment, remembering Officer Berchard and Clotilde—the way they'd protected each other without hesitation, the way they trusted each other, even when they disagreed. A knot formed in her throat. She was fooling herself, she chided. That had never been a possibility.

Still, she had to force her eyes down to the page to read.

Helena Moriarty's first partner had been hit by a stray bullet on a train on the way to Cardona to deal with a vampire haunting the crystalline mines of Salt Mountain. There had been a train robbery, apparently, and only two shots had been fired, both of which missed their intended target, one of which ended up splattering her partner all over the inside of the carriage. Dr. Moriarty had dealt with the vampire swiftly, before returning with the corpse of her former partner to London.

The investigation afterward turned up no obvious connections with the Fenians or her father, other than that the train robbers said they'd been tipped off to a large monetary shipment. When asked where they'd heard that, they simply shrugged.

He's a whisper of information, Hel had said of her father, *a nudge on someone's baser instincts.*

Her second partner had been trampled to death by flower-bedecked cattle on the way to a small alpine nunnery in Austria, where a drude had been crushing the life out of the nuns. Something had startled the drowsy parade into a stampede right when Dr. Moriarty's partner had bent over to examine a strange print in the mud. He'd died on the spot. After gathering what she could of his body and carting it to the nunnery, Dr. Moriarty had taken no time at all in dealing with the malevolent nightmare spirit.

The attempt to uncover what had startled the cattle led to a hunter, who swore they'd seen a *wolpertinger* in the Alps, and had shot at it at exactly the same moment as Dr. Moriarty's partner had bent over to examine that odd print. The wolpertinger, if it ever existed, was never found—and with a hare's head, a squirrel's body, a deer's antlers, and the wings of a pheasant, members of that species tended to stand out.

A finger on a domino whose effects spiral out in unseen designs.

Dr. Moriarty's third and final partner, before Sam, that is, had fallen overboard in the middle of the night while they searched Lake Ladoga for a sailor-killing rusalka—those beautiful revenants of violently drowned women, who were said to seduce young men and pull them beneath the waves with their tangled hair.

It was theorized the man was the rusalka's latest victim, until her partner's waterlogged head came up in a fisherman's net—a choice piece with which the rusalka would never have parted. It was later determined that he had simply been stung by a bee, to which he was deathly allergic, and fallen overboard. An incident that never would have occurred had an enterprising apiarist not been shipping his hives that very day, by boat, to the new, larger fields he'd unexpectedly lucked into.

He doesn't order attacks—he manipulates the circumstances so that the attacks happen without ever having to dirty his hands.

Whispers, dominoes, manipulations. Hel's father wasn't trying to murder her, of that, Sam was certain. That was too direct, too obvious for a man who moved people like pieces on a chessboard. But then, why did all of Hel's partners end up dead?

Sam read on. It took a bit longer to finish that one up, only because Dr. Moriarty hadn't killed the rusalka, as Society policy dictated—she'd avenged her. Sam frowned, checking to make sure she'd read that right.

She'd read the theory of course, that rusalkas didn't have to be slain to stop the bloodshed, that they were like enough to unquiet ghosts that they could be laid to rest if the one who'd murdered them was killed. But that was only a theory—*untested!*

Or so she thought. The date on the file was well before Sam had read the Society's policy on rusalkas. The report indicated Hel's efforts had been successful—Hel had shot and killed a man in front of God and country, been charged with murder, and cleared with the dissipation of the rusalka and the Society's purchase of new fishing vessels for the village.

But if it worked—if avenging a rusalka laid them to rest—then, why hadn't Society protocol for rusalkas changed? Sam knew from chatting with the women in the records department that Van Helsing had dispatched at least twelve rusalkas in the years since Hel's report, every one of which he'd destroyed as per protocol. It was as if the Society had missed Hel's report, but that couldn't be—they were the ones who'd given it to Sam.

The phone rang. Sam picked it up. "Samantha Harker."

"Miss Harker," Mr. Wright said.

"Mr. Wright, I was hoping to speak with you," Sam said quickly, before he could start.

"Oh?" Mr. Wright asked, his chair creaking.

"Mr. Van Helsing is in Paris," Sam said. "He claims to have finished his assignment and has taken it upon himself to follow me. I was hoping I could prevail on you to speak with him—"

Mr. Wright's chuckle cut her off. "Miss Harker, you're a clever young woman. I'm certain you can think of a reason a young man might want to spend time with you."

"But—"

"I'm afraid there's nothing I can do," Mr. Wright said. "What a man does on his own time is his business. Besides, it's not a bad idea, really, having Van Helsing there. So long as you're not violating any rules, you have nothing to worry about, and if things with Miss Moriarty get dangerous . . . Well, Van Helsing will be there to step in and help." Because of course that was why he had called. Mr. Wright hesitated then. "You *have* had a chance to read the file, I trust?"

Guilt snaked around her throat. "I have."

"Good, good." His voice was fat with satisfaction. And why shouldn't it be? Sam was back in her place, playing her part in *his* story. In the past, it would have given her relief: it meant she was invisible, it meant she was *safe*. But safe from whom?

From *him*, a small voice whispered. And the realization made her sick.

"Thank you for passing the files along," Sam made herself say. "I'll update the rusalka file as soon as I return."

"That will be unnecessary," Mr. Wright said dismissively. "Miss Moriarty's actions, while effective in that instance, resulted in the unacceptable loss of human life and substantial cost to the Society."

"Wasn't he a murderer?" Sam protested.

"He was still a human." Mr. Wright spoke over her, as if truth might be measured in decibels. "She, on the other hand, was a monster."

But Sam wasn't done. "There wouldn't even *have been* a monster, if he hadn't—" Footsteps sounded outside the door, a hand rattling the knob. Hel. "Dr. Moriarty is coming," Sam whispered in a rush. She hung up on Mr. Wright.

The door opened. Sam scrambled to hide the file, but not fast enough. Hel swept in, her long tan coat swishing around her hips, only to stop dead when she saw Sam.

"You're reading my file," Hel said flatly.

"The rusalka," Sam said, unrepentant. "Why did you do it?"

Hel shrugged. "I suppose I felt punishing the perpetrator rather than the victim worth the risk."

"But what if you were wrong about the rusalka?" Sam pressed. "If you'd killed the wrong man, or if avenging the rusalka hadn't worked, she would have gone on to kill again. Not to mention, you would have killed an innocent man."

"Did the file tell you what I found on that 'innocent man'?" Hel asked. Sam shook her head. Hel snorted. "Of course it didn't. Let me enlighten you: The man who killed Synnöve Håkansson, the woman who became the rusalka, once dragged her out of a pub by the hair in front of all her friends. He didn't permit her to attend her father's funeral—or her sister's a year later. And one late September day, when she tried to leave, he tangled her in his casting net, tied the handline to a rock, and threw her into Lake Ladoga. Even if it didn't free the rusalka, that man deserved to die."

"But if that's true, why wasn't he prosecuted?" Sam protested.

"The courts decided there wasn't proof it was anything more than the man claimed: a boating accident. Only the whispers of women," Hel said. Sam's heart ached; they both knew how well those stood up in court.

Sam couldn't trust Hel. Not when she seemed intent on lying to Sam, and not when she seemed all too willing to trust every dark-alley criminal who claimed to have the answers over her partner.

But, despite that, Sam realized she believed in Hel—that however many rules Hel broke, or secrets Hel kept, she always did what she thought was right, and what Hel thought was right was often the same as what Sam herself thought.

Except when it came to Sam.

"What did you find?" Hel asked.

Sam settled on the bed, tucking her legs under her, and pulled out her notebook, smoothing the paper out with her hands. "The victims weren't involved with werewolves at all, but they were involved with attempts to eliminate the shadow market, the further separation of church and state, and the displacement of people in the poorer arrondissements."

"There's a motive," Hel murmured.

"Or three," Sam said.

Hel sat down next to her on the bed, leaning to read over her shoulder. Sam traced the numbers with her fingertip. "The prefecture had pictures of the graffiti at every crime scene, excepting the incident in the carriage. I translated them and put them in order, starting with the numbers recovered from the first murder."

Hel frowned. "Twenty-seven. It's the third number in one of the triplets for every one of these ciphers."

If Sam and Hel were right, if this was a book cipher, then the first number was for which page in the book, the second for which paragraph on that page, and the third for which word in that paragraph. Which meant only that the twenty-seventh word was used at least once in all five sets.

Sam frowned. "Is that significant?"

"Statistically? Yes," Hel said. "The chances are exponentially low. But what makes it even less likely are the other two numbers."

"Twenty-eight and eight. One and nine. Seven and nine. Eight and nine. Ten and nine." Sam's head snapped up. "Hel, those are the dates of the murders!" All except the first attack, which had taken place on the twenty-sixth of August, and the fourth attack, on the fourth of September, as no graffiti had been found at the scene of the prior murder.

"Dates hidden in plain sight, in the pattern of the cipher," Hel said, standing and pacing. "The twenty-seven is the marker for the triplet with the date—that way they can shift the location of the date, so it's not as obvious."

And that last date, the one transcribed from the graffiti on the wall of Le Meurice the night before: ten and nine. A shiver coursed through her.

"Hel, this is tomorrow night!" Sam said. The murders were accelerating. "We have *no* idea where the murderer will strike next."

"But we know who might," Hel said, and Sam swore she could almost see the gears spinning in her head. "Come on, I have a plan."

"For what?" Sam said, flustered. "Where are we going?"

"The Cabaret du Néant." Hel smiled sharp as broken glass. "Clotilde sent us a telegram. We're to meet her there by sundown. If Officer Berchard is telling the truth, the Wolves of God have known the details of every murder before it happened. They have every reason to want the French parliament dead. And they're throwing a party tonight. If we want to find out where the next murder is, we need to get ourselves invited."

CHAPTER ELEVEN

Montmartre, Paris

The Cabaret du Néant was in Montmartre at the bottom of the butte, where the streets were still paved with cobblestones and the buildings less ramshackle—the grimmest member of a trio of cabarets.

The first, the Cabaret du Ciel, was a tawdry vision of the heavens, replete with young women dressed as angels playing harps. The second, the Cabaret de l'Enfer, was the very mouth of Hell, with effigies of the souls writhing, pushing their way out of the stucco, and the father of all sin there to damn you at the door.

The last of the three—the Cabaret du Néant, the Cabaret of the Void—looked like nothing so much as a morgue, with boarded windows, an entrance draped in black mourning crepe, and a priest to walk you to your final resting place—for the evening, in any event.

It was also the favored haunt of their quarry.

The Wolves of God.

Sam fiddled nervously with the silver-and-iron knife Hel had given her, running her thumb over the ivory grip. It was the only weapon in Hel's collection that fit in the silk jersey dress with which Clotilde and her fellow midinettes had adorned her for the evening: an ephemeral arsenic-green dress that clung to her body like a serpent's half-shed skin. The midinettes were artists of appearances, and the dress was absolute perfection for their gambit—the latest fashion in Tout-Paris. And if it left their canvas feeling vulnerable? Well, that suited the role she was to play just fine.

Hel still wore her customary black suit. "Men don't tend to go for me," she'd said dryly when Sam had pressed her. So she was going as Sam's chaperone for the evening.

The false priest swept open the funerary doors of the Cabaret du Néant.

"Entrez, mortels de ce monde pécheur, et entrez dans les brumes et les ombres de l'éternité," he intoned, turning dramatically to lead the way inside. *"Et que Dieu ait pitié de vos âmes!"*

Church bells tolled as Sam and Hel passed the threshold into the narrow dark. A tinny-sounding funeral march played, piped in from somewhere in the walls. Ahead of them was a shadowed room, decorated with bones and corpses in grotesque positions.

The sole light came from wills-o'-the-wisp, swirling above coffins, as if caught in invisible vortexes. It put Sam in mind of one of the other names for wills-o'-the-wisp: *corpse lights*, those omens of death seen hovering over fresh-turned graves and by those soon to be buried in them.

There must, Sam thought, be a radio signal emitted from each coffin. A clever trick, and one that made her glance nervously at Hel once more.

A pallbearer seated them at one of the coffins as if it were a table, and handed them each what couldn't possibly actually be a *human skull*, sloshing with beer.

Hel grimaced. "A pun," she said. "The French word for beer and bier is the same."

An apparition melted through the wall, as solid looking as Hel except for the fact that she passed *through* the coffin table between them. Sam gasped, but the apparition seemed not to notice, murmuring soundlessly to herself, only to look up at something Sam could not see, and fade away.

Sam touched her beer—but it was still lukewarm, not frosted as it would be in the wake of a proper ghost. Not to mention, she was fairly certain the nails in the coffin were iron, and would disrupt anything of a ghostly nature.

A vision then? "Did you see—"

"Pepper's Ghost," Hel said as another apparition emerged to startle a coffin of gentlemen on the other side of the room—a half-drunk gaggle of bourgeoisie. "It's a trick of light and glass. To add something that *isn't*, you just have to reflect the desired addition at the right angle, and the eye can't tell the difference."

Sam thought she understood. It was just the way Officer Berchard hadn't been able to see his cousin Clotilde, not truly. The version of Clotilde in his head—an amalgamation of assumptions and societal expectations—had gotten in his eyes and overlaid her like a ghost. Until Clotilde had changed his perspective, forced him to see *her*.

Sam knew this trick. She had weaponized it—used it to hide inside other people's assumptions, to keep them seeing the ghost of their own expectations instead of her. It worked on just about everyone.

Everyone but Hel.

"It doesn't fool you," Sam said hesitantly.

"Misdirection takes advantage of your assumptions," Hel said. "I was raised not to have them."

"But . . . how does that even work?" Sam asked, and then immediately regretted it. That was too personal. Information on

Professor Moriarty and how he might be trying to murder them was one thing—Hel's childhood trauma was another thing entirely. "I'm sorry, I shouldn't have asked, I—"

"It's easy," Hel said softly, and Sam fell silent. "You watch a person, study them. Isolate their assumptions. And one by one, you take them away. Your home is safe. Your book isn't poisoned. Your friends will keep your secrets. The town you live in is real. The brother you've tried to protect wants to escape."

"You have a brother?" Sam said, startled. As notorious as Hel's family was, she'd never heard of Professor Moriarty having a son.

"Only by blood," Hel said, with an unspoken *Blood can be split.* "He's my father's shadowed left hand. He doesn't officially exist. Anytime my father needs to act directly, he sends Ruari in his place. I was never going to be my father's favorite, but Ruari ensured it."

"Too much his father's son?" Sam asked.

"A son," Hel said simply.

"And your mother?"

Hel just looked away, her jaw tightening.

Sam's heart cracked. "Hel, that's *awful.*"

Expectations could be blinding, but they also defined the world as it existed in your mind. They gave you something to hold on to, made you feel safe. *Water is wet. Fire is hot. My father loves me. He will still love me tomorrow.*

If every expectation instead made you feel unsafe, made you feel as though you'd made a mistake . . . Sam thought she understood, at least a little, why Hel didn't trust Sam—even if Hel believed in her.

"Who is *that*?" Hel interrupted, blatantly changing the subject. Sam looked at Hel for a moment, to let her know she knew exactly what Hel was doing, and then let her, following her gaze.

Sweeping through the door like a dark-crowned Helen of Troy was Évangéline St. Laurent. She was dressed in silver satin and a blue-and-black ruffled coat that never seemed to make it to her shoulders. Her sultry brown eyes looked as if they might sink ships, her lips curled in a perpetual almost smirk that said she knew it, and her dark hair, both scandalously short and artfully disheveled, said she didn't care what you thought about it.

Mlle St. Laurent had just stolen a gentleman's cigar and taken a long drag, tipping her head back and wreathing herself in smoke before returning it to him, the scarlet print of her lipstick on the end. He moved it reverently toward his lips.

"That's Évangéline St. Laurent," Sam whispered back, suddenly overwarm as she remembered the last time she'd seen Mlle St. Laurent—at the morgue, watching with horrified fascination as Sam arched on the floor, dragging her fingers through the frost. She probably didn't remember that, Sam told herself. Sam was nobody. "She's the lead soprano in the Paris Opera."

Men clamored for her attention, eager to be shipwrecked on her shores, but Mlle St. Laurent had eyes only for the women—gracious as a patron saint. The midinettes gathered around her, all wearing the same burgundy lipstick Mlle St. Laurent had worn that morning, at the morgue. Sam wondered if, upon seeing Mlle St. Laurent's scarlet lipstick, they'd change their hues tomorrow.

Hel frowned. "Why is she here?"

Sam considered the question. It wasn't entirely shocking that the starlet was in the cabaret. Born in poverty but with a voice as rich and honey-bright as the Lorelei, rumor had it Évangéline had gotten her start at the Moulin Rouge, another one of the cabarets in Montmartre. She had reportedly shocked audiences for days with her shimmy in the production of *Carmen*.

Since then, Évangéline had made a way for herself through Tout-Paris, sharp-eyed as she played the fools who thought they could possess her, working to secure herself a future as a rich man's wife, before the petals fell off her rose and they abandoned her to the streets from which she'd come.

What was strange—and somewhat scandalous—was that Évangéline was here without her fiancé, M. Poulin.

But before Sam could formulate a response to Hel, Clotilde sidled up to their coffin, cradling a cracked skull of beer.

"Oh good, you're here," Clotilde said in a low voice. She wore an embroidered black half cloak, the hood shadowing her features. "So, what do you think?"

Sam pulled her gaze from Évangéline and glanced around. "It's . . . different. Not what I expected."

"It's a reminder," Clotilde said, rubbing the crown of a human skull grinning out of the wall. "We all die in the end. Even Tout-Paris. In that, we are the same."

She could have done it, Sam found herself thinking. This woman who once ran with the Wolves, who did what needed to be done to keep her family safe, who drank beer out of a human skull and spoke of equality in death. This woman to whom M. Barrere had given fake garnets. She could have killed him.

Sam might have believed it, too, if Clotilde weren't helping them catch the killer.

"One of the Wolves of God is drinking at that table over there." Clotilde nodded at a coffin in the shadowed corner, with a view of the entire room. A young man in a sack coat and flat-cap looked up at the same time Sam glanced over, and their eyes locked. "Cyprien Renouard."

A frisson of electricity spidered over her. Something about the way the man held himself, the easy sprawl of him, the cocky smile that didn't quite reach those canny eyes. The man was gorgeous—and dangerous.

"Be *careful*." Clotilde leaned in, breaking her gaze. "Cyprien—he might seem a scoundrel and a skirt chaser, but he's too clever by half. He's seen it all. One wrong word, and he'll see through you, too. We should try another night, when another of the Wolves of God is here."

"And wait until the Wolves of God throw another party?" Hel said. "No, it needs to be tonight."

Sam bit her lip. "What if he doesn't go for me?"

"Sam, you're a confection." Hel snorted. The line between Sam's brows deepened. "Just bat your lashes and give him that smile you do—the one like you have a secret. He'll bite. Trust me."

"Oh, he'll go for you," Clotilde agreed, but she still looked nervous. "You're exactly his type."

Whatever was Sam doing? She didn't belong here, poured into a dress so clingy you could see the curve of her undergarments, talked into seducing a scoundrel in the hopes that he'd take her to an illegal party.

What if it didn't work? Worse, what if it did, but he didn't want to let Hel go along, and Sam was stranded five stories below the streets of Paris where no one could hear her scream?

At a party, she told herself. It's just a party. Sam had heard of parties in the catacombs before. Parties so wild they'd made international news and the police had begun to lock the catacombs up tight. Not that it had stopped them. Music. Dancing. *Flirting.*

Whatever happened after flirting.

"I can't do this!" Sam gasped. "Here, you wear the dress. We can change in the washroom."

Hel squeezed her hand under the table. "It will be fine. You're more capable than you think."

"All right," Sam managed, taking a deep breath. "OK."

Clotilde left, her cloak pulled low over her face, disappearing into the dark narrow passage that led into the night.

"Remember—wait until you've left the building before 're-membering' your chaperone," Hel said, putting some money down on the table. "That way it will be harder for him to say no."

"Yes, yes, of course," Sam said.

"I'll be waiting right outside."

And then Hel disappeared as well, surely as Pepper's Ghost, leaving Sam alone with the wills-o'-the-wisp, hoping she wasn't making a terrible mistake.

But no sooner had Sam stood up, intent on trying that lash-batting exercise Hel had recommended, maybe figuring out what Hel meant by the way Sam smiled, than someone bumped into her roughly, a hand taking hold of her bicep.

"What exactly do you think you're doing?" a low voice growled.

She *knew* that voice. *Van Helsing.*

"I'm enjoying my time off," Sam said with forced lightness. "You might try it sometime."

"You're being used, Miss Harker," Van Helsing said. The gravel in his voice made her glance back at him—was he *flushing*? He didn't like to think of her as a woman, Sam realized, and with what Sam was wearing . . . well. It was impossible to think of her as otherwise. "I suggest you reconsider whatever course of action you're intending to take. You are not a field agent."

"I have it on good authority that what I do on my time is my business," Sam retorted, and she twisted out of his grasp. Van

Helsing snatched after her, only to catch hold of her dress, which he dropped so fast you'd have thought it burned him. He didn't try again.

That, Sam thought with perhaps a little more satisfaction than was entirely appropriate, had been fun.

Except Cyprien had vanished. Where had he—?

Sam turned to see Cyprien walking over to her, two beers in his hands. Only that couldn't possibly be called walking. That was sauntering at the least, something about the way he moved drawing her attention to his hips. Now it was Sam's turn to blush, as she tugged her attention up, her ears so hot she thought they'd burn right off.

"*Vous risquez de vous faire arrêter . . . votre beauté m'entraine en état d'ivresse sur la voie publique . . . quell délit délicieux,*" Cyprien said, pressing a beer into her hands.

Sam hadn't the slightest idea what he was saying, but his voice was so buttery smooth she wanted to close her eyes just to listen. *Oh*, she was in trouble.

"Bonjour," she answered, exquisitely aware of how poor her French sounded next to his. How had she thought she could do this? It was some spell of Hel's, she was sure of it. The woman wasn't a detective, she was a witch. "Or is it *bonsoir*? I'm so sorry, I'm mangling your tongue. I'm Samantha."

"Cyprien. And it's been through worse," Cyprien confided, his voice practically a caress on her eardrums—which were not things she'd previously thought in need of caress. He took her other hand and gently pulled her toward to his table. "Though, if you feel guilty, you could always kiss it, and make it better?"

It was so bold that Sam laughed. She could feel Van Helsing scowling at her from across the room, his face red as beets. "Do you talk to all women like this?"

"Only the ones who dress like you." His gaze swept over her appreciatively, and Sam's arms were around herself before she could stop them.

"Honestly, I don't know why I'm wearing this," she confessed, tittering nervously.

Mischief flashed in his eyes. "Did you need help taking it off?"

"No!" Sam blurted. Cyprien raised an eyebrow. Could everyone on this earth who wasn't Sam raise one eyebrow? At this rate, Sam was going to get a complex. "I mean, the midinettes chose this for me. I'm not—this is not the sort of thing I usually wear."

"Ah, they are playing a joke on you, then," he said, settling back, studying her like a painting. "You look like a siren. Glorious and dangerous enough to break a man. But that isn't what you are at all, is it?"

"I could be," Sam said defensively.

Cyprien spread his hands. "Ah, but you're not. You're kind. Aren't you?"

"And sirens can't be kind?"

"Of course they can. But they are breaking my heart, so it is hard to see them so. You would not break my heart, I don't think," Cyprien said, and Sam's cheeks pinked. He'd seen right through her, *knew* she was no flirty coquette from Tout-Paris looking for a little fun, no bold seductress in search of her latest conquest. Just as Clotilde had warned her he would. "It's nothing to be ashamed of. Some of my best friends are kind."

"You're—"

"A scoundrel?"

Sam gave him a sharp look. "I was going to say surprisingly nice."

"You wound me," Cyprien said, laying his hand theatrically

over his heart. "Perhaps I'm only saying what you need to hear to trust me."

Sam arched her eyebrows. "And telling me all about it?"

He leaned in, conspiratorial. "Is it working?"

Sam laughed. "A little," she admitted. His eyes sparkled.

And she realized it *was* working after all—not Cyprien's flirtations, though those were working better than she cared to admit, but this game of hers and Hel's. Cyprien knew her to be playing a game, just as he was—there was no way Sam could have hidden that, not with her inexperience. She was too clearly ill at ease playing the part of a siren.

But Cyprien had nothing but experience, and he was used to being the cleverest person in every room. So when he saw Sam, dressed to seduce yet unbalanced by his affections, he thought *that* was the game, and didn't bother to look for another.

Sam hadn't failed—not yet. She could still make this work. And so Sam played her part, drank a couple of beers, flirted badly, and watched his surety grow—that he was winning, that he'd already won. Having fun, despite herself.

"Is it true there's a party in the catacombs tonight?" Sam whispered at last, leaning in close, head tipped toward his. "Music and dancing amidst the bones of the dead?"

Cyprien leaned in just as close—for a moment, she feared he was going to kiss her in front of God and everyone, but he brushed past her, whispering in her ear. "Would you like to come with me?"

Got him.

Sam *would.* And he would very much like to be alone with her in a crowd, in the dark where no one would see or care what they did. They paid for their drinks and, laughing, went out into the night in a shower of envy.

Almost as soon as they left the cabaret, he swept her against the wall of the alley. She gasped, her heart racing. "Now, this party is very secret, very, how do you say, *illegal*," he murmured, putting a finger to her lips, and nodding at a pair of policemen passing by. "So it is very important we are not seen, and that you tell no one of what you see tonight."

"Well, that goes without saying, doesn't it?" Sam said, a little breathless.

"Exactement." The Wolf's teeth flashed in the dark as he led her from the alley and into the streets. He twirled her under a streetlamp, her green dress glimmering like the ocean at night, and for just a moment, Sam felt like a goddess—no, like a *siren*.

Where was Hel? She was supposed to be waiting right outside. Sam tried to pick her out, only to find her entangled with Van Helsing, preventing him bodily from chasing after Sam, only for him to turn on her, gesturing fiercely, his face a thundercloud. Nerves fluttered in Sam's chest, and she glanced up at Cyprien.

"My chaperone," Sam protested. "I can't leave her behind."

"Do not worry," he said, with a sly smile. And he pulled her away. "Your chaperone won't be bothering us this evening."

"Oh!" Sam said, hoping it sounded excited and not terrified.

Sam had to do something. If Hel succeeded in delaying Van Helsing long enough to ensure he couldn't follow Sam, then Hel wouldn't be able to follow either. She needed to leave her a trail of breadcrumbs, or Sam would get to the mines all right, but well and truly alone—with a man who had designs on her she had no intention of fulfilling.

But perhaps Sam could use that.

Sam reached out to brush the stubble on Cyprien's cheek, her touch so light he had to turn to push into it, and was gratified when his eyes locked on hers. Taking advantage of his distraction—running her fingers down his jawline—she slipped her lipstick out of her purse and palmed it. And when he moved to lead her deeper into the night, Sam stumbled on a cobblestone and let herself fall.

Sam gave a little yelp, only half faked, grabbing her ankle with one hand and surreptitiously smushing the velvety rose-colored lipstick off on the bottom of her left shoe heel with the other.

He was at her side in an instant. "Are you all right, *ma chérie?*"

"It's just these heels," Sam managed, standing before he could notice what she'd done. "I can't seem to walk in them." She raised her skirt to bare the ankle and unpainted heel.

"How could you?" he said, and she was surprised to hear his voice a little rough. "Heels like that are meant for lying down."

This time, when he led her onward, Sam followed, her heel print leaving smart red dots behind her on the cobblestones. *Not bad for a researcher,* she thought. She cast a glance back at where Hel was still caught up with Van Helsing, just in time to see Hel throw a punch. Sam winced.

It would have to be enough. Hel was clever. She'd figure it out.

Cyprien led her down such a tangle of streets, Sam didn't think she could unwind them if she tried, down to an abandoned brewery and into its cobwebbed basement. There he rolled aside a cask, revealing a hole in the masonry that looked as if it had been chewed out of the concrete.

"A gift from the Romans," Cyprien whispered, for all there was no one there but the spiders to hear them. "An old quarry entrance, long forgotten."

He wriggled through the hole on his belly, and for a moment,

Sam could have sworn she heard bones crunching, saw his legs thrashing, blood spilling across the floor—and then, all at once, it was gone. And there was nothing but that ragged, dark hole that looked so like a mouth.

Sam drew in a deep breath, wishing her vision had chosen a different moment to be so unnerving.

And then it was her turn. Sam lowered herself to her belly, whispered an apology to the Society for ruining the dress they'd afforded her, and wriggled after him. After an agonizing squeeze, inching her way along, pushing and squirming, it widened just enough for her to crouch.

Cyprien was there waiting for her, his grin flashing in the dark.

"Almost there," he promised as he lowered himself down out of sight. Sam looked after him to see iron rungs hammered into the stone walls, leading the way down a dark and narrow chute that looked as if it burrowed to the center of the earth.

She leaned over the chute, the breath of the earth raising goose bumps on her skin. Hitching her clinging dress up around her knees, Sam put her foot on the first of the iron rungs and descended.

"Stay close," he cautioned as she dropped down beside him. A lantern flared in the dark, lighting his face like a hollowed gourd and casting the narrow tunnel in shades of grey. "A man can get lost here, in the dark, where there are no sounds but your heartbeat and the echoes of your footsteps. A man can die down here, a hundred meters from the exit, if he does not know the way."

And she shivered, as he'd no doubt intended, and clung tight as he led her deeper into the tunnels beneath Paris.

The ceiling arched overhead like a church near the entrance, the stone-block walls covered in graffiti, a macabre reflection of the Venetian mirrors of Lapérouse. Only instead of the graze of diamonds, these were names, carved over and over each other until they lost their meaning and at the same time became something more: a lace of lives lived and lost, of people who had been here and were no more.

More recent graffiti was scrawled in grease pencil, not just names but artistically rendered quotes, a portrait of a woman smoking, a series of stylized skulls, and of course, one of the black wolves that the Wolves of God had drawn at the crime scenes—those hollow eyes watching all who dared enter the realm of the dead, those legs dripping down onto the broken crown, under the light of a rayless star, with the now-haunting words: *Car la solde du péché, c'est la mort.*

Sam took a step toward the wolf and almost slipped, steadying herself against the wall. She looked down. On the ground was the barest sheen of something wet, something viscous.

Cave slime. *Eeuch.* Sam's brother went into raptures at the mention of mucous bacterial growth, which was why Sam knew, rather against her will, that cave slime thrived on gypsum crystals—and gypsum had been the primary mineral mined in Montmartre.

Sam still thought it looked like cave snot.

A scraping sound echoed somewhere distant. Sam whirled, but there was nothing there.

"What—what kinds of creatures live down here?" Sam asked, hoping Hel had managed to get away from Van Helsing, that she'd found the marks Sam had left her and was still coming and not just trusting Sam to handle this one. Sam didn't really need that kind of trust.

Cyprien chuckled deep in his throat and set down the lantern, wrapping an arm around her shoulders.

"Oh, *chérie*," Cyprien purred, brushing a stray curl out of her face and tucking it behind her ear. "You are safe here, with me. The party's not far, I promise. Though first, what do you say we do something about that uncomfortable dress—"

"I think not." Hel's voice rang out as she dropped down into the tunnel behind them.

"Hel!" Sam cried.

Shit, Cyprien mouthed to Sam, as if agreeing with her, before turning to Hel. "Ah, the chaperone. A little late, aren't you? What were you thinking, leaving a woman alone in a place like that? You are fortunate I—"

Hel ignored him, tossing Sam a pair of sensible shoes.

"Oh, thank goodness!" Sam said, slipping off her heels and casting them aside. She had been fairly certain she was going to break an ankle on the uneven footing, and then she'd never be able to climb her way out again.

"Quick thinking with the lipstick," Hel said.

"Wait—what is going on here?" Cyprien said, frowning at the lipstick on Sam's shoes, and back at Hel. His eyes widened. "*No*—I know you! I saw you at Lapérouse. You're working for the police. I will not take you anywhere. You will have to leave without me."

Clotilde had been right—he was too clever by half.

"We don't work for the police," Hel said. "We're tracking a monster. All we need from you is for you to lead us to that party. That's it."

"The Beast," Cyprien said. "You're here for the Beast."

"We just want information," Sam assured him, hoping it was true, that they weren't involved in the actual murdering. Somehow, she couldn't imagine Cyprien involved in something like that, for all he was a rake.

"Ah, so this was none of it true?" Cyprien said to Sam,

dismayed. "This was all just for . . . what, directions? You could have just asked, you know."

"And what, you would have told me?" Sam said tartly.

"Ah, no," he said, flashing a grin. "It's only I was falling for you a little. And that's embarrassing, when you were only after one thing, after all—and not the one thing I was hoping for."

"You were not," Sam protested, blushing. "It was as much a game to you as to me."

Cyprien winced theatrically. "And here I thought you wouldn't break my heart!"

"We'll pay for the privilege," Hel said. Five silver coins flashed between her fingers—a week's wages. Cyprien reached for the francs, and Hel disappeared them with the ease of a street magician, holding up empty hands. "Just as soon as we get there. And again when you lead us safely out."

"Will you do it?" Sam asked, looking up at him.

The look Cyprien gave her then was calculating. If he said no now, there was no risk for him, but also no reward. If he said yes, he would get paid, and have a chance to shape their suspicions as to the nature of the Beast. And if they played him false? Well, the mines were dark and damp and full of Wolves.

Besides, it was just a party.

"How could I say no to the opportunity to spend more time with you?" Cyprien said. He swept up Sam's hand, circling his fingers on her palm. "And, *chérie*, should you change your mind—"

"She won't," Hel said flatly.

Cyprien chuckled, letting her hand go. "Well, you'll know where to find me."

CHAPTER TWELVE

The Mines Beneath Paris

Water slopped with their every step, scattering the lantern light and seeping between their toes. At least, Sam hoped it was water. It was cloudy and brown, and occasionally, Sam swore she could feel something hairy and wriggling brush up against her bare calf.

"Oh, do not worry, they are only rats," Cyprien promised her when she asked about them, chuckling when Sam shuddered. Hel rolled her eyes.

Sam started to dream she was trapped in the Labyrinth of Minos, deep below all the people who lived unknowing in the city above, winding her way ever closer to the monster at its heart. In places, Sam heard the rumble of the Metro above. In others, graffiti or seashells decorated the walls. But the old mining tunnels seemed to go on forever, and there were long stretches without any sign of human ornamentation at all.

The current passage would have looked almost natural, if not for the rotting beams holding the ceiling from collapsing. This was a good thing, given the unnerving frequency with which buildings collapsed into the mines, and yet the fact that the beams were rotting seemed to *invite* the possibility more than would the beams' absence.

Even with Hel's suit jacket, Sam was shivering by the time Cyprien led them out of the water and through a half-collapsed passage. Suddenly, her hands came down on something long and curved and smooth as—

Bone. She'd just grabbed a human bone. Sam cried out, scrambling for new purchase, but they were everywhere. Horror bloomed in her throat as she skidded down the spill of femurs and fibulas and slack-jawed and staring skulls, flinching at the clatter of bone on bone, until at last, she fell on her hands and knees on stone that was thankfully not covered in murky water.

Cyprien, for all he was a self-professed scoundrel, looked as if his stomach had turned at the gruesome sight, his hand trailing on the wall, steadying him as he made his way down. Hel, of course, crunched down on the bones, hands shoved in her trouser pockets, as if she did this sort of thing every day. Which, if Sam hadn't known better by now, she might even have believed.

The crawl emptied out into a large T-shaped chamber, with broad flat stones piled into makeshift columns and three steps of a spiral stair that rose up to nothing. Trembling from cold and revulsion, she pushed herself to her feet.

Liquid dripped from somewhere in the darkness, and there was another sound. . . . The skittering of—she snapped her head around and caught sight of beady eyes, long, furless tails—rats, crawling up the rotting beams. Just rats. Exactly as Cyprien had said.

"Merde." Cyprien turned slowly, looking at each of the three passages leading forward, and then back the way they'd come.

"Are we lost?" Sam said, panic rising in her chest. They'd had to take a different route than intended, due to a sizeable police presence on the main route.

"What? No. Of course not," Cyprien said. "I know exactly where we are. More or less."

Hel snorted. "Right."

Cyprien snapped something at Hel, who shot back a response, but Sam had stopped listening, her gaze hooking on the mound of human bone. The cave slime was particularly thick here, dripping off the bones like an enormous sneeze. But that wasn't it. There was something *off* about them, beyond the cave slime and the rats. Quietly, Sam crept toward the pile of bone.

"You would think the police have enough to do," Cyprien complained. "But they do hate it when we have a party."

As Cyprien gestured, the lantern light hit the knobby end of a humerus. Sam frowned, leaning closer. It was as if someone had painstakingly carved a segmented spiral around the bone, snaking down the length of it. The light shifted again, and Sam gasped. It wasn't the only one.

Swallowing her revulsion, Sam dug deeper, bones clattering to the floor as she shoved them aside. All of them—every single one of the bones—had that same spiral. It wound down the length of femurs, through the gaping sockets of eyes, across the flare of craniums and hip bones, like a snake's trail through sand. And was that a strip of *tendon*? And there, a belt buckle. A pitted coin.

A wristwatch.

Oh, no. *No no no no no.*

These bones, she realized, her whole body going cold as mud-slicked ice, they weren't the ancient bones interred in the catacombs, or spillover from plagues since. These bones were *fresh*, and all of them dripping with cave slime.

No—not cave slime. *Carcolh slime.*

"Hel, come here," Sam said quietly, afraid to talk too loud for fear it would bring her suspicions down on them like an avalanche.

Hel was there in an instant, her voice soft as Sam's. "What is it?"

"Look at the spiral markings on those bones," Sam said. "There are only a few things that can cause markings like that. Put together with the slime, there's only one."

"The carcolh." Hel cursed.

"That's impossible," Cyprien scoffed, not bothering to keep his voice down. "You are just scaring yourselves. The carcolh lives in Hastingues, so far south it's practically Spain. These tunnels stretch far, but not that far."

Sam had thought about that. The carcolh was too big to leave its cave, and even if it had found a way, someone would have spotted the enormous shell of the tentacled, serpentlike snail as it crossed practically all of France, not to mention the winding ribbon of thin brown grass that grew in its wake.

But impossible or not, Sam knew what she was looking at.

There was that soft shush of movement again. Sam whirled, but there was nothing there.

"What was that?" Sam said, but it came out as a whisper as she shuffled backward, eyes darting as they tried to look everywhere at once.

"I told you, it's just rats—" Cyprien started.

And then Sam looked up.

"Hel!" Sam shrieked. Hel and Cyprien turned just in time to see Sam tumble backward, foot catching on the tangle of bones, as a hairy tentacle, fat as a baby's arm and *glistening*, shot through where Sam's head had been a moment before.

Hel spun, firing her revolver, and the tentacle flinched back from Sam. But it didn't retreat. Instead, it lashed out at Cyprien, the tentacle snaking up his leg to kiss his thigh.

Cyprien had just enough time to say, "Oh, fuck." And then he was being dragged backward into the dark. He clawed desperately at the stone floor, but there was nothing to catch, and then the ground was bones that came away in his hand, a foretaste of the feast he'd become.

"We can't lose sight of him," Sam cried out, scrabbling up the pile of bones.

The carcolh's tentacles stretched for miles. That was how it hunted—it stayed underground in its cave and sent out viscous, hairy tentacles to snatch prey and pull it back to smash against its shell and swallow whole. And then, when there was nothing left for miles around but a pile of bones—like the ones they'd found in that tunnel—the carcolh left and found a new haunt, and sent out new tendrils. At least it had, until it had gotten too big.

There was no telling how far it would drag Cyprien. And if they couldn't get to him in time, if they couldn't save him, not only might they fail to find the Wolves of God—they might never find their way *out*. They'd be trapped down here, in their wet and honestly insufficient clothes, with just one lantern, and no food.

Not to mention the distinct possibility they might *become* food.

That wasn't going to happen to them. Sam wouldn't let it.

"Help!" Cyprien cried, and she heard the thump of flesh on stone. His arms were braced against the narrowing walls, trying to keep from being pulled back through the crawl. The hairy tentacle pulsated as it snuck higher up his thigh. "I thought you said you hunt monsters!"

"What do I do? How do I stop it?" Sam cried. She'd researched the carcolh, but she'd never read of any particular weaknesses.

Salt perhaps? It was like enough to a snail, even if it was also a snake—except she'd spent her bag of salt on that grindylow, and there was nowhere in her magnificent dress to keep it anyway. Vinegar worked, but she didn't have any on her—

"Just cut it off," Hel shouted back, pulling out her revolver. Right! She had a *knife*.

Cyprien murmured prayers in French as Sam hiked up her dress and pulled out the silver-and-iron knife from her garter, and then hesitated. If she slipped even an inch, she'd drive her knife straight into Cyprien's thigh. Sever the femoral artery and he could bleed out in seconds, and even if she missed the artery—a wound like that, underground?

"What are you waiting for? Cut it off!" Cyprien cried.

Sam squinted and turned her face away, lashing out at the tentacle on his thigh with the iron blade. Blood squirted out all over her face and Hel's suit jacket—hot and viscous. The muscles in the tentacle squirmed, threatening to pull the knife from her grip should she let it.

Sam drove her knife into the glistening tentacle again and again and again, splattering them both all over with blood, until the tip of the tentacle released his leg, falling to the bones, still squirming like a worm that had been cut in half. And for a moment, she was sure she'd made a hideous mistake—that it was more like an earthworm than a snail, and this, *this* was how new carcolh were born. But the remainder of the tentacle retreated, and Cyprien collapsed to the pile of bone.

"Oh, thank Mary," he said, finding his feet, and taking her face in both hands, running his thumb over her jaw. It would have been almost romantic if they weren't both entirely saturated with monstrous snail gore. "You saved my life."

The sound of Hel's revolver cracked in the dark, the rotten

wood of the support splintering beside his head. "Get away from there," Hel ordered.

Cyprien released Sam, holding his hands up. "Oh, have pity, woman, I—"

Before Sam could so much as gasp, a flurry of tentacles shot out of the dark, wrapping Cyprien up like a present—binding his legs together and his arms to his chest. One tentacle slipped up to ring his neck and squeezed. He gasped, his face purpling.

Sam rushed forward with her knife, but another tentacle lashed out at Sam. She threw herself backward, but it caught her foot, snaking its way *up*. Sam shrieked and slashed at the laces of her shoe. It came loose in an instant, and she fell back down the pile of bones, absent her shoe and her knife.

"Sam, out of the way," Hel ordered.

"Don't shoot!" Cyprien choked out as Hel lined up a shot. "You'll hit me!"

But Sam understood what Hel intended at once, diving out of the way as the old mines echoed with gunfire, bullet after bullet hitting the rotting beams, the wood splintering, *weakening*.

Giving way.

"Get ready to run," Sam shouted at Cyprien. As if in answer, the rotting beam burst into kindling, and the earth groaned, a trembling running up the soles of her feet into her bones, dust pattering from the ceiling like tears.

And then all at once, the ceiling came crashing down behind Cyprien, pebbles and hunks of stone pelting the tentacles that stretched out of the crawl. The tentacles wrapped around Cyprien looked almost comically panicked, dropping him onto the mound of bones.

"Come *on*." Sam reached out for the dazed man as pebbles and stones rained down around them, dust choking the air. "We have to get out of here." Heaven only knew how far the ceiling would collapse.

Cyprien tried to get to his feet and slipped on a bone, letting out a sharp cry. Sam leapt the distance between them, grabbing his hand. He clasped hers back, grinning past the pain as they ran, his teeth grey with dust. "Ah, *chérie*. You're going to make your partner jealous."

Sam laughed despite herself. What an absurd—

A tentacle slipped around his ankle. Her laughter caught in her throat. Cyprien had just enough time to meet Sam's eyes— and there was a moment when Sam could have done something, bolstered her grip, pulled him free, whispered *I'm sorry*. But she did none of those things. Instead she hesitated, eyes wide with horror. And then he was ripped from Sam's grip, the tentacle dragging him under the ceiling as it came crashing down.

"Cyprien!" Sam cried. His body was briefly visible through the falling boulders—it looked unreal, more like a paper doll than a man, the way he *crumpled*. And then all that was left was his hand, reaching out of the rubble.

"Sam!" Hel shouted. "Don't you dare leave me!"

Sam tried to follow Hel, but her eyes snagged on Cyprien's hand, reaching out, reaching for *Sam*. And she couldn't shake the feeling that he was calling out for her, that he needed help, that she needed to *help him*.

Hel caught Sam's wrist, and Sam snapped back to herself. The ceiling was coming down on them both.

"What are you doing?" Sam cried.

"Saving your life."

They ran, hearts screaming, through the sting of rocks and splintered bone, and a good ways past it, not stopping until the rumbling ceased.

By the time the dust settled, they'd found themselves at a crossroads.

"We have to go back!" Sam started toward the collapse, but Hel was still gripping her wrist and held her fast. "We have to help Cyprien, he's under there—the carcolh, it grabbed him, I couldn't stop it, and now he's—"

"Dead," Hel said.

"He can't be dead!"

"It's generally what happens when two hundred tons of rock fall on you."

"I saw his hand. It was, he—" Sam couldn't finish that thought, not without remembering the way his body had crumpled. The way she'd hesitated.

A real field agent wouldn't have hesitated.

"The ceiling is still unstable, we need to keep moving," Hel said. "Besides, if we don't track down the Beast and stop it before tomorrow night, more people will die."

Sam wavered. "But it's entirely *my* fault. Cyprien's dead because of me. He never would have been here, if I hadn't—"

"He never would have been here if he hadn't been a member of a criminal organization."

"How can you be so cold?" Sam accused.

"I meant it when I said there's a world of blood and pain and death outside your books," Hel said. "What did you think being a field agent would be like? Did you think it would be without risk?"

"I thought the risk was only to *myself*," Sam said.

"Right," Hel said dryly. "That's why every one of my partners before you has died."

Sam felt the knife of her words as surely as if Hel had twisted it in her guts. She yanked free of Hel's grip, only to stumble after her first step toward the collapse. *Wet*, why was her foot—

She looked down at her bare, muddy foot. *Oh.*

Her shoe. Somehow she'd forgotten: she'd cut it from her foot to free herself from the carcolh. It had been buried alongside Cyprien in the collapse. And for some reason, despite everything that had happened—Cyprien, the carcolh, and the whole bloody mess of the Beast—it was the sudden thought of being barefoot in the old mining tunnels, walking through what you hoped was muddy water, when she was already so *cold*, that brought tears to her eyes.

Cyprien was dead. They had no map, no street signs, and no guide. They couldn't backtrack if they wanted to, not with the ceiling collapsed, and the people of Paris had been tunneling under the city for over *seven hundred years*. It was an anthill, an uncharted maze that went on for nearly two hundred miles, five stories under the crust of the earth.

And Sam just *couldn't*. Save Cyprien, find her way out, stop the Beast, find her grandfather—go on, take your pick. *I can feel things and still deal with them*, she'd admonished Hel. But she *couldn't*.

There was a sound, like cloth tearing. Sam looked up in time to see Hel standing there in just her white pin-collar shirt, damp with sweat, cutting a long, wide strip from her coat with her knife. "Here." She held the cutting out to Sam. "Wrap this around your foot."

Sam hesitated. "Hel—" First she'd taken Hel's suit jacket because of the chill in the mines, and subsequently ruined it with monstrous snail gore. Now she'd ruined Hel's coat as well. Sam wasn't entirely sure Hel had another of either. She never seemed to change her clothes. "I can't."

"Take it." Hel shook the strip of cloth and looked away. "It's at least a little waterproof. Besides, it's not like I can stick it back on again."

Sam sat down on a fallen bit of rock, and began winding the cloth around her toes.

"Not like that." Hel knelt and took the strip back from Sam. "Here, let me."

"How do you do it?" Sam said as Hel carefully wrapped the strip around the ball of her foot, working her way up toward Sam's ankle. "How do you keep going, after . . ."

"After you get someone killed?" Hel answered for her. But no sooner had she asked than understanding blossomed. Sam knew exactly how Hel handled it—she had been doing it the whole time.

Hel had sworn to keep Sam from getting hurt. She kept secrets. She left Sam behind.

Mr. Wright had told Sam she'd need to *convince* Hel to take her as a partner. Hel wasn't in want of partners—she was *rejecting* them. She'd taken a chance on Sam, but some part of her was still afraid she was going to get Sam killed. That was why Hel didn't trust Sam. Not entirely.

"I'll tell you if I ever figure it out," Hel said.

"Hel . . . ," Sam started, when suddenly, something caught the corner of her eye. *Light*, delicate as cobwebs, playing in the dark. She gasped, pointing. "*There.* That faint light, do you see it?" But by the time she said it, the light was gone.

Hel frowned. "No."

"This way," Sam said, grabbing Hel's hand and pulling her after.

The tunnel curved like a cat's tail, the floor glimmering with slime. As they came around the bend, Sam caught her breath. The darkness teemed with ethereal blue flames, like stars caught beneath the skin of the earth, a whole river of them.

"Wills-o'-the-wisp," Sam said. She reached out to touch one of them. It eddied, as if she'd disrupted the current, and circled around to light on her fingertip, cold as winter's kiss.

"*Ignis fatuus*—luring foolish travelers to their deaths." Hel studied them as another will-o'-the-wisp melted through the ceiling overhead and drifted after the rest, as if caught in the same invisible current. "But why are there so many?"

"There must be a radio signal somewhere up ahead," Sam said, hope sparking in her breast.

"A radio signal? Down *here*?"

"I know, radio waves don't go through stone," Sam said. "It's useless as a communication device. But wills-o'-the-wisp are solitary creatures by nature. They don't come together like this without good reason. What's more, they're all caught in the same current. Something is drawing them in."

And if it was a radio signal, that meant people—that meant a way *out*.

It might also mean danger. Someone had purchased a carcolh on the shadow market and hatched it in the catacombs. Given the size of the tentacles, the carcolh's shell was almost certainly too large to fit through the tunnels. It was stuck in a cavern somewhere, starving—guarding the area around it from anyone who dared pass by.

Sam could think of only one reason a person might do a thing like that, outside of abject cruelty. They had something to hide—something they were willing to pay dearly, in blood and money, to keep secret.

But Sam didn't have to guess. Whatever the carcolh was guarding, they were about to find out.

CHAPTER THIRTEEN

The Mines Beneath Paris

Sam and Hel walked deeper into the mines, down tunnels she was certain Cyprien had never seen, the wisps eddying around them like the souls of the catacombs' uncounted dead.

It reminded Sam eerily of the River Styx, as if they'd crossed over to the Underworld somewhere back along the path, as if they'd died alongside Cyprien and simply not realized it yet.

Sam shivered, feeling oddly like she'd stumbled into someone else's story. Except, for perhaps the first time in Sam's life, the story wasn't anyone's but hers, the darkness and delights and death included.

It was terrifying and thrilling, like standing at the edge of a precipice, toes curled over the edge, with a voice in her head urging: *Jump.*

Then, all at once, the wills-o'-the-wisp stopped—the whole wide river of them.

"No—no no no no no," Sam said as the wisps in front of her drifted away, melting back through the wall. But the others were all doing the same thing, seeping into the stone, leaving the darkness deeper for their absence. "The radio signal must have been cut off. Where do we go now?"

Hel raised the lantern. "I think I know."

The light spilled across a chamber that glistened with carcolh slime. Bones hung from the ceiling like wind chimes, candle wax dripped from the eyes of skulls set in the walls, and straight ahead was something that looked as out of place as Sam felt: a *door.*

Not a rusted-out mining door with a handwheel, either, but a proper wooden one, carved with Medusa's head, the snakes of her hair twisting, her eyes like pits. The wood swelled with the damp of the earth, a strange, bronze mold flowering across it with hairs that quivered in an unseen breeze.

Sam hesitated. "Should we . . . knock?" Just because this person dwelt in the carcolh's territory didn't mean they were responsible for it. It could be why they had a *door.*

Hel shrugged and rapped her knuckles on the rotting door. It pushed open.

Light spilled from the chamber. Not the flickering warmth of kerosene, but Mr. Edison's cold, unstinting electric.

Some enterprising individual had patched into power lines on the surface and routed them through the twisting passages along the cave ceiling, all the way down here. Power lines they might be able to follow out of the mines.

"Hello? Is anyone here?" Sam called out from the threshold. There was no response. Just the hissing of steam and the soft popping of burbling liquids.

Sam and Hel exchanged a glance.

At Sam's nod, Hel led the way into the room, revolver braced on the arm holding the lantern, Sam following close behind.

The walls were charred black, with vast swooping lines drawn in white grease pencil, all emerging from and returning to an eight-pointed star that looked as if it were meant to be in five dimensions, like a trap set for time and space. And within every intersecting space was drawn a strange sigil. Triangles with lines through them, circles with curled horns, and crescent moons.

Dizziness struck Sam as she stepped into the room, and the walls juddered. Sam gasped, stumbling against the doorframe.

"Sam?"

"I'm fine," Sam managed, pushing herself upright again.

The lines on the wall were vibrating so fast, they left trails in the dark, humming a note Sam had only heard in her dreams. Not a vision. More like . . . the lines on the walls were imbued with power, like the magic imbued in the Wolfssegner's bread.

Sam shook her head, cradling it in her hands. Whatever it was, it felt like a migraine. "This room—the lines on the wall. I think they're magic. *Dark* magic. That or the fumes are getting to me."

The room looked as if it should have fumes—everything about it seemed chemical and illicit. Bare bulbs hung from patched-up wires along the wooden beams that supported the ceiling. Copper retorts hissed on a door-turned-table alongside glass beakers and coiling tubes. Behind all that was a rusting metal cabinet and a sealed glass container the size of a casket, filled with something dark and viscous. White grease pencils were scattered across the floor.

"Someone was here recently," Hel murmured, her eyes fixed on the chemistry equipment. The flames had been snuffed, but the liquids still simmered.

"What is this place?" Sam asked uneasily.

She'd read about brewing operations in the secret tunnels beneath Paris, whole drums boiling mash, with fumes enough to kill a man, and once the police had run across a dead end decorated with stolen art. Then, of course, there was the so-called library—filled with rotting arcane books and absinthe fountains with their tiny cups and slotted sugar spoons.

But this looked more like a pharmaceutical operation. She remembered the files she'd read—the sixteen casks of alchemical concoctions seized at the docks in Calais. This, perhaps, was where some of those casks might have come from.

Her eyes caught on a portable radiotelegraph—like Sam's, except in far worse condition. There was a leather strap attached to the table beneath it that looked as if it was made to snap over the transmission key. But that meant it wasn't so much transmitting a code as sending out a continuous radio wave.

Sam stepped deeper into the room, peering around the glass container filled with dark liquid to the desk behind it, her eye catching on a book: *Der Wolfssegner*. It was bound in faded yellow leather, impressed with a strange elongated creature somewhere between a demon and a wolf, arching like a prancing lion on a coat of arms.

Sam touched it gingerly, and a horrible sensation coursed over her, her head feeling as if it were crumpling in on itself, as if it were *melting*.

Sam gasped, the sweltering heat of the kitchen enveloping her, the scent of burning bread sweeping through her like a hot gust from the oven. And suddenly, Sam could *see* bread under her hands, see it break, blood pouring out, finger bones wriggling their way free of the dough like worms from meat—

"Sam!" Hel caught Sam around the wrist and pulled her off the book.

Sam's lungs belled as she gulped in air, struggling to catch her breath. The images lingered a moment longer, and then faded.

"What did you see?"

"It was strange," Sam said, running her hands up and down

her arms as she told Hel about the bread, the blood, and the finger bones. For all the vision had been too hot, in its absence, she couldn't seem to get warm. Hel took off what remained of her long tan coat, wrapping Sam in its warmth, the familiar scent of gunpowder and resin chasing out the last of that burnt toast smell.

Hel frowned. "The Wolfssegner?"

Sam nodded tightly. It was like the dark version of what she'd felt when she'd touched the Wolfssegner's bread wards—only far more ocular. Her episodes were getting worse, affecting her more strongly. Perhaps she'd been using her powers too much and she was beginning to pay the price.

Sam reached out for the book again—it would have the answers, she was sure of it—but couldn't make herself touch it. "Can you?"

"Of course."

The pages were fragile, crumbling at the edges as Hel turned them. It was handwritten in German, and filled with stanzas of what looked like poetry, save for the mystical diagrams and lists of ingredients. On the inside of the cover was the ex libris of Moritz Knie, with a familiar Latin phrase inscribed in calligraphy: *Omnes angeli, boni et mali, ex virtute naturali habent potestatem transmutandi corpora nostra.*

"I've seen those words before," Sam said. "On the broadside in the Wolfssegner's home. The Wolves of God's sigil was on its back. Do you know what it means?"

"All angels, good and evil, have the power to transmute our bodies," Hel translated. "It's a quote by St. Thomas Aquinas, arguing that not all werewolves are the morning star's own. That some monsters might be on the side of God. His hounds in the fight against evil."

"The Wolves of God," Sam breathed. "Officer Berchard said they hadn't been called that until recently. What if the Wolfssegner is working with the Wolves of God? What if that's when they changed their name?"

That would explain the broadside and the ex libris. What's more, it made sense: an underserved people had stumbled upon a man who could give them the power to take back what was theirs. A man who happened to be a shadow-market alchemist.

That was motive, on all parts. But they still didn't know *how*.

"Let's keep reading," Hel said.

On examination, the spine of *Der Wolfssegner* was broken in three places. The first of these opened to an ill-used flour-crusted page with stanzas of ritualized poetry and wood-block prints of bread, wine, and ointment, as well as a print of wolves fleeing into the forest.

Wolfssegen, enchantments to drive wolves away.

The second was much the same as the first, excepting the absence of flour, and that the wolves in the wood-block print were running out of the forest and attacking a sheep.

Wolfbann, enchantments to call wolves to attack.

And the third had a complex alchemical equation, and a wood-block print of a man spreading an unguent on himself, his back already arched, his face elongating into a howl.

Wolfsalben, enchantments to call the wolf out of the human—to change a person into a Beast.

The subsequent pages confirmed it, showing diagrams of the swooping lines, a continuous radio wave moving through a vat of black liquid, which moved in response.

"The police file said Moritz Knie was kicked out of Germany on suspicion of attacking the flocks of his neighbors in the form of a wolf," Sam said. "The French assumed it was a translation error, that he'd been calling wolves to attack his neighbor's flocks with ensorcelled loaves of bread, the evidence of which was devoured by birds in the morning, and threatened him with exile should the same happen to any flocks in Montmartre. But what if it wasn't? With this unguent, you can turn yourself into a Beast."

"Or someone else," Hel said grimly.

"The mistresses!" Sam said. A mistress would be alone with her man in a secluded environment, at times and in places that would never make it onto his calendar. She would be overlooked. *Underestimated.* Even, it appeared, by Hel and Sam.

The fact that M. Gauthier did not remove his wedding ring, that he didn't have smears of cosmetics on his suit, didn't mean he didn't have a mistress. His lover might have been a man.

"Of course." Hel cursed. There had been rumors that the Beast of Gévaudan was actually several Beasts, working in concert. "That's why we couldn't find a single person who was at every crime scene—because it's someone different every time."

It explained the tears.

"Which would mean Clotilde did kill M. Barrere," Sam said. "But it can't have been on purpose. She *helped* us."

"Did she?" Hel said. "As far as I can tell, she lured us down here, where the Wolves of God have us outnumbered and outgunned."

"Except Cyprien wasn't in on it," Sam pointed out.

"Which may be why she tried to cancel when she saw him," Hel said. "Thirty thousand Wolves of God. They couldn't all be in on it, or it wouldn't be much of a secret, would it? Then there's the issue of the unguent. An unguent is something you spread on your skin. It's hard to do that accidentally."

That was a fair point. How was the Wolfssegner getting the unguent onto the mistresses? What's more, one assumed the mistresses were still human when they met their gentle-men, which meant it had to be something applied during their encounter.

"Maybe," Sam said slowly, "they don't know what it is."

Hel furrowed her brow. "So the unguent is, what, a face cream?"

Sam shook her head. "Everyone uses face cream, but not in the middle of dinner. More likely it's lipstick or perfume, some-thing they might not apply before arrival for fear of—"

"Get down!" Hel shouted, drawing her revolver.

Sam hit the floor, following the line of Hel's aim past the al-chemical equipment to the massive black wolf standing in the open door. Oh, why had they left the door open! It snarled, all bared teeth and claws and nightmare, and adrenaline doused her in a rush.

The Beast. It was here.

The animal scent of it rolled over her, blood and musk with a hint of amber.

Amber—that wasn't a Beast's scent, Sam thought. That was the scent of the man beneath the monster—or rather, the *woman.*

"Wait!" Sam cried, pushing Hel's arm down as Hel fired, flinching at the sharp retort of the revolver. The bullet went astray, lodging in the container of black liquid, cracks spidering up the glass like lace. "Don't hurt her!"

They needed to save the mistresses, not murder them.

"It's not a mistress," Hel answered as the glass container groaned, the cracks spreading.

Of course.

What were the chances a mistress just so happened to be idling in the alchemist's secret lab guarded by a carcolh in an abandoned mine beneath the city streets, all so that the alchemist might transform her to attack anyone who might stumble upon his lab? No, this was not one of the mistresses.

This was the man who made the unguent. The man who transformed the mistresses against their will and made them murder. This was the alchemist, the Wolfssegner: Moritz Knie.

With a final resounding *crack*, the glass container exploded in a shower of scintillating glass and dark, viscous liquid. Hel yanked Sam down just as there was a horrid wet *thump*. And despite her every instinct screaming to the contrary, Sam looked.

Sam had seen a weasel once, preserved in formaldehyde. It had smelled like chemical death, but it had looked peaceful, curled up as if it were merely sleeping and might dash off at any moment. Its fur still enviably soft, its eyes still bright.

This was nothing like that.

Collapsed in the shattered glass, black liquid running from its nose and eyes, was the emaciated, tarry corpse of what looked like it might once have been a wolf, its body mutilated in a now-familiar fashion: eyes clawed out, ribs cracked open, lungs pulled out, with nothing but a wet cavity where its heart should have been.

"What is *that*!" Sam cried.

Hel fired again at the Beast and this time Sam didn't stop her. There was a spray of blood and an animal yelp, and the Beast disappeared around the corner like smoke.

Hel was already making for the door, silver bullets flashing between her fingers as she reloaded her revolver. Sam scrambled to follow, wishing she had her knife, that she had something, anything to put between her and the jaws of the Beast. She glanced back over her shoulder, her gaze hooking on the power lines.

They might be able to follow those power lines out, back to the surface from which they'd come. If they followed the alchemist, the labyrinth beneath Paris might swallow them whole—if the Beast didn't get them first.

"Lipstick!" Hel said, as if she could read the thoughts on Sam's face. And Hel ran, her eyes locked on the Beast, her ruined scarf flying behind her. It took Sam a moment to register what Hel meant.

Then, *Right.*

Sam was out of lipstick—she couldn't pull the same trick she'd used on Cyprien to let Hel follow—but she grabbed one of the white grease pencils from the floor and sprinted after, her eyes locked on Hel, dragging the grease pencil along the walls as she ran. This was their chance to get answers, to end this, if only they didn't flinch. And Sam refused to be the reason they failed.

They chased the alchemist through the Gorgon door and into the chamber beyond, the eerie percussion of the bone wind chimes accompanying their footfalls as they skidded down the passage they hadn't yet taken and into the unknown.

The passages thickened into chambers and constricted into crawls, twisting like the bowels of a beast. It didn't take long until Sam had no idea where they were, and after the fifth bifurcation of their path, she'd lost all sense of whence they'd come.

In the form of a monstrous wolf, the alchemist should have left Sam and Hel in the dust. Sam *knew* wolves—her parents' stories of Dracula's wolves had haunted her nightmares for years, and in lieu of sleep she'd memorized every fact about them, as if it would keep her safe. Wolves sprinted at thirty-eight miles per hour—five times faster than Sam could run, and that was in proper footwear, which a bandage made from a coat was *not.*

It shouldn't have even been a contest. But every time Sam thought it had gotten away, they caught a glimpse of its tail, a spatter of its blood upon the stone.

Hel's bullet slowing it down. Though Sam couldn't shake the feeling, deep in her gut, that it *wanted* them to follow it.

"Why . . . was there . . . a preserved wolf . . . in that vat?" Sam panted. The mutilated wolf hadn't been in the wood-block prints in *Der Wolfssegner*. Sam would have remembered that much.

Hel raised an eyebrow. "You can't wait until after we're done running?" she said, the words coming easily, as if they hadn't been running forever.

"Abso . . . lutely . . . not!" Sam said, leveling Hel with her best glare.

"I don't know." Hel looked troubled. "The mutilations were exactly the same as on the victims. That can't be an accident. Some sort of compulsion, perhaps?"

"You think he's changing . . . the recipe?"

Sam began to see signs of human habitation. Wax dripped down the walls and candles melted into their alcoves. Graffiti shrouded the walls—first a familiar mix of names and nudity and death, then hollow-eyed wolves, their legs dripping down onto broken crowns, drawn over and over again.

The candles in this room were lit, casting the broad-bellied chamber and fat columns in flickering shadows. Sam could just make out a low stone block scattered with tarot cards and what looked suspiciously like skull fragments filled with ash and the butts of cigarettes. One of the cigarettes still trailed a thin ribbon of smoke.

Up at the arch ahead, the shadows jumped alarmingly, the candles beyond twinkling like stars in the dark. Sam could just make out the faint strains of music—violins, trumpets, clarinets, and drums. The scent of sweat and cigarette smoke twined in the air.

People dancing, Sam realized.

"Is this the party?" Sam asked, a curious mix of relief and fear washing over her.

"The alchemist led us straight to them." Hel frowned. Her question hung in the air: *Why?*

Because there are thirty thousand of them, and only two of us, Sam thought. *Because Hel was right and we were never meant to escape these tunnels alive.*

But then, why hadn't the alchemist just killed them? She didn't like it.

"We should go back," Sam said, turning around. They could follow Sam's grease pencil lines back to the laboratory and trace the power lines up to the surface. They'd lost the alchemist, but without his unguent, there was no Beast. They had to destroy his laboratory, root out his supply. Tracking the alchemist could wait until after.

"Agreed," Hel said. But it was too late.

"Hé, Henri. Je ferais mieux d'inspecter cette bière!" came a man's voice out of the darkened archway, his shadow struck large across the floor. *"J'ai la dalle en pente."*

Sam froze.

"T'es saoul, c'est pas Henri," came another man's voice, a second shadow joining the first. *"Y en a deux."*

"Et ce sont des femmes," said a third, in a voice Sam didn't much like at all. And he blocked out the last of the light from the party.

She could feel the frisson of their gazes on her skin as the three Wolves of God eased into the room.

The first man was young, his eyes bright with drink. Nature had failed to furnish him with a chin, but he made up for it with a roguish scruffiness and a floral scarf around his neck. He plucked up the cigarette from the fragment of skull and took a long drag, wreathing them in smoke.

The second was older, with a scar across his hollowed cheeks. He looked as if he might envy Van Helsing's boots, in his leather vest and sack coat, a gunslinger's belt low and tight across his hips.

But it was the third who caught Sam's attention—a soulful looking man, well heeled, a gentleman in everything but his eyes. Those burned like pitch, sticking to her skin as he looked her up and down. He smiled and her heart went cold in her chest.

"Come on," Sam murmured, hooking Hel's arm in hers. "Let's go."

The youngest man stepped forward and hooked Sam's other arm, easy as if he were dancing, and pulled her so close she could smell the beer on his breath. "So soon? But the party is just getting started."

The cowboy laughed, but not the gentleman with the devil's eyes. He just kept smiling, and watching. This was a test, Sam realized. He wanted to see what they would do—how far they could be pushed. And a thread of fury slipped out.

Sam shoved him away. "Are all Montmartre men so polite?" Sam said sharply.

"Oh, *désolé*." The young man bowed, all false apologies. "You're in the wrong part of town for polite. We're all men down here." He straightened, his cigarette clamped between his teeth, revealing a wolfskin beneath his coat, and brass knuckles welded with clawlike knives on his hands.

Hel snorted. "Right, that's why you're dressed like animals."

He went a deep red—this wasn't part of the script. "What did you say?" He turned to the others. *"Qu'est-ce qu'elle a dit?"*

"We're leaving," Hel said loudly, starting back the way they'd come. And Sam released a pent breath as she turned to follow.

"Wait just a second," the cowboy said from behind them, his voice the kind of rough that came from years of hard drink. "Those are the women Cyprien was with earlier, at the cabaret, aren't they?"

The bottom of Sam's stomach dropped out. *Oh no.*

"Cyprien?" the young man said, the puff going out of him.

Hel slowed, her hand straying inside her coat to where the revolver nestled against her ribs.

"Yeah," the cowboy said, gaining confidence as he took in the ruin of Sam's dress. "Almost didn't recognize them, with the state of her. What game is Cyprien playing? Where's he hiding?"

"Merde! I wasn't going to touch them, Cyprien! I swear," the young man cried, fumbling his knuckle knives off his hands, and snuffing his cigarette. And surprising grief flashed over Sam. Cyprien had been a scoundrel, but he had also been surprisingly kind. He hadn't deserved to die.

"He's not coming, is he?" the gentleman with the devil's eyes said, catching Sam's eye. And Sam felt every inch of the blood soaking her dress.

"Cyprien is dead," Sam said, and Hel looked at Sam incredulously. But Sam held her ground; they were his friends, they deserved to know. "He led us down here, and then we were attacked by a carcolh. The two of us managed to escape—but Cyprien didn't. We're lost without him—and we're just trying to find our way home. I'm so sorry."

"Des conneries," the cowboy said, his face twisted up like old leather. "I might not know much, but *lou carcolh* is in Hastingues. Not here. Is that Cyprien's blood?"

The young man let out a strangled cry. "They killed him!"

"Fine," Hel muttered. "We'll do this the hard way."

The cowboy lunged at Hel, she leaned out of the way, hands in her pockets, letting his arm shoot past her. Sidling up behind him, she stomped on the back of his calf. He fell to his knees, letting out a feral yell. When he next looked up there was murder in his eyes and a pair of those brass knuckle knives on his fists.

"The party!" Sam shouted. They could lose the men there in the press of bodies and the dark.

The young man swiped at her, like a scrawny, drunk bear. Sam's heart jackknifed into her throat as she danced around the makeshift table, throwing everything she could get her hands on at his face—tarot cards, candles, ash-filled skulls. He cried out as the ash blinded him, and Sam ducked behind one of the fat columns, by the candles burning in puddles splattered across the ground.

The young man growled as he swung wildly, his eyes streaming as he tried to clear them. The cowboy cursed as Hel led him into the young man's fist.

Sam had a straight shot to the party—they were almost free.

But no sooner had she thought it than the gentleman grabbed Sam's arms, twisting them roughly behind her back and walking her out from behind the column. Pain stabbed through her shoulders.

Sam gasped. He laughed at her impotence, the way people laugh at the fierceness of house cats, teasing them even in their rage. And suddenly, Sam was more afraid than she'd ever been before.

"Freeze," he commanded Hel, and to Sam's horror, Hel froze as the tips of four knives kissed Sam's throat.

CHAPTER FOURTEEN

The Mines Beneath Paris

"Hel—!" Sam started, her breath taken from her as the gentleman with the devil's eyes twisted her arm behind her back. *Don't,* she pled silently. Sam knew the way the story went if you stopped fighting back. It never got better. But Hel wasn't looking at her.

She removed her hands from her pockets, holding them high. Sam's heart fell. *No.*

The gentleman smirked. *"Attrapez-la."*

The cowboy yanked Hel's unresisting arms behind her back and shoved her face against a column.

Hel's lips quirked beneath her fall of red hair.

"Qu'est-ce que—"

Shadows spilled across the floor, and a spray of hot liquid hit the back of Sam's neck. Sam stumbled free, the gentleman releasing her, scouring the air with curses as blood gushed from the side of his head.

A woman in blood-spattered yellow silk stood behind him. She had a kind face, round cheeked with laugh lines and soft brown eyes that were currently contemplating the brass knuckle knives on her hands, the gentleman's ear caught between two of the blades like a scrap of meat between teeth.

A man and a woman that looked as if they couldn't have been older than seventeen stood in her wake. They each wore the same yellow silk blouse with a wolfskin over their right shoulder like a pauldron, and they each had the same striking black eyes, their tightly coiled hair done up in braids. Their brass knuckles had snub-nosed guns soldered onto them, both pointed almost lazily at the gentleman.

"Eulalie!" the gentleman with the devil's eyes spat, holding the side of his head, as blood painted his arm red. No one outside of Sam seemed the least bit undone by this development. *"Merde, alors!"*

"We've talked about this, Romain," Eulalie said. Without taking her eyes from Romain, she held out her claws. The first of her lieutenants deftly plucked the severed ear from between her knives, placed it in a small wooden box, and handed it to the second of her lieutenants, who tied it up in a yellow satin ribbon before placing it in Eulalie's waiting hand.

Eulalie shoved it against Romain's chest. "Go home and give this to your wife, along with your apologies, and never act this way to a woman again. Or next time, it won't be your ear in that box."

"But they killed Cyprien—" Romain whined.

Eulalie's eyes narrowed, and she flicked her claws, the blood spattering on the floor with a *slap*. Whatever words Romain had been about to say dropped and shattered on the ground like glass. And Romain, the cowboy, and the young man turned tail and ran.

This was the leader of the Wolves of God, Sam realized, and her sudden violence was a *message*, not just to Romain, but to Hel and Sam.

More of the Wolves of God melted out of the dark, their

brass knuckle knives glinting. Hel's hands were reaching for the revolver she hadn't needed for the likes of Romain. Sam pressed herself to Hel's side as tension gathered electric in the air.

"Peace," Eulalie said, slipping off her knuckle knives like satin gloves. She gave Hel and Sam a smile that said she enjoyed teaching children and embroidering hearts on handkerchiefs, which was to say, Sam didn't trust it at all. "These women are friends of Clotilde, aren't they?"

"Yes, we are," Sam said, at the same time as Hel said, "Not really."

Eulalie's smile deepened, as if their dissent had given something away.

"And how is our little Clotilde doing these days?" Eulalie asked idly.

"Why don't you ask her yourself?" Sam said carefully.

"I would," Eulalie said, "but we aren't close anymore. If we ever were. Have you ever had a friend like that? Someone you thought you knew, someone you trusted—only for them to do something that makes you question whether you ever really knew them at all?"

"She's been better," Sam said, instead of answering.

"Ah yes, her lover was murdered, wasn't he?" Eulalie said. "Is that why the three of you were talking with the police?"

The air went out of the room. The murmurs of the Wolves rose around them like a growl. Sam had misestimated the situation. Eulalie hadn't stopped Romain out of kindness, but because it would have given him *power*. Officer Berchard had spoken of how he knew them before they became the Wolves of God. How they'd been little more than thieves.

Eulalie was a new leader—she was in a tenuous position. And that meant so were Hel and Sam.

"Did you kill Barrere?" Hel asked bluntly. Sam's heart leapt into her mouth.

"Me? No, no, of course not." And a slow smile crept across Eulalie's face. "But *we* did."

"How did you do it?" Hel pressed.

"Hel," Sam hissed. You couldn't just *ask* a murderer how they killed someone. That was a good way to invite them to *show you.*

"These mines, long since abandoned by Tout-Paris, like the people who dwell here—"

"No." Hel waved her hand impatiently. "I know all that. I meant *how.*"

Eulalie laughed, a harsh bark of a sound at odds with her sweet appearance. "How do you think?" Eulalie held up her knuckle knives—still red with the blood of the gentleman's ear.

Oh, Sam realized suddenly. Eulalie had even less of an idea as to how the murders were taking place than Sam and Hel did. There were paw prints at the murder scene and wounds left by teeth. Even leaving aside the unguent, Eulalie's lie was laid bare at the first glimpse of the crime scene.

"They didn't do it," Sam said.

"I just said we did." Eulalie's voice grew hard. But the Wolves shifted behind her, knuckle knives lowered, glancing at each other.

Eulalie hadn't just lied to Sam and Hel—she'd lied to her own people, claiming credit for the murders in order to elevate herself to leader of the Wolves of God.

"Sam's right," Hel said, pressing their advantage. "The wounds on the victims were made by a large canine's incisors— two inches long. Your knives are six inches."

"Not to mention set in a tidy row," Sam added.

"So unless you were using *just the tip—*"

"Enough! You two, with me," Eulalie snapped to Hel and Sam. She turned in a swirl of yellow silk, snapping at the Wolves closing in around her. *"Vous attendez quoi? Tirez-vous!"*

Her lieutenants waited and watched, their knuckle pistols still drawn but not pointed at anything in particular, murmuring softly to one another in French.

Hel brushed up against Sam. "Are we in?" she murmured. They could still fight, Sam heard in her question. They could still flee.

Sam hesitated. She did not want in. She wanted out. Sam was exhausted and filthy, the aftermath of adrenaline leaving her limbs hollow and spent. She wanted a hot bath, proper shoes, and a clean dress. She wanted to be back in her beloved library, putting together the puzzle pieces others pulled from the blood and gristle of a dangerous world.

But more than all that, Sam wanted answers. She didn't think she could walk away now if she tried.

Sam gave a minute nod. Hel's hand eased off her revolver.

Eulalie led Sam and Hel down a winding candlelit corridor, to a pitted iron door with a rusted wheel. It squealed open to reveal an irregular chamber with walls so covered in graffiti they looked like stained glass. The corners were clotted with lockboxes, the walls decorated with maps of the mines. In the center stood a makeshift desk made of metal siding.

Eulalie set her lieutenants outside, standing guard, and closed the old mining door behind them, tightening the rusting wheel until it groaned.

Sam's every nerve awakened at the sight of the grease pencils scattered across that desk.

It doesn't mean anything, she told herself. But still, she was drawn to them, her fingers drifting like a dowsing stick toward water.

Eulalie rounded on them, and Sam snatched her hand back.

"Who *are* you?" Eulalie demanded.

"What, you don't know?" Hel said, and Eulalie scowled.

"I'm Samantha Harker and this is Dr. Helena Moriarty," Sam cut in quickly, mustering a smile, "representing the Royal Society for the Study of Abnormal Phenomena."

"You're hunting the Beast," Eulalie said after a pause.

"I assure you, we have no interest in monsters of the human varietal," Hel said dryly. "Excepting the man making monsters, of course."

And those who sell them, Sam added silently, thinking again of the grindylow, of Hel's father and the family business.

"The man making monsters?" Eulalie shook her head, as if she didn't even want to know. "Why are you here?"

"We need your help," Sam said, before Hel could open her mouth. "Please—help us get to the surface. Help us stop the man behind the Beast before he kills again."

Eulalie laughed long and hard. "Wait—you're serious. Why on earth should I do that? The Beast is killing the bourgeoisie, putting the fear of God in them. I'd like to buy his beer, and you talk of stopping him? What possible reason is there for me to help you?"

"Because," Sam said, "if the police pin the murders on you, which they very much want to do, the Senate will use it as an excuse to empower the police to drive you out of Montmartre—out of your homes. And you know they won't stop with you. Your families, your friends—you're putting them at risk for crimes you're not even committing."

"It's already happening, isn't it?" Hel said, and Sam recalled the laughter of the bourgeoisie in Montmartre, the dark look Clotilde had given them. "The rich come to Montmartre to strut in your cabarets and gawp at the way you live. The Wolves of God have always been careful. You know what would happen if you pushed too far—what the police would do, if something happened to one of them while they were playing poor. What changed?"

"Nothing," Eulalie said flatly. "That's the problem." But she looked away—at the table, where mixed among the grease pencils there was a small curl of paper no bigger than a wood shaving. And again Sam felt that *pull.*

Sam reached toward the curled paper, her fingertips brushing it. A feeling like mist broke over her and she gasped, as black liquid seemed to ooze out of Eulalie's ear.

Eulalie snatched the paper out of her hand, and the black ooze burst into spiders that skittered away, hiding in the folds of her sleeves. But it was too late. Sam had caught sight of what was written on it.

"It was you, wasn't it?" Sam said, and she remembered what Officer Berchard had said, about catching one of the Wolves scrawling that cipher into the graffiti. Sam had been certain he'd recognized the culprit, for all he wouldn't tell them. "You're the one hiding the Morse code around the star in the graffiti at the crime scenes. Officer Berchard recognized you, but he wouldn't give you up."

This time, Sam recognized the flush in Eulalie's cheeks at the name, the way she looked away. They had *meant* something to one another, still did—otherwise Berchard wouldn't have let her go. And he'd had the temerity to give Clotilde trouble for staying friends with the Wolves of God.

Hel glanced at the curl of paper in Eulalie's hands. "The code on the wall at Lapérouse. Who gave you those numbers?"

"I don't know what you're talking about," Eulalie said.

"The man behind the Beast has already betrayed you," Hel said. "He does not deserve your protection. How else do you think we found you, in the hundreds of miles of mines beneath the streets of Paris? He means for you to take the fall."

Eulalie crossed her arms. "That would require him to know where we—wait, you said *he*. You know who it is, don't you? Who is it? What is his name?"

"You first," Hel said. "Who gave you those numbers?"

"Tu me casses les pieds," Eulalie muttered, pressing her palms to her eyes. "Fine. He came to me with an offer. A young man, I never got his name. He claimed he'd overheard my conversation and handed me an envelope. I thought he meant to threaten me—the things I'd said were nothing short of treason, as far as our former leader would have been concerned. . . . But it was just a series of dashes and dots."

"Morse code," Sam murmured.

"He said there was an opportunity, that he'd like it to be for me," she said. "All I had to do was ensure that code got in the morning paper. I told him I wasn't interested. He gave me an address, in case I changed my mind. I thought the address was for him. But that night was the first of the Beast murders, and I realized what he meant. If I could claim credit for the Beast murders, the Wolves of God would follow me. I could take control, make it better. And now . . ."

"You can't stop," Hel said grimly. Because if she did, it would at once become obvious the murders weren't perpetrated by the Wolves of God, and all her power would crumble.

"How do you get the code and locations now?" Sam asked.

"You can't track him," Eulalie said. "He sends me the codes and locations glued to the backs of bees."

"The carriage murder?" Sam pressed.

"It wasn't supposed to be in the carriage," Eulalie said. "It was supposed to be in the Olympia, the night of the symphony. They never arrived. By the time we realized where the murder had happened, police had the whole area locked down. We actually did mark a warehouse nearby, but it didn't make the papers."

Sam frowned. A murder this complex—and the Beast couldn't help but kill the man early? That didn't make any sense.

"This young man," Hel said intensely. "What did he look like?"

"I don't know." Eulalie shrugged. "He kept to the shadows. But . . . he sounded like you."

Which was to say, *Irish*.

Sam felt as if she'd been dropped off a cliff, her grounding falling away as new details swam into focus. *Bees, book ciphers, and the shadow market.*

A whisper of information, a nudge on someone's baser instincts.

An Irish accent.

Sam looked at Hel. But Hel didn't seem to see her.

"And you just did what he asked?" Hel said, sounding disgusted.

Eulalie lifted her chin, her voice steely. "You don't know what it was like before. I made things better—made *us* better. I gave us something to believe in. If I didn't do as he asked, I would never have become the leader of the Wolves of God."

"And how long do you think that good behavior will last when it comes out that you were lying to your own people?" Hel demanded. "And trust me, it will come out. Men like that don't leave pieces on the board. Not when they might lead back to them."

Eulalie cut Hel a sharp look, her fingers gripping the metal of the desk so hard her knuckles went white. She looked as if she'd like to kill Sam and Hel both, and be done with it, but if she did that now, her people would know she was hiding something from them.

"Your turn," Eulalie said, wrapping her grace around her like a cloak. "Who is the man behind the Beast? Who betrayed me?"

"Moritz Knie," Hel said. "He's creating an unguent that can transform a person into a Beast. We think he's using it on the victims' mistresses. But we don't know how."

"The Wolfssegner," Eulalie cursed, but didn't question her further. "I knew the German was trouble when they let him in. Of course the police wouldn't let him live in the heart of Paris. And now he brings trouble to our home."

Sam neglected to point out that Eulalie was the one bringing trouble home. That without her, the police would never have looked to the Wolves of God—let alone Montmartre.

"The police promised they would cast him out if there was so much as a single wolf attack," Eulalie said.

"And there hasn't been," Hel pointed out. "Not in Montmartre."

"So, will you help us reach the surface?" Sam asked. The time they'd spent—it must be well past midnight. If they didn't catch the Wolfssegner soon, the Beast would claim another victim that very night.

"Where's your proof?" Eulalie asked.

"The laboratory," Hel answered. "We left a grease pencil trail that should lead you straight to it."

"We saw the alchemist there, in the form of the Beast," Sam explained. "With all manner of pharmaceutical equipment, strange sigils, and . . ." She didn't know how to describe what that desiccated wolf was—flesh black as tar and mutilated in the same manner as each of the victims. It filled her with an overwhelming sense of *wrongness*.

Hel shook her head. "We should have destroyed it when we had the chance."

"You'd shot the alchemist," Sam returned. "We couldn't let him get away."

"But we did."

Eulalie opened the door and spoke rapidly to her lieutenants. Sam heard them trotting away.

"My lieutenants have gone to verify what you've said." Eulalie went over to one of the lockboxes and pulled out a pair of knuckle knives more ornate than any Sam had seen. The sides of the brass blades were elaborately filigreed with religious iconography, and the blades were edged in silver.

"So you'll help us?" Sam said.

"If you're telling the truth, and this man has betrayed me, worked black magic, and led trouble to our door, then I am going to tear out his throat myself," Eulalie said as she slid the ornate knuckle knives over her fingers, reverent as a queen with the royal jewels. She flexed her fingers, and the blades flashed in the candlelight. "No one will stop you from following."

CHAPTER FIFTEEN

The Mines Beneath Paris

After Eulalie's lieutenants returned to verify Hel and Sam's story, the leader of the Wolves of God furnished Hel and Sam with a pair of wolfskins. They smelled of wet dog, but they were warm. Eulalie spoke quickly to her lieutenants in French, and they fell into place behind them, their snub-nosed knuckle guns hidden away.

"Are you sure you can trust them?" Sam asked nervously, drawing her hood deeper over her face. Eulalie's lieutenants had not only located the lab but, horrified by the alchemical sigils and mutilated wolf, set it ablaze.

It wouldn't be enough to stop the alchemist—they hadn't found any sign of the unguent in the laboratory, which meant he stored it elsewhere—but the destruction of his laboratory should at least slow him down.

"Them? They're my children," Eulalie said offhandedly as she swept past them. "If I can't trust them, I deserve what I get."

The pieces clicked: Striking black eyes. Tightly coiled hair. The pricks of heat on Eulalie's cheeks when Sam mentioned Officer Berchard.

"Does he know?" Sam blurted, startled into saying the first thing she thought.

Eulalie's expression cracked. "I'm sure I don't know what you're talking about." And she sped up, so Sam had no breath to spare to ask troublesome questions.

No, then, Sam thought.

"Not our responsibility," Hel murmured.

"I know, but—"

"The alchemist is murdering people, Sam," Hel said. "Besides, we don't know the whole story. Officer Berchard could be more of a ratbag than we know."

"Maybe," Sam said, unconvinced. Because, at her heart, Sam was a romantic. They still cared about one another, Sam was sure of it—the heat in Eulalie's cheeks; the way Officer Berchard hadn't given her up despite suspecting her of murder, when it could cost him everything he'd built.

This terrible business of how to survive a world divided into the haves and have-nots had come between them. Not the quality of their affections. Sam was sure of that.

Sam could sense the Wolves of God stop their dancing and carousing to watch as they passed. Every hair on her body lifted, but Sam kept her head down, and their gazes skipped off their wolfskins and passed on by. Thirty-thousand Wolves. No one knew what all of them looked like. It was why Eulalie's lies had worked to begin with.

Turn by turn, Eulalie led them through the mines, until they emerged in hidden underground fields tended by bent-backed farmers with handheld lanterns and baskets filled with mushrooms.

"Rosé-des-prés," Sam breathed. "It's said they were a favorite of King Louis XIV. Supposedly they taste sublime when grown

beneath the streets of Paris—but when grown anywhere else, they taste of water."

"How like a monarch to enjoy the fruits of his dead," Hel said dryly.

Beyond them was a large basket—big enough for a person—attached to a pulley system, the ropes swaying slightly with the distance.

"You can't be serious," Sam said as Eulalie stepped into the basket. Eulalie just gave her a flat look, took hold of the rope, and pulled herself up and out of sight, the basket swaying and the rope creaking.

"Devrions-nous l'encourager?" Eulalie's son whispered to his sister.

"Non." The sister cast a rather judgmental look back at Sam. *"Mentir c'est un péché."*

The sister went up next, followed by the brother, who clapped Sam on the shoulder once, before leaving Sam and Hel alone in the fruiting fields of the city's dead.

"I can't do this," Sam said, panic threading her voice. Hel might be fine with hauling her own body weight up hundreds of feet. Hel was brilliant at things involving monsters and bullets and biceps. But Sam's biceps were almost entirely decorative. "There has to be another way."

Hel stepped into the basket, hooked an arm around the rope, and leaned out. "Come here."

"I, what—" Sam took Hel's hand and to Sam's surprise, Hel pulled her stumbling into the basket with her.

The basket was clearly not meant for two—it creaked and swayed pendulously, Sam tightening her fingers in Hel's sweat-slick shirt, but it held. She felt the basket jolt as Hel pulled on the rope. The basket rose by inches. The walls of the throat-like passage were so close she could have leaned out and licked them.

"You're going to have to help," Hel grunted.

"The heaviest thing I've lifted in years is a dictionary!" Sam babbled.

"Then pretend I'm a dictionary."

Biting her lip, Sam reached out and grabbed the rope below Hel's hands, pulling down when Hel pulled. Reaching up and trying again, pressed against each other to keep from over-balancing and falling.

Her arms trembled and her biceps felt about to come undone. But to her surprise, the swaying basket rose, faster than before. And Sam reached up, striving to be in sync with Hel, and pulled again, and again.

Until at last, gentle moonlight broke over the top of the tunnel. Three more heaves, and they crested the top. Hel braced the basket as Sam stumbled awkwardly out and onto solid land, feeling as if she were about to collapse.

The breeze kissed her face; Sam's cheeks were wet. She wiped them with the back of her hand, staring up at the stars that brushed across the sky like heaven's own dust. Some part of her had been certain she was never going to see the surface again.

"Come on," Hel said, drawing alongside Sam and grabbing hold of her hand. "This isn't over."

Right. The alchemist. Sam scrambled for her bearings. Dirt roads, slumbering chickens, and silhouetted against the horizon: the Basilica of Sacré-Coeur.

Montmartre.

And there, on the dirt road winding up the side of the butte, were the dark shapes of Eulalie and her children, their weapons glinting in the starlight.

They were going to tear the Wolfssegner apart.

A flutter of panic went through her chest before she caught herself. The Wolfssegner was the alchemist. He had caused the murder of six people. What else did she think they were going to do? Have a nice chat where everyone went home and agreed not to murder each other?

This was always going to end badly.

Sam and Hel caught up with Eulalie and her lieutenants outside Moritz Knie's cottage. There was smoke coming from his chimney and light shining behind the curtained windows: the Wolfssegner was home.

This was it. If they could stop the alchemist here, it would be over. No one else had to die, and Sam might finally get her answers. About her grandfather, and the book cipher. About what it all meant.

If.

"Whatever are you—" Sam began, only to cut off as Eulalie held up a hand for silence. There was a *thump*, followed by a clattering. Then a low, rumbling snuffle and a wet, tearing sound. Eulalie's children looked at each other, eyes wide.

One. Eulalie signaled. Sam's legs tried to do that shucked-stocking thing again. What was she even doing here? She'd lost her knife. She didn't even have proper footwear, for goodness' sake.

Two. "Just stay behind me," Hel murmured, hand resting on her revolver. Sam wanted to say *Don't kill him,* but the words stuck like fish bones in her throat.

Three.

Eulalie kicked open the door. It slammed against the far wall—setting the keys Sam knew hung there to jangling. It hadn't even been locked.

The scent of burning bread rolled over them, and then Sam

was hit with that familiar, sickening humidity pressing against her skin, earthen sweet with a metallic tang.

"Oh no," Sam said softly.

As if in answer, there was a startled snort and thundering of hooves. A wild boar charged out of the cottage, its eyes rolling, its tusked mouth frothy with blood, forcing Eulalie and her lieutenants to leap out of the way.

"Is that him?" Eulalie demanded.

Sam shook her head mutely. *I don't know.*

There was a lot, Sam was realizing, that she didn't know. Things that weren't in the Society's sanitized libraries: things they didn't know about, things that weren't supposed to exist, and things they chose not to catalogue.

But Hel raised an eyebrow. "Do you want to take that chance?"

Eulalie cursed, barked an order, and she and her children sprinted after the boar, the sharp retort of those snub-nosed guns cracking the peace of the night sky like an egg. The boar screamed and rounded on them, charging Eulalie's daughter with his blood-foamed tusks.

"Quick, before they're back," Hel said quietly, pushing her way into Herr Knie's cottage. Hel, Sam gathered, did not think the Wolfssegner had changed shape into a wild boar.

Sam followed Hel inside. Immediately, she regretted it, turning away and covering her mouth with the back of her hand. "Mother of Mercy," she croaked.

Moritz Knie was there all right—on the ground by the scattered books and on the wooden table. But most of him was over by his formidable oven, which was still in the process of burning something Sam hoped to the heavens was bread. The rest was terribly familiar—his eyes hollow as a jack-o'-lantern, his rib cage cracked wide, his lungs pulled out and *chewed on*, and a wet cavity where his heart had been.

Dough had crusted over on the wooden table. He must have been kneading it when he'd been attacked. The hand-carved crucifix hanging off the hood was spattered with blood, and something pink Sam didn't want to guess at was stuck to the cheery kitchen towels.

Everything Sam thought she knew about the alchemist's motivations and methodology came apart in an instant.

"The Beast murdered the Wolfssegner," Sam said in disbelief, staring at the mutilated body of Moritz Knie.

"Or else someone wanted very badly to make it look that way," Hel agreed.

"But who?" Sam said. The Wolfssegner was supposed to be the one making the unguent that turned people into the Beast—he had done it before, it had gotten him kicked out of Germany, and there was no doubt it had been his book in the catacombs. And her vision . . . "Did one of the women he changed into a Beast turn on him?"

"Maybe," Hel said. It seemed clear the alchemist didn't have precise control over when the women transformed, or else the incident in the carriage never would have happened.

But the idea of Moritz Knie being eaten by his own creation sat uneasily with Sam. It was too . . . poetic. Too easy.

Hel opened the door to the cast-iron oven. Smoke billowed out. Choking, Hel quickly shut the door to the oven again, but not before Sam caught sight of what was within: the remnants of bread smoking like the pyres of the dead.

The Wolfssegen—the wards against wolves. And it wasn't just one loaf, but dozens. The oven was stacked with them, like the bones behind the carefully curated walls of the catacombs. Not a whole arrondissement's worth, but enough.

It didn't make sense. Surely the Beast wasn't intending on attacking more targets in Montmartre. The people of Montmartre weren't anything like the other victims.

"What if he had a partner?" Hel said.

"Someone who had access to his books," Sam said, warming to the idea. "Someone who turned on him."

Her visions had clearly indicated Moritz Knie was the one behind the unguent, and they hadn't steered her wrong yet—but that didn't mean it was *just* Moritz Knie. And whoever had murdered Moritz Knie had known his wards for what they were.

"A second Wolfssegner in Paris," Hel said.

"But who?" Sam said. "And why didn't Herr Knie tell us?"

Hel let her gaze drop to the mutilated corpse. And Sam knew without asking what Hel was about to say.

Sam's gorge rose. *"No."* She didn't think she could take more claws in her belly right then, more jaws around her throat. Besides which, she had a horrible feeling that the reason her visions were getting stronger was because she was getting weaker. "You don't know what you're asking."

Hel looked at her steadily. "This is what we've been waiting for: the murderer's first mistake. Moritz Knie was a poor exiled immigrant, one mauled sheep away from being kicked out of France, with no particular influence with the Parisian parliament. He's the first victim who breaks the pattern. Moritz Knie almost certainly knew the person who killed him. You might learn who."

"We *know* who killed him," Sam retorted. It was the Beast, and the visions had never started early enough to get a vision of the murderer before they became the Beast. Then again, they'd never come across a corpse this fresh before.

"You might learn *why.*"

Sam hesitated—*that* was a good reason. Sam bit her tongue against the curse that came to it. She really had been spending too much time with Hel.

"You're right," Sam admitted.

"Of course I'm right," Hel said cockily, "it's me."

"Keep going if you want me to stop," Sam said tartly, and Hel gave her that crooked smile. "I'll do it, but if I—if something goes wrong . . ."

"I'll pull you away before you go too deep," Hel promised, glancing over her shoulder out the open door, where Eulalie tore into the wild boar with her silver-kissed knuckle knives. "Quickly now. We don't have much time."

Sam knelt by what was left of Moritz Knie, her fingers curling against her palm of their own volition. She couldn't look at the Wolfssegner's face, so she stared at the kitchen floor next to him, at the flour spilled across it.

Then, every fiber of her being pulling against her, Sam opened her hand and reached out for the Wolfssegner's apron. Her fingers brushed the fabric and feeling fluttered over her skin like moths. All at once, she could *see* the Wolfssegner alive with rage, shouting, though she couldn't hear the words, looking *down* at a slender figure, their face obscured with smoke, the scent of burning bread filling the room like incense.

Time seemed to skip, and then her vision vanished and it was sinking teeth into the back of her neck, her head smashing on a corner of the table, stars filling her eyes. There were no tears, only pain as the world bled down the sides of her throat.

"Sam—Sam!"

Sam sat up, gasping—when had she fallen? Hel knelt in the blood beside her, hands on Sam's shoulders, her eyes locked on

Sam's face. Sam lay next to Moritz, in the exact same position as him, her fingers entwined with his.

Sam gave a little cry, scrambling back across the blood-slick floor.

"What did you see?" Hel asked intently.

Sam shook her head, wrapping her arms around herself. "I—*he* was arguing, looking down at someone, furious. I don't know who, I couldn't make out their face. He turned his back and—" Sam shuddered. The rest had been familiar enough.

She didn't like it. The feeling of being murdered was bad enough. Now Sam was seeing, smelling, and feeling the emotions of the dead. It felt like losing herself.

The front door banged against the wall again. Standing in the doorway, painted in blood like Artemis, goddess of the hunt, Eulalie shrugged off the boar's corpse, and it thudded to the floor.

"It wasn't him," Eulalie said flatly, walking into the kitchen, flanked by her equally blood-spattered children. And then her gaze smacked into the mutilated corpse, and Sam and Hel clutching each other in the puddle of blood. "What the—you know what? I'm not going to ask."

"Moritz Knie wasn't the alchemist," Hel explained matter-of-factly, as if she sat in puddles of blood every day.

"Obviously," Eulalie said. "Then who is?"

"We don't know," Hel said.

"What are we going to do?" Sam said. "We have no idea who is behind all this, and even if we did, we don't know who they're going to transform into the Beast, how they're going to change them, or where they're going to strike. And the Beast is due to kill again tonight."

"That's not entirely true." Eulalie produced a tiny slip of paper.

Sam recognized it immediately: one of the encoded messages, delivered by bees. Gingerly, Hel took it, smoothing it out on her knee. Sam leaned over to read beside her, her heart pounding.

There was a single line of Morse code written in a tight, cramped hand—another book cipher—and a location: *the Palais Garnier.*

The opera.

This was it. The next location of the Beast's attacks. And with it, an approximate time. They had a chance.

"Well, I think this has been enough excitement for one evening." Eulalie shouldered the boar again and turned toward the door. "Don't take this the wrong way, but I hope we never see each other again."

"Likewise," Hel said as Eulalie walked out the door.

Sam and Hel watched as Eulalie and her children wound their way not down toward the mines through which they'd come, but up the butte, in their bloodstained yellow silk, toward the wooden steeple of a simpler church than the Basilica of Sacré-Coeur.

"Right," Hel said. She was filthy from scrambling through crawls in the mines, her white pin-collar shirt slicked to her body with sweat and streaked with blood from where she'd sat with Sam in the puddle of Moritz Knie, but her eyes were alight with that familiar fire. "We have roughly seventeen hours. We need a carriage. First we'll head to the Palais Garnier—"

"Hel—"

"Scout out the location, and figure out what the likely entry points are—"

"*Hel*—"

"Then go over the guest list, it will hardly be complete but should give us—"

"Hel, *no*," Sam said, and this time Hel stopped and looked at Sam, confused. Sam spread her arms. "Look at us. We can't go anywhere like this."

Hel glanced down, then back up. "Right. Clothes. We can get cleaned up at the hotel, and then—"

"And then *I'm* going to sleep," Sam said.

"We don't have time to sleep." Hel's gaze was so focused, Sam felt dizzily like she would catch fire. "You can be sure whoever's behind this is not sleeping—he's making plans. This is the first time we've been ahead of him. If we want to have a chance of catching him, this is *it*."

It was always "it," as if the investigation leapt from one fevered stone to the next, the path crumbling behind, the quarry always one step ahead.

"Hel, I have been up since yesterday morning," Sam said.

"That's what coffee's for," Hel scoffed.

Sam chose to ignore that. "Since then, I've been almost killed at least three times, seen two men murdered, and been lost beneath the streets of Paris, sure I would never see the sun again, which, mind you, I still haven't. We have the location and date of the next murder. Surely the rest can wait a few hours."

"We don't know who the man behind the Beast is," Hel pointed out.

"We don't need to right now. We need to know who he's going to—" Sam started to argue, only to stop herself. *A nudge on someone's baser instincts.* This was what Hel wanted, drawing her back in so that she wouldn't want to go to sleep. And for an unkind moment, Sam saw the Moriarty in Hel. Hel might have turned against him, but at the end of the day, she was her father's daughter.

"I am not a piece on your game board, to move about as you

please," Sam said sharply. "You keep going if you want. I can't stop you. But I'm going to bed."

There was a pause, in which Sam was sure Hel was going to answer—she was always so quick on her feet, with an argument for everything—but whatever swords Hel had been ready to draw, she swallowed them.

"All right," Hel relented, her breath curling in the cold night air. "Let's get you some sleep."

You, she'd said. Not *us*. But it was enough.

CHAPTER SIXTEEN

The Grand Hotel Terminus, Paris

Sam sat in the claw-foot bathtub, hot water lapping at her collarbones. Steam curled around her, until the events of the evening felt more like a dream than reality.

Except there was still blood crusted under her fingernails.

"Cyprien Renouard and Moritz Knie," she heard Hel tell the police over the hotel phone, and she let the words detailing their deaths wash over her. They would be headlines by morning.

Sam wished her father were there. He never said much when she was upset. Not like her grandfather, who'd spin her stories; her brother, who would try to make her laugh; or her mother, who'd comfort her. But whether Sam was nine or nineteen, her father would mix her a cup of hot cocoa and sit with her on the back porch. Just . . . sit.

Jonathan Harker knew not all horrors could be talked away. That sometimes, you just had to sit with them, until you could bear it.

Sam turned off the taps and towel dried, the tile floor cold under her bare feet, and after a moment sprayed her perfume on the inside of her wrist, the scent of her library washing over her. When Sam closed her eyes, she could almost believe she was there.

Hel and Sam had come to Paris to stop the Beast from killing, and thus far, all they'd done was get two people killed. She kept seeing flashes of Moritz Knie's face, bloody sockets where his eyes should have been. Her fingers curled against her palm. She kept seeing Cyprien's hand, reaching out of the rubble, toward her.

You are not a field agent, Van Helsing hissed in her ear. She climbed in bed and slipped under the covers, feeling raw as a newborn, and unexpectedly conflicted.

Life was so much more complicated than books.

Hel's father might be motivated by money, but Sam had a feeling the people he used to commit his crimes had other reasons entirely. Reasons he used like puppet strings. But what strings had he pulled with the alchemist? There were, Sam thought, so many to choose from.

It was a golden age for men of wealth and taste in Paris by anyone's measure—the City of Lights afire with poetry and fashion and art, as they led France into a new era of enlightenment. But Sam had seen how everyone else lived. It was as if Tout-Paris itself were a Beast that fed on the blood of the poor.

Was it any wonder someone had decided to fight back? Even without Professor Moriarty's machinations.

No—Sam wasn't doing this right now. Honestly, she was nearly as bad as Hel. Her mind was coming apart at the edges, and still she was trying to pick apart the puzzle. She squeezed her eyes shut. She needed to *sleep.*

Some unlucky woman had doubtless already been chosen to be the Beast at the opera that evening, and if Sam and Hel were going to catch her without murdering her or being murdered in turn, Sam was going to need to be at her very best. Perhaps even better.

Sam succumbed to sleep to the shush of Hel sinking into the bathwater.

A calloused hand touches the side of her face, thumb brushing across her lips.

"Ah, chérie. You're going to make your partner jealous," the thumb's owner says. "Dreaming of me like this."

Cyprien. *Sam's heart thrills.*

"You're alive!" Sam exclaims, laughing, kissing him the way she never would in life, their bodies merging like they are made of paint, only to split apart again. "I thought we'd lost you."

"I am not so easy to get rid of as that," he chuckles, spinning her in her goddess-green dress under a forest of streetlights. "But I am dead."

And suddenly the streetlights snuff out, luminous tentacles undulating in their place. Cyprien looks up and catches one, wrapping the tentacle around his throat, before pausing and holding out the end to Sam. "Oh, I'm sorry. Should I have let you—?"

It yanks him back into the nothingness that surrounds them, like a fish on a hook, leaving nothing but laughter in his place.

No! *Sam reaches after him, only for her hands to hit glass. She's in the laboratory—white lines swooping dizzily over the tar-black walls—except this time, Sam is the one trapped under glass, where the mutilated wolf had been, black tears leaking out of her eyes.*

She watches herself, in her tattered dress and bloody suit jacket, her foot wrapped in a strip of Hel's coat, as she steps gingerly into the room.

Adrenaline flashes through her body, as she remembers *what comes next. The alchemist, escaping. The Beast, killing Moritz Knie.*

"Look behind you!" Sam shouts—or tries to. She almost forgot: she's drowning. She shouts anyway, her lungs filling with the darkness closing in on her. "Turn around! Please—"

The other Sam touches the glass. A man's shadow falls over them.

No! *Sam cries; the other Sam jerks up, her wide eyes meeting Sam's own.*

Sam gasped awake, blinking blearily into the sunlight, the remnants of the dream burning in her veins. She was, to her embarrassment, sprawling over the entirety of the bed, one leg thrown over the bundled-up covers like a lover. Hel was nowhere to be seen.

Sam's heart squeezed. *You keep going if you want,* she'd said. But Sam had hoped Hel wouldn't. The phone rang. Sam picked it up, the brass fitting cool against her ear.

"Samantha Harker," Sam answered, hoping against reason that it was Hel. The dream—it was just a dream—had unsettled her.

"Miss Harker," Mr. Wright said, his voice deep with displeasure. It seemed the hotel staff was keeping him well informed.

Sam could only imagine how she must have looked walking into the foyer in that scandalous dress, made more indecent by the rips and tears and clinging fabric, wet with blood and dirt and carcolh slime.

And then there would be the morning newspapers, plastered with the deaths of Cyprien Renouard—which was entirely Sam's fault, even if only Hel's name made the news—and Moritz Knie, the latest victim of the Beast, who should never have been a victim at all.

"I can explain." Sam scrambled. Indecent *and* inept. It was as if she were going for extra credit.

"I certainly hope so," Mr. Wright said. "Because I found myself woken up out of bed, having to explain to a very unhappy widow at four in the morning why exactly it is my agents are spreading rumors about her recently murdered husband's supposed mistress—and in the morgue of all places!"

"This isn't about the deaths?" Sam ventured.

"Deaths happen," Mr. Wright said. "You know what doesn't happen? The Society being invited to France to aid in hunting down abnormal phenomena. And thanks to your actions, it might never happen again."

But how—?

Van Helsing, Sam realized. That must have been what he was up to when Sam and Hel were fighting for their lives in the catacombs. Sam couldn't prove it, of course, but how else would a French widow find out who Sam was or whom she answered to? Let alone secure Mr. Wright's personal phone number.

"But he *did* have a mistress," Sam started to say, only for Mr. Wright to cut her off.

"Of course the man had a mistress," Mr. Wright said dismissively, as if he couldn't possibly imagine such a woman being the Beast. Which, perhaps he couldn't. "That doesn't mean you have to throw it in his widow's face. I expect such indiscretions from Miss Moriarty, but I had thought you had some sense in you."

"I'm sorry, sir," Sam said. "It won't happen again."

"You're right," Mr. Wright said. "It won't. You and Miss Moriarty are off the case. I'm assigning Jakob Van Helsing to finish what you started. I expect your full cooperation in getting him up to date on the case, and your subsequent return to London."

No.

Sam felt as if a ghost had gone through her.

Van Helsing was the kind of man who looked at wild things like they existed to be conquered, as if conquering them somehow made him more of a man. The kind of man who was content to murder the monsters, and let live the man who'd made them. Which would only ever create more monsters.

As, it was becoming apparent, was Mr. Wright.

What did you expect? a voice that sounded an awful lot like Hel said in the back of her mind. More monsters was good for business.

She'd *expected* they'd be heroes, she was embarrassed to admit. That they'd help people. But if Van Helsing had his way, he would shoot whatever poor girl the alchemist had transformed into a Beast and return home, another notch on his revolver, and the only people that would be helped were those who least needed it.

"He should be in touch shortly. I've booked him the room next to yours," Mr. Wright was saying, then he cleared his throat. "As for Miss Moriarty, I'm sure you'll be pleased to hear you won't have to deal with her much longer. The hotel staff monitoring your room have managed to intercept two encoded messages sent via wireless telegraphy from that location. What I need you to do—"

Sam could not allow Mr. Wright to take Hel away from her and leave Sam alone with Van Helsing. She *wouldn't*.

"Oh, *that*," Sam said offhandedly. Mr. Wright paused, as Sam had intended, and she made a big show of quieting down. "I'm sorry, you had something you needed me to do?"

"What do you mean, 'that'?" Mr. Wright said.

It would make him feel clever, to uncover a discrepancy—and if he felt clever, he'd believe it, better than if she told him the truth, because it would reinforce the stories he told himself.

"Oh, it's nothing." She smiled, and lied through her teeth: "You were going to tell me more about the radiotelegraphs I sent?"

"*You* sent them?" Mr. Wright said incredulously.

"Of course," Sam said. "You remember my grandfather Murray—his love for radiotelegraphy. I suppose I kept up with it to feel close to him after his disappearance." And because radiotelegraphy was *fascinating*, but Sam had a part to play.

"It's a request for some research documents, from an old colleague," Sam confessed, remembering how like a library classification system the book cipher had seemed. Mr. Wright, Sam thought, rarely saw the inside of a library. The various library classification systems would be as arcane to him as all the bobs and bits of revolvers were to Sam.

"You don't say," Mr. Wright said faintly.

"We have a shared interest in radiotelegraphy," Sam continued, as if she were confiding in him, and he were the mentor she wished he was. "She works for a private collection, and that's the classification system their archives use. In fact, I meant to ask you to look up those same references for me as well. Do we have anything on Wolfssegners or alchemy? Mr. Van Helsing might find them of use, given that he's taking over the case. I didn't remember our library having them in there, but if I'm wrong . . ."

"You of all people should know you're supposed to go through the internal system for such things," Mr. Wright said, frustration cutting his words jagged. *He believed her.*

Give someone a problem to fix, and they won't look any deeper.

"I'm sorry, sir," Sam said. "I'll be sure to follow the proper protocol next time."

"I should hope so," Mr. Wright grumbled. "I'll put in the request."

"Of course." Relief welled in her chest. "Thank you, sir, I appreciate—"

"I do hope you aren't letting your fondness for Miss Moriarty get in the way of your good judgment," he cut her off, his voice soft. And Sam wondered if he had bought her story quite so well as she'd thought. "Miss Moriarty is a subtle knife that has found her way between the ribs of many a good field agent, and Mina— your mother would never forgive me if something were to happen to you."

Was that a threat? No, it couldn't be. This was Mr. Wright she was talking about, the director of the Society. He was only worried about her. Still, victory soured on Sam's tongue—she didn't like her mother's name in his mouth.

"I'll see you in the office shortly," he said. And then he hung up, before Sam could so much as formulate a response. Sam returned the handset to the cradle, a little shaken, and looked up in time to see the door swing open. Hel wore a clean coat and suit, which was a mystery in itself, as there was no earthly way she might have repaired it given the state Sam had left it in, but not one she was intent on solving right then.

"Sam—" Hel started. How much had she overheard?

Sam realized she didn't care.

"Mr. Wright is taking us off the case." The words were out before Sam could stop them. And she felt her eyes begin to prickle—again. Oh, for goodness' sake, why did every strong emotion seem to leak out of her eyes? "Mr. Wright is giving it to Van Helsing. We're to tell him what we know when he arrives, and then go home."

"Well then," Hel said, every line of her sharpening. "We'll just have to solve the case first, won't we?"

"But we know almost nothing about the identities of the alchemist, his next victim, and the mistress who will be the Beast!"

Hel shrugged. "I've done more with less. And back then, I didn't have you. Besides, we can't leave until he finds us. Otherwise how are we to give him what we've uncovered?"

"But that will take no time at all!" Sam said.

"Then I'll get a second room at the hotel." Hel shrugged, and Sam stared at her. "Mr. Wright said he expects our full accommodation when Van Helsing comes to us for a briefing. He didn't say we had to make it easy on him. We'll use a new line of credit, put the room under new names, and leave everything we don't absolutely require there. Then we relocate to a different hotel—one without telephones. That should buy us some time."

It was clever. Of course the Grand Hotel Terminus would fold the moment Van Helsing asked after an Irishwoman in a suit and a spectacularly dressed American woman rooming together—they didn't have the funds to afford discretion. But their new room was a poisoned pawn. Once Van Helsing saw their equipment within their new room, he would think he'd overcome their attempt to lose him, and that it was only a matter of time before they returned.

Even if he saw through it, it would take hours to check all the other hotels, the Grand Hotel Terminus being one of the only hotels in Paris equipped with telephones.

It wasn't perfect, but it should, as Hel had said, buy them

some time. And with any luck, they wouldn't need much: the opera was that evening.

Sam felt a surge of gratitude. "Hel—"

There was an answering squeak, and Sam's eyes widened.

"What," Sam said, "was *that*?"

"Oh, right." Hel reached into her long tan coat and pulled a rat out of her pocket. "I almost forgot."

"A rat!" Sam exclaimed. "Does the hotel know?"

Hel raised an eyebrow. "I don't know, were you planning on informing them?"

"Tell me you didn't just bring that in from the sewer," Sam said. "No, wait—don't. I don't want to know."

"Hardly." Hel snorted as she let the rat run up to her shoulder. "He's courtesy of the Golden Dawn. We know mistresses are being transformed into the Beast by way of an unguent— we just don't know *how*. I thought it best we test on something that wasn't one of us. The Golden Dawn assures me this rat has been ritually prepared to react to alchemy in the same fashion as a person. We should be able to test whether it was Clotilde's perfume or lipstick that held the unguent. I should have a cage somewhere around here."

Hel rooted around in her luggage as Sam imagined a pint-sized Beast gnawing at the bars of a rodent cage. As terrifying an image as it was, it would be nothing compared with if Hel or Sam transformed.

"So he's a magic rat," Sam said, creeping closer to where it nestled in Hel's hair. It didn't look like a sewer rat. It was small for its kind, black furred, with a blaze of white that ran up its nose, and odd eyes—one red and one black.

"If you like."

The rat stood on its hind legs, paws raised in supplication. In spite of her reservations, Sam reached out her hand, and the rat ran up her arm to perch on her shoulder like a little pirate. Sam let out a squeak nearly as high as the rat's as it sniffed behind her ear and burrowed in her hair.

"What's his name?" Sam said, pushing the rat's tail out of her face.

"He doesn't have one," Hel said. Sam followed her into the washroom.

"Don't be ridiculous," Sam said as Hel began to construct a wire-frame cage in the bathtub. "He has to have a name. How else will we refer to him?"

"Test subject A."

"Absolutely not!" Sam said.

Hel raised an eyebrow. "First you don't like him, now you want to name him?"

"I never said I didn't like him. Only that the hotel might not," Sam said, and she turned to the rat, cooing. "You're a Heathcliff, aren't you? Everyone believes the worst of you, but you just want to be loved."

Hel laughed. "That was *not* the moral of that story."

"Says you," Sam said primly. "Heathcliff was rejected by society. What else could that do but turn a man into a monster?"

"Not everyone who is rejected by society turns into a monster," Hel said. But she looked away when she said it.

"Hel," Sam said, reaching out for the other woman, catching hold of her hand. "You're not a monster."

Hel scoffed. "As if I'd trust the word of someone who thinks Heathcliff is the victim."

"I'm serious," Sam said, squeezing Hel's hand.

"Then why does it feel like everyone's waiting for me to show my teeth?" Hel looked up at her, her eyes open, vulnerable.

"Because," Sam said fiercely, "as a wise woman once told me, men are entirely too quick to call a woman mad or monstrous just because she can do something they can't. Don't do it for them."

Hel barked out a surprised laugh. "Wise now, am I?"

"You had better be," Sam said. "If you're wrong—"

"You're not a monster, Sam," Hel said, squeezing Sam's hand back.

"I know," Sam said, though it was a lot easier to believe when she was saying it about Hel.

Hel released Sam's hand, offering her own to Heathcliff. The rat obligingly scampered into the palm of Hel's hand, and she deposited him in the wire cage.

First, Hel offered the crimson lipstick to the rat, sticking it through the bars of the cage. The rat sniffed the lipstick delicately before taking it in both paws. Clearly appalled, Heathcliff fell to licking his paws and running them over his muzzle, trying to scrub them clean. He threw Hel a resentful look, his face appearing as if it were covered in gore.

"Sorry, Heathcliff," Sam murmured.

Next, Hel withdrew a slim glass perfume bottle, chased in gold filigree and inscribed with the words *L'Heure magique*. The Golden Hour. She sprayed Heathcliff with the perfume, and the scent of magnolias filled the room as if a tree had sprouted right there and shoved its blossoms up their nostrils.

At first Sam was confused—that was most definitely not the perfume she remembered from Lapérouse—until she recalled what Arsène Courbet had said about the top notes.

Hel coughed, waving the air in front of them. "How do people live with all that stink on them?"

"Some of us prefer to smell like more than gunpowder and resin."

"You mean how you like to smell like old books?" Hel said.

Sam's cheeks heated. "It's comforting!"

"So's gunpowder," Hel said dryly.

Before long, the top notes had faded, revealing the more familiar gardenia, jasmine, tuberose, and lily. It still smelled just as dangerous and wild as it had the first time, but nothing happened.

Heathcliff was still just a rat in lipstick—albeit one that smelled better than most denizens of the order Rodentia.

"So the unguent isn't in the lipstick or the perfume," Sam said, trying to hide her disappointment. It would have been so much easier if it had been.

"It's possible it's a time-delayed reaction," Hel said. "It's the product of alchemy, a mixture of chemistry and raw magic. Chemical kinetics alone could produce a delayed reaction." Then, at Sam's blank look: "Like the iodine clock—two colorless solutions that when first combined have no reaction, only to turn dark blue after a set interval of time."

So they still didn't know how the unguent was being applied to the mistresses—nor how the transformation was triggered. Unless, of course, the answer was time. Which meant all they could do was wait.

Sam went to fetch breakfast at their new hotel—the Hôtel du Louvre—as Hel moved their belongings into the decoy room at the Grand Hotel Terminus.

Juggling a carafe of coffee and a basket filled with breakfast pastries in one hand, Sam riffled through the pamphlets at the front desk with the other, until she found one about the opera that evening: Gounod's *Roméo et Juliette*.

"Are there tickets left for the opera this evening?" Sam asked the gentleman at the front desk, holding up the pamphlet.

The gentleman shook his head. "*Non.* That opera has been sold out for weeks. I'm sorry, perhaps I can help you with dinner reservations, or—"

"No, thank you," Sam said. That was problematic. Not for Hel, of course, she'd probably be delighted at the opportunity to sneak in. But Sam would rather not have to keep an eye out for both security and the Beast if she could avoid it.

When Sam returned, Hel was spreading the blueprints of the Palais Garnier over the desk in their new room at the Hôtel du Louvre. She must have obtained it sometime during the night— though the libraries couldn't possibly have been open. Also, libraries didn't tend to lend out blueprints. Sam looked at Hel sidelong. She *had* been busy.

"All right, what do we know about the opera?" Hel asked, as Sam grabbed an *escargot aux raisins* and placed it deliberately in Hel's hand. She was nearly certain the woman was running on coffee fumes alone at this point.

"The opera opens at seven thirty this evening," Sam said, tearing off a piece of her pastry and feeding it to Heathcliff. That gave them nine and a half hours to put together some sort of plan. "The opera in question is Gounod's *Roméo et Juliette*. It's entirely sold out and should run for approximately three hours."

"At some point during which, the Beast will attack its next victim," Hel said. "Our goal is to locate the mistress in question— preferably in advance of her murdering anyone—and resolve the issue of the Beast before Van Helsing finds us."

They both knew what would happen if they failed and Van Helsing saw the Beast. Silver bullets. Blood. Death. Another victim taking the fall for the perpetrator.

The only thing missing from their plan was a way to capture

the alchemist behind it all, or at the very least, to discern his identity. Having no clues, Sam and Hel would have to play that part by ear—if they were offered the opportunity at all.

"It won't be easy," Hel said, her fingers playing over the stolen plans. "Setting aside the matter of tickets, the Palais Garnier seats one thousand nine hundred eighty-nine guests. It has six floors, two secret passages—here and here—outfitted with thin metal ladders that lead from the belly of the basement to the fourth floor, and countless hidden alcoves sufficient for cover."

"We need help," Sam argued. "She could be anywhere. She could be any*one*."

"We can't ask the police for help," Hel said flatly.

Sam wanted to argue—the police could certainly get them access to the theater. Besides which, it felt irresponsible not to warn them, when they knew where the next murder would take place. But she knew Hel was right. The police were hardly versed in abnormal phenomena. Asking them for aid would go about as well as asking Van Helsing, except with more death, largely on the part of the police.

But if they failed to stop the Beast, the picture was similarly bleak. The opera had its own security, who would inevitably try to help and inevitably die. And when Van Helsing arrived, the poor young woman who had been changed into a Beast against her will would inevitably die with them.

"Besides, we know where the Beast will be," Hel said. "Or rather, where she won't be."

"The Beast doesn't strike in the open," Sam realized. That still left a great number of possibilities. But this was the opera, and she was a rich man's mistress. "She'll be in one of the boxes."

It was still nearly a hundred possible sets of people—there

were four floors of boxes on three sides of the auditorium. But it was something.

"We also need to stop the Beast from escaping the opera house, once it enters," Hel said. "That will limit the space we have to search."

"The Wolfssegen—the bread wards—from Montmartre," Sam said. "We can sneak the unburnt ones into the opera ahead of time, slip out shortly after the opera starts, and place them around the performance hall."

"Good idea," Hel said approvingly.

The bread wards had worked well enough to keep Clotilde from her house after she'd transformed into the Beast. They should work to trap this Beast within the auditorium.

Provided, of course, whoever was instigating the transformation of the Beast didn't recognize Hel and Sam and decide to hold off on the attack until the victim was in the washrooms—which had been a bit of a problem as of late.

"What are you planning on wearing to the opera?" Sam asked.

"I don't *plan* on wearing anything." Hel opened her suitcase to reveal three identical black suits and crimson ties. "That's the point."

Sam's head spun. Though that did solve the mystery of Hel's attire. "Don't tell me you only have the one suit."

"I don't. I have three," Hel said. "It's efficient, and means I don't have to spend time thinking about things that are ultimately unimportant."

"Unimportant?" Sam squawked. Fashion was a whole language, a way to communicate information at a glance. "You *can't* wear that suit to the opera. You'd stand out like a gun at a flower show, not only on account of being perilously out of fashion—"

"How perfectly terrifying."

"But also on account of the law against women wearing slacks in Paris—which you received special dispensation to flout," Sam persisted. "Why do you think two of the Wolves of God recognized you and not me? We need to blend in, or we'll have no hope of catching them at all. Besides, you'd be surprised at the number of things you can hide in a proper skirt—and in being underestimated."

"All right, fine," Hel groaned. "That still leaves the matter of tickets."

"There is *one* box available," Sam said reluctantly, remembering the rumors she'd heard. "Or rather, it's reserved for someone less . . . corporeal."

"Box number five," Hel said. Seven years ago, a stagehand had been found hanged in box number five. It was rumored that his ghost had cut the line on the seven-ton bronze-and-crystal chandelier, sending it crashing down from the auditorium ceiling, killing the concierge who dared seat people in his box. It had been reserved for the phantom ever since. "We'd have to appease the phantom. We don't have time to discover what binds it here. Can you get us access?"

Sam thought about it. They needed someone with connections. Someone who held sway with Tout-Paris.

"Arsène Courbet," Sam breathed.

"Who?" Hel said.

"The perfumer," Sam explained. "He creates perfumes for the brightest stars of the city and stage. He has connections everywhere. I bet he could get us in."

"Why would he help us?" Hel frowned.

"I, um . . ." Had Sam imagined the connection between them?

She might have, she allowed. But she hadn't imagined the perfume he'd given her. "I got the impression he wouldn't mind my company again, in more . . . private circumstances."

"You have a date?" Hel exclaimed. "When did you have time for that?"

Sam's cheeks heated. "It's not a date! I just, Arsène and I—"

"Oh, *Arsène*, is it now—"

"Don't tell me you're jealous," Sam said, her flush deepening.

"Don't be absurd," Hel scoffed. She *was* jealous! But surely not of Arsène. She hadn't even met the man! "And I suppose I would go as your chaperone again."

Sam lifted her chin. "Unless you have something else in mind. It's the perfect cover. If Van Helsing arrives, or the alchemist recognizes us, they will see what they expect to see: a gentleman on an outing with a lady and her chaperone."

Hel cocked her head. "You'd use him?"

Sam bit her lip. "You're right." She wouldn't use someone like that when the risk was all too real that they would end up dead—not after what had happened to Cyprien. "We'll have to tell him."

CHAPTER SEVENTEEN

The Palais Garnier, Paris

Arsène Courbet, it turned out, was thrilled to hear of Sam's interest in the opera and was enticed by the promise of a secret mission.

"It would be my honor to assist you," he said seriously, his voice tinny through the public phone at the train station. Out of anyone else's throat, it would have sounded ridiculous, but from his, it had sent a flutter in her belly. "One of my clients is in *Roméo et Juliette*. She is always asking me to come, and I always make my excuses—a love story is a terrible thing to see alone. She will be delighted I have accepted her offer at last."

"You shouldn't be in any danger," Sam assured him, worrying the edges of the card he'd given her and keeping an eye out for Van Helsing. "You're not her type."

"Her?" His voice lowered. "You don't mean to say you think the killer is a woman? Did the midinettes help you identify her?"

"After a fashion," Sam hedged.

Hel, on the other hand, was less thrilled at her preparations for the opera, *suffering* the ministrations of the midinettes at Paquin in the truest sense of the word. It was the Harrowing of Hel.

"This is a waste of time," Hel said, standing on the dress platform, stripped down to her pin-collar shirt and slacks. She waved away a gossamer violet number that Sam thought would look quite well on Hel, if she'd been anyone other than who she was. "There will be plenty of suits at the opera."

"But none of them on women," Sam said. "Imagine the world's a stage. Clothes signal what part you play, writing you into the stories other people tell themselves about the world around them. You can use them to blend in or stand out, to signal allegiance, to express your mood, and even to advertise what kind of person you are. Fashion is a whole secret language."

"A language I don't speak," Hel grumbled.

"That's the thing." Sam laughed. "You do—you just have no idea what you're saying."

That got Hel's attention. She looked over the dresses the midinettes offered—and the dresses the midinettes wore—a new thoughtfulness in her eyes. And when she waved away the next dress, a black number that clung to her like an oil slick, she offered direction.

"More structure. The color's good, though."

After the midinettes at Paquin coerced Hel into the dress least offensive to Hel's sensibilities and the Society's budget, Sam and Hel returned to their room at the Hôtel du Louvre. There, Sam pulled out her needle and thread. She sewed pockets in the folds of Hel's skirts for salt and a flask of holy water. She sliced the dress weights out of the hemline and replaced them with silver bullets. She padded Hel's jacket so she might hide her pistol along her ribs and fitted her with garters strong enough to hold silver-and-iron knives.

Sam examined Hel critically as the hour to go drew near.

Hel was bent over on the floor in their hotel room,

disassembling and cleaning her pistol in a black dress with tulle trim and a smart black jacket. Her ginger curls were already falling into her face, escaping Sam's attempt at pinning them beneath her black trilby hat with birdcage mesh. A silver-tipped black cane lay on the floor beside her, which in Hel's capable hands would more than suffice as a weapon.

Somehow, Hel managed to stand out just as much in that dress as she had in a suit, but it would do. There was no use putting her in an outfit that discomfited her—that was a shouting all its own.

Sam herself chose an ephemeral, feminine piece from her suitcase for the evening—champagne chiffon with silver beading on the hem, like starlight shimmering on sand, that glittered when she moved. It was eminently fashionable and entirely impractical, though her seamstressing had gone a long way to improving that, sewing in a small silver knife, salt, chalk—all the essentials.

She finished it off with the perfume Arsène had made for her—the scent of the library wrapping around her.

"You were right," Hel admitted. She selected a slender engraved revolver with pearl grips from her collection and compared it against the measure of Sam's thigh. "You can hide a lot in these skirts."

"I don't know about this," Sam said nervously as silver bullets flashed between Hel's fingers.

Hel snorted. "If I can wear a dress to the opera, you can bring a weapon to a fight."

"Perhaps you should keep it," Sam said. "The last time I used a revolver, I nearly took out a light fixture. I believe the hole's still there, home to a small colony of ants."

Besides, Sam found, in the secret hollow of her heart, she didn't *want* to shoot the Beast.

Hel gave her a level look. "Even if it means Arsène goes the way of Cyprien?"

Sam bit her lip. *Right.*

Hel strapped the revolver to Sam's thigh beneath the froth of champagne chiffon.

"Sam . . . about this morning," Hel said. "You lied to Mr. Wright for me."

"You were right about him," Sam said shortly.

Hel raised an eyebrow. "I was?"

"We can't trust him to do the right thing," Sam said.

Mr. Wright hadn't cared about the highwaymen on the road to Dover. He hadn't wanted the file on rusalkas updated with the method Hel had discovered for laying them to rest. He hadn't even cared that Sam and Hel had gotten two men killed—only that they'd spread the *rumor* that the victims of the Beast had mistresses. And now Mr. Wright was sending Van Helsing out to take over their case.

Hel let out a pent breath. "I'm sorry."

Sam looked at Hel suspiciously. She had never apologized before. Not with words, in any event. "For what? You were right."

"I know."

It was a half-mile walk from the Hôtel du Louvre to the Palais Garnier. The sun was just setting, dripping over Paris like candlelight. Anxiety played the strings of her nerves like a violin, warming up for the opera.

In Paris, in the year 1903, the Palais Garnier was the stage on which Tout-Paris played, a game of glances and gleaning that revealed who was favored and who was scorned.

And what a stage it was: a bombastic wedding cake of a building, a harmonic explosion of Beaux Arts and neobaroque architecture. It was as if Achilles had been stuffed in a bridal gown and dipped into liquid gold instead of the River Styx— gilding his physique where it wasn't already marble.

Its grand columns were topped with the busts of famous composers. Gold figures of Harmony and Poetry crowned the façade, and Apollo stood cast in bronze between them, holding aloft a golden lyre.

Then there was the opera.

"Assassination attempt," Hel said, nodding her chin toward the building.

"What's that?" Sam had never seen a building so extravagant.

"The Palais Garnier," Hel said. "It was only built on account of the near assassination of Napoleon III—"

Sam yelped, slapping a hand to her neck. It hit something bristly and too sharp, her neck stinging, and in the palm of her hand, when she pulled it away: a bee, with a small scroll of paper attached to its back.

Cold poured down Sam's veins.

"Hel," Sam managed, uncurling her fingers so Hel could see.

Hel drew in a sharp breath and scanned the people on the streets—men and women in long wool coats, braving the cool autumn night. No one close by. No one so much as looking at them.

One of them must have sprayed her with the queen bee's pheromone, as the Irishman had Eulalie. But they'd been moving through crowds—it could have been anyone. It could have been any *time*.

That was part of the message, Sam knew. Their adversary was showing them just how easily he could get to Sam—how easily he could *touch* her.

Fingers shaking, Sam carefully broke the wax and unrolled the message. It was in Morse code, like the others. Sam pulled out her notebook and carefully transcribed it: *fxg1=N+.*

No book cipher here. Sam looked up at Hel, who was peering over her shoulder. "Is this—is it another code?"

Hel had gone white. "It signifies the Lasker Trap. It's a chess move in which the opponent sacrifices lesser pieces in order to promote a pawn to a knight in your back line. It forces you to either sacrifice your queen to regain control of the board or put your king out of position—putting yourself at an incredible disadvantage."

Sam shook her head. "I don't understand."

"It's in English notation," Hel said, as if that explained everything. "Anyone from France would use the German notation, fxg1=S+." She paused. "My father used to send me instructions in chess notation when I was a child."

"We need to tell the Society," Sam said at once.

"I thought you didn't trust them?" Hel accused.

"Scotland Yard, then," Sam said, waving her hands. "If there's a chance Professor Moriarty is really behind this—"

Hel shook her head. "You don't understand. Every piece you put on the board is a piece he can use against you—a piece he might already be using against you, in a game you don't even know you're playing."

"You're saying you think Scotland Yard is compromised?" Sam said.

"I'm saying they might not even know it if they were," Hel said grimly.

Sam squeezed her eyes shut. "What's the message then? What does the Lasker Trap represent?"

"He wants me to know that it was him," Hel said. "That any

successes we've had were actually pieces he willingly forfeited in order to force me to sacrifice my queen if I want to regain control of the board and continue the game."

The pieces he forfeited . . . The mistresses. The underground laboratory. The Wolves of God. The Wolfssegner.

"Sacrifice your—" The words caught in Sam's throat. "Wait, who is your queen?"

Hel just gave her a look.

Sam. Sam was Hel's queen. Sam could feel her calm melting, thinning, like arctic ice. *I am not a piece on your game board,* Sam had told Hel, never suspecting how near it had been to the truth.

Hel's expression cracked. "I—"

"Mlle Harker," Arsène Courbet called. Sam watched as Hel folded up whatever she'd been about to say and tucked it back inside. "Over here!"

Sam turned, forcing her most brilliant smile. M. Courbet was waiting for them at the entrance to the Palais Garnier. Like Hel, he had a cane, a plain black affair tipped in gold. He wore the suit Hel would have wanted to wear—a black suit with a tie the color of heart's blood.

"Thank you so much for offering to help," Sam said. "We couldn't have done this without you."

"I am grateful for the opportunity to see you again," Arsène said gravely, drinking her in as they approached. Her cheeks pricked with heat. Sam had told Hel this wasn't a date—but this felt very much like a date. What if he had only agreed because he wanted to see her again? Was that any better than the way she'd tricked Cyprien? "You look . . . different."

Still, a small voice in the back of her head said, *He could have anyone, and he chose you.*

"I'm just trying to fit in," Sam managed.

"I wish you wouldn't," he said, brushing his lips to her knuckles. A thrill shivered down to her bones as he straightened, looking down at her with those Darcy-dark eyes. She'd forgotten how tall he was. "I liked you very much the way you were."

"Oh, I don't know," Hel said dryly. "I don't think she looks that bad."

"Hel!" Sam whispered, giving her a sharp look. *Play nice.*

Hel gave her a look right back. *Him? Really?*

"I have arranged for us to be seated in box number five, as requested," M. Courbet said. "I have assured them you can appease the phantom?"

"Don't worry, we'll protect you," Hel said.

"Excellent." Arsène eased back a step under the weight of Hel's disapproving gaze and offered Sam his elbow. Sam took it, resting her fingers lightly on his forearm. "Then if you'll follow me?"

But Hel was already striding toward the opera house, leading the way.

Arsène leaned close, the scent of sunflowers washing over Sam. "I don't think she likes me much."

"Don't take it too hard," Sam said. "She doesn't like much of anyone."

Arsène chuckled, deep in his throat, so softly Sam was certain Hel hadn't heard it. Like a secret just between the two of them.

If the outside of the Palais Garnier was a wedding cake, the inside was a confection. The grand staircase swept upward, diverging into two flights halfway up and hewn from Italian marble with red-and-green marble balustrades. Female torchères lined the stairs, lifting glittering candelabra to the stars as if celebrating Prometheus's theft of fire.

Sam's dress glittered like the sun on warm sand under all that golden light. She knew she should banish the awe that swept over her then. The brightest flames of Tout-Paris were ascending those stairs, in the most luminous of dresses and the sharpest of suits; eyes were already finding them, painted lips whispering about who that woman was on Arsène's arm. But she couldn't.

It wasn't a date, she reminded herself. Still, a petty little part of her hoped the smug Frenchwoman who'd been so *embarrassed* for Sam she'd had to say it twice was there to see her on Arsène Courbet's arm.

"M. Courbet," the concierge said as they approached. "Mlle St. Laurent wishes to speak with you. May I take you to her?"

"Of course," Arsène Courbet said. Then, explaining to Sam, "She is the client I told you of, and our benefactor this evening."

"Mlle St. Laurent," Sam squeaked. "Are you certain she didn't expect your attentions? I could just—"

Arsène chuckled. "Her dancing card is full. All of Tout-Paris wishes they were on her arm—or will after they see her tonight. I am merely her armorer, against the amorous hordes. She will be glad of you, believe me."

He left Sam no choice. Sam swallowed against her clambering fear, holding on to the hope that Mlle St. Laurent wouldn't recognize her.

The concierge led them up the stairs, into the grand foyer, a chamber that looked as if someone had distilled Versailles's Hall of Mirrors and infused it with music.

Chandeliers the color of antique gold hung from a ceiling painted with scenes that depicted the history of music. A clever trick of windows and mirrors created the illusion of the expansive hall and gave the gilded room a golden glow. A massive fireplace in red-and-green marble crackled at the end of the hall.

It was designed as a meeting place where paupers might mingle with princes, provided said paupers could afford the price of admission, of course, but in reality it was the salon where Tout-Paris gossiped and mingled.

They found Mlle St. Laurent at the entrance of the Salon de la Lune, luxuriant in her crowd of admirers, in a dress the color of sea glass, the hem foamy with gold. Her dark hair was cropped short and artfully disheveled, as if she'd just rolled out of bed, and her curled lips were painted the same scarlet as they had been the night before at the cabaret.

Sam braced herself as Mlle St. Laurent turned, her eyes lighting up.

"M. Courbet!" she said, parting her sea of admirers. *"Je n'osais pas espérer vous voir ce soir!"*

He took her hand, kissing it lightly. "Mlle St. Laurent, how could I not, when it was you who invited me?"

Évangéline took both Sam's hands at the fingertips. "Arsène is a true artist," she said in halting English, as if this were the first time they'd met. And Sam let out a breath. "I have tried to get dear Arsène to come for years, and this is the first he has showed up. You must be a very special person."

"She is," Arsène said gravely.

Hel snorted.

"What, you don't think I'm special?" Sam murmured, amused, as Évangéline continued her conversation with Arsène in French.

"No, no, it's not that," Hel answered, her voice low in Sam's ear. "It's just that I'm somewhat allergic to flummery."

"Flummery!" Sam protested. "Then you *don't* believe I'm special."

"For attracting a man's attention?" Hel scoffed. "Of the many things 'special' about you, that wouldn't make the top ten."

Sam flushed at the unintended significance of Hel's words. "What about for attracting *your* attention? The notorious Lady M can't possibly keep all that many people in her affections. It would ruin her reputation."

"Who says I like you?" Hel said.

Sam looked over her shoulder sharply, to find Hel smiling crookedly back at her. She swallowed a laugh.

"Vous l'avez apporté?" Évangéline was asking as they returned their attention to the conversation.

"Of course," Arsène said, switching to English. And he pulled out a bottle of perfume with Évangéline's picture painted on the front, rotating it to show the gathered men. "I have striven to capture your essence, though I am certain I have fallen short, as even the greatest of history's painters can only hint at the perfection of God's work."

Évangéline's eyes lit up, her cheeks flush, as he deposited it in her hands with a flourish.

"Ah, you are a marvel, Arsène," Évangéline cooed, before switching to French.

Sam was just about to ask Arsène what scents he'd chosen to capture Évangéline, when he touched her shoulder. Warmth bloomed from his fingertips, like flowers.

"Pardon me, Mlle St. Laurent, Mlle Harker," Arsène said apologetically. "I see more clients I must attend to."

Sam and Évangéline followed Arsène's gaze over to a woman Sam recognized from the playbill, holding court in the Salon du Soleil: Josephine Heroux, the evening's Juliette.

If Évangéline was a dark-crowned Helen of Troy, Josephine Heroux was Persephone when Hades first saw her in that garden, eyes uncertain as a fawn's, her golden curls falling down her back.

Her dress was a column of moonlight, golden vines creeping up from the hem as if they, too, craved her touch, with an overskirt like spider silk gilded with the first light of dawn.

"Look," Hel murmured, pointing with her chin. Sam followed her gaze and caught her breath. There, in Josephine Heroux's court, was the man she'd seen at the morgue on Évangéline's arm: M. Poulin, one of the most influential men in Parisian politics, and Évangéline's apparently *former* fiancé.

A look flashed over Évangéline's face, brief as a shadow. She caught Arsène's hand before it could alight on her shoulder. "Not you too, Arsène," she said softly, searching his gaze.

"Alas," Arsène said, "I cannot deny what she is."

"And what is that?"

"A queen, like yourself." Arsène stepped back, so her hand fell away. And then he was heading to the other queen's court, a gift of perfume in hand.

"I'm sorry," Sam said, not knowing what else to say.

Évangéline stared after Arsène for a moment. She turned to Sam, and seemed to see at once the way Sam looked at Arsène. Sam quickly averted her gaze.

"You are sweet, aren't you?" Évangéline said with an emotion Sam couldn't quite place. "Allow me to offer a word of counsel: never trust a man, especially a rich one. Men are like bees. They will call you their queen, offering you nectar and adulations, all while they are grooming your successor behind your back. And when her time comes, believe me, they will not hesitate to sting you and sit her on your still-warm throne."

Sam and Hel exchanged a glance, and three things occurred to her at precisely the same time. One, Évangéline knew an awful lot about bees. Two, Évangéline knew far more English than she'd let on before. Because of course she did—she was an opera

singer. Évangéline likely spoke three or four languages semiflu-
ently. That she hadn't before had been an act so as not to intimi-
date her admirers.

And three, like the people of Montmartre, Évangéline had
reason to be unhappy. Évangéline had not been born to wealth.
She depended on the kindness—or rather the want—of men for
that. And she was watching her star fall and a new star rise in
her place. Already she was to play the Nurse to her successor's
Juliette, when just last season she would have played the lead.
Her lover and benefactor had abandoned her for her rival's court.

All of which meant that Évangéline's time in Tout-Paris was
almost up, before she'd even turned thirty. And she was utterly
helpless to do anything about it.

"Thank you," Sam managed, but Évangéline had already
turned back to her admirers, tilting her head back to laugh as if
nothing had happened at all.

Sam looked back over at Arsène, to find he'd finished with
Josephine and was striding off toward a group of tall men in dark
suits by the marble fireplace. They welcomed him in with laughter and a glass of champagne. He pulled out another bottle of
perfume.

Sam felt foolish. Of course he wasn't coming back for her yet.
She should have expected as much. This was a business trip for
him, just as it was for her.

Hel leaned in to Sam and hooked her arm. "See if you can
sort out which are the mistresses."

"How?" Sam whispered back. They all looked the same—
dressed like goddesses fallen from Heaven. And she hadn't taken
into account the fact that nearly everyone wore gloves to the
opera, which meant she couldn't look for rings. Which, honestly,

should have occurred to her. There was a reason they were called *opera* gloves.

Hel raised an eyebrow. "Isn't there something about perfume or cosmetics?"

"It's the *opera*," Sam said helplessly. Even wives painted their lips and slipped into dresses that clung to them like dew. Drama was always in season at the opera. "I don't think—"

Sam cut off, frowning, as she saw a familiar figure slide past Arsène, moving toward a circle of young women gossiping amidst themselves. Lina, one of the midinettes who worked at Paquin, the one who had told Sam how no one else cared when they went missing and to bring Clotilde back safe. She was nearly unrecognizable in her own wares, dressed in chartreuse embroidered with silver, her black hair pinned in a chignon, her lips painted the same exact shade of scarlet Évangéline had worn the night prior at the cabaret.

Looking around, Sam picked out more of the midinettes, dressed in borrowed finery, clustered amongst themselves or hanging off the arms of swaggering men—their lips all painted that same shade of scarlet.

"Hel, you're brilliant," Sam breathed.

"*That* we knew already," Hel said. "Go on."

"That's Lina, the midinette who picked out the dress I wore to the cabaret." And a mistress. "Look at her lipstick."

Hel frowned. "It's red. Just like everyone else's."

"It's scarlet," Sam corrected excitedly. "The exact same shade, in fact, that Évangéline wore last night at the cabaret."

"That," Hel said frankly, "I never would have noticed."

Ordinarily, the choice of lipstick would have meant nothing. What Évangéline wore one day, everyone else wore the next—at least to the opera, where the boundaries of propriety broke down for one evening. Except that no one had been at the cabaret to see her except for midinettes and mistresses, and all the wives were still wearing burgundy.

"This is how we'll know who to watch," Sam said. "This is how we'll count the mistresses." Or rather, how Sam would. All red! As if there weren't a world of difference between burgundy and scarlet.

By the time the chimes rung out, signaling it was time for the audience to take their seats, Sam and Hel had noted two dozen young women of particular interest. It was still too many, but it was better than the hundred it had been before.

"Shall we?" Arsène Courbet offered Sam his arm. Sam startled; she'd been focusing so hard on the midinettes she'd nearly forgotten he was there.

"Is everything all right?" He lowered his voice, glancing around as if the Beast might be behind him, enjoying a bay-leaf sorbet and chatting with Évangéline St. Laurent. "Have you spotted the culprit?"

"No—I mean yes, everything's fine," Sam said.

"All right, then," he said as she rested her hand on his arm. "If you say so." He led them up the stairs to a dark wooden door with a round window like a ship's cabin.

The key turned, the door creaked open. It was as if they'd opened the door to one of the chambers of the heart. Everything was a rich, deep red: the satin walls, a floral burgundy; the carpeting, a plush carmine; the scattered chairs, sumptuous vermilion.

It was located only one floor above the stage, hidden between two columns—the perfect place to watch the audience without being seen. If the box hadn't been reserved for the phantom that haunted it every night, Sam would have expected it to be the location of the next murder. Who would hear you scream, with the orchestra wailing?

"Are you ready?" Hel murmured, eyes locked on the room. It appeared empty, but Sam knew that to be a trick. Ghosts could go unseen when they willed it—and often when they didn't.

Sam nodded, not trusting her voice. She'd never appeased a ghost before.

"Should I—" Arsène began, but Hel had entered the room. Sam shrugged at Arsène helplessly and went after Hel. After a beat, Arsène followed.

The mirror frosted as they passed. Hel knelt on the floor, pulling her gloves off with her teeth and producing a knife from one of her hidden pockets. With neat, precise cuts, she freed a few of the objects Sam had sewn into her skirts.

Sam turned to the mirror. Tentatively, she reached out with a fingertip and drew a word: *hello.*

A handprint appeared in the frosted glass, obliterating the letters. Sam looked up into the mirror to see a man behind her, his mouth opening inhumanly wide, beetles skittering—

Hel flung a handful of salt from her pocket. The ghost splintered into fragments of shadow, with a shriek Sam was fairly certain was only in her mind until she saw Arsène wince.

"She has enough men haunting her, thanks," Hel said irritably. Arsène cleared his throat awkwardly. "Find someone else."

It was only after she felt them melting down her cheeks that Sam realized tears had frozen in her eyes.

Hel knelt back down, trickling salt around her in a circle. Then five unlit tapers went inside the salt. At last, Hel gestured for Arsène and Sam to join her.

"You are not what I expected," Arsène told Sam.

"You aren't what I expected either," Sam confessed. She'd a

notion he'd be horrified—magic in any form tended to have that effect on people. But Arsène leaned forward, watching intently.

Hel drew her knife again. Arsène flinched, but Hel just nicked the pad of her middle finger. She milked blood from the cut into a silver saucer, then held up the saucer of blood.

The phantom materialized outside the salt. A tall, almost preternaturally thin man dressed in a suit and top hat, his face smeared.

"I have a bargain for you, phantom," Hel said, holding the saucer right inside the salt. The phantom swiped for it, his hand hissing into ash as it passed over the line of salt. He wailed, a high-pitched sound like the wind on the moors, a stark contrast to his appearance. "You will get your taste of life, and in turn, you will stay quiet, until the last of these candles has blown out."

The phantom hissed, the whole of his attention on the offered blood.

"Is that a yes?"

The phantom jerked his head up, and Sam swallowed a shriek. But he only nodded and held out his hand.

Hel pushed the saucer outside the circle of salt. The phantom descended on the blood, ravenous. Sam felt a tone resonate through her body, and all five candles burst into flame. By the time the note had faded, the phantom was gone, the saucer licked clean.

Sam shivered.

"You surprise me, M. Courbet," Hel admitted, standing. "Most men would have called that witchcraft."

"I'm pragmatic, Mlle Moriarty," Arsène said. "I'd rather not be eaten by a ghost. And I'm glad to have improved your opinion of me, as I suspect it is necessary if I wish to see Mlle Harker again."

Sam blushed.

"Let's not get ahead of ourselves," Hel said dryly, pulling his attention back to her. And she tossed him a book of matches. "Now, whatever you do, don't let those candles go out."

"Who, me?" Arsène said, his eyebrows rising. Hel had that effect on people. "What are *you* going to do?"

"*Sam* and I are going to stop the Beast."

CHAPTER EIGHTEEN

The Palais Garnier, Paris

The amphitheater was sumptuous—the red-velvet heart of the Palais Garnier. Five levels of seating, the walls gilded and intricately carved. A three-tier cascading crystal chandelier adorned with lyres, illuminating a ceiling like the inside of a Fabergé egg. Lavish, red velvet curtains pouring from the ceiling, rimed with antique gold.

"An illusion," Hel murmured. "It's just painted canvas." But it looked so *real*, the velvet weighty enough to smother.

From their seats in box number five, Sam and Hel could see nearly the entire ground level and, if they twisted around a bit, all the other boxes as well.

Sam scanned the shimmer of dresses, the dark patches of suits. If it was difficult to tell the mistresses from the wives in the grand foyer, it was impossible from this distance, even with the opera glasses Arsène had lent her. Instead, Sam focused on locating the boxes of the mistresses they'd already identified, knowing that it could very well be someone she'd missed, writing down the numbers in her notebook.

"If this murder follows the pattern, the mistress won't transform in sight of the audience," Hel murmured. "She and her lover will withdraw to the back of the box first, where they're out of sight."

"That doesn't give us a lot of time," Sam worried.

"No. But it's all we've got."

The lights lowered. Hel set out to close the trap of the bread wards. Once she was through, the entire auditorium would be enclosed in Moritz Knie's protection against wolves.

If they were lucky, the mistress who would become the Beast was there in the auditorium. As soon as she transformed, she would be trapped. The people could all flee, but she would not be able to escape. Theoretically, in any event—the wards hadn't protected Moritz Knie, in the end. But then, whoever had attacked him had come to him in human form; she'd seen as much in her vision.

If they were unlucky, the mistress was meeting her man outside the auditorium, in some hidden nook, where no one would hear him over the rumble of the opera. And then they might never find him, not while he was alive, for was there anywhere a besotted young fool wouldn't go, if it meant getting time alone with the object of his affections?

Sam felt a twinge in her chest. *Cyprien.* She was hardly better.

Sam didn't let herself think on it. They *had* to be successful, or else the next young woman who changed into a Beast would be murdered—and Van Helsing would probably get a promotion.

Hel returned as the music swelled and the curtains lifted.

"Any sign?" Sam whispered.

Hel shook her head, her brow furrowed.

The stage was set with Corinthian columns and false windows looking out into a painted night. Stairs on either side of the stage led to a balcony, and in the center of the stage was an enormous vase embellished with golden masks and bursting with red roses.

A masked ball in the courtyard of the Capulet palace. It felt eerily apt. They were all playing at something, weren't they? Every player on the stage and in the stands.

One of them was the alchemist.

Another was the Beast.

The music was dramatic, the clashing orchestral number giving way to flights of violins as Roméo and Juliette were drawn together and then pulled apart. The chorus sang of two houses, alike in dignity, and of ancient grudges breaking to new mutinies.

Sam kept her eyes on her boxes. Then, suddenly, one of them was empty. "Hel! I lost sight of the couple in box number twenty-seven. Is that—"

"Lina," Hel said grimly. "I'll go." Hel rose. Sam made to follow, but Hel shook her head. "Stay here. In case we're wrong."

"But I can help," Sam protested. She was a part of this, too. "I—"

Hel was already gone, disappearing into the dark like a phantom.

Sam resumed watching the boxes, returning again and again to box twenty-seven in case they reappeared.

"I thought you were partners," Arsène murmured beneath the soaring instrumentals.

"We are," Sam said. Her thoughts raced with reasons she should follow Hel.

What if Hel needed Sam's help?

What if Hel couldn't convince Lina in time?

What if the mistress was already the Beast, and she killed Hel? She could well imagine Professor Moriarty's response: *A daughter who can't survive a Beast is no daughter of mine.*

"And yet she left you behind?" he said, disapproval heavy in his tone. "What if I had ill intentions?"

Sam choked out a laugh, then looked over at him to make

sure he wasn't affronted. "That would be the least of our worries. Honestly, there's not much I could even do, were I with her. I'm not a fighter. And"—it felt a jinx to say it—"I'm hoping there won't be any fighting."

M. Courbet arched an eyebrow. "You'd spare the Beast's life? After all the lives she's taken?"

"I don't think it's her fault," Sam said, eliding the fact that there were multiple Beasts, that she was nearly certain the alchemist behind the Beast was changing the mistresses without their consent, and that Professor Moriarty was behind *him*. "But if it is, if she's doing it on purpose . . . I suppose I think she has reason to be unhappy."

A pause. "And is Mlle Moriarty of a similar mind?"

"She's the one who convinced me."

M. Courbet made a soft *hmm* in his throat.

"You have a kind heart, Mlle Harker," he said.

Juliette and Roméo were singing a duet. Their voices were so different—the bright sweetness of the lyric soprano, the smooth heat of the lyric tenor—but in this way, they complemented each other perfectly, making something new in the harmony between them. Something greater than the parts.

And Sam felt a terrible yearning in her chest, not for love— she had entirely too much to do to concern herself with love— but for such a complement. To be worthy of it.

"You and Mlle Heroux—" Sam started.

"Just business, I assure you," M. Courbet answered, and Sam bit her lip. That hadn't been what she was about to ask. He cleared his throat. "What happens if you don't catch the Beast tonight?"

"We'll be off the case." Technically, they were off the case already, only their trick with the hotel rooms had worked, and Van Helsing hadn't found them yet.

"Perhaps that isn't so bad," Arsène suggested. "This matter of the Beast—it's not for young women with kind hearts."

Sam shook her head. "You don't understand. Van Helsing— the man they're sending in our place—he won't see it the same way we do. He'll *kill* the Beast and consider it a job well done."

There was a pause. "Ah," he conceded. "That *is* unfortunate."

Josephine Heroux next took the stage in a white ballet dress, her lips painted rose, her eyelids starlit grey. She danced alone in the darkness, small on the empty stage, until at last, Roméo appeared to answer her, turning to Juliette like she was the sun.

A feeling shivered through Sam then like the breath of winter, every hair on Sam's body standing up at once. And suddenly, Sam could *see* blood trickling down the curves of Josephine Heroux's cheeks, the same way it had trickled down Clotilde's, the same way it had trickled down Sam's in her dream last night. Like tears.

A vision.

"Oh *no*," Sam said, standing up. It wasn't real, she knew it wasn't real. But it would be, if she didn't do something about it. The scent of burning bread swirled around her like the ghost of Moritz Knie. "No no no no no."

M. Courbet's brow furrowed. "What's wrong? Are you all right? Should I fetch a doctor?"

"I need you to find Dr. Moriarty as fast as you can," Sam said, her words tumbling from her mouth almost faster than she could form them. "Tell her the Beast isn't in the audience. Tell her—" She couldn't make herself say that the Beast was Josephine Heroux. "Just tell her to come as quickly as she can!"

"You can't be serious," M. Courbet objected. "Dr. Moriarty should never have abandoned you, but seeing as she has, I can't possibly leave you *alone*—"

"Please," Sam begged. "We don't have much time."

M. Courbet looked as if he would protest further, but something in her voice must have convinced him, for he nodded tightly and left.

Sam stole a glance back at the stage, at the bloody tears running down Josephine's face, and her eyes caught at last on the piece she'd been missing this whole time.

The unguent. It wasn't lipstick or perfume—Heathcliff had given proof to that.

It was *eyeshadow.* That shimmery grey eyeshadow. How had she not seen it before?

The police had a theory. They thought the murderer would come to see his work. And who had been there but Évangéline St. Laurent, watching in fascination as Sam scratched a dead man's words into the frost?

Évangéline had been at the cabaret as well, the midinettes crowding around her, their faces painted reflections of Évangéline's. It would have been easy to convince one of them to wear the grey eyeshadow. It would have been an honor.

And Évangéline had reason to be unhappy—she had told Sam never to trust a man, especially not a rich one. Her star was falling in favor of Josephine Heroux, a woman who had not only stolen the role of Juliette from her, but also the affections of her fiancé, M. Poulin.

Here was a woman with a great deal of anger at men—particularly at men who were rich . . . and unfaithful.

The man behind the Beast, slipping unguent into eyeshadow to transform mistresses into murderers—it wasn't a man at all.

It was *Évangéline.* Or at least, she was a part of it. Whether she was the alchemist herself or not remained to be seen.

Oh, one of these days, Sam was going to have to stop underestimating women!

Josephine Heroux let out a terrible cry and convulsed. Sam's hands gripped the railing so hard her knuckles went white, but the crowd was calm as fur shivered over the singer's limbs, bones shifting, pressing against her skin, making tents and hollows of her flesh.

It's just the vision, Sam told herself. *It's not real.* She still had time before it became reality.

Sam stole a glance back at the doors, but of course Hel wasn't back, and Arsène had just left.

The vision that followed wasn't so much a transformation as an unleashing, as if the singer's rib cage had cracked open, the wolf pouring out in a rippling of muscles and fury, tearing the shell of the young woman apart as easily as her dress.

The Beast's lambent eyes raked her admirers, and she let out a cry of rage and fear, the voices of woman and wolf twining with each other as Roméo's and Juliette's had moments ago.

To Sam's horror, an answering howl echoed in her own chest, as if there were a wolf inside her too, a rage so incandescent it couldn't possibly be hers. Quick-fingered, she folded her feelings back up before she could know them, and stuffed them back in the locked box of her heart until it ached.

A fear filled her then, not of the Beast, but of what was inside her—what the monsters were making of her, that she might identify with that *rage*.

This was what happened to channels. Channels got visions from monsters, and those visions led them astray. And if they were not careful, then everyone they cared for would suffer for it.

And Sam had been anything but careful.

Oh, Mary, Mother of God, Sam couldn't do this. She couldn't.

Hel had trusted Sam to handle this, but if Sam's visions were true—if Josephine transformed into the Beast—there was nothing Sam could do.

Hel. She needed Hel. She would know what to do.

Sam turned to run.

Shoot her.

Sam stopped in her tracks, her hand on the doorknob. The voice was low and sweet, the kind of voice Sam imagined talked Eve into that apple.

This, Sam thought, was not the time for strange voices. She turned the knob and flung open the door.

Shoot her, before she transforms, before it's too late.

The image of Cyprien's hand reaching out of the rubble flooded her mind. Visions playing in her head of Hel shooting and failing to stop the Beast, of Hel with her eyes hollowed and her lungs pulled out, her hand reaching for Sam, all because Sam wouldn't shoot.

It's just a vision, Sam told herself for a second time. It's not real.

But it would be. And Sam couldn't lose someone again. Not when she could stop it.

You're the only one who can save her.

Sam's hands found the revolver Hel had strapped to her thigh, beneath the cloud of her skirts. She slipped it loose. It was heavier than she'd expected, cold and unforgiving.

Sam closed her eyes, her breath fast in her throat. There was no practical way Sam could do this. She hadn't been able to so much as graze the target at the shooting range—this was so much farther than forty paces, and the target anything but still.

This is not the time to find out you don't have what it takes!

Sam raised the revolver and took trembling aim before giving a little cry and pulling the revolver back down.

She couldn't do it, she couldn't make herself shoot, no matter what the visions showed her. Sam didn't want to shoot Josephine Heroux; she wanted to save her. She was as much a victim in all this as the man she'd murder.

Now! the voice commanded. *You have to shoot her now!*

Her visions had never steered her wrong. But this—this was not a normal vision. It was practically an illusion, the way it claimed her senses. Her visions were getting stronger. The thought knotted in her gut.

A compromise then: She wouldn't shoot Josephine Heroux. She would shoot to get everyone's attention, to make them listen. Then Sam could tell Hel what she'd seen, and Hel would know what to do.

Sam raised her revolver high, but not so high as to catch the chandelier, and pulled the trigger.

The retort was swallowed in the swell of sound, the recoil sending her bullet wild, ricocheting off something in the dark to hit the enormous rose-filled vase. It shattered with a crack, taking the vision of the Beast with it and leaving behind only a horrified Josephine Heroux, roses raining down around her, petals scattering over the stage like blood.

The crowd was in an uproar. The revolver slipped from her fingers.

The door to the box slammed open and a man rammed into her from behind, arms wrapped around her, bearing her to the ground. Another scooped up her revolver.

"Hel!" Sam cried, her heart pounding painfully. "Hel, it's in the eyeshadow—"

The man shoved her face into the plush red carpet. Sam could taste blood. And suddenly, she realized what it must have looked like to everyone else: Sam pulling a revolver from her skirts and shooting not at the ceiling, but at Josephine Heroux.

"Je la tiens!" the man holding her down shouted. Tout-Paris craned their necks from their boxes, trying to catch a glimpse of Sam pinned to the carpet in champagne chiffon.

The doors opened, and Sam heard the clink of American-style cowboy boots on the floor, could see the hardware and pointed toes, the sun-kissed bronze scales too large to have come from any terrestrial lizard. Jingling with every step. Sam knew those boots.

Van Helsing.

No, Sam thought impotently. But of course she had *known* Van Helsing would track them down, had known it was only a matter of time before he realized their trick and found the right hotel, before he asked reception about Sam and they remembered she'd inquired about the opera.

Now she'd shot at the stage, and Hel wasn't there, and no one was listening to her.

"It's her eyeshadow—!" Sam cried. "It's—"

The man holding her cursed, and pushed her head down into the carpet until she couldn't draw breath.

When at last he let up—just enough for her to breathe—Sam gasped in air.

Arsène Courbet was by Van Helsing's side, his tie askew, his forehead slick with sweat. It lent the sunflowers of his cologne a strange, sharp note of desperation, like an animal hunted. Hel was nowhere to be found.

"Arsène—" Sam pleaded. His gaze fell to her, flooding with horror as if *she* were the Beast, and she felt as if she would collapse in on herself in shame. "Tell *her.*"

He flinched.

"What's going on in here?" Van Helsing demanded. He didn't sound mad about it so much as eerily calm. As if all this time he'd been waiting for Sam to prove herself the monster he knew her to be, and finally she'd cracked. "Why is Miss Harker being restrained?"

A dozen voices tried to answer in French, until one of the police officers stepped forward.

"She drew a revolver and shot at the stage," the officer said. "It's unclear who she was shooting at—"

"It was perfectly clear!" a waspish voice said in unsteady English. It was an older woman who had been sitting in the box to her right, who had fixed her with the evil eye when she'd shouted for Hel. She threw up gloved hands. "She wanted to kill our Juliette. She shot right at her!"

"I didn't—"

Sam cut off with a gasp as the man holding her twisted her arm harder, until she was silent. *"Ferme-la."* Tears stung her eyes.

M. Courbet went ashen. "Mlle Harker questioned me earlier. She wanted to know whether I was interested in Mlle Heroux, whether she should be jealous."

Sam's face flamed with the implications. An eager murmur eddied across Tout-Paris. The jealous lover. The beautiful siren. An omen of death followed by attempted murder. It would be the story of the night.

"Sir," the police officer said warily. "We must arrest her for attempted murder. Take her to prison."

"Of course," Van Helsing said, not taking his eyes from Sam. She saw the tension leave the police officer. "She tried to kill an innocent woman. The Society won't stand in the way of justice."

"Thank you for being so understanding," the police officer said.

"It's only right." Van Helsing clapped the police officer on the back. "I'll be honest with you: we never should have sent women to do a man's—"

Hel pushed open the doors looking like an angel of death. Van Helsing nearly swallowed his tongue. Relief poured into Sam; Hel was here. At last, Sam wasn't alone.

"Hel—!"

The man holding her twisted her arm again, and Sam hissed and fell silent. Hel walked right past Sam, turning to face the police officers.

"Ah, Miss Moriarty—" Van Helsing began formally.

"*Dr.* Helena Moriarty," Hel cut him off. Her voice was dispassionate, clinical, the curiosity Sam had come to expect pulled from it like color from the night. It was as if she were an entirely different person. Except Hel was terrible at pretending to be someone she wasn't—she'd nearly blown their cover on the way to Montmartre with her bad acting.

Was this, then, the real Hel? Had she lied about being bad at lying?

It sounded like the kind of thing her father would do. The same father who had ordered Hel to sacrifice Sam if she wanted to regain control of the board. And while Hel did not answer to her father, she'd proved time and time again that she was her father's daughter.

A calculated sacrifice, so Hel could stay in the game.

A cold hand closed around her heart as she recalled just how much she'd confided in Hel.

You have to promise me, Sam had said before confessing her visions to Hel. *Promise me you won't tell anyone what I'm about to tell you.*

"Don't," Sam heard herself beg. Don't tell them. Don't turn on me. Don't be the villain everyone said you were. Except she wouldn't be the villain, would she? She'd be the hero. "Please."

Hel made no sign of having heard her, instead addressing the police. "Mr. Van Helsing asked me to keep an eye on Miss Harker out of concern that she might be channeling."

No. A ringing filled her ears as Sam stared at Hel, willing her to take the words back, to laugh, to cut Van Helsing down to size, the way she always had before. Hel's lips parted—

"Yes," Van Helsing admitted slowly, frowning. "Though I can't say I approve of your methods. I could have sworn—"

"They were effective, weren't they?" Hel's voice cut through Sam's hopes like a knife. This couldn't be happening, this was *wrong.* Sam knew Hel, and this wasn't her. "More flies with honey, and all that."

This whole time . . . Hel had been working for Van Helsing? The awful things Van Helsing had said about Hel nothing but misdirection to, what, incline Sam to trust Hel? To befriend her?

Heaven help Sam, but it had worked.

"How could you?" The words were out of Sam's throat before she could catch them. She was embarrassed, it was embarrassing, on the floor in front of all these people, but somehow the only person in the room who mattered right then was Hel. And Sam couldn't bring herself to fold back into the little box she'd lived in before she'd met Hel, to be the person who could talk her way out of this, if that person even existed at all. "I *trusted* you!"

"And I appreciated your trust," Hel said, tossing Sam an unreadable look.

Appreciated my trust? Sam had stood up to Mr. Wright for

Hel, had risked her career by lying for Hel when he'd found reason to accuse her of treason. She'd told Hel . . . everything, things she hadn't even admitted to herself, and Hel *appreciated her trust?*

A growl rose from somewhere deep within her chest.

Surprising even herself, Sam surged at Hel—thinking to . . . she didn't know what, but something—only to collapse as the man restraining her yanked her back down. The carpet ground into her cheek, Sam helpless to do more than glare at Hel.

This wasn't the way the story was supposed to end. For the first time in Sam's life, she hadn't been alone. She'd been with someone who'd seen her, understood her, even liked her, because of and not despite the parts of her that usually drove people away. And in the end, Hel had betrayed her, the way everyone had always said she would.

To think, Sam had regaled Hel with the benefits of pretending to be someone else, never knowing Hel had been doing it the whole time.

Sam never should have stopped pretending. Never should have taken off her mask. Tears leaked between her lashes. Sam turned her face so Hel couldn't see them.

"Well then," Van Helsing said, his blue eyes glittering with anticipation. He'd been waiting for this moment since he was fifteen and they'd been whispering to each other at a Society party. No, since that day in the forest, when he'd run. "What is your recommendation?"

"When you reached out to me, you requested proof that Miss Harker was acting on her visions," Hel said. "I think this evening's events should suffice, don't you?"

"We can't just let her go," the officer said stubbornly.

"Of course not," Hel said. "I wouldn't dream of asking. Merely to sharpen your aim. Miss Harker is not a murderer, she's a broken channel. Take her to the Salpêtrière. They have the means to deal with her kind there."

The police officer nodded slowly and looked to Van Helsing, who also nodded, then said, "Well done . . . partner."

The Salpêtrière.

The asylum.

CHAPTER NINETEEN

The Salpêtrière, Paris

Sam lay on a steel-frame bed, in the darkness, in a cell that, for all the walls were papered and the floor tiled, reminded her more of the catacombs than any place meant for the living. Her cell was otherwise bare—she'd checked, walking the circumference, one hand trailing on the wallpaper, the path worn smooth with the ghosts of women past.

As asylums went, the Gunpowder Hospital was not the worst. Located in the southeasternmost part of Paris, it was one of the most extensive establishments of its kind in all Europe, staffed by caretakers with a reputation for being compassionate and gentle. Those who proved themselves capable of nonviolence were allowed to wander the village-like complex as they willed, so long as they never left. It even had a chapel—Sam could hear the bells tolling every hour.

Of course, it hadn't always been so. There were whispers of years past, when the women of the Salpêtrière had been kept in shackles, tormented in the name of science, and gawked at by the rest of society who found their vulnerability titillating.

But by 1903 the Salpêtrière was, in many respects, a refuge from society. The focus was on psychology, and tourists weren't permitted. The patients—then as now—were mostly the women whom society didn't care for anymore. Women society deemed hysterical or unfit by their husbands, elderly women with no one else to care for them, impoverished women seeking an escape from violence and exploitation, and, of course, broken channels.

The Salpêtrière was *safe*, and therefore it wasn't the worst. But it was also in France, when Sam spoke little French, and Sam was still a prisoner.

So she hadn't struggled as they led her to the carriage that would take her to the Salpêtrière. Nor as they led her to her cell— the window shuttered and barred, the heavy door locked. Only when Hel had tried to say good-bye, grabbing at her hand, did she act.

"I should never have trusted you," she'd whispered poisonously.

"I promised," Hel had reminded her meaningfully.

Sam snatched her hand away. "I wish you hadn't."

Darkness and solitude, they said, would quiet her mind. But they didn't. Instead, her thoughts raced like horses in the night, going through every conversation, every confession she'd made to Hel.

Do you need to touch things to get these feelings of yours? Hel had asked.

Yes, she'd answered. And it had been true. But last night Sam had touched nothing at all.

Sam had seen her diagnosis. A broken channel, they were calling her. Her mother had warned her. *Trust in the rules. They will keep you safe.*

It was a terrible thing, having your reality questioned, because it wasn't just her visions: it was everything. Every waking moment. Every assumption. It felt as if her world were unraveling stitch by stitch.

Sam had been so certain of what she'd seen: that Josephine Heroux would be that evening's Beast, that Évangéline St. Laurent was the monster behind it, that the iridescent grey eyeshadow was the unguent.

Sam had shot at the stage because the visions had told her it was the only way to save Hel's life and because her visions had always proved true, and then everything had gone wrong.

It felt, awfully, like her own mind had betrayed her. But that was what happened to channels, wasn't it? They had visions that led them astray. Hel might even have been right to betray her, to send her here, where she couldn't harm anyone else. Sam had, after all, asked Hel to stop her, should she turn monstrous.

Sam simply hadn't believed it would happen.

Sam pressed the heels of her palms into her eyes. How many of her visions were even true? All Sam and Hel's leads, all their discoveries, hinged on her visions. If Sam's visions weren't true, none of it was.

If Sam's visions weren't true, they had no idea who the killer might be.

— —

In the morning, Sam was given a generous portion of bread and butter and soft-boiled eggs.

But no sooner had she taken a bite than the door opened a second time. She squinted against the light as what looked like a new set of clothes was tossed in, landing on the floor of her cell.

Her chewing slowed, her world narrowing to that slice of

light pouring from the door. She scrambled over to the clothes, licking the yolk from her fingers as the door closed, taking the light with it. Sam felt at the pile in the dark, making out a simple chemise, corset, and overdress.

"Hello? Is anyone there?" She hammered on the door, frustration lighting up her veins. "How do you expect me to do anything in the dark?"

"They don't," a muffled voice said in the cell to her left.

"I'm sorry," Sam said automatically, sitting back on her heels. "I just thought—"

"Do you always think with your mouth?" the woman snapped, and this time, Sam caught a whiff of perfume through the cracks in the walls—thick and green as if she knelt in a tropical garden instead of on the hardwood floor of her shuttered cell. "How embarrassing for you."

A shock of recognition went through her. "I know you."

There was a pause. "You must be mistaken."

She wasn't. This was real, and she clung to it. "I asked you about perfumers, at the Gare Saint-Lazare. You recommended Arsène Courbet." She had claimed he wouldn't see Sam—that he only worked on canvases displayed in the right places.

A dismissive snort. "So would anyone. He's the *only* perfumer in Paris worth mentioning."

Sam hadn't seen the other woman at the opera. It wasn't something to be proud of, but she'd *looked*, hoping the woman would see Sam on Arsène Courbet's arm. But while all Tout-Paris had turned out in their glittering best, she had been nowhere to be found.

"Why are you here?" Sam asked, before she could think better of it. It was as if being imprisoned had undone what remaining shreds of restraint she had left.

A strangled laugh. "You can't just ask someone why they've gone mad." Not a broken channel then. Broken channels were corrupt, but they weren't mad. Not precisely.

"Are you?" Sam asked. "Mad, that is?"

"What does it matter?" the voice said coolly. "Everyone else thinks I am."

If everyone else thought you were mad—did it matter that you weren't? Reality was built on a foundation of stories, everyone's interwoven together. Always before, Sam had walked the strands of other people's truths, careful not to catch herself in society's web.

Until Hel.

Feelings Sam wasn't prepared to deal with threatened, rolling within her like a black and shipwrecked sea.

"It matters to me," Sam said evenly.

The other woman seemed to think about this for a moment. "You're very strange."

"So I'm told," Sam said. She was, at this point, resigned to it.

They were both quiet for a few moments, and Sam had expected that to be the end of the unfortunate business of their conversation. But then the woman's voice came again, slipping through the cracks in the wall like a mouse: "Marcelline Frossard."

"I'm sorry?" Sam said.

"My name," Mme Frossard repeated. "I assume you're acquainted with the concept? If we're going to be shouting at each other through the wall, we should at least do it properly."

Sam warmed. She leaned against the wall, tipping her head back. "Samantha—"

"Harker," a new voice said, stealing the words from her mouth. The new voice was coming from outside her cell; Sam recognized it from the night before. One of the caretakers, then.

The key was jangling in the lock. The door opened, and Sam had to squint against the light. A woman dressed in the hospital's black and white frowned down at her. "Get changed."

"With you watching?" Sam said incredulously.

"Now," the woman said. "The doctor is ready for you, and he has a very busy schedule."

A frisson of fear skittered over her nerves.

"Of course," Sam said, changing just as quickly as she could, her cheeks burning under the weight of the caretaker's gaze.

"Follow me."

The caretaker scooped up her clothing and led her out of the strange locked hallway she was in—the ward for broken channels and hysterical patients with violent tendencies—and into another building entirely. There, she was led through a large room fitted with dozens of hardwood chairs around a clear central space, like a lecture hall. Lining the wall were paintings of doctors demonstrating the fainting and the fury of broken channels before crowds of curious men.

Sam balked, sure for a moment she would be part of the show. That people were going to be invited to watch as the doctor articulated all the things that were wrong with her, peeling back her flesh to reveal the corruption of her soul.

But the caretaker led Sam through a door in the back, heels clicking on the hardwood. The good doctor was waiting in a well-appointed office, the walls covered in framed photographs and diplomas and shelves of medical texts.

The doctor himself was young—practically her age, which was as unwelcome as it was unexpected. He sat behind a heavy wooden desk, his hands steepled like a caricature of a much older man. His hair was curly and brown, his nose slightly crooked, and his suit of a traditional Parisian make, freshly purchased—she could still see the creases where it had been folded.

The doctor gestured for her to take a seat on the divan.

The caretaker left, closing the door behind her; chaperones were only for women with honor left to lose. The doctor leaned forward.

"Miss Harker," the doctor said. His eyes had an intentness to them that itched at the back of her mind—familiar, somehow. "I'm glad to be making your acquaintance at last. I'm Dr. Morgan."

"You're not French?" Sam said, startled.

Dr. Morgan smiled crookedly. "I'm on loan from Wales. We thought you might be more comfortable with someone who speaks English."

Her eyes flicked to the diplomas on the wall—the Cardiff University School of Medicine, Wales. The black-and-white photographs of the doctor and his colleagues at what looked to be a university campus, not looking much younger than he was today.

"But we're not here to talk about me," Dr. Morgan said, withdrawing a journal and pen to make a note, probably about her paranoia. "We're here to talk about you. Why don't you tell me what happened last night?"

Sam sat very still as the black sea welled again, and she tasted salt. "I'm sure you've heard it from the police."

"We are trying to get a look inside your mind, my dear Miss Harker," Dr. Morgan said. "To find out why the monsters have found their way in. It is the only way we shall ever uncover how to shut them out again. So, if it's not too much trouble, I'd like to hear it from you."

Sam could do this. She just had to be normal. She could do normal. She'd been quite good at normal once. She wet her lips and really looked at him—at the part he expected her to play. But of course, the doctor expected her to be a broken channel, and she couldn't play that part. It would only seal her fate.

She had to prove him wrong.

"I asked M. Courbet to the opera," Sam said slowly, measuring each word out twice before she gave it breath. "He accepted. Dr. Moriarty went with me as my chaperone."

Dr. Morgan made a note in his book. "But you weren't there to see the opera, were you?"

"No," Sam admitted. "We—that is, Dr. Moriarty and I—were there on behalf of the Royal Society for the Study of Abnormal Phenomena. We hoped to catch the Beast."

"Catch. Ah, right. I understand you sympathize with the Beast." He flipped through his notes, read a line. "That you believe she has reason to be upset."

He must have talked to Arsène—because of course he had. The black waters surged within her again. Sam swallowed against the sea, trying to keep from drowning.

"I sympathize with a great many people."

"Just not Josephine Heroux," Dr. Morgan pointed out. "Why did you shoot at Mlle Heroux, Miss Harker?"

"I didn't!"

But the memories kept slipping between her teeth.

Mlle Heroux in that white ballet dress—

Blood dripping down her cheeks like tears—

Fur shivering over her limbs—

Bones making tents and hollows of her skin—

"A concert hall full of people beg to differ," he said gravely. And his words—oh, they were the current, the way they kept pulling her under. "In addition to a revolver with your fingerprints on it."

The gun in her hand, and the voice in her ear.

"I did shoot, but not at her."

Dr. Morgan raised an eyebrow. "You missed her by *inches*."

The illusion shattering with her bullet, rose petals raining down—

That unreadable look in Hel's eyes as she turned Sam in.

Maybe Sam *was* a broken channel. Maybe this was where she belonged. And suddenly, Sam was tired of pretending.

"You don't know what it's like," she found herself saying. She was crying; when had she started crying?

"Help me to understand," Dr. Morgan said intently.

"At first my visions were just . . . things I felt, glimpses of the past. I didn't want to believe them, but they were always right. So when I started *seeing* things . . ." Sam swallowed. She still couldn't tell him about the possession. It seemed too obvious that she should have known that was wrong. "At first it seemed an advantage. But then last night . . ."

Everything had gone wrong, and Sam had become the monster Van Helsing had always known her for.

"And what did Miss Moriarty think of all this?" Dr. Morgan said, his voice soft.

Sam looked up, confused. "You—you want to know what Dr. Moriarty thinks?" She was reminded, oddly, of Mr. Wright, when she'd tried to tell him about the grindylow and he'd swerved the conversation to Hel, seemingly out of nowhere. As if grindylows being sold to brigands were of no concern.

"I'm just trying to understand," he soothed. He offered her his pocket handkerchief. "What did she tell you about the things you saw? It's important."

The itch of familiarity blossomed into suspicion. *It couldn't be.*

Sam reached forward and took the offered handkerchief—

creased and new as the rest of his clothing, as if he knew of her gift and didn't want her to glean any memories from it—and extended her fingers at the last moment, brushing his hand.

Sam gasped, her bones shivering, and suddenly she could *feel* the buzz of bees vibrating the air around her. She breathed in and her lungs filled with smoke and something resinous—

Dr. Morgan withdrew his hand quickly, but it was too late. Bees. A smoker. Shellac.

This vision felt different from the one she'd had the night before at the opera. It was a *feeling*, a collection of sensations that were, rather than a moving picture of things that *might be*. There were no voices trying to convince her it was true, and yet it resonated in her bones, as if it came from within rather than without.

It felt, for lack of a better word, *true*.

Sam began to see patterns in her visions. In her earliest visions, she brushed her fingers over an object and got a *feeling*, experiencing sensations from the object's past, sightless as Tiresias. This was what had happened when she'd touched the severed arm in the suitcase and felt the man's death as if it were her own, and again when she'd touched the garnet between the cushions, the slip of silk caught on the window frame, M. Barrere's cold dead fingers.

Occasionally, Sam had flashes of uncanny insights, but they were neither literal nor lingering. The bloody newspaper she'd seen in the streets of Paris. The skulls in the secret passage from Lapérouse. The bloody tears running down Clotilde's cheeks.

But the vision she'd had of Mlle Heroux hadn't been a *feeling* at all, but a moving picture, showing her a literal vision of the future that had seemed to go on and on. And Sam had hesitated, for she hadn't believed it, not in her bones.

A moving picture that had smelled, incongruently, of burning bread. Just like in the catacombs, when she'd touched the Wolfssegner's book and seen bread oozing blood and finger bones—which was doubly odd, seeing as those images were precisely what Sam had invented when she'd tried to imagine what she might see if the Wolfssegner was guilty, before she'd ever gone to the catacombs or known about the Wolfssegner's book.

Ice crystallized up her spine.

False visions.

Sam had known from the start it was a possibility. This was what monsters did, as Van Helsing was so fond of reminding her, they sent you visions and led you astray.

Only these false visions were not from monsters. A false vision from a monster would be indistinguishable from a true vision. That was why they were so dangerous, why it was so easy for a channel to fall into temptation. To *break*.

Which meant whoever was sending Sam false visions was *human*. All to do what, break her sense of reality? To imprison her?

Sam thought about the bees and the book cipher, about what Hel had said in the Cabaret du Néant regarding her father and the way he undermined her expectations, her trust that what she saw was real, so that he might supplant her reality with his own. About the man her father sent in whenever he needed to act directly, a man who did not officially exist.

About her *brother*.

Sam sat back, eyes dry. "You're not a doctor."

"The other doctors and caretakers here would beg to differ," the man said, as if this were an amusement between the two of them.

"They're not looking," Sam agreed, and now that *she* was, she could see it, even without her vision. Like a changeling, he just wasn't quite right. "You are not a decade older than the man in those ten-year-old photographs—"

He chuckled. "Why, thank you. I'm telling you, cold cream will be all people talk of in the future—"

"And yet your hairline is different," Sam pressed, even more certain now that he was deflecting her. She was right; she *knew* she was right. She couldn't let him throw her off. She would wrap both hands around her reality, and not let it go for anything. "You have a mole on your neck that isn't in your pictures—"

"My, do you think it's cancerous?"

Sam's fingernails bit into her palms. He still wasn't taking this seriously—wasn't taking *her* seriously. He'd probably killed the doctor whose place he took, she realized. He'd *killed* to have this audience with Sam, and now he was refusing to be straight with her.

"Why are you here?" Sam demanded. "You've already won. You've silenced the six loudest voices in the efforts against the shadow market—as well as for the separation of church and state, if your father ever even cared, if this wasn't always just business. You told Hel to give me up and she has. I'm locked away, Hel is alone, and the investigation into your crimes is closed. What more does Professor Moriarty want?"

He didn't speak this time, he just leveled a disappointed look at her that sent a small voice inside her into whispering that she was wrong, that Sam herself had just admitted she had a hard time telling reality from whatever fancies the monsters sent her, that she was making a fool of herself. Again.

But the voice didn't sound like her own—it didn't resonate in her gut—so she set her jaw and lifted her chin. "Well, Ruari?"

At last, the man who would be Dr. Morgan closed his

notebook over his pen and set it aside, then removed his glasses.

"I'm impressed," said Ruari, and his accent melted away to something very like Hel's. And despite the danger she was in, Sam felt a small thrill; she'd been right. "You're clever, probably cleverer than most people give you credit for. I can see why my sister likes you—why she tried to keep you from us. And she must like you, if she told you about *me*."

Except Hel had been hunting her brother from the start—she must have been. Ever since she'd asked where a well-heeled man would buy a suit. A traditional, Parisian suit like the one across from her, creases still fresh.

All of which meant Hel had *known* her brother was involved, had seen what happened when she left Sam in the dark, and still she hadn't told her.

"To answer your question," Ruari continued, "Father is not *unsympathetic* to the Catholic cause, but yes, this is just business. And perhaps a matter of . . . motivation."

Professor Moriarty might not care about the people of Montmartre, or the separation of church and state—but the fact that others did? Certainly made it easier to get people like Eulalie and the Wolves of God to do what he wanted.

"And Hel?" Sam pushed.

"I won't deny that the opportunity to outplay my sister once again isn't motivating, but she picked this fight, not me." Ruari shrugged. "I will never understand her. Why bother running away at all, if you're only going to obsess over us?"

"The way I understand it," Sam said, "you never gave her a chance to get away."

Ruari snorted. "Only because my sister cares more about her pride than her freedom. If she had failed and Father had kicked her out, that would be one thing, but my sister *left*. Turned her back on him. Now she will never be free. She will be alone, without allies or lovers or friends, until the day she comes home. Father will make sure of it."

Sam's heart squeezed. Oh, *Hel*. Was this why she had given Sam up? Because she didn't believe she had a choice? Because her father had conditioned her to believe that everyone she loved would be taken from her?

It still wasn't fair to Sam. But . . .

"But this isn't about my family," Ruari continued. "This is about yours. Tell me, Miss Harker, do you want to see your grandfather?"

Sam felt as if she'd been struck. "I visit his *grave*."

"My sister told you about me, and not him?" Ruari said. "I'm sorry, I just assumed. It was your radiotelegraph she used to send the, what, two messages asking after him? I hope she's not expecting an answer from her friend. My family doesn't tolerate disloyalty, as everyone in our employ well knows."

"You're lying," Sam said reflexively. But Hel had sent at least two telegrams, Sam knew she had. And Hel had told her of how her friends had all betrayed her in the past, how she'd confided in them and they'd reported her secrets to her father. And still, Hel had tried, for Sam. "If my grandfather were alive, he would have visited, or sent a telegram, or—"

"Written the same Morse code numbers that had been coming in through your grandfather's radiotelegraph the day he disappeared on the side of a building in Paris, near a grisly paranormal murder for which the Society was sure to be called in?" Ruari supplied.

"What? No, that's absurd," Sam said. Though now that she thought of it, the chances that her grandfather's numbers would be exactly the same as those used to order murder at a specific date and place in Paris were infinitesimally low. She should have known it for a trap. "I meant he might post a letter."

"And yet it *is* why you left the library for the field, isn't it?" Ruari said. "Do you want to know what it means?"

Sam's mouth went dry. Her grandfather's numbers. Here were the answers to everything she'd sought for the last ten years. "Yes," she whispered, and even that felt like a betrayal of Hel.

Hel had betrayed her already, Sam reminded herself.

Ruari smiled, sharp as the edge of a knife. "It was an invitation, much like yours, except he understood it. He came to us *willingly*, and faked his own death so no one would look for him."

"I don't believe you," Sam said instinctively, but deep inside, the answer fit. He'd always been secretive, relaying strange messages across the world in Morse code.

The night he disappeared, he had left the radiotelegraph where Sam would find it—where she would hear those numbers. Was this part of the plan, even then? Pulling Sam into the fold?

Sam swallowed. It was too much. She couldn't fit the questions inside her head, let alone make room for the answers.

"What would you have done if I hadn't noticed the numbers?" Sam asked.

"Well, then you wouldn't be worth the trouble of claiming, would you?" Ruari said. It was a test, Sam thought dizzily, it had all been a test. "Don't give yourself so much credit. You were never the point of this endeavor—you're just a bonus. And if we'd sent a letter, you wouldn't have come. Not without telling entirely too many people, and not at all if you knew Father was involved."

"Don't pretend you know me," Sam said sharply.

"I don't have to. Your grandfather has told me everything about you," Ruari said. "I know that you have a scar on your left calf from a púca when the trap you built actually worked—you were five years old and needed seven stitches. I know you had a fever when you were eight, and that your grandfather kept you from crying by reading from a book of Greek myths, and that after you'd recovered, you made your classmates call you Circe, the witch of Aeaea, for a solid six weeks.

"I know that you are a channel," he went on, "that it was magnified by the vampiric influence over your mother during her pregnancy. That your mind is peculiarly receptive, like the radio-telegraphs you so treasure. And that you cannot tell the difference between the false visions and the real.

"And, Miss Harker, I know you need help," Ruari finished.

"What, and you're the one to give it?" Sam said incredulously. After everything he'd done to her?

"Don't let propaganda cloud your mind," Ruari said. "We are more aligned in our beliefs than you think. We have a library you wouldn't believe; we're always in need of good researchers. We will always be there to tell you what to believe, and what to ignore. We can help you. *Trust me.*"

Sam would be lying to herself if she didn't admit that she was tempted, despite everything. It would be so much easier if someone just told her what was right and what was wrong. If she didn't have to constantly try and fail and reexamine and strive as people shouted at her that she shouldn't pay attention to the things she saw even if they might prove true, even if they might save someone's life. It would be so much easier to just supplant her reality with their own.

She could be useful. She could be wanted. She could stop fighting, and just *be.*

But that wouldn't really be living, would it? And at her core, it wasn't what *she* wanted.

Which was why, when he reached out his hand magnani-mously, as if he truly expected her to take it, Sam couldn't help but feel that he was, at that moment, perhaps the greatest ass on the planet, which was saying something.

"No," Sam said. It was true that she'd set out from her be-loved library at the barest shred of hope of finding out what had happened to her grandfather. But since then, she'd braved grin-dylows and carcolhs and phantoms and Lady M herself. She'd set herself on fire, gotten lost in the mines beneath the streets of Paris, and followed wills-o'-the-wisp to a secret laboratory. She'd watched a man die and almost died herself. She'd found the an-swer to her grandfather's disappearance: Professor Moriarty.

A part of her still wanted to see her grandfather more than anything. He had been the only person besides Hel who had ever seen Sam's visions as something other than a curse, for all it hadn't endeared him to Sam's parents. But then he'd left with-out saying a word—leaving her to grieve for *ten years*, visiting his grave every February, on the anniversary of that day, of those numbers. She didn't know whether to hope he'd left under du-ress or by choice. Either way, if he was working with Professor Moriarty . . .

Sam wasn't ready to see him. "Not like this."

Ruari leaned back, looking disappointed but not surprised.

"Think about it." Ruari rapped the desk with his knuckles. "We have all the time in the world." Without taking his eyes from her, he called the caretaker back in.

The door opened at once. "Yes, Doctor?"

"You can take her back now," Ruari said. "Darkness and soli-tude still, I'm afraid. She's not ready yet."

CHAPTER TWENTY

The Salpêtrière, Paris

It was raining.

Sam was pacing in her darkened cell, trying not to listen to the rain, to her grandfather's numbers *tap-tap-tapping*.

Her grandfather, who was still alive. Her grandfather, who was working for Professor Moriarty—whether of his own accord or by force.

Sam needed to get out of there. She needed to tell someone about Évangéline St. Laurent, and about Professor Moriarty's son, who was almost certainly the man behind the numbers on the wall, the man directing the alchemist who to kill next.

Not that it would do her any good. Who would believe her, even if she could break out? Mr. Wright? He hadn't been inclined to believe her on the best of days, let alone when she'd escaped from an asylum. Besides which, he seemed unusually content to hunt monsters and let the men who made them go free. Better for business and all that.

Officer Berchard? No, Sam's actions and subsequent diagnosis as a broken channel had quite effectively sapped her credibility to any ordinary person.

Hel? No, Sam wouldn't make that mistake again. She had

trusted Hel, despite what everyone had told her, only for Hel to turn around and betray her—spying on her for Van Helsing, calling her a broken channel, and getting her committed, when she knew very well that was Sam's worst fear.

"I hate you," Sam whispered, even as her heart ached—this must have been what Hel had felt like when her friends had betrayed her to her father. When Hel had learned she couldn't trust anyone.

"You should," Mme Frossard said from the cell next door, as if Sam had been speaking to her.

Sam squeezed her eyes shut. "You don't even know what I'm talking about."

"You're talking about the person who put you here," Mme Frossard said. Then, at Sam's sharp intake of breath, "What? It's not that mysterious. And do stop. You shouldn't give them the smallest piece of your attention. You can be sure they're not thinking about you anymore."

"You don't know that," Sam retorted. "Maybe they just wanted to help."

Mme Frossard laughed. "You want to know how I was discovered to be mad? I walked in on him. He'd always been friendly with the midinette who was my particular helper at Paquin. Well, after you and I met at the train station, I caught a carriage home, a day early from Provence, to find him being friendly all over the midinette's face. And her mouth. And her hair."

"Oh, that's awful." All this time, Sam had been jealous of Mme Frossard.

"It's normal," Mme Frossard said dismissively. "I don't even think I mind that he *fucked* her, it's so pedestrian, so unimaginative. But the disrespect, to do so in our marriage bed. To not even close the door."

"What did you do?" Sam asked.

Sam could hear the shrug in Mme Frossard's voice. "I threw a vat of pig's blood on them."

"You *didn't*," Sam said, shocked and a little awed despite herself.

"I *did*," Mme Frossard confirmed, with a glimmer of pride. "Which is also pedestrian, but the cook had just slaughtered a pig and saved the blood for *sanquette*—they hold a surprising amount of blood, pigs—and I couldn't help myself. He doesn't deserve me at my most inventive anyway.

"But I shouldn't have. I should have ignored it, closed the door, and pretended it wasn't happening. Gone to dinner at Beauvilliers, worn a fashionable dress from Paquin, bought a new necklace from Fouquet. Ordered the most expensive wine on the menu to make him pay, like every other wife does when she inevitably has her heart broken by the man who promised to take care of her, to love and cherish her, until death do you part. And everything would have been *fine*."

"But it wouldn't," Sam pressed. "He'd only do it again, you know he would."

"But I wouldn't. Be. Here."

"What an absolute ass," Sam said, rage wicking to life inside her, the way it had when the Beast in her visions had howled—incandescent not because it wasn't hers, she realized, but because it had been pent up for so long. It hadn't been safe before. But what else could they take from her now? "I hate him."

"You don't know him," Mme Frossard said contemptuously.

"I don't care," Sam said, too worked up to mince words. "I hate him for you. I hate what he did to you. Not just the cheating, which would have been reason enough—but discarding you like this, locking you away in an asylum, because he was done with you. He took away your whole world to account for his sins, and I hate that he *could*."

For a long time, the other woman didn't say anything, and Sam thought she'd gone too far. But she found she wasn't sorry for it. Someone ought to be mad at him, for what he'd done. It was the least he deserved.

Then . . . "Take one of your hairpins," Mme Frossard said. "Slip it between the bars. The latch on the shutters is simple— you have only to lift. Then you can push the shutters open."

Sam pulled a hairpin from her collapsing coiffure. It took her a few tries, standing on her tiptoes to reach the window, her aching fingers trying for deftness, but she unlocked the shutters and gingerly pushed them open—not all the way, she needed to be able to close them again should someone check on her—just enough that a narrow strip of light fell across the floor of her cell.

It wasn't much, but somehow, that single ray of light loosened the bands around Sam's chest. Sam's eyes prickled, her rage melting away. She tilted her head back in the light. Kindness, she decided, was much more moving than cruelty.

"Thank you," she said, just as soon as she was sure her voice wouldn't wobble.

"Don't let them see," Mme Frossard warned her, "or they will find a way to take this from you, too, and I will deny everything."

Sam was going to get out of there. She wasn't a broken channel. Professor Moriarty was manipulating her, playing on her fears to try to control her, through his son. But now Sam knew the trick of telling the false visions from the true. And she wasn't afraid anymore.

Well, that was a lie. Sam was utterly terrified. Honestly, she was lucky her legs weren't doing the shucked-stocking thing just from thinking about attempting to escape. But someone had to stop Hel's brother and Évangéline St. Laurent, and Sam was the only one who could.

Before she could hatch a plan, footsteps sounded in the hall. Sam hurried over to the window with her hairpin, fumbling to catch the slats of the shutters and pull them closed.

Darkness descended just as the keys jingled in the lock.

"I thought I heard voices," the caretaker said, looking around the room with narrowed eyes.

"Did you?" Sam said innocently, holding the hairpin behind her back and standing as nonchalantly as she could. "You should ask the doctor about that."

The caretaker scowled. "The doctor has ordered that you be kept silent. If you are unable to keep your words to yourself, we will move you where no one can hear you. Am I understood?"

"Entirely," Sam said, and she had never been so relieved to hear a door close.

— —

By the time night fell it was raining again. Sam still hadn't found a way out, and had, in fact, exhausted herself just *thinking* of escape plans.

She pulled her pillow over her head, trying to muffle the rain before her brain started picking out patterns in the slow drops beating against the shutters—before it started translating those patterns into letters.

E-M H-?-M H-E-? H-E-M—

Sam sat bolt upright. That wasn't random. It was a word.

No, it wasn't, she chided herself. What was more likely: that it was her imagination, or that someone had scaled the building and was lying on their stomach in the rain, carefully dripping water onto her windowsill? Sam squeezed her eyes shut. She couldn't tell anymore.

But it was easy enough to check. Fingers trembling, she felt along the bottom of her dress—*there!* A long shape, sewn into the hem. Sam tore at the stitches first with her fingernails, and then her teeth, until they came free and she found herself holding her escape in her hand: a heavy iron skeleton key.

She looked sharply back up at the window.

. . . How long had it been "raining," exactly? More importantly, how had Hel ensured Sam would receive that particular dress? Her mind filled with images of Hel spilling canteens of soup on piles of dresses, or painstakingly sewing copies of the key into every skirt. Of Hel in a maid costume . . .

Never mind—there was time for that later. She had to escape, and regardless of Hel's intentions, this was the best chance Sam was going to get. The tricky part would be sneaking past the guards that patrolled the locked ward. Most of the patients were allowed to wander. No one would look twice at her after that, until she reached Salpêtrière's iron gates.

She palmed the key, hiding it in the fold of her waistband. Then Sam climbed on her bed and rapped quietly on the bars.

K-E-Y K-E-Y K-E-Y.

The "rain" paused.

B-E-?-L-?-E-L-L B-E-L-L.

Sam furrowed her brow. She really needed to teach Hel to talk in sentences, but then, it might not have worked. Usually you were working with less signal loss than with water dripping onto a windowsill.

Bell. The chapel had bells that tolled the hour, Sam recalled. Hel must be asking her to leave during the sounding of the bells.

Sam waited what felt like forever, but at last the church bells rang. Hands sweat-slick and shaking, she slipped the key into the lock and turned it, using the clamor of the bell to disguise the sound of her cell door opening. There was no one in the hall. She quickly closed the door behind her and locked it.

The hallway was dark, the gas lamps extinguished, the only light from the streetlamps outside.

What now, Hel? she thought desperately, sure a guard would come around the corner at any moment, afraid to move for fear of going the wrong way. *I'm* not *going back in that cell.*

As if in answer, a will-o'-the-wisp came floating through her cell door, where she'd been moments before—followed by a trickling of more wills-o'-the-wisp, like the beginnings of the starry river that had guided them to the alchemical laboratory in the mines.

The radiotelegraph. Hel had remembered.

But just as Sam took her first step toward freedom, she heard the muffled sound of crying: Mme Frossard.

She couldn't just leave her.

There were no bells to cover the sound as Sam slipped the key into the lock this time, nor to cover the *kerchunk* as she turned it. She heard the shifting of fabric somewhere down the hall—someone had heard her. But there was nothing for it. Sam eased the door open. It creaked like a bird warming up for its evening sonata.

Sam winced and ducked inside, closing the door quickly behind her, holding it shut. She heard footsteps as the guards paced by outside, suddenly grateful their doors had no windows.

Mme Frossard sat up in bed.

"*Qu'est-ce que vous faites là?*" Mme Frossard said sharply. "*À cette heure de la nuit.*"

She was barely recognizable as the elegant woman she'd met

on the street, who had been so embarrassed for Sam's French. She sat in a tangle of sheets, her hair knotted, her eyes red rimmed and puffy with crying. Her fine dress had been exchanged for one as "efficient" as Sam's own.

"What—*you*," Mme Frossard said. "How—"

Sam held a finger to her lips, cocking her head and pointing to the door.

The footsteps stopped outside their cell, and Sam and Mme Frossard held their breath, the light from the gas lamp sweeping under the crack in the door and then back again. She heard the guard mutter a prayer at the sight of all those corpse lights crowding the hall, and then the footsteps faded.

Sam waited a ten count and cracked the door. The hallway was empty once more, save for the wills-o'-the-wisp.

"Come on," Sam whispered. "Quickly now. We're getting out of here."

But Mme Frossard didn't get out of bed. "What's the point? There's nothing for me out there—it was all in my husband's name. Everything I own belongs to him. What would I do? Where would I go?"

"Anywhere you want, I imagine," Sam said impatiently, keeping an eye on the hall, hoping this wasn't a mistake, "which is a far sight better than here. Surely you have friends."

"I'm not sure I do," Mme Frossard said. "Friends of my husband, friends of my position, sure."

"All you need is one," Sam persisted. "A friend who believes in you when you don't believe in yourself. Who challenges you when you're being unfair, and doesn't require you to be anything other than exactly who you are." The friend she'd thought Hel to be. The friend Sam couldn't help but hope Hel might still be, despite everything, given that she was helping Sam escape.

"A friend I haven't seen in a long time," Mme Frossard murmured, but there was something different about her now—a light in her eyes. "And when they catch us?"

"And do what, throw us back in?" Sam said, and had to fight the irrational urge to laugh. There was something unimaginably freeing about seeing your greatest fears come to fruition, and finding yourself on the other side, still *here*. "The worst has already happened. Now, are you in or out, because I'm on a bit of a schedule."

Mme Frossard was up at once.

The wills-o'-the-wisp led them down the darkened hall, past the guards patrolling an intersection—Sam and Mme Frossard ducked into the shadows until they passed. Sam let out a shuddering breath. Hel had timed the escape well.

The wills-o'-the-wisp led them to the end of the hall, into an empty but still-lit office with one window and one door. A mug of tea sat steaming on the desk.

The guard station. A will-o'-the-wisp sailed through the room and melted through the window, into the night.

Right.

"We have to move quickly," Sam said, but no sooner had they closed the door behind them than another door opened, and a slender, balding man in a suit walked in, flipping through a file.

"Hé!" the man shouted, dropping the file, paper scattering all over the floor. *"Pourquoi vous n'êtes pas dans vos cellules?"*

The guard.

"Merde!" spat Mme Frossard.

Sam's heart leapt into her throat; she couldn't fail now, not when she was so close. "The window!"

The guard reached for them, braced as if they were wild

animals. Sam took two running steps toward him, and then slid, skidding on scattered papers right through his legs.

The guard made a swipe for her and missed, regained his bearings, and lunged for the phone. But before Sam could act, she heard an unmusical smash of typewriter keys—once, twice. Sam turned just in time to see Mme Frossard holding a typewriter overhead, the imprint of the keys on the guard's cheek, his eyes and mouth open in surprise. He collapsed in a heap.

"Violent tendencies," Mme Frossard said with a shrug, putting the typewriter back onto the table. "Symptom of hysteria. Now come, help me tie him up. He won't be out forever."

They tied him up with the ribbon from the typewriter, and helped each other out the window and into the gaslit courtyard.

Running now, they chased the wills-o'-the-wisp across the grounds, the frosted grass tickling their ankles, the crickets falling silent at their approach. Sam could see their destination, wills-o'-the-wisp spiraling into the sky above the darkened building, like a beacon.

This was why Hel had asked her to wait, she realized. So that Hel might move from the roof to a location that allowed the wills-o'-the-wisp to travel in a straight line.

And it struck Sam then, how like a love letter this whole escape was. The key, sewn into the hem of her skirt. The Morse code, dripped on the windowsill. The wireless telegraph, which Sam had shown her how to operate, and using radio signals to draw in the wills-o'-the-wisp. Every step showing Sam that Hel had been listening.

That she cared.

When at last they reached it, the wills-o'-the-wisp disappeared through the door. It had to be one of the oldest buildings on the grounds. There were burn marks on the stone, and Sam could still smell the lingering scent of gunpowder, and for a moment, she was back in the firing range, Hel looking up at her for the first time. . . .

Scent is a powerful thing, Mlle Harker.

"What are you waiting for?" Mme Frossard whispered.

Sucking in a deep breath, Sam reached for the door. It opened before she could touch it.

Hel stood on the other side in her black suit, long tan coat, and crimson tie, holding Sam's radiotelegraph. Her red curls clung to her neck like vines, absolutely sopping because of course she hadn't used an umbrella; she never did. Hel lit up at the sight of her. Sam's belly tightened. And the next thing Sam knew, she had flung herself into Hel's arms. A heartbeat, and the radiotelegraph clattered to the ground, Hel's arms wrapping around her.

Hel looked down at Sam, surprised for perhaps the first time, as Sam knotted her fingers in Hel's wet curls and pulled her close, as she *kissed* her. And for the longest moment, Sam feared she had gone too far, that Hel didn't want her like that, that she'd made a terrible mistake and ruined everything, when a soft sound came from Hel's throat, her arms tightening around Sam.

And Hel closed her eyes and kissed her back.

CHAPTER TWENTY-ONE

The Salpêtrière, Paris

"How could you?" The words left Sam's mouth like a slap as soon as they parted, the taste of Hel's mint tea still tingling on her lips. Mme Frossard hissed something in French and shoved them into the old building, closing the door behind them. Dust filtered down from the rafters. "Working with Van Helsing this whole time. I trusted you!"

"I said he *asked* me to spy on you," Hel said, off balance in a way Sam had never seen before, not even when they were being attacked by a grindylow. Hel started to raise her hand to her lips, then dropped it. "I never said I would."

Sam's heart was still racing from the kiss, her thoughts still in a jumble. She remembered Van Helsing's slow response as he'd admitted it was true that he'd asked Hel to spy on Sam, but *I could have sworn . . .*

Hel had cut him off before he could finish.

"But, the things, what you said," Sam said, her words tangling like they never did. She shook her head, as much at herself as Hel. "You *promised* not to tell. You knew being committed was my worst nightmare."

"Van Helsing was going to send you to prison for attempted

murder," Hel said, as if this were something Sam should already know, as if she were a piece on a chessboard, and this simply the most logical move. And Sam began to realize that Hel might be incapable of recognizing why Sam was upset. Hel shrugged. "It was easier to break you out of here."

"By letting me think that either I'd broken or you'd betrayed me to Van Helsing?" Sam burst out. "Why didn't you say something?"

"What are you talking about?" Hel looked honestly confused. "I gave you *the look*."

"The look?" And then it sank in. That unreadable expression after she'd said *I appreciated your trust.* The meaningful look before she'd handed Sam off. "You can't express all that with a look!"

"Can. And did," Hel said. She led them deeper into the old building, then out a back door and into the asylum's gardens, the dark shapes of topiaries silhouetted against the night.

Sam would much rather have had this conversation face to face, but they had to get clear of the beacon Hel had made of the wills-o'-the-wisp before someone came to investigate. Thus they whispered as they worked their way toward Hel's escape route, keeping to the shadows.

"Besides," Hel said. "It's not like I could just out and tell you the truth, Van Helsing was right there."

"Not that," Sam said. "Your father told you to sacrifice your queen—and when you did, he was ready for me. Why didn't you tell me your brother was involved? He was waiting for me, and—"

"My brother is *here*? In the asylum?" Hel's demeanor changed in an instant, her intensity suddenly frightening. "I should have known."

Hel unholstered her revolver. It glinted silver in the

moonlight, reminding Sam of gunfights, of last stands and revenge. Hel had already stepped out of the shadows of the garden
wall before Sam found her voice.

"You're not even going to give me a look this time?" Her fingers curled into her palms. "I thought we were—" She stumbled.
It was just a kiss, it was the heat of the moment, it didn't mean
anything, she didn't even know how Hel felt about her. "I thought
we were partners."

Hel seemed to still herself by force of will, a bit of her old self
coming back into her eyes, as if called to her body by the sound
of Sam's voice.

"There is knowledge, the knowing of which is dangerous in
and of itself," Hel said. "My brother is one of those things."

"Hel, we've been over this!" Sam said. "No one was ever safer
for being kept in the dark. You promised—"

"To keep you safe," Hel snapped, and then, with effort,
evened out her voice. "None of the leads I had on him paid out. I
had begun to suspect he wasn't involved, that it was another dead
end, like all the other cases I've taken. You don't understand, the
games he plays, how long I've been tracking him.

"But if he's here . . . My brother—he's my father's shadowed
left hand. He must be the one sending the numbers, setting up
the kills on my father's behalf. Sam, this is the closest I've ever
been. I need to stop him."

Sam drew a deep breath. "Hel, we can't. We've just escaped
from our cells in an asylum *you* broke into—and they think he's a
doctor. No one will believe you."

"I don't need them to believe me," Hel said grimly. "I just
need a clean shot."

"Don't be a fool." Mme Frossard's tone made it clear she
thought they were both being fools, and that she was very much

regretting what she'd gotten herself into. "I know what it is to be tempted by the prospect of making a man pay, but he'd suffer only a moment, and you'd suffer the rest of your days in prison."

"I have no choice," Hel said stubbornly.

"It's not just you," Sam said. "If you do this, none of us escape, and there would be no one left to stop Van Helsing or the Beast."

Hel tossed her head. "The moment he hears of your escape, my brother will *know* what happened. He'll know I know, and he'll be gone, like blood in water."

"Then we'll be sharks," Sam said fiercely. "But this is not the time."

Hel's hand tightened on her revolver for a breathless moment—this was why Hel was here, Sam remembered. Every case was another chance to thwart her family. This was why Hel didn't have friends, why she didn't take partners. Moriarty had taken them from her one by one.

Here was her first chance for revenge, and Sam was asking her to give it up.

"This is just like the Lasker Trap," Sam said. "Your father is baiting you, offering to sacrifice his bishop for your king. That's not a trade you can survive. You need to play the long game."

At last, Hel's expression cracked. "You're right." Sam let out her breath as Hel holstered her revolver.

"You're not a game piece to me, you know," Hel said, unwilling to meet Sam's eyes, and a tangle of emotion knotted in her throat.

"Except . . . I *am*," Sam said. "It's just that I'm a game piece you happen to care about, which is not the same thing as being partners. Partners trust each other. They don't keep secrets from each other."

And they don't betray each other.

Hel sagged, leaning her head back, looking as young as Sam had ever seen her—and somehow so world weary, all at once. "I . . . don't know if I can be that for you," Hel said in a low voice, and Sam knew she was thinking not just of partners, but of that kiss. "I'm not sure I know how."

"All I ask," Sam said evenly, "is that you try."

"I will. I am," Hel said, and she looked away. "When we get out of here, I'll understand if you want to go home."

"Don't be ridiculous," Sam said. She was sore at Hel, not done with her. "I'm not going anywhere."

Hel drew a deep breath through her nose and let it out. "Good."

"I'd like to go somewhere," Mme Frossard put in. "Preferably out of here."

"Follow me, it's just—" Hel turned and then cursed, quickly ducking back behind the garden wall. The dark shapes of men strode across the field, their lanterns blinking in and out of sight as they swept across the courtyard.

The guards were coming for them.

"This isn't right," Hel said. "They shouldn't have checked the cells until morning. Something must have alerted them."

Sam winced. "We, um, might have run into one of the guards."

"With a typewriter," Mme Frossard added.

"A couple of times," Sam finished, her cheeks pinking.

Hel raised an eyebrow, looking highly amused. Sam shot her a hard look: *Don't start.*

See, you can *say complex things with a look,* Hel's crooked smile said in response.

Sam was just about to return with a look that said, *That's not a complex thought and you know it,* when Mme Frossard cut them off.

"*Pour l'amour de Dieu!* We don't have time for—" Mme Frossard waved her hand, at a loss. "Whatever it is you think you're doing." Mme Frossard turned to Hel: "You said you had a plan for our escape."

"I did." Hel nodded with her chin. "It's on the other side of the courtyard."

The shapes of the guards came clear, at least ten of them. They'd spread out over the whole of the garden—there was nowhere left to hide. Fear splashed through Sam's veins.

"We'll never make it," Sam said, her bravery melting away like fat in the pot. Hel might be able to outrun them all, but Sam? Her legs were scarcely better than her biceps.

"Don't be ridiculous, of course you will," Mme Frossard said.

"How? I'm a terrible sprinter, and—"

Hel cleared her throat and, when Sam looked at her, nodded to Mme Frossard.

You. Mme Frossard had said *you.*

Mme Frossard lifted her chin, pulling her pride on like armor. "I'll run across the field and distract them, pull them away from here so you can escape."

"No," Sam said at once. "I'm not leaving you."

"Don't be foolish, then we'll all get caught," Mme Frossard said. "Don't worry about me. You said yourself: the worst has already happened."

Sam could hear their voices now, calling out for them—their long shadows flickering across the lantern-lit field. Her eyes pricked.

"We'll come back for you," Sam promised.

"You're sweet, but please, don't," Mme Frossard said as she stepped past them to the edge of the garden wall. She looked back, over her shoulder, and offered Sam a half smile—the first she'd seen on the woman. "When you get out, send a message to Audrey Bellamy of Provence, tell her where I am, and . . . and that I need her help. You were right. She'll come for me."

"We will," Sam said, pressing the skeleton key into Mme Frossard's hand.

Mme Frossard stepped out of the shadows. Sam watched, her heart in her throat, as she ran into the frost-limned field. It didn't take long before one of the guards' lights fell on her, and he started to shout: *"Je la vois! Elle est là!"*

At that, every light in the field fell on her, as if she were the soprano in an opera and it was her turn to sing. And sing she did—letting out such a howl as to startle the birds from the trees; they scattered, black shapes cut out against the sky, crying out their displeasure. If any of the guards hadn't been looking at her before, they were now.

All eyes on her, Mme Frossard whirled, feet flashing in the dark as she sprinted across the frozen grounds. After a moment of shock, the guards gave chase, shouting into the night like hounds braying after a hare: *"Attrapez-la! Ne la laissez pas s'échapper!"*

"I can't watch," Sam said, unable to peel her eyes from the figure of Mme Frossard as she tripped, as the guards closed in.

"Come on." Hel gently pulled her by the hand. "Don't let it go to waste."

Mme Frossard's sacrifice did its work: Sam and Hel had no trouble evading the guards and making their way to an old saltpeter processing building. They slithered in through a window, and Hel led them down to a rusted iron door, the locking mechanism of which looked to have been melted clean off.

Sam stared at the puddled metal. "How did you—"

"Chemist, remember?" The hinges glistened; the door opened, quiet as a whisper, stale air wafting out.

The mines. Sam shivered.

"There's a path through here that lets out into an alley in the Latin Quarter to the north. We can catch a carriage from there."

Sam balked, the ghost of Cyprien in her ear:

A man can get lost here, in the dark.

A man can die down here, a hundred meters from the exit, if he does not know the way.

Her body remembered what it had been like to be lost in that lightless labyrinth, in the claustrophobic dark, under the terrible weight of all that earth.

But she banished the feeling. This time was different: Hel had come through this way, and therefore presumably knew the way back out. And even if she didn't, Sam and Hel had found their way out of the dark before—Sam was certain they could do it again.

Behind the door was a narrow rocky tube, so tight it pressed her arms to her sides, and she had to inch her way through it like a caterpillar. Her hips got stuck at the end, scraping the skin through her skirt, and then she was through, stumbling into the unremitting blackness of the mines. She heard the clang of metal as Hel slid the door shut, and then, after a bit of scuffling, dropped down beside her.

Hel sparked a gas lantern, before handing Sam her coat, which Sam accepted gratefully. The light threw shadows on uneven walls. There was an unnerving rust-red color splashed over them, in which Sam thought she could make out handprints, and a few tumbled bones underfoot.

A part of her yearned to brush her fingers against the remnants of the old blood—to uncover its secrets, curious how far her visions extended—but she curled her fingers into her palms. She'd had quite enough trauma for one day.

Hel glanced at the handprints. "A few of the doctors tried to escape down here when the revolutionaries stormed the Salpêtrière," she explained.

Sam shuddered. "It was monstrous, the things the doctors did back then. I don't blame the revolutionaries."

"It would have been nice if they'd spared the women who were their victims, but yes," Hel agreed.

"Wait, they killed them?" Sam said. "But I thought they broke in to *save* them."

"They did," Hel said. "This way."

Sam followed Hel through the dark and winding tunnels, following the trail of chalk Hel had left behind on the walls.

"So . . . what happened during the rest of the opera?" Sam asked.

Hel made a face. "You were right. The Beast that evening was Josephine Heroux."

"I was . . . right?" Sam said.

"I arrived back at the Palais Garnier just in time to see it," Hel said. "The director invited one of the show's sponsors onstage after the performance—a politician named M. Poulin. Mlle Heroux was applauding along with everyone else until he reached over, drunkenly grabbed her by the waist, and kissed her. She transformed into the Beast right there onstage, and *ate his face off*."

M. Poulin. Évangéline St. Laurent's ex-fiancé—the man who'd left her for Josephine Heroux.

"Is he . . . ?"

"Dead? Very."

"And Josephine Heroux?"

Hel shook her head. "Van Helsing caught her twice with silver bullets as the audience fled, but Josephine managed to crack M. Poulin's chest, pull out his lungs, and eat his heart before Van Helsing could even slow her down."

So the vision had been right about that much—only Hel hadn't been the victim.

"Once everyone was clear, I shot down the chandelier to trap her. I managed to convince Van Helsing not to finish her off," Hel said. "She's going to be shipped back to the Society in London for interrogation and eventual autopsy. They're very keen to understand how a werewolf transformed without the full moon."

"Except she's *not* a werewolf!" Sam protested, suddenly feeling sick about what the Society did—about what she'd helped them do.

"And it's a good thing Van Helsing doesn't know it," Hel said. "Or Josephine Heroux would already be dead. This buys us some time to prove her innocence."

If only the events of last night had proved Sam's innocence. If the charge had been attempted murder, she would have been set free at once. But proving she wasn't a broken channel was a far trickier feat—particularly when your doctor had a vested interest in keeping you confined.

"It's not even her fault," Sam said. "It's Évangéline St. Laurent. Josephine Heroux was her rival, and M. Poulin—"

"I know," Hel said as she pulled herself up through another crawl, this one taking them all the way to the surface. "But half of Paris saw Josephine transform into the Beast. She ate M. Poulin's face off *onstage*. That has a tendency to remove any doubts as to who the culprit is."

Sam fell silent from sheer exertion as she pulled her way up after Hel.

"My vision last night," Sam said, a little breathless from the climb. "It shouldn't have been right."

"What do you mean?" Hel said. She wasn't even sweating.

"Someone's been sending me false visions," Sam said, steadying her voice. "They're different from the true ones. They feel wrong—they look like moving pictures, and they have this particular smell, like burning bread. The vision I had of Josephine Heroux was false. Which meant whoever's sending them *wanted* me to know she was the Beast."

If it was Évangéline, perhaps it was only that she wanted her rival dead. And with Van Helsing's capture of "the Beast"? The case would be closed, and the Society would pull out entirely. The French parliament would declare victory in the papers, just as they had a century ago, when the king's men had shot a random wolf and called it the Beast of Gévaudan. A tad premature, given that the Beast had kept on murdering.

All of which was to say, if Sam and Hel were going to defeat Évangéline St. Laurent, they were going to have to do it themselves. It gave Sam the queasy feeling that everything they did was just playing out a game of Professor Moriarty's design, that the dominoes were still falling.

No. Sam couldn't think like that. Men like Hel's father, they tried to make you believe everything that happened was by their plan. It made it easy to give them credit where they'd earned none, to give up before you'd even gotten started. But he was just a man like any other, and that meant he could be beaten.

Hel cursed. "I *left*, and still I end up playing my part. There's nothing I've achieved that wasn't according to his plan."

"That's just what he wants you to think," Sam protested.

"Even you," Hel said, waving a hand. "You said my brother was waiting for you. My father must have meant for us to meet, for me to take you with me. I should have known when he only sent a dehydrated grindylow to take you out. I thought he'd just underestimated you, but he wanted you on this case."

"*I* wanted me on this case," Sam snapped. "So it doesn't really matter what he wanted, does it?"

"It matters, because it means I can't stop him," Hel said, slamming her palm against a streetlamp. The light wobbled. "I keep trying, but I can't beat him."

All at once, Sam's anger melted. She felt as if she were see-ing—truly seeing—Hel for the first time. The way Officer Berchard must have felt, looking at Clotilde what seemed like years ago.

Hel was brilliant, fierce, and driven, but she was only human, trying to fight the sins of her father, when everyone around her couldn't seem to see past her last name.

Sam took a deep breath to steady herself. "Listen," Sam said, taking Hel's hands in her own, pulling her into the pooling light beneath the streetlamp. "Your father might have tried to stick us together for his own advantage, but if he did, he made a terrible mistake. You are the cleverest person I've ever met—"

"You haven't met my father," Hel said dully.

"Shut *up*," Sam said. Professor Moriarty didn't rule the world, but let him into your mind and he may as well have. "You are the cleverest person I've ever met, and while your father might know my family, he doesn't know *me*. You might not be able to stop him alone—but *we* can. Even if we can't get your brother this time, we can still save Josephine Heroux. We can take down Évangéline St. Laurent. And we can send back a message of our own. Trust me."

Hel shook her head. "Why are you helping me? I betrayed you to Van Helsing. I used your radiotelegraph to contact a source in my father's home, I got you committed—"

"I'm still mad about that," Sam admitted. To be honest, *mad* was an understatement. "But I understand why you did it, even if I'd rather you had told me—both times, using words. And I believe in us. I believe in you." *Even if you don't believe in yourself.*

"Sam—"

"Get it together," Sam said as much to herself as to Hel. *Don't cry.* "Van Helsing is about to send an innocent woman back for autopsy, because her rival wants him to, and we are the only ones who can stop her—and only by solving this case. I need you to trust me."

Hel let out a shuddering breath, and when she opened her eyes, she was herself again. "You're right."

"Of course I'm right, it's me," Sam said, echoing Hel's own words back at her. "Now, where do you think Mlle St. Laurent might be at this time of night?"

At last, Hel cracked a smile. "Oh, I don't think we'll have any trouble with *that.*"

CHAPTER TWENTY-TWO

The Hôtel du Louvre, Paris

The streets of downtown Paris near the Hôtel du Louvre were crowded with revelers—it was as if all Tout-Paris were drinking and dancing. Sam sidestepped a man vomiting into an alley as they turned onto Place du Théâtre Français.

"What's this about?" Sam asked.

"Didn't you hear?" he slurred. "The police caught the Beast! They're selling tickets to her viewing. I bought five."

He tried to toast her, slopping champagne on Sam's sensible dress. Hel caught Sam's elbow before she could say something they'd all three of them regret. "It's not worth it."

"You're probably right," Sam said, tamping down on the fury uncurling within her. When had Hel become the sensible one?

Ever since that Beast had roared onstage, Sam thought. Ever since it had awoken something in her—something she hadn't thought she had in her. Rage, simmering just beneath her skin, no matter how hard she tried to shove it down.

It's not real, she told herself. It was the Beast's, not hers. But those thoughts felt like lies, and the rage felt like truth.

Sam allowed Hel to lead her as they cut through the riotous crowds, the revelers swirling away from Hel, her long tan coat snapping in the wind behind her. They hurried through the empty hotel lobby, up the stairs to their hotel room—Sam sure any moment someone would catch sight of her, would realize she should be in the asylum and put her there. But no one did. No one paid them any attention at all. It was as if the news of the Beast's capture had drawn all the eyes in Paris.

Sam unlocked their hotel room, eager to change into something a little less institutional, and swung open the door—only to slam it shut again.

"Hel!" Sam whispered urgently. Inside had been a woman *tied to a chair*. A woman with scandalously short dark hair and one of Hel's crimson ties for a gag. Her sultry brown eyes had been molten. "Why is Mlle St. Laurent tied up in our hotel room?"

"I told you we wouldn't have any trouble finding her."

"You just *left* her there?" Sam said incredulously. "While you went about the whole business of rescuing me?"

"I may have been slightly upset with her at the time," Hel allowed. For what happened to Sam, she realized. It was almost sweet, except for the part where it was still absurd.

"You can't just tie people up in your hotel room and leave them there!" Sam said. Even if they were murderers.

"If I hadn't tied her up, she might be halfway to Spain by now," Hel said. "I needed her to stay put while I broke you out of the asylum."

"Someone could have come in and seen her!"

"But they didn't," Hel said, opening the door.

A familiar jingling sounded, accompanied by footsteps, coming around the corner. *Van Helsing!*

There was no time for Sam to hide. Hel barely had time to slam the door as Van Helsing strode around the corner, his cowboy boots clinking. And Sam said a small prayer of thanks that he still wore those gaudy boots, and that they were so very loud.

"Miss Moriarty! I thought I heard your voice," Van Helsing said. "Where have you been? You haven't been to your room all night. You were supposed to give me your notes. I can't get anywhere with—" He startled, seeming to see Sam for the first time, and his face went white. He was afraid—she could see that now. But rather than make Sam feel powerful, it made her nervous. The worst things people did, they did because they were afraid. As if intent on proving her right, Van Helsing scowled, crossing his arms. "What's *she* doing here? Shouldn't she be in a cell somewhere?"

Hel raised an eyebrow. "Should she?"

"She's a broken channel," he said flatly. "She shot at the stage."

"At *Mlle Heroux*," Hel corrected, which was factually true, even if it wasn't what Sam had intended. And Sam began to see what Hel was setting up. "Who Sam claimed was the Beast. In which case, so did you. If she had better aim, a man would still be alive tonight."

Van Helsing went very still, then turned to Sam.

"Fair point," Van Helsing said, his voice deceptively calm. If Sam had learned Mlle Heroux was the Beast from her visions— as, indeed, she had—and if Hel had broken her out, as was very clearly the case, then Van Helsing might catch two monsters that day.

But if Sam hadn't acted on her visions, she wasn't a broken channel. If she hadn't acted on her visions, she deserved to be free.

"But you shot at her before she transformed," Van Helsing said. "How did you know it was her?"

Sam held his eyes, pressed her hands to her skirts to keep them from shaking, and leaned forward. *"Tapetum lucidum."*

"What?" Van Helsing said intelligently.

Behind her, Sam could hear the muffled bumping of Évangéline, knocking her chair about the floor. Van Helsing frowned.

"*Tapetum lucidum,*" Sam repeated, loudly, drawing his attention back to her. "According to the research I've done, it's a thin reflective layer behind the iris of the eye that reflects the light, and is the first part of the werewolf to change, generally when the werewolf starts thinking about transforming, the way a human's heart rate quickens in anticipation of exercise—"

It was utter bunk was what it was. Josephine wasn't a werewolf, for one thing. For another, even if the change Josephine had gone through was similar, her eyes would have only started reflecting the light once the transformation had been triggered and was, at that point, irreversible. Which was to say, your throat would be torn out before you could cry wolf. But Van Helsing didn't have the years of research Sam did nor the scientific understanding to question it—he was, after all, only a field agent.

"Why didn't you say so?" he demanded.

"You mean when that man had her grappled face down on the ground, and twisted her arm out of its socket when she tried to talk?" Hel said dryly. "You mean why didn't she just talk then?"

There was a loud *thump* from behind the door. Hel winced. Van Helsing looked at the door sharply.

Sam's heart flipped inside out—he was going to open the door, she could feel it in the shifting of his feet, of his focus. She had to get his attention back, or he was going to see Évangéline tied to that chair, and Sam could only guess at what would happen then.

So she did the only thing she knew worked one hundred percent of the time.

"I—I'm sorry," Sam said, letting her voice crack, her eyes flooding with tears. And she was glad for once at how easy it was for her to cry. Van Helsing swore under his breath and looked away. For all he'd made her break down countless times, he never could stand to watch, as if some part of him knew what he was doing was wrong. "If I'd been able to think straight, then maybe . . ."

"She's a *researcher*, man," Hel said.

"You have no business being in possession of a firearm," Van Helsing said, which was the first thing he'd said in years, if not a decade, with which Sam wholeheartedly agreed. He tossed his briefcase at her, his lip curling when Sam barely caught it and then stumbled under its weight.

"What's this?" Sam asked. It was heavy. Unusually so.

"Tissue samples from the victim and the werewolf," Van Helsing said, sounding tired. Sam nearly dropped the case. As right as she'd been when it came to sensing clues, it didn't do her constitution any favors. Nor her lunch. "Go back to London and the libraries, Miss Harker. You're a liability here. I will finish up."

"Finish up?" Hel prompted.

"There's . . . been a complication," Van Helsing admitted. "Miss Heroux arrived in Paris from Belgium the morning of her performance at the Palais Garnier. There were witnesses. Apparently, she was onstage the entire week prior."

"You don't say?" Hel said, exchanging a look with Sam.

"The other murders must have been done by other members of her pack," Van Helsing said sourly. "But she won't give them up, despite my best attempts at encouragement. Whatever varietal of lycanthrope she is, it's not lunar. While she has a strong reaction to silver in her wolf form, it does not extend to her human form, and her regenerative properties appear to be exclusively lupine as well."

He was so sure of the story he'd sold himself about her, so sure she was a werewolf, that all the evidence to the contrary wasn't enough to make him see how he was wrong.

God save the world from people like him.

"Is that why you were looking for me?" Hel asked. "You wanted me to try?"

"Heavens, no," Van Helsing said. "If I couldn't get her to talk, I highly doubt you could. I came for your notes. Someone left a tip at the hotel this morning—apparently a mushroom farmer saw wolves in the catacombs."

Hel and Sam exchanged a glance. They had passed mushroom farmers on their way out of the mines in Montmartre, and it was possible the farmers had caught sight of the Beast's flight, but the mushroom farmers were in the mines. The *catacombs* were a small section of the mines that was kept safe and clean, the bones of the city's dead laid out in complicated and ornate designs in the walls and columns. It was a tourist destination—there were *tours*.

It was probably a translation error—but that was fine. The catacombs were safe, and would keep him distracted, giving them room to pursue the case.

Hel pulled out a folder from her coat pocket and handed it to him. "Here you go."

"Right, then," Van Helsing said, flipping through the folder. But still, he didn't leave. "You know, Miss Moriarty . . . you could come with me."

"How generous," Hel said. "But I'm off the case, remember?"

"I'll ask Mr. Wright to reassign you," Van Helsing said, with the ease of a man used to getting what he wanted. "Nothing simpler. Now suit up. We'll have to leave immediately. Bring tracking equipment—we're probably already too late for the sighting in question, but we can track them to wherever they're holed up."

"You misunderstand," Hel said. "I'm leaving with Miss Harker."

"You're what?" Van Helsing demanded. "You can't leave, the job's not finished!"

"Oh, come now, surely the Butcher of Bran Castle can handle a few werewolves on his own," Hel scoffed. "I leave it in your capable hands."

"But—" Van Helsing started. He needed an explanation, Sam realized. One that would let him keep his pride, or he'd keep pushing.

"We were attacked by a grindylow on the way to Dover," Sam confessed.

"A grindylow?" Van Helsing said. "In Southern England?"

"Highwaymen." Hel shrugged, like *What can you do,* effortlessly picking up where Sam had left off. "I abandoned her once and look what happened. I'm not going to do it again. My loss— all that work, and you get the glory, right, Van Helsing?"

Van Helsing's nostrils flared, but they'd woven their story too well. It fed into all the things he most wanted to believe. This case would be groundbreaking; it would make his name. If, that is, werewolves still really existed. Which they didn't.

Sam almost felt bad for him.

"Your loss," Van Helsing agreed, and he took off back down the hallway.

As soon as the sound of his boots had faded, Sam and Hel opened the door to their hotel room, slipped inside, and slammed it closed just as fast as they could, locking it after them.

Lying on her side on the floor, red faced and gagged, Évangéline St. Laurent looked less Helen of Troy and more like any other woman from Montmartre. Hel righted her as Sam dumped the briefcase on the bed and slid the remaining chair over from the fireplace and propped it under the doorknob.

"You know he'd have blamed me, if he'd opened that door!" Sam said.

"Now there's an interesting question," Hel mused. "Who does Van Helsing hate more at this point, do you think? You or me?"

"It's hardly a competition!"

"Not with that attitude, it's not." Hel snorted, and she looked at Évangéline, who glared back at her. "Believe me. You'd rather deal with us than the official channels. The man who came knocking would like to murder Josephine Heroux. I can only imagine what he'd do to the alchemist who was the reason he just made a fool of himself proclaiming werewolves still exist."

Évangéline went very still at that, her eyes widening. She had, Sam realized, heard everything. Sam's cheeks pricked with heat. Well, at least she wouldn't have to explain what she was doing out of the asylum, or why she supposedly shot at Josephine Heroux.

Hel untied her gag. And, to Sam's surprise, Évangéline didn't scream, but took a deep, steadying breath.

"Just because I am not sad he is dead," Évangéline said evenly, "that does not mean I did it. You *saw*—"

"The eyeshadow," Hel cut her off.

"I—my *eyeshadow*?" Évangéline said incredulously.

"It's a shimmery blue grey," Sam supplied.

"Oh, you can't be serious!" Évangéline turned to Sam: "I was *kind* to you. I—"

"Now," Hel interrupted. "Or we can turn you in to Van Helsing and tell him what you told us about men and bees."

Évangéline let out a searing string of French that Sam was grateful she didn't understand. Hel raised an eyebrow.

"*No.* Don't. Not him," Évangéline huffed. And she let out a helpless breath. "It's in my clutch."

Hel nodded at Sam. Sam went over to Mlle St. Laurent's clutch and pulled out a pot of silk-paper wrapped lipstick, a vial of perfume, and, at last, the eyeshadow.

"I have it," Sam said, turning the eyeshadow to catch the light. It really was a beautiful shade. Almost otherworldly. She should have known from the start there was something special about it.

Hel nodded. "You know what to do."

"What? What is she doing?" Évangéline said, craning her head around.

Sam went into the washroom. Heathcliff squeaked as soon as she entered, standing on his hind legs, his paws against the cage. His face was still a scarlet mess, and what she was about to do would hardly make it better. She knelt by his cage in the claw-foot tub. "I'm sorry, Heathcliff."

Selecting one of her own cosmetic brushes from her kit, Sam dabbed the end in the eyeshadow.

"I'm applying the eyeshadow now," Sam said, her voice un-steady. This was it. The moment of truth. She stuck the brush through the bars of the cage. Heathcliff must have understood what was happening, for he squeaked in protest, running around, trying to dodge the brush. Sam's heart squeezed.

"I'm sorry," Sam whispered again. But it was the safest way. At least Heathcliff wouldn't be able to destroy more than the bed-ding of his cage. If Sam or Hel tried it . . . "I will buy you the best cheese in Paris after this, I promise."

At last, Sam cornered him with the brush, and dabbed the eyeshadow on Heathcliff's head. "Got him!"

"Nicely done!" Hel called from the other room.

"Did she just put my eyeshadow on a *rat*?" Évangéline demanded.

Sam and Hel ignored her, holding their breath. Heathcliff started cleaning himself, licking his paws and running them over his head, glaring at her reproachfully.

But at last Sam had to exhale. Nothing had happened.

"It's not working," Sam said. But she had been so *sure*.

"It's a popular shade," Évangéline said. "I wore it in Wagner's *Tristan and Isolde*. A gift from M. Courbet. The department stores at the Louvre have been sold out of it ever since—"

What had Hel said, about chemical kinetics? There must be something that activated it. Josephine Heroux had worn that eyeshadow for three hours and not transformed until she took her bows. Until that sponsor had grabbed her.

Hel turned on Évangéline. "What are we missing? What makes her turn into a Beast? Is it sweat? Adrenaline? A kiss?"

"A kiss," Évangéline said dryly. "Yes. That's it. How could I have forgotten? You must kiss the rat. Both of you."

Sam was close to understanding—she could feel it. In the beginning, the stories she could spin from the puzzle pieces she'd picked up had seemed near endless. But now, the pieces she had *didn't fit*, and between them, they sketched the dark shape of what she was missing. Sam could almost grasp it.

Sam leaned in closer to Heathcliff, studying him, looking for any sign of change—and with her next breath, Sam found it.

Amber and musk.

A terrible suspicion crystallized in her gut.

"What is it?" Hel called.

But Sam wasn't listening. She opened the suitcase Van Helsing had brought. Inside was a fragment of Josephine's white ballet dress, saturated with blood and the familiar perfume of gardenia, jasmine, tuberose, and lily—L'Heure magique. Beside it was a man's forearm torn off at the elbow, wrapped in the rest of the suit jacket. She leaned in and sniffed.

"Hel, we have to let her go," Sam said. "It's not Mlle St. Laurent,"

"I *told* you it wasn't," Évangéline said.

"Are you certain?" Hel said. "She could be lying."

"I'm sure," Sam said. Hel nodded tightly and pulled out a knife. Évangéline, to her credit, didn't flinch. Hel knelt and cut the singer free.

Évangéline stood at once, rubbing her wrists. "You know, I could have you locked up for this."

Hel snorted. "Bold words for the woman without the knife."

"Mlle St. Laurent," Sam said, giving Hel a sharp look. "We are so sorry. And you're right, you could have us locked up, if that's what you think is right. But we're on your side. These murders—someone is framing the midinettes. We want to protect them. Trust us."

"First Arsène, and now you. I don't think I shall be trusting anyone ever again," Évangéline said tartly. "But . . . the midinettes do. So I suppose I can make an exception just this once."

"Thank you," Sam said. Honestly, she wasn't sure what they'd do if she'd refused.

"Don't borrow trouble," Hel warned her, opening the door.

"I know how this works," Évangéline huffed, and by some trick of posture, the woman from Montmartre faded, and the queen of Tout-Paris walked out of the Hôtel du Louvre and into the night, without ever once looking back.

"Right, then. Explain." Hel pierced Sam with her undivided attention. Once, Sam had found it intimidating. Now, she hardly noticed.

"I know who the alchemist is," Sam said.

It seemed impossible Sam hadn't realized it before, it fit so perfectly.

A Beast had attacked Hel and Sam in the alchemical laboratory. It had to have been the alchemist. Sam had caught a hint of his scent then—amber and musk—but she hadn't been able to place it.

Until she'd smelled it on Heathcliff.

Amber and musk were the base notes of L'Heure magique— the perfume they'd borrowed from Clotilde. It had also suffused Josephine's dress. But the perfume on its own wasn't sufficient to instigate the change, or Heathcliff would be a Beast by now. It was, as Hel had suspected, a matter of chemical kinetics.

Je sens le sapin, M. Barrere had written in his own heart's blood. I can smell the fir trees.

A euphemism for death—but that's not all it had been. It had been *literal.*

All the victims had worn a cologne that smelled like evergreens, like pine, like *fir trees.*

Moritz Knie had tried to warn Sam and Hel: he'd told them someone was calling wolves in Paris. Given the presence of *Der Wolfssegner* in the laboratory, and the fact that Moritz Knie didn't mention its loss, there seemed little doubt that the Wolfssegner had been working with the alchemist at the start. It wouldn't have taken much for the alchemist to find him, nor to convince him to help. Life was hard in Montmartre, and every man had his price. But the old man must've loved his adopted home too—enough at least that he drew a line at Clotilde.

Unfortunately, by that point, he knew too much.

The alchemist had hoped Sam and Hel would think the burning of the bread was just to get rid of the Wolfssegner's wards, when it was really because he didn't want Sam to scent the perfumes used to instigate the change. He knew *exactly* how good Sam's nose was, because she'd told him herself. Just as she'd told him how she knew there was a mistress, and what their plans were for catching the Beast.

And when Sam was being forced to the ground for firing a revolver at the opera, he had abandoned her utterly, spinning a story for the police that would have landed her in prison had Hel not intervened.

"Arsène Courbet," Sam said. "He uses one perfume for the Beast, and another for the victim."

And after he'd said he didn't know who made the perfume the midinettes wore!

Taking her little silver-and-iron knife, Sam cut a strip of cloth off the man's suit, infused with that same fir scent. Then, careful to hold it at its end, she dropped it into Heathcliff's cage.

Curious, Heathcliff ran over to it at once. No sooner had his nose touched the cloth than he started quaking and squealing, his bones shifting, fur shivering out of his tail, his mouth sprouting more teeth, until Sam and Hel were staring, disbelieving, at the tiniest, most furious wolf.

The beastly Heathcliff squeaked in rage and tore the strip of fabric to shreds with his teeth.

"So that's how he's marking his victims," Hel said. The

Wolfssegner had tried to warn them—wine, bread, or *ointment.* "And I'll bet they pay handsomely for the privilege."

"Perfume has a delayed reaction," Sam said. "Arsène told me how it changes after five to fifteen minutes, revealing the heart, and then again at twenty minutes to an hour, exposing the base, which can last for days."

"It's the iodine clock all over again," Hel said. "His would-be Beasts can wear that perfume every day and not change. But once the base has been revealed, once it mixes with the perfume of his victims—it changes."

And so, too, did the women into Beasts, which was why Josephine had changed at that kiss.

No wonder Arsène Courbet selected mistresses for his assassins—not only did the young women embody his victims' sins, they were also the ones most likely to activate the unguent in a secluded environment.

And suddenly, Sam recalled the way Arsène Courbet had talked about the midinettes. . . . Like they were lost souls, tempted into a life of sin by Tout-Paris—somehow patronizing and condemning at once. Like they were *disposable.* All because what, his father had cheated on his mother with a mistress? Fury flared through Sam's veins.

Who was *he* to judge them? Turning young women struggling to make a living into literal *monsters* on account of their supposed sin, using them to murder men he considered wicked, and thinking himself righteous for it, thinking himself *clever.*

For the wages of sin is death.

As if Arsène weren't attempting to murder his way through parliament! Murder was still a sin, last Sam had checked, and a capital one at that. Mother of Mercy, Arsène must be so full of himself, to work with Hel and Sam when he knew what they were about, so confident in their inability to figure out he was behind it.

"Sam," Hel said slowly. "Arsène Courbet made *you* a perfume."

"Oh God," Sam said.

The alchemist had made Sam a perfume. A perfume she'd found so comforting, she'd worn it every day, even as Hel teased her for smelling like old books.

And every time Sam had received a false vision, it was after she'd touched something. The broadside. The book. Moritz Knie's corpse. All things he would have had time to prepare with the catalyst.

And then, at the opera, Arsène *himself.* He kept offering her his arm. And she, besotted fool that she was, kept taking it.

Sam had asked him if a perfume could make you fall in love. Her cheeks burned at the memory.

"What a fool he must think me," Sam said.

"More the fool him," Hel said, coming up to stand by her side. "You're the one who figured him out. Now, let's make sure he doesn't get away with it."

CHAPTER TWENTY-THREE

La Parfumerie du Papillon, Paris

The sun was just rising by the time Sam and Hel arrived at La Parfumerie du papillon, the red dawn's light catching on the frosted windows. The trees were skeletal and grasping, the last of autumn's leaves skittering over the streets.

La Parfumerie du papillon was closed, the lights out, even though it had been due to open half an hour ago. In an unspoken accord, Hel moved to pick the lock, as Sam shielded her from view. The door opened, and Sam and Hel tore inside, the bell tinkling.

"Arsène!" Sam cried. Glass closed them in on all sides—cages filled with a vast array of perfume bottles, mortar and pestles with drops of ambergris and myrrh, vast teak cabinets with their tiny drawers, and that desk on its platform at the end.

But there was no perfumer with Darcy-dark eyes. No Arsène Courbet.

"There must be something here," Sam said, checking his heavy wooden desk for scratch marks that might reveal secret panels. If they could just find evidence they might bring to the police, or something to trigger a vision . . .

Arsène was getting away, Sam felt sure of it. He was on a boat to America, his dark hair perfectly ruffled with the salt from the sea air as he sipped a martini and chuckled at the thought of Sam in the asylum and Hel trying to get her out when she could have been going after him. But this wasn't a vision; this was just her imagination.

And then Hel's soft intake of breath. In Hel's hands was yesterday's newspaper.

Sam felt faint as she saw the photograph under the headline "Affaire de meurtre à l'opéra," Murder at the Opera: a hollow-eyed black wolf standing on a broken crown, under a five-pointed star, over the now-familiar words of *sin* and *death*. And around it: *numbers*.

He wasn't done. Professor Moriarty had pushed Arsène to perform one last murder.

Hel looked as if she wanted to rip the newspaper apart—they must not have found it until after Hel had left to liberate Sam. "The date is September 12. That's *today*. But this time we have no way of telling where."

Arsène and Ruari must have intended on Sam and Hel being occupied with the business of the asylum. But Ruari knew Sam had escaped. He must have known they'd find his cipher. And if Ruari had told the perfumer . . . Arsène would be ready for them.

"We have to find the key to the book cipher," Sam said. "The newspaper is here, which means the key can't be far."

Sam searched the drawers of the desk, and then the cabinet of tiny drawers, but nothing. She needed a vision—she needed to touch something. But what? Not the newspaper . . . Her eyes landed on the desk, on a pen still uncapped on the table.

Sam could see it in her mind's eye, Arsène Courbet jotting down words on a piece of scrap paper—there, a notepad, one sheet recently torn off. He couldn't be expected to keep it all in his head. She brushed her fingers over the notepad.

"Anything?" Hel murmured.

Sam shook her head. He hadn't pressed hard enough to leave the impression of the words beneath, and the vision didn't come.

Sam reached for the pen.

As soon as her fingers touched the polished wood, she heard singing. Women's voices, twining, drawing her in as surely as sirens pulled ships onto the rocks. She followed them, her hand tracing a path worn into time like a groove on a record, letting them guide her to a large painting that covered a whole panel of the wall. Then they faded.

"It's here," Sam gasped, uncurling her hand and letting the pen roll off her palm to drop to the floor.

Hel tore down the painting. Behind it was a hollow in the wall, and nestled within it, like eggs in a nest, were books. Far too many books.

Sam picked up a copy of *Les Fleurs du mal*, a black bound book gilded with a skeleton in a garden grown from human skulls. She had heard of it. It was, by all accounts, an obsessive screed of sin and death and disgust toward evil and oneself—and aspirations for a world ideal.

The margins were clotted with Arsène Courbet's tight handwriting, as if he'd read all that death and sin and taken it for marching orders. Cleansing the world of those who sinned like his father had against his sainted mother.

Which was to say, murdering them. Her stomach curdled.

"There's too many," Hel said. "We don't have time to check them all."

"Then it's a good thing we don't have to," Sam said, realizing even as she said it that it was true.

Hel frowned. "What do you mean?"

"The perfume he made for the victims—it's a French euphemism for death," Sam said as she scanned the titles. Rimmel's *Book of Perfumes*, *The Call of the Wild*, *The Migration of Birds* . . . "He murders the men he accuses of indulging in the sin of lust with their own mistresses. And he tried to convince us the alchemist had been murdered by his own creation. Which means Arsène won't have chosen just any book for his key. He'll have chosen something *poetic*."

At last Sam's eyes fell on a slender volume she'd almost skipped right past. A book of myths entitled *The Riddle of the Sphinx*.

Perfume, he'd said, *is like the riddle of the sphinx: she has a dawning, a noontide, and a twilight.*

"It's this one!" Sam said, plucking the book from the shelf. "I'm sure of it."

"Well done. I'll read. You search."

Sam flipped through the book as Hel called out the numbers from the opera house murder, piecing together the message, number by number.

Where—the—dead—sleep—Dutch—man—in—snake—skin—boots.

"*Van Helsing*," Sam said. Trust Van Helsing to have boots so notorious that even Hel's brother had heard of them.

"That tip this morning," Hel said. "He's headed to the catacombs."

Ruari must have left that tip at the front desk, all to get Van Helsing into position so Arsène could murder him. And she'd thought it just the mushroom farmers, catching sight of the Beast as he fled ahead of Hel and Sam.

"But why?" Sam asked. "Van Helsing seems like exactly his sort of pawn."

"Oh, that *fool*," Hel cursed. "Van Helsing called himself my partner at the opera."

At first, Sam didn't make the connection. Then her stomach dropped as she remembered what Ruari had said: *She will be alone, without allies or lovers or friends, until the day she comes home. Father will make sure of it.* Hel had been surprised when all her father had thrown at Sam was a dehydrated grindylow—and then, of course, it had turned out to be because her father possessed other intentions for Sam. She supposed she should be grateful. It was likely the only reason she was still alive.

"That's—" Sam was at a loss for words. What an awful way to show your affection for someone, by killing anyone else who gets too close. Honestly, it was a miracle Hel let anyone in.

"Come on," Sam said, tossing the book. Hel snatched it out of the air. The tip hadn't specified a time, and they couldn't have known when Van Helsing would receive it, or when he would answer. Besides which, the catacombs—the parts they let tourists in, anyway—only went for about two miles before connecting to the mines beyond. It would take Van Helsing and the Beast time to find each other. "We can still save him."

"Or," Hel suggested slowly, turning the book over in her hands, "we could be too late."

"What are you saying?" Sam said.

Hel gave her a look that said, so clearly Sam couldn't pretend she didn't understand, *You know what I'm saying.*

We could let Van Helsing die.

They wouldn't even be killing him. All they had to do was be . . . less than competent, and Van Helsing would go away, and never threaten Sam or hurt an innocent woman he deemed a monster again.

Mr. Wright wouldn't even blame Sam and Hel—the book cipher was supposed to be impossible to break, and they were supposed to be on their way back to London. A fourth "partner" of Dr. Moriarty's would join the list in Hel's file, and they could be very sad.

Sam couldn't pretend it wasn't tempting. Van Helsing had been waiting for Sam to turn monstrous since they were eleven years old. But—

"No," Sam said finally. "We have to at least try."

"He won't thank you for it," Hel warned. "It might even make things worse for you."

"We're not doing it for him," Sam said, thinking of Clotilde Auclair, of Josephine Heroux, of the other young women whose names she didn't know. "We're doing it because whoever the poor girl is that Arsène Courbet has made into his monster this time—she doesn't deserve to have Van Helsing's death on her hands. And because you don't need another name on your list, either."

And perhaps a little bit for the boy Van Helsing used to be. The one who had been Sam's friend.

Hel gave her a consternated look.

"What?" Sam protested, feeling self-conscious.

"My father wasn't the only one who underestimated you," Hel said simply.

Sam cleared her throat, not knowing quite what to say to that. "I'll contact Officer Berchard and explain what's going on. We're going to need help from someone who can actually do the arresting. Someone we can trust—who can make sure Arsène won't escape."

Hel raised an eyebrow. "And you trust Officer Berchard? You are on the run from the police regarding the incident at the asylum, if you recall."

Sam hesitated. "He's loyal to those he cares about. And Arsène made a murderer out of his cousin. He'll want justice as much as we do."

Sam sat down at the desk and pulled out Officer Berchard's card. She had to wait a bit, as the officer who answered the phone went searching for Officer Berchard, watching as Hel riffled through the discarded books. But before she could ask what Hel was looking for, Officer Berchard's voice came over the phone.

"Good morning, Mlle Harker," he said, sounding slightly aggravated. "What is it you have to tell me, and only me? Are you calling to turn yourself in?"

"I'm afraid not, Officer Berchard," Sam said crisply. And she explained the situation, skipping the bits about Professor Moriarty and concentrating on the parts that connected Arsène Courbet to the murders—the books, the Wolfssegen, the alchemical laboratory, the perfume that turned young women into Beasts, and the cologne that marked men for death.

Officer Berchard, Sam thought, *must* have known something when he'd found Clotilde, bloody mouthed and bloody handed in that private salon at Lapérouse, standing over the corpse of M. Barrere. She must have looked like a werewolf—he'd been so nervous when they'd wanted to test her.

But Officer Berchard had known his cousin, known she would never do something like that. So he'd protected her, hoping he wasn't harboring a monster.

Here, at last, was a way out. A way to finish the story where his cousin wasn't a monster, but a victim. A way to clear his cousin's name. All he needed to do was catch Arsène Courbet.

"I will contact Eulalie," Officer Berchard said at once. "I don't agree with her methods, but—Eulalie cares about this city, and the Wolves of God know the mines better than anyone. They can keep Arsène Courbet from escaping that way, drive him toward the surface."

Officer Berchard wasn't like Van Helsing, Sam thought. He didn't just follow the law as it was written, because the law didn't help people—at least, not all people. He had his own justice.

It was a dangerous road, one that required him to sacrifice many of the things he loved—but one that gave Officer Berchard the power to help people in ways he couldn't from the outside. Sam wondered if this, then, had been what had driven Officer Berchard and Eulalie apart.

"What about the police?" Sam said.

"I will start the case against Arsène Courbet as soon as I'm done with Eulalie," Officer Berchard said.

"Start the case—" Sam protested.

"Perfume? A book of myths? We work on evidence, Mlle Harker, and you've given me none," Officer Berchard said. "There is nothing that directly connects him to the case, nothing I can charge him with. But if it's there, I will find it, I promise. Now go save that other young woman—before she does something she regrets. And . . . do me a favor. Don't get caught."

— —

The difference between the catacombs and the mines was that of a veil and a shroud. The entrances to the mines were sores in the crust of the earth—ragged and illicit and legion.

The entrance to the catacombs, on the other hand, was singular: an unassuming green metal building. It even had a sign.

There was no guard—but then, the sturdy metal door was supposed to be locked when there weren't tours going on. Van Helsing had apparently taken care of that, too. The door swung loose from its hinges, creaking in the breeze.

Hel glanced at Sam. "You're sure you don't want to be too late?"

"We might already be," Sam said, for all a part of her shivered at the creaking door, at the long stair down to a labyrinth where a monster waited. Not Ariadne this time, but one of the hunters. "Come on."

They sparked their lanterns.

It was 131 steps down, down into darkness as the air around them grew cold enough to raise gooseflesh on their arms. The walls around them were proper stone blocks, even and set with mortar. It felt more like descending into a subterranean Metro station than an ossuary, until they came to the sign: *Arrête! C'est ici l'empire de la Mort.*

The bones of six million Parisians lay behind that entrance, stacked on top of each other in designs that the Church had named alternatively profane and divine. Oceans of bones lay behind them, leaving a slender path for the living through the land of the dead.

There, beneath the sign, was a large wolf's bloody paw print. Arsène Courbet was nothing if not poetic and macabre.

Hel knelt and ran a finger through still-bright blood and sniffed it. "Sloppy. It's not even blood."

"It's a trap." Any woman would know it couldn't possibly be real. "Van Helsing has to see that, doesn't he?"

He would. Van Helsing was many things, but he wasn't unintelligent. Nor, unfortunately, was he a coward.

Exchanging a look, Sam and Hel hurried faster, down past

lines of grinning skulls, and monuments to the dead, and columns painted like castles in a game of chess. There were no worries about losing their way this time—the paw prints were always there, right when they thought they might have lost their way, the bloodiest trail of breadcrumbs. They didn't even have to break their stride.

Until at last, they heard a scuffling up ahead, just past where the catacombs ended and the mines began. Sam stopped, her heart drumming in her ears. *What was that?* Hel set down her lantern and loosened the revolver in its holster.

Their lanterns illuminated a room filled with columns and loose stones, with an exquisite painting of the *Aphrodite of Fréjus* on the wall over a large cenote, around which someone had written the words *Qui se souvient?*

Who remembers?

It was all of it spattered with blood. Only, not just blood. It was mixed with a kind of goo, and bits of tentacle lay still twitching on the floor—the thickest of them sprawling out of the well like vines.

The carcolh. Van Helsing must have killed it.

Sam almost felt bad for the monster. The carcolh had been trapped, put there by a person and left to starve unless it fed. It was, in a way, just another casualty of Professor Moriarty and Arsène.

But then, it had murdered Cyprien.

The scuffling continued.

"Van Helsing?" Hel called into the dark, pacing forward. "Is that you?"

The scuffling stopped.

"Miss Moriarty?" Van Helsing's voice echoed back. Sam let out a shaky huff of relief. *We made it.* No one had to die. But where was he? "What are you doing here? I thought you were taking Miss Harker to the train station."

"It's a long story," Hel said, letting her jacket fall back over her revolver and picking up her lantern. "Where are you?"

"Down here," he said, his voice still echoing oddly. Sam and Hel stepped into the room and peered down the cenote to see Van Helsing collapsed on a ledge, the telltale marks of a carcolh tentacle winding up his pant leg, just as it had the bones in the catacombs. His usually cocky face was pale and sweaty, his hair stuck to his forehead with snail goo. Past his small ledge, the cenote continued into the darkness. Far below, she could just make out the mottled shell of the carcolh, and, winking in the lantern light, the Nemean Lion–claw dagger, driven straight through its head.

Van Helsing was lucky he'd managed to land on a ledge. He might not have survived if he'd fallen all the way. Certainly, Sam and Hel would never have found him.

"There was a carcolh, of all things," Van Helsing said. "I thought I had it, but it wrapped a tentacle around me, right at the end, and pulled me down here."

Sam couldn't suppress a pang, remembering the look on Cyprien's face as that tentacle slipped around his ankle. Her hesitation, costing him everything.

She wouldn't do that again.

"Miss Harker?" Van Helsing tried to scowl, but it crumbled into a wince of pain. "What on earth were you thinking bringing her here? Tell me you haven't given her a gun."

"Why? Tempted to put yourself out of your misery?" Hel said.

"Don't joke about that," Van Helsing said. "With a firearm, she's a danger to everyone, and she's a liability without."

"I know I'm a fascinating topic, but we can discuss me later, once you're out of here," Sam said crisply as she dug in her bag for her rope, please let her have remembered the rope. "Which we have to do, now." Before he was marked with perfume, before the Beast came to devour him whole.

"I can't." Van Helsing grimaced up at them. "My leg's twisted. It won't take my weight. You need to get help—someone to pull me out of here."

"There's no time," Hel said, looping Sam's rope around a column and feeding the other end down into the cenote. They could do this. Van Helsing was not a small man, but surely he wasn't heavier than Sam and Hel together, and they'd managed that much before.

"You can't seriously be expecting to pull me up yourselves?" Van Helsing exclaimed. "If you drop me—"

He would break more than his leg.

"That's a risk I'm willing to take," Hel said, and Van Helsing swore at her.

"The tip was just bait, to get you here," Sam explained. "Someone's trying to kill you."

"You think I don't know that?" Van Helsing said irritably. "It's not a trap if you know about it. It's an opportunity."

"We need to get you out of here, before they realize you've killed their carcolh and come to finish you off," Sam argued. "You are in no condition to fight."

"Not if I have to protect *you*," Van Helsing said stiffly, as if he might take on a pack of werewolves, while stuck down a hole, unable to so much as stand. *Honestly.* "All right—just don't drop me."

With an undue amount of grunting, Van Helsing roughly splinted his leg with the bandages and wood Sam lowered down. Then he looped the rope around himself and gave it a tug.

Sam and Hel braced themselves against the column and started to pull. The rope sawed on the column, and dust sprinkled from the ceiling, sticking in the sweat on Sam's arms. She felt her biceps tremble. Still, she braced herself and pulled.

By the time they had Van Helsing almost to the top, Sam was finally beginning to believe that they might succeed, that Sam could save Van Helsing, with her noodley biceps, and hold it over him forever, when Sam sucked in a deep breath. Underneath the acrid stench of human sweat and slaughtered carcolh, the unmistakable scent of fir trees blossomed around her, as if there were a hidden forest in that cenote, buried beneath the crust of the earth.

They were too late.

Hel cursed. "He's been marked."

"It was a trap," Sam cried. Not just for Van Helsing—for Sam and Hel.

"We already knew that," Van Helsing grumbled. "Don't drop me, I'm warning you."

"We have to pull him up now," Hel said. "Double-time."

Sam braced herself. "All right!" They could do this. She could—

"That's far enough Mlle Moriarty, Mlle Harker," a familiar voice said, and Sam's and Hel's hands froze on the rope. Arsène Courbet stepped out from behind one of the chess-painted columns on the far side of the cenote, hands playing with a bottle of perfume.

Sam gave a cry, skidding forward a step as Hel let go of the rope with one hand, reaching inside her jacket for her revolver.

"What are you doing up there?" Van Helsing cried. "Don't drop me!"

"You heard the man," Arsène said. "Don't drop him."

"Why shouldn't I?" Hel said, one hand straining on the rope, the other over her revolver. "He'll survive."

"That's debatable," Arsène said, glancing down in the darkness of the cenote. Sam stumbled forward another step, her arms trembling uncontrollably now, her hands stinging as salt broke new blisters. "But say you do. Then what? You can't shoot me. You don't have any evidence."

"It's never stopped me before," Hel said.

Please, whatever you're going to do, do it now, Sam thought as Hel stared down Arsène. She couldn't hold this much longer.

"Then do it. Shoot me. End this game right here and now." Arsène spread his arms wide. But still, Hel didn't drop the rope. And Arsène smiled. "You can't, can you? Because even if the threat of prison and killing your friend won't stop you, you're not sure what I know about your father."

"Tell me," Hel demanded, a hunger in her voice that Sam hadn't heard before. This was why Hel was here—this was what Hel was hunting. Information on her elusive father and the family she couldn't seem to escape.

"No. I don't think I will," Arsène mused. "You never appreciated the gift you've been given in your father. He's a great man, a true believer, working to make the world a better place. Not all of us have had such inspirations."

"He's a monster," Hel said scornfully.

Arsène shrugged. "It takes a monster to hunt a monster."

"I used to think that, too," Hel admitted. "But I was wrong."

"Hel, please—!" Sam cried, the rope slipping through her fingers, tearing the flesh of her hands. Van Helsing let out a little cry and jerked down a step. She thought for a moment that she would overbalance and follow Van Helsing down into the cenote headfirst, but Hel swore and put both hands on the rope. It steadied.

"That's a good girl," Arsène said.

"Please, let him go," Sam said as her arms vibrated with the strain. "He has no influence over the French government. You have no reason to hurt him."

"Mlle Harker, I'm surprised at you," Arsène said, turning those soulful, downturned eyes on her, and Sam hated herself a little for ever getting lost in their depths. "You're the one who told me what kind of man Van Helsing was. You're part of the reason he's on the list."

"This isn't what I meant!" Sam said, trying not to think about what Van Helsing was making of all this, of what he'd tell Mr. Wright when he got out of here—if he got out of here.

"I must admit, I'm disappointed," Arsène said. "I thought you, of all people, would understand what I am trying to accomplish—that we had a *connection*. You confided in me at the opera how you sympathized with the Beast, how you believed she had reason to be unhappy, and how you intended on sparing her once you caught her. Is your opinion so changed, just because I'm not a young woman?"

"That is hardly the same!" Sam said. "Mlle Heroux didn't act on account of her ideals—because you acted for her, *through* her, without her knowledge or consent, turning her into a Beast and forcing her to murder a man. She was your friend, and you *used* her, and when she got caught, you let her pay the price for your sins."

Arsène scoffed. "I assure you, Josephine was a woman of sin long before I came along—as were all the others. I would never have subjected a woman like you to that."

He was, Sam realized, one of those men for whom women came in two varieties: sainted like his mother, or sinful like the woman with whom his father broke his vows.

"I am no different from them," Sam said, fury rising in her like a tide.

Arsène shook his head, as if she were a child making a child's mistake. "That's where you're wrong. You're a good woman, if perhaps a bit too clever." And Sam remembered the way his fingers had brushed her saint medal when she'd nearly fainted that first time they met, the way he'd disapproved of her more fashionable attire at the opera. The way the Beast had spared them in the tunnels. "I want you to know that I never wanted it to come to this. You were supposed to be out of the way by now, in the asylum, or back home in London. When a little bird told me you'd broken free . . . Well. A gentleman is always prepared."

"Don't kill him," Sam said, panic rising in her. "Please—"

"Oh, don't worry, I won't," he said with a smile. "You will." A jet of liquid leapt from the bottle of perfume. Sam threw her hands up in front of her face, dropping the rope. The perfume splashed against her crossed forearms, her hands, her chest. The scent of magnolia filled her senses, the top note of L'Heure magique.

Hel cried out, "Sam!" And she, too, dropped the rope. Van Helsing fell, cursing. Fortunately, he'd been slipping through their fingers, and the distance to the ledge wasn't so far now. He must have made it, otherwise she'd have heard sounds a lot worse than cursing.

"I'm all right," Sam said, pressing her hand against the strange fluttering in her chest. It was fear, that's all it was. "It won't do anything. We know how this works. It takes time for the base notes to be exposed. Minimally twenty-five minutes. And even then, it needs to touch the catalyst. We're safe." For now.

"Right," Hel said. And she drew her revolver, for she still

didn't have evidence and he still had information about her father, and clicked the safety off. "Stop right there."

But Arsène just chuckled, his eyes locked on Sam. "Clever girl." He walked forward slowly, keeping Sam between him and Hel. "Allow me to let you in on a secret."

Hel stepped sideways, trying to line up a shot. "Sam, get away from him." Sam took a step backward, and then another.

"The base notes don't emerge from nothing," Arsène confided in her, even as the top note faded. He crossed the distance between them until he was so close he could kiss her. "They're always there, underneath the layers of propriety—the Beast inside us just waiting to come out." Then, at last, he stopped.

Too late, Sam noticed where she stood. "Don't—!" she cried, her eyes wide with fear.

He smiled, pushing her over the edge, and the scent of gardenia, jasmine, tuberose, and lily devoured her whole.

"Sam!" Hel leapt after Sam, throwing herself onto her stomach and reaching out. Sam slipped through her fingers, Hel looking after her, agonized, as she fell, screaming.

Van Helsing, the fool, caught Sam.

"Don't touch me!" she cried, trying to push away, panicked.

Van Helsing scowled, his arms tightening on her instinctively. "I *saved* you, you thankless—"

His hand brushed hers, and suddenly the black and shipwrecked sea that had awoken within her at the Beast's howl turned *molten*, filling her chest. Her spine curled and her teeth lengthened, her skin needled with fur and her fingernails sharpened. Until at last, she dropped to all fours and howled, fury pouring through her, reckless and wild:

Fury that she had to live in fear that someone would uncover what she could do and imprison her for the sin of having a power that didn't come from them.

Fury that the Mr. Wrights of the world forced her to play the part they'd written for her in their stories—because it was always *their* stories. Never hers.

Fury that the world forced her to choose between being herself and being safe.

And this time, Sam couldn't pretend the anger wasn't hers. Where had her rage been, all this time?

Here, it had always been here.

And that *smell*—it pulled her lips back from her teeth, pulled her toward the nightmare before her, who sometimes wore the face of Van Helsing, and sometimes Mr. Wright, and sometimes Ruari, and sometimes her own.

Clotilde and Josephine had been wrong. The smell was worse than rancid, worse than sulfurous. It was the smell of death—and not a pretty metaphor of fir trees and caskets, but of a three-day corpse that had sat out in the sun.

She could feel her control slipping away. This was how the alchemist controlled the Beast—how he ensured it killed his target, and no one else. The change into a Beast might have been chemical, but the targeting was by scent.

Which meant, Sam realized, it could be broken—because of course it could. The alchemist had changed himself into the Beast in the tunnels, and had spared Sam and Hel. But there were only a few heartbeats before Sam lost control, before she became a mindless Beast and tore Van Helsing apart like a rabbit in a snare. How in the world was she going to find a scent strong enough to—

Oh.

"Tea!" Sam screamed, the subharmonics of the Beast's howl echoing in her voice. She hoped Hel knew what she meant. She had to—Sam was out of time, her bones shifting inside her skin, tears springing from her human eyes before her tear ducts melted away.

A fishhook of searing pain shot through the back of her skull, and a rotting ache rooted in her limbs. She could still hear people talking, but dimly, as if through water: A woman shouting. A man screaming. The retort of a revolver, in slow motion.

For all he'd talked of hunting monsters, Van Helsing was entirely taken by surprise when Sam lunged. A bullet tore through her shoulder like a biting gnat, and then she had him pinned, back to the rock, his revolver pressed uselessly to his side while he flopped like a fish on the docks—already dead, he just didn't know it yet.

First crush the throat.

Sam's jaws gaped—she could taste the salt of his skin—when something hit her on the nose.

Sam yelped, then sneezed as a riot of mint overcame her senses, crisp as winter's breath on her tongue and up her nose—*tea*, she remembered—and all at once the nightmare shattered.

In its wake, Sam was still a Beast—pinning Van Helsing to the ground, her jaws around his throat—but her strings had been cut. The targeting scent had been overwhelmed with the scent of mint tea, and her rage was her own.

"Soft without your father's influence," Arsène was saying to Hel, his voice no longer muted. "You could have shot me there, had you not let yourself get distracted trying to save a man you don't even care for."

"I didn't do it for him," Hel said.

Arsène had his back to the cenote—Hel's gun in his hand. Hel was holding her shoulder, blood leaking between her fingers. He'd *shot* her. A growl rose in Sam's chest.

Arsène scoffed. "That's even worse. You knew Mlle Harker would heal as soon as she became the Beast. And now, I'm the one with the gun."

Sam leapt, springboarding off Van Helsing's chest, barreling out of the cenote and into Arsène Courbet, knocking him over, a growl resonating through her whole body. She snarled, snapping at his wrist that held the revolver, and he dropped it. "What are you doing? You daft Beast!"

This time, his were the eyes wide with fear, and it thrilled Sam somewhere deep and terrifying inside her. This man had transformed vulnerable young women into Beasts—women who thought him their friend, but whom he'd always seen as less than.

He had forced them to mutilate and kill men they knew intimately, if not cared about, because he'd thought those men responsible for France's descent into sin.

This man had shot Hel, had turned Sam into a Beast and nearly forced her to kill Van Helsing—the very fate she'd sought to avoid for whatever young woman he'd chosen this time. Her jaws were around his throat.

This man was also the best chance Hel had at finding her father. Sam raised her gaze to Hel, but Hel just nodded. It was, Sam realized, Hel's gift to Sam: she was giving her the choice.

Hel had always given Sam the choice.

With a whimper in her throat, and more difficulty than she cared to admit, Sam removed her jaws from Arsène's neck.

"There's a good girl," Arsène said, his breath unsteady as he tried to pull together the shreds of his charm. And he looked at her with those dark eyes as if she were still a woman and not a Beast. "I knew we had a connection."

Sam huffed and placed a paw on his chest, keeping him from sitting up. She hadn't done it for *him*.

"Thank you," Hel murmured as she pulled out a pair of handcuffs.

— —

After, Sam took the rope between her teeth and hauled Van Helsing out of the hole. No sooner had he crested the top than he had his own revolver out and aimed at Sam, as if on instinct, before slowly lowering it.

"She's not a werewolf, is she?" Van Helsing said.

"Werewolves don't exist," Hel confirmed.

Van Helsing looked at Sam, then back at Hel, before holstering his revolver. He watched Sam warily, as if he still thought she might take his throat between her teeth, even with everything he'd seen and heard.

Even when she'd saved his life.

"You," he said to Hel, "have a lot of explaining to do."

Sam realized then that it didn't matter how good Hel's explanation was—if people saw Sam right now, she would be a werewolf, and there would be a panic. If the police saw her, there would be violence. As much as Sam hated to admit it, they needed him.

"All right, Van Helsing," Hel said. "This is what's going to happen. This is Arsène Courbet. You're going to take him to the police and make sure he gets arrested for the murders ascribed to the Beast. The women involved, they're innocent. Not werewolves. Not monsters. Victims. Make him tell you where his alchemy laboratory is—that should give them all the evidence the police need.

"I'll give you this case. You can have the glory, I don't care. Just clear the women's names, and don't mention Sam to anyone, or there won't be enough left of you to ship back to Mr. Wright. Are we clear?"

"You are out of your mind," Van Helsing said.

"Is that a yes?" Hel asked.

"Yes."

"Good," Hel said. "I wish I could say it's been a pleasure, but it's just been."

"Wait," Van Helsing called after Sam and Hel as they moved deeper into the mines. "The things M. Courbet said about Miss Harker—she didn't really want to kill me, did she?"

Sam and Hel exchanged a look. "If she wanted you dead, you would be."

CHAPTER TWENTY-FOUR

The Catacombs

Hel led Sam deeper into the mines beneath the streets of Paris, her fingers tangled in the ruff at Sam's neck, until at last they reached a small chamber. A stained-glass window was set into the rock—a woman with her head bowed in prayer, naked save for the halo of a saint.

"We can wait here until it wears off," Hel murmured, and she released Sam's ruff.

Sam nosed Hel's hand in assent, and after sniffing the room for anything untoward, she curled up on the floor, resting her snout on her paws. A whining yawn escaped before she could stop it, and she looked at Hel wildly, standing up, ears flopping.

"Don't worry." Hel laughed, and reluctantly, Sam settled back down. "I'll keep watch."

For the first time, Sam was the one with the bigger biceps, and so a not insignificant part of her wanted to be the one to protect Hel. But . . . she really was tired. She closed her eyes.

The last thing Sam remembered before she drifted off, so distantly it might have been a dream, was Hel curling up beside her, her fingers laced in Sam's fur, as if she never wanted to let her go.

Sometime later, Sam woke with a start—thoroughly human,

if a bit sore and utterly starving. Also, naked. Hel's coat lay over her like a blanket, and Sam pulled it on gratefully, tying it around her like a dress, breathing in the scent of gunpowder and resin. Hel was right: it *was* comforting.

Puddled on the ground beside her were her clothes from the prior evening. Like Clotilde's, they were torn beyond repair. Despite everything that had happened, Sam groaned. Being a field agent really was hard on one's wardrobe.

Something shifted in the shadows, and Sam sat up so quickly her head spun, her mind full of snail monsters and grindylows and perfumers with Darcy-dark eyes, and a small part of her missed being the Beast.

But it was only Hel, leaning against the wall, her suit jacket slung over one shoulder, her revolver held loosely in the other, keeping watch as if she'd been there all night.

"It's a shame about your dress," Hel said awkwardly.

"I thought you didn't care about fashion," Sam said, trying for light.

"I don't," Hel answered. "But you do. And . . . I may have garnered something of a new appreciation."

"You can hide a lot more in skirts than a suit," Sam said sagely.

"*So* much more."

"How did you stitch the hem of that skirt so fine?" Sam continued. "I could have sworn it was original! One would think you'd been sewing for years."

Hel shrugged. "It's not so different from flesh."

Sam winced, remembering the way the needle had flashed in Hel's hand.

"Now you've done it," Sam said. "Now you have to stick around, and teach me how to sew people up, too." Just in case.

Hel didn't answer. At first, Sam thought she'd offended her, but Hel just watched the leaping shadows of the lantern. Then, "I'm sorry I didn't trust you."

Whatever Sam had been expecting, it wasn't that. "I understand. The way Mr. Wright and the Society treat you—the way your own family treats you—I don't think I'd trust easily either."

"It doesn't excuse it," Hel said firmly. "You can handle a lot more than anyone gives you credit for. You change your mind when presented with new information—which is a far rarer trait than it ought to be. And you manage the trick of feeling things, even amidst all the blood and pain and death."

Sam's cheeks pinked. "If it's any consolation, I didn't trust you either."

"I didn't make it easy," Hel said.

"No, you didn't," Sam admitted. "But I trust you now. You always fight for what you believe in—even if it's harder, even when other people will condemn you for it. You don't care what anyone else thinks. And you don't expect me to be anything other than I am."

Hel turned away, and Sam thought her cheeks might actually be flushed, though perhaps that was just the light of the lanterns playing tricks. Sam thought again of that kiss, and wondered if Hel was thinking of it too. When Hel spoke again, her voice was soft. "I'm not used to having a partner this far into a case."

And Sam's heart ached as she again remembered Ruari's words: *She will be alone, without allies or lovers or friends, until the day she comes home.*

"Well, you'd better get used to it," Sam said lightly, "if we're going to keep working together."

"You're going to continue doing fieldwork?" Hel asked

guardedly. "I thought you might want to get back to your library, after all that."

She did. Sam missed the library like she missed home. The rabbit holes of research and piecing together puzzles from the warm comfort of the stacks, and that old-book smell—though given recent events, she could probably go without that for a bit. She even missed the flickering gas lamps, which were honestly a fire hazard and should be replaced, but were so like the one by which she'd read late at night as a girl that she couldn't bear to see them go.

And a part of her wasn't sure she could handle the world beyond her books. She had almost died a lot more in the past few days than she had in her entire life. Before, death had seemed a faraway thing, something that happened in beds and hospitals. Here in the field, death felt close as your shadow—only one day this shadow would swallow you up, and you wouldn't know it until your foot didn't hit the ground.

To say nothing of the deaths of other people.

But there were worlds out there beyond her books, not just of blood and pain as Hel had described, but of secrets and wonder. Of spells baked in bread and alchemical laboratories hidden beneath the city streets, of wills-o'-the-wisp following mysterious radio signals and book ciphers hidden in the graffiti on the walls.

Then there was the matter of the omissions from the library, omissions Sam was fairly certain were intentional. It made her wonder about what else the Society might have been hiding from her—or about her.

Sam had to return to the library at least long enough to uncover whether there was a forbidden section she simply hadn't had access to—or whether there was a clandestine curator, removing all the dangerous bits of the world they didn't want their second-level researchers to know, for what reason Sam could only begin to guess. And she still had to locate Audrey Bellamy of Provence for Mme Frossard, to secure her freedom.

But after that?

"I promised to help track down Professor Moriarty," Sam said. And Sam's grandfather, which was apparently the same thing. She reached out and gave Hel's hand a squeeze. "I'm not going anywhere."

EPILOGUE

Holyhead, Wales
October 1903

The sky was marbled with clouds, and gusts rolled off the ocean, carrying with them the scent of salt. Sam and Hel stood on the creaking dock in Holyhead, waiting for the steam-packet service that would take them to Dublin, Ireland. Hel's long tan coat whipped behind her as she stared out at the tumultuous dark of the ocean, toeing the very edge of the dock, Heathcliff perched on her shoulder.

Sam stood by her side, looking the other way—past the neat line of row houses to where ships crowded the shore, as if the ocean had dried up and left them behind. Once again, Sam was snug in her white wool and velvet traveling dress with matching gloves, her curls pinned up under the broad-brimmed hat she'd bought in Paris to replace the one she'd lost to the grindylow—this one festooned with a cloud of white feathers.

It had taken her hours to get the smoke and grindylow out of her skirts, and she'd needed to replace the petticoat entirely, this time with a less flammable material. Already, she was certain it was covered in a fine sheen of road dust, the fishy smell of the docks wriggling its way into the wool. She was beginning to suspect white might not be the best color for travel.

Hel, of course, remained in her black suit and *scarlet* tie—the only nod to her new appreciation for fashion she seemed like to make. It was, Sam reflected, a good color for her, even if current sensibilities argued against redheads wearing red. Though she was, perhaps, biased. And if the ability to differentiate reds was the only thing Hel took from her adventure in fashion, aside from sewing things in skirts of course, it was well worth it.

Sam studied Hel, who seemed bent on looking everywhere but at Sam, her lean figure all at angles, as if Hel feared Sam might read the truth of her in her eyes before Hel knew it herself. A feeling Sam was entirely too acquainted with.

"What are you reading?" Sam asked, nodding to the book peeking out of Hel's coat pocket.

"A book," Hel said. "One would think you'd have seen one before. Being, as you are, a researcher."

"I'm in recovery," Sam returned primly. "Is it about the case? I think I—hold on!"

The folded pages, the places Sam had gotten a bit too enthusiastic and cracked the spine . . . That was no research book, that was *Raphael Slade and the Devil's Fiddle*. One of the romantic detective novels that had first made Sam wonder if the scent of rosin meant Hel played the violin. Which, in fact, she *did*.

Sam recalled one scene in particular, in a train car, handprints in the window steam, amidst the remnants of a basilisk. . . . It was . . . affecting. She blushed, wondering if Hel had gotten that far yet—if she felt the same way.

And Sam thought again of that kiss in the gardens of the asylum, a phrase that lived in capital letters in her head. *That Kiss.*

In stark contrast to Raphael Slade's romantic adventures, nothing more had happened between Sam and Hel after that night. Which Sam had half convinced herself was good. Hel still didn't know how to be a partner. Not really. She didn't know how to trust someone and not think of them as a game piece. Besides, Hel didn't want more. . . .

Unless Hel did, and Sam had missed some sign. And then Sam would think about That Kiss all over again, this time, in more detail.

"Where did you get that?" Sam blurted.

"It was on your desk," Hel said with a one-shouldered shrug. "I got bored."

Sam raised her eyebrows. "And you're still reading?"

Hel gave her a crooked smile. "I've never been one for quitting."

Except, of course, for the one thing she had.

"Are you sure you're up for this?" Sam said quietly.

Mr. Wright hadn't wanted to give Sam and Hel the case. Not at first. At first, they'd been assigned a number of thoroughly unextraordinary cases in the greater London area, in punishment for their handling of the Paris murders, she supposed. Sam had never thought the business of being a field agent might be boring, but there it was.

Then this case came up, and the Irish weren't keen on the English. Hel would be able to go places and talk to people the rest of them never could—even if it meant running up against Hel's family.

"We could always tell Mr. Wright no," Sam suggested. "I'm sure he'd figure something out."

"And deal with more boggarts?" Hel snorted. "Not a chance. Besides, this is what I've been waiting for."

Hel had been brooding ever since her brother had sent a bee

to sting Sam farewell, promising he'd see them soon.

But for all Hel had drawn a revolver at the mere mention of her brother's name, Sam wasn't entirely certain Hel was prepared to face him down—or any of them, for that matter. They were still her family, even if they were awful. And as Hel wasn't the sort to talk about her feelings, let alone admit to having them, Sam suspected Hel and her family had a lot of . . . unfinished business.

In the end, though, it didn't matter. Sam had promised Hel she'd help her track down her brother, so if Hel wanted to do this, Sam would be by her side. Besides, there was the matter of the book.

It had appeared on Sam's doorstep three days prior, wrapped in brown paper and string like a thing out of a fairy tale. With it was a note.

> Dearest Samantha,
> I would not have you walk this path, but as you have chosen to walk it anyway, know that I am with you.
> All my love,
> Mom

Sam's hands had shaken as she'd opened it to see a slim, worn volume of Irish fairy tales—exactly like the one her grandfather had read to her when she was a child that had her trapping púca in her backyard.

Sam had nearly dropped it, an ocean of numbers surging in her ears.

Seventy-four. Ten. One hundred three. Twenty-eight, eight, twenty-seven. Forty-four, one, fifty-six . . .

This book . . . it was the key to the first book cipher. Sam had felt it. Had her mother known, all this time? She must have. But what did that mean? Hands shaking, Sam had translated, not even bothering with a pen and paper.

Don't—Follow—Me—Saint—Hide—You—Keep—You—Love—Always.

Sam's fingertips alighted on the medal of St. Brigid at her throat. It had kept her grandfather safe for decades. When she was ten, he'd gifted it to her for Christmas, saying it would keep her safe in turn. Sam had hesitated, even then, asked didn't he need it. Her grandfather had just chuckled and said she needed it more.

But then shortly after, he'd disappeared. Was abducted, she amended, for that wasn't the sort of note you left when you were going of your own free will.

Don't follow me. Saint Brigid hide you and keep you safe. Love always, Grandpa.

Nor was it the one you sent when you hoped for a rescue. Though Sam's grandfather had to know she couldn't just leave him, not once she had confirmation that he was alive, that he was a prisoner. He had to know Sam would come for him.

Which led Sam to wonder if it wasn't her mother who had sent her the book at all, but Professor Moriarty. Speaking of which . . .

"Shouldn't something have tried to kill us by now?" Sam ventured.

For the entire month they'd worked cases in London, it had been nothing but snapped ropes and runaway trains and venomous snakes well outside their accepted range. But since Hel and Sam had departed for Ireland, Professor Moriarty hadn't whispered or nudged a single death into their path—and not because

Sam and Hel had caught the mole feeding him information, because they most assuredly hadn't. They were hardly out of the woods yet, but he was . . . late.

Was this how Hel's father showed his approval? By ceasing his attempts to murder you and your friends?

There were easier ways, Sam thought with a little pique. A nice cheese platter never went amiss. But the Moriartys, Sam got the feeling, were not a cheese platter kind of family.

It made Sam nearly as nervous as the book. "It's a trap, isn't it?"

"Almost certainly," Hel agreed.

"He knows we're coming."

"Probably arranged it himself."

"But we're still going," Sam said.

"Wouldn't miss it for the world."

At long last, Dr. Helena Moriarty—wayward daughter of the notorious Professor Moriarty—was going home. And Sam was going with her.

ACKNOWLEDGMENTS

Everyone always says writing is a solitary pursuit. And it is, really! You spend a lot of time alone writing, thinking about writing, and sometimes unwriting. But at least in my case, it is also true that there are a seemingly endless number of people who have helped to bring this story to life.

Here is a short list of some of those people.

Thank you to my amazing agent, Jennifer Azantian, and to Wesley Chu for introducing us. I could not have done any of this without Jen's astonishingly astute editorial insight and exceptional strategic guidance—not to mention her endless support. Thanks must also go to Alex Weiss at Azantian Literary Agency, Jen's assistant extraordinaire, for keeping on top of *Strange Beasts'* submissions and everything else, and to Ben Baxter for his keen editorial insights. When I first started this journey, I could not have possibly known what a wonderful agent and agency I would end up with, but I'm so grateful to have ended up with you.

Thank you to Kathryn Budig, publisher at Inky Phoenix Press, for taking a chance on me, and for being such a passionate and innovative advocate and advisor throughout this whole process. So much of this journey has been kismet—I feel so lucky to have gotten to work on this book with you. Thanks also to Kate Fagan for offering such fantastic support, and to Kathryn's Inky

Phoenix book club, for being such a wonderful and welcoming place to launch a book.

Thank you to the spectacular team at Bindery Books—Meghan Harvey and Matt Kaye, founders of Bindery, for their amazing guidance and direction; to CJ Alberts for her deft hand at marketing and her constant updates; and to Charlotte Strick for her fantastic art direction and design. And thank you to Zach Meyer for reading my book and pulling out of it the most phenomenal cover art. If people judge a book by its cover, then I have nothing to worry about.

Thank you to everyone at Girl Friday Productions. To Kristin Duran for managing the whole project with precision and flexibility. To Clete Smith for a wonderfully incisive editorial letter, for believing in my book, and for helping me capture the soul of Van Helsing. You have made my book so much better. To the proofreader Nicole Brugger-Dethmers and copyeditor Valerie Paquin for helping correct my many mistakes and making it much more readable—especially the timeline. If there is anything right about the timeline, it is because of Valerie. To Paul Barrett for exceptional interior design and art direction. To my publicists, Brittani Hilles and Amelia Possanza at Lavender Public Relations, for helping spread the word about *Strange Beasts*. And to Dr. Stacey Battis for not only correcting my high-school-meets-Google-Translate French but making it period appropriate as well.

Thank you to Calah Singleton at Hodderscape for being the first editor to believe in my book, and for that utterly brilliant editorial letter and line edit. I feel so fortunate to have ended up in your hands. You truly captured the heart of Sam and Hel, and this wouldn't be half the book it is without you. I cannot wait to work with you on book two. Thank you as well to the wonderful team at Hodderscape. To the editors Molly Powell, Natasha

Qureshi, and Sophie Judge for your invaluable insight and support behind the scenes. To Natalie Chen in design and Katy Aries in production for bringing my book to beautiful life, to Kate Keehan in publicity and Laura Bartholomew in marketing for ensuring people hear about it, and to Jessica Dryburgh and Sarah Clay in sales for making sure you can find it on the shelves.

Many thanks go to Corry L. Lee, Erin M. Evans, Rhiannon Held, and Shanna Germain for their invaluable help with the first draft of *Strange Beasts*. Additional thanks to Jaleigh Johnson for her incredible insight on my second draft, helping me to breathe life into Sam and Hel's relationship, and to Rashida J. Smith for helping me not only with my first draft, but also with refining the beats of *That Kiss*.

Special thanks to Kate Alice Marshall for helping me to sharpen my aim before I even began the book, and for her exceptional insight throughout every stage of the process.

All the thanks to my Bindery siblings—S. Hati and her nuanced exploration of power and loyalty in her searing climate fantasy *And the Sky Bled*; Kay Synclaire and the beautiful and raw expression of grief and love that is *House of Frank*; and Tiffany Wang and her utterly captivating tale of intrigue and rebellion in *Inferno's Heir*. Our group chat was everything during the wild ride of this year! Thank you for all the support.

I would be remiss if I didn't offer thanks to Carolyn H. Morris (hi, Mom!) for her excellent critique of *Strange Beasts*, and for always reading my writing and encouraging me; to Dr. Robert E. Morris (hi, Dad!) for his aid in researching radio waves and teaching me that chemistry is like magic; and to Rachel E. Morris (hi, sis!) for playing *Monster Hunter* with me when I was stressed and grounding me in the world outside my books. Additional thanks must go to Dr. Brigitte Andrejs and Hans Andrejs for cheering me on, and for making sure at least a few books will find their way into the homes of readers in Germany.

Thank you to my partner, Axel, for all his incredible support throughout this whole process, including but not limited to buying me consolation and celebration cupcakes, listening to me ramble about my book on an uncountable number of walks, answering far too many questions about Europe, and being the reason I learned German (and so could research Wolfssegners properly). I could not have done this without you.

Thank you to Sir Arthur Conan Doyle and Bram Stoker, for inspiring generations of young writers, and without whom my book wouldn't be possible. Their books are still amazing—everyone should check them out.

And thank you to you, the reader, for taking a chance on this book, and for staying with me until the end. Truly, you are the reason for everything. ♡

DISCUSSION QUESTIONS

1. *Strange Beasts* is about hunting monsters—but the deeper Sam gets, the more she begins to question who the real monsters are. What do you think makes a monster?

2. Hel is famously aloof. How has this impacted her professional and personal life? Do you think she is satisfied with this, or does her time with Sam make her question her choices?

3. Sam doubts herself, even as she is piling up impressive victories. Where do you think this doubt stems from?

4. What is feminine strength? How is it different from masculine strength, and how does this play out in the story?

5. Werewolves in literature often echo the struggle between civilization and our own wild natures. What do you think the Beast represents?

6. Jakob Van Helsing and Sam have a tumultuous relationship. What do you think the root cause of that is, and how do you think he feels about her now?

7. What draws Sam and Hel together? What makes them afraid to get close?

8. Hel says channels like Sam are feared because men are jealous of any power that does not come from them. Sam would say it's because her visions come from monsters—though the visions they give her have always proved correct. How do you think this illustrates the experience of women in patriarchal societies?

9. Hel doesn't trust anyone. Where do you think this stems from, and why do you think she trusts Sam?

10. Sam feels like she is forced to choose between being safe and being herself. How do you think this has impacted her professional and personal life?

11. Sam thinks Heathcliff (from Emily Brontë's *Wuthering Heights*) was rejected by society, but that he just wants to be loved. Hel believes rejection is no excuse for being a monster. Does a good enough reason excuse harmful actions?

12. Hel takes tremendous risks but isn't totally fearless—in fact, she always keeps mint tea on her to settle her nerves. What do you think Hel is afraid of, and how does it shape her life?

13. Hel points out that the people of Paris have reason to be unhappy, and that change rarely comes from asking nicely. But Hel and Sam also work to stop the murders of the rich, powerful men perpetuating their unhappiness. How do you think change should be instigated in an unfair system?

14. Arsène Courbet looks down on the socially progressive women to whom he sells his perfumes. Do you think they would still purchase his perfumes if they knew how he felt about them? How much do the opinions of an artist matter, when it comes to purchasing their work?

15. Hel mentions that fashion isn't a language she speaks—and Sam tells her that she does, she just has no idea what she's saying. How do you think this illustrates the different experiences of appearance and femininity of the characters?

16. Wills-o'-the-wisp are a recurring theme in *Strange Beasts*. Harmless, unless you follow them into the dark, they appear in several instances:
    - When Sam uses the radio telegraph (and wonders if wills-o'-the-wisp are just trying to find their way home)
    - On her way to the second murder
    - At the cabaret
    - When Sam and Jakob are children
    - In the catacombs
    - And perhaps most notably at the asylum when they lead her to Hel

    What do you think the wills-o'-the-wisp represent?

17. In the beginning, we learn that Hel's nickname is "Lady M"—a reference to Shakespeare's *Macbeth*. When asked to call her Hel, Sam immediately makes the connection to *A Midsummer Night's Dream*. What do you think this exchange signifies, and why is it so meaningful to Hel?

THANK YOU

This book would not have been possible without the support from the Inky Phoenix community, with a special thank-you to the Inky Inner Circle members:

Aimee Letto
Aniela Kuzon
Ann Levine
Annie2023
Brit Liegl
Carolyn Hanson
Deni
Emily Williams
Erin Tonda
Esh
GrettyVB
Hollyn Cook Chapman
Jessica Limbach
Kacy Fleming
Karine Lairot
Kathleen Fagan
Kyleanne Hunter
Lindsay Warren
Marguerite White
Marion Kathryn Nielson

maryfrances
Mary Jane Goodman-Giddens
Monkimiles
RaeBroderick
Samantha Bassler
Shawna Hawes
Stephen Johnston
Sweet Lu
Tess Carver
Tiffany Curren

ABOUT THE AUTHOR

Photo by Daniel Stark www.starkphotography.com

SUSAN J. MORRIS is a fantasy author and editor best known for a writing-advice column featured on Amazon's *Omnivoracious* blog and her work editing Forgotten Realms novels. Susan delights in running workshops for Clarion West and in moderating panels for writing symposiums. She lives in Sammamish, Washington, with her partner, two cats, and entirely too many plants.

When not writing, reading, or wading through said plants, Susan indulges in playing video games such as *Hades*, *Oxenfree*, and *Baldur's Gate 3*; training in Pilates (which is better for her shoulders than jujitsu was); and experimenting with new plant-based food recipes.

Strange Beasts is her debut novel.

Inky Phoenix Press is an imprint of Bindery, a book publisher powered by community.

We're inspired by the way book tastemakers have reinvigorated the publishing industry. With strong taste and direct connections with readers, book tastemakers have illuminated self-published, backlisted, and overlooked authors, rocketing many to bestseller lists and the big screen.
This book was chosen by Kathryn Budig in close collaboration with the Inky Phoenix community on Bindery. By inviting tastemakers and their reading communities to participate in publishing, Bindery creates opportunities for deserving authors to reach readers who will love them.

Visit Inky Phoenix Press for a thriving
bookish community and bonus content:

inkyphoenix.binderybooks.com

KATHRYN BUDIG is an internationally celebrated yoga teacher, author, and founder of the online community Haus of Phoenix and the Inky Phoenix book club. She's known for curating magical realism, historical fiction, and dark fantasy with a focus LGBTQ+ and BIPOC themes and authors. Cohost of the Webby Award-nominated podcast *Free Cookies*, Budig is the author of *The Women's Health Big Book of Yoga* and the bestselling wellness guide *Aim True*. She lives in Charleston, South Carolina, with her wife, Kate Fagan, and their dog, Ragnar.

INSTAGRAM.COM/KATHRYNBUDIG

FACEBOOK.COM/KATHRYNBUDIG

YOUTUBE.COM/@KATHRYN-BUDIG